Kiss Me Quick

DANNY MILLER

ROBINSON

Constable & Robinson Ltd
3 The Lanchesters
162 Fulham Palace Road
London W6 9ER
www.constablerobinson.com

First published in the UK by Robinson,
an imprint of Constable & Robinson Ltd, 2011

A copy of the British Library Cataloguing in Publication
data is available from the British Library

ISBN: 978-1-84901-516-5

Printed and bound in the EU

1 3 5 7 9 10 8 6 4 2

To Josie Miller

ACKNOWLEDGEMENTS

I would like to thank Veronique Baxter at David Higham for picking the book up and going with it. Krystyna Green and all at Constable & Robinson for putting it out there. Cressida Ellis for looking at early drafts with her red pen. My mother Josie Miller for being a voracious reader and inspiration, and all my family and friends.

PROLOGUE

JACK, FOREVER

24 December 1939. Brighton. The middle of the night.

The driver glanced in the rear-view mirror as the man in the back seat ignited a cigarette with a gold lighter. As the flame burned, the man rubbed his thumb over the cartouche that had been etched with: 'Jack, Pour Toujours'. It was a gift. She knew that he would appreciate this inscription, because Jack Regent was in the habit of putting his mark on the things he owned: monogrammed shirts from Jermyn Street, engraved silver cigarette cases from Aspreys and gold lighters from Dupont.

Jack snuffed out the flame and drew slowly on the cigarette, pulling the rich pungent smoke deep into his lungs. Then he steadily exhaled, and plumed a chain of smoke towards the mirror that the driver, Henry Pierce, was watching him in. Caught out, Pierce averted his eyes. He knew Jack didn't like being stared at. He knew he wanted to be alone with his thoughts. The cigarette was Jack's first real taste of freedom, and he was enjoying it.

They were sitting in a maroon 1936 Rover 8: red leather upholstery, walnut dashboard, top of the range. Less than an hour ago Jack Regent had stepped out through the gates of Lewes prison to find Pierce already waiting for him. He had been released early, with a commendation from the Governor. Jack had

1

stopped a prison riot, one he'd organized, incited, then heroically ended. Jack also saved a screw from a beating – a beating he'd ordered, planned, then courageously prevented. It was all just a set-up, resulting in seven years being commuted to eighteen months.

Jack had been sent down for a malicious wounding. A book-maker had refused to pay up, so a razor was pulled out and drawn across his face. Jack left his mark. The choice of weapon, the open razor, was not typical of Jack, however. He had always thought razors childish, a twee English affectation. You could never put enough force behind a razor to do the real damage. It acted more as a warning. Regent didn't hold with the idea of warning his enemies, therefore the bookie was viewed as a mistake. A mistake he promised himself he would never make again. A promise he was going to keep tonight. Jack took one last hit of his cigarette, then stubbed it out.

That gesture was Henry Pierce's cue. Pierce opened the car door, unfolded himself from the driver's seat and expanded to his full bulk: six foot five inches and 230 pounds. An imposing figure sheathed in black from the brogues on his feet to the Homburg on his head. He reached into the pockets of his long black chester-field overcoat and took out a pair of kid-leather gloves – black – that fitted over his large, brutal hands like a second skin.

As an ex-pro wrestler, Henry Pierce appreciated the import-ance of a good costume and putting on a performance. He'd once toured the country, playing to packed houses under the guise of a Red Indian; entering the ring in a full feather headdress, warpaint, a tomahawk tucked into his trunks and a squaw by his side, to the accompaniment of tom-tom drums and loud boos from the crowd. Pierce was the arch villain of the ring, and a top draw until one night he got carried away and almost killed a fel-low wrestler. Pierce treated life as if he was still in the ring, still the arch villain, still the performer. He'd just swapped the feather headdress and buckskins for black.

The sharp sodium wind pricked Pierce's scarred face. Scars he'd picked up years ago, but somehow they'd never weathered, just remaining smooth, shiny and pink. A long stripe running from an ear lobe to his top lip sectioned off one quarter of his face. A spider's web on his cheekbone where the business end of a broken stout bottle had been plunged. His left eye resembled a rare bird's egg sitting in a nest – a nest of scars. A shard of glass had penetrated it, leaving it completely redundant: a speckled, marbled jelly with streaky blue and red blood vessels running through it. Sometimes he wore an eyepatch, other times he liked the feeling of unease it gave people when he looked at them. And for his line of work it was as good a tool for intimidation as a knife or a gun. He'd long decided that he liked his bad eye better than his good eye, but appreciated the fact that he needed the good eye to witness just how monumentally unpleasant the bad eye looked. He wouldn't swap it for the world, never mind for another good eye. And this is how Henry Pierce viewed the world.

He opened the rear door.

Jack Regent stepped out of the car, one foot hitting the pavement lightly, and one heavier foot following. The left foot was clubbed; he had a certain gait when he walked, but the club foot with its built-up shoe never affected his swiftness, never impeded him from what he had to do. And, like Henry Pierce, he'd learned to appreciate his physical disadvantage, but the club foot signified more than a few scars could ever achieve. For Jack had been born with it: a gift from God that marked him out.

The wind-driven snow had been falling steadily and had dusted the street white. A scattering of windows were illuminated with decorous Christmas fairy lights. The tall Georgian terraced town houses that lined St Michael's Place had long taken a beating, been slummed over and turned into walk-up flats. One- or two-bedroom dwellings with shared bathrooms and toilets located off shabby hallways.

The front door of number 27 had a red and green festive wreath attached to its heavy brass knocker. The door was off the latch and the two men made their way inside to the dark hallway. Without turning on the light, Jack made his way up the stairs. It was on the stairs that Jack's heavy-booted foot pronounced itself, the light foot levering its way upwards, while taking the weight off the other, which then landed with a distinctive thud.

Four floors up and they were on the desired landing. Jack stood at the door he was about to enter and listened for signs of life . . . All he heard was his own breath, measured and calm. The climb had taken nothing out of him, nor did the thought of what he was about to do unnerve him. He stepped back a couple of paces, raised the clubbed foot, then hammered it home, sending the door flying off its lock.

Inside, the startled voices of a man and woman rudely awoken were heard. A light went on in a bedroom. A sliver of it escaped under the door and feebly illuminated the living room where Jack and Pierce now stood.

Jack scanned the room, which was tatty and depressing. Threadbare carpet, damp and mottled peeling wallpaper, cheap painted furniture. As an attempt at seasonal cheer, a small tinsel-covered Christmas tree stood in the corner of the room, shedding pine needles on to a handful of wrapped presents. Some cards stood on the mantelpiece.

'What the bloody hell is—!' A woman's voice, fearful, as she started getting out of bed and pulling on a dressing gown. The doorknob turned. Jack bolted to the door and entered the room before she could exit. The door slammed shut.

'No . . . please, God, no!' Her panic-pitched voice scorching the ceiling, but going nowhere.

Jack grabbed her hair and reeled her in towards him. Her long, shiny auburn tresses were wrapped around his hand like silk rope as he forced her to her knees. Her head was pulled back, the long white neck exposed, her green eyes wide open and so alive. Jack's other hand gripped the ebonized hilt of a long slim knife. Her cries quickly muted to gargles and bubbled out in blood as the knife sliced back and forth; fast, savage, severing the spine. Her lifeless body, almost in two parts now, fell to the floor.

Jack then turned his attention to the corner of the room.

And there he crouched, cowering on the floor. Bollock-naked and well and truly backed into a corner. He still had the sweat of his exertions with the woman upon him. No doubt he was cock-sure, felt he could handle himself in the right circumstances. These weren't the right circumstances. He looked up at Jack, and the inevitability of it all took away some of the fear. He knew what was coming, because he knew Jack Regent.

Jack held the man's gaze as he approached, then slowly drew the knife down to the level of his face. With a steady hand he placed the tip of the blade on to the black pupil of the man's hazel eye. The pupil dilated and contracted – flashing on and off like an emergency signal. The tip of the blade slowly punctured the membrane that covered the jellied lens, yet still the man didn't squeeze his eyes shut, or even blink. He couldn't take his gaze off Jack, and time slowed for the kneeling man. His life didn't flash before him, because what he was watching was so much more compelling than anything that went on before – a front-row seat for his own execution.

Jack gave the man a soft smile, almost an *adieu*. And in one swift, powerful movement drove the knife into his eye, through the soft grey matter until it reached the bone at the back of his skull. His body juddered and twitched as Jack rotated and twisted the blade buried in his head; skewering his brain, shutting down the fear, the thoughts, the memories, until his life faded like a diminishing signal . . . over and out.

Jack came out of the bedroom, switching off the light. Henry Pierce eyed him admiringly. Hardly a drop of blood on the long, perfectly tailored camelhair overcoat. Pierce knew what came next. Whilst it wasn't exactly routine, this was how they'd done it before. Jack would depart and leave Pierce to get on with his work: the clean-up, the getting rid of the bodies. The tools were in the car. Cut them apart and bury them at sea. Pierce cracked his knuckles inside the black leather gloves, showing his readiness for the task ahead.

But Jack didn't go immediately, and leave Pierce to his work. He held out the knife and fixed him with a challenging look.

Henry Pierce took the weapon simply because it was offered to him. This unexpected gesture threw him slightly, and his heavy brow furrowed in confusion. He didn't know what came next, so he looked to Jack for further instruction.

Jack didn't say a word. He pulled out his silver cigarette case, took out another of his French cigarettes, put it to his lips and fired it up with the engraved gold lighter. The flame illuminated the dark hallway. Jack inhaled the rich smoke, then plumed it like an instruction towards the door.

Pierce was no longer confused; he had got the message. Sweat prickled his top lip. He quickly wiped it away with the back of one leather-clad hand. He knew Jack might take that for weakness – maybe even insubordination, a questioning of his judgement. Pierce gave him three slow, considered nods and conceded that it was the right thing to do. The only thing to do. By the time he reached the third nod, he wondered why he hadn't thought of this himself. But that was Jack, always one step ahead. It would join them, bond them in blood: a shared deed they would carry together to the grave. Pierce savoured this morbid thought. He gripped the knife tighter in a hand which still trembled. He reckoned even Jack could forgive him this minor weakness, considering what he was tasked with . . .

Jack left the flat. Pierce listened as those uneven footsteps faded away, heading down the stairs. He then headed towards the bedroom door and pressed his ear against it. The only sound he could hear was his own jagged breath. He opened the door. The room was pitch-black, seemingly windowless. No light from the street lamps below or the three-quarter moon above made its way into the room. But darkness, and whatever it held, never bothered Henry Pierce. Dressed in black, as always, he even felt an affinity with it.

The long knife in his hand remained steady now, as he stepped over the threshold and closed the door behind him.

CHAPTER 1

LONDON

12 January 1964. Soho, London. Evening.

Detective Edward Tobin stepped into the Peek-A-Boo Club on Wardour Street. He badged the doorman, a slender young man in a cheap tux that left lots of spare room around the collar. Tobin badged him more out of habit than necessity. They'd met before, and the doorman knew his profession. He was expecting him. As Tobin was led through the club, he reflected on how Soho muscle wasn't up to much these days.

Tobin, on the other hand, measured five foot eleven inches, weighed in at about sixteen stone, and possessed noticeably more muscle than fat for a man who was a year off his police pension. He'd fought middleweight in the army and for the Met, and as they say – *and they always say* – he could have been a contender. He looked like an ex-pug. Punched and paunched out, with half-closed, narrow eyes, a spread nose, fat lips and – as he found out when he got his ticket out of Palookaville and fought Freddie Spinx at the Royal Albert Hall – a glass jaw.

The club was empty. Dark, low ceilings, cavernous. Small stage, about ten tables. The walls were lined with horseshoe-shaped booths recessed into faux-rock effect walls, with heavy black-velvet curtains that could be drawn around them for more privacy. Tobin looked around the club. He'd been there many times before, but never with a dead body lying on the floor.

'Where's Duval?' he asked.

'In his office.'

'Then go and get him. And tell him to have my envelope.'

The slender bouncer sloped off.

Tobin went over to inspect the body on the floor. Male, mid-thirties. Suited. Thick head of brown hair on top of a thin, drawn, cadaverous face – which, of course, it now genuinely was. He had smooth skin which just served to accentuate the scores of scars he carried on his face, all varying in size and distinction. Three long razor cuts down his left cheek looked like the latest addition to this collection.

Tobin knew the corpse: Tommy Ribbons. He was 'a face' and a fixture in Soho. Tommy had a place in Berwick Street, the Author & Book Club. A two-room dive with a bar and a betting parlour upstairs. The only authors that hung out there were the authors of their own misfortune, in hock to books that carried columns of odds and wagers, not prose and poetry.

Ribbons wasn't his real name. He'd been given that nickname due to the scars he'd picked up over the years – literally cut to ribbons. His real name, long forgotten apart from on his exten-sive form sheet at West End Central, was Smithson. Thomas Albert Smithson. The extensive razor cuts to the face hadn't killed him, they were merely wounds he'd picked up two years previously. Tobin knew that because he had worked the case. Ribbons had close ties with the Maltese: he was married to a Maltese girl, and worked as muscle protecting their prostitution rackets in Soho. The Maltese were then trying to get a foothold in the lucrative West End slot-machine business. But two brothers from south-east London already in that business wanted to keep the monopoly, and had sent their emissary to etch their intentions clearly across Tommy's face.

What had killed Tommy Ribbons was plain to see: a twelve-inch carving knife buried to the hilt in his chest.

'Looks sort of funny, doesn't it?' said the voice behind Tobin.

Tobin looked around hoping to find Duval, but instead he found Detective Treadwell.

'I double parked,' said the young detective, knowing that would displease Tobin. It did.

Tobin wanted Duval here in the room before he wanted Detective Treadwell, because he wanted the envelope. That's why he'd sent Detective Treadwell off on a parking expedition.

'What the fuck's so funny about it?' he snarled.

'Laid out like that, looks sort of staged. A theatrical depiction of a murder victim.'

Tobin shook his head in mild disgust, major annoyance. 'What is this, then, some of your poncified university humour? What they call it – satire? Beyond the Pale?'

'Fringe, Eddie. *Beyond the Fringe*,' replied the young detective thoughtlessly, as he knelt down for a closer look at the body.

'Smart-arsed bunch of disrespectful public-school irons, the lot of them.'

'That's as maybe, Eddie, but you wouldn't get this going on in the Establishment Club.' He continued inspecting the body.

'Talk straight, Treadwell.'

'OK, how's this? The knife obviously stopped his pump straight away, accounting for the small amount of blood around the wound and hardly any on the floor. No signs of a struggle. His tie's still in place, so doesn't look like he's been in a fight. No cuts to the hands or arms, suggesting he didn't raise them to protect himself. Probably didn't think he had to. And by the time he did, it was too late. I'd say not only did he know his attacker, but he trusted him.' He glanced up at Tobin. 'Don't you think?'

'Nice way to start the New Year,' interrupted Lionel Duval, emerging from the beaded curtain that separated the back room from the main club. Sleek as a shark in a slate-grey suit, his perfectly coiffed silver hair put him in at around fifty; his smooth boyish features put him in at under forty; and the gold-framed tinted glasses that covered those cold dead eyes put him in as a night-time operator. 'The Fourth Estate will love this shit. That Duncan Webb of the *People*, he'll be all over it like a bad case of the pox. Always looking for intrigue, that man.'

The irony wasn't lost on the young detective. As he stood up to greet Duval, he couldn't help but smile. 'A scarred-faced gang-ster found with a knife practically nailing him to the floor of a Soho clip-joint isn't exactly "cat stuck up a tree" material, Mr Duval.'

Duval was a study in indignation. 'Clip-joint? Eddie, who's the adjunct?'

'This is Detective Vince Treadwell and . . .' Before Tobin could finish, Duval had reached into his jacket pocket and pulled out a wedge-heavy manila envelope. Tobin cut dead Duval's indiscretion by dipping his brow into a furrowed frown, raising his voice and putting him straight. 'Otherwise known as "Vinnie Clean Face".' Not subtle but effective. Duval went into reverse and slipped the envelope back into his pocket.

Tobin then felt the need to clarify the nickname, 'We call him that on account he's so young and fresh faced. A college boy.'

It was an apt description of the young detective, but a risible explanation of the moniker. Vince registered the point with a small cynical laugh, accompanied by an equally disdainful shake of his head.

'Oh, nice to meet you, Detective Tread . . . ?'

'Treadwell. Detective Vince Treadwell.'

'Tread-well. Detective Vince Treadwell,' Duval echoed, making a show of committing it to memory. Satisfied it had sunk in and been stored away, he pulled a big convivial grin, showing rows of expensively capped teeth. 'And please call me Lionel. All my friends call me Lionel.'

'You need Murder Squad, Mr Duval.'

Duval understood the message, but kept on grinning.

'So how come you called DS Tobin?' continued Vince.

Duval looked at Tobin for a lead, but none was forthcoming. Tobin wasn't that fast on his feet – not even in his boxing days.

'I called Eddie here because, well, he's an old acquaintance. And I knew he'd follow the correct procedures, deal with it in the proper manner. Murder Squad, Vice Squad, they're all much of a muchness to me. All you boys in blue, pinstripe, houndstooth or Harris fucking tweed for that matter are, like I said, Vince, friends of mine.' Laughing now, Duval offered Vince his hand.

Vince pointedly ignored it, gestured to the body and asked, 'So what happened here?'

The continued snubs appeared to be water off the shark's back. Duval's grin stayed fixed as he replied, 'Well, from what Colin told me—'

'Who's Colin?'

'The doorman,' replied Tobin.

Vince took out his notebook and started writing.

'Tommy Ribbons came in with two mates,' continued Duval. 'Maltese guys – dark, swarthy-looking buggers from all accounts. Nattering away in their lingo, ten to the dozen, you know how they do. They sat in the booth.' He pointed to the booth. 'Then they ordered some drinks off one of our lovely hostesses, the only one on duty at the time as it thankfully happens. When she returned with the drinks, the two swarthy fellas were gone' – Duval glanced down at the body '– and only he was left.'

'Where's the girl?' asked Tobin.

'I sent her home. She was in floods. In floods, she was, poor cow. She's new and she comes from Luton. Never seen a dead body, let alone one like this. Nice introduction to the bright lights, eh?'

'We'll need to talk to her,' said Tobin, 'and see if she got a good look at the dagos.'

Duval tut-tutted and shook his head, not in admonishment but simply to rectify that last statement. 'They were Maltese, Eddie. Dagos are Italians.'

'I thought Italians were wops,' replied Tobin. 'What's the difference?'

It was Vince's turn to shake his head. 'Nothing, Eddie. I think Mr Duval is just looking after you, wanting you to get your racial epithets right.'

Duval issued a mirthless laugh, then looked Vince up and down, reappraising the young detective. 'Oh, you're cute. Whippet-smart, and good-looking, too,' he said, nodding in wary admiration. 'Double cute.'

Vince ignored all this and carried on studying the stiff, kneeling again to take a closer look at the weapon that had put him there. 'Big knife, not the kind you'd carry around with you,' he said, looking up at Tobin, who knew Soho like the back of his fist. 'There's a hardware store on Greek Street sells kitchen supplies, right?'

Tobin nodded, his slitty eyes showing no enthusiasm for what Vince was saying.

'Maybe it wasn't planned. They saw Tommy, went and bought the knife, invited him for a drink somewhere dark and empty,' he continued, switching his attention to Lionel Duval. 'Somewhere not too many questions get asked, because they don't like the publicity, and they killed him there.'

'What's the adjunct saying, Eddie?'

Vince stood up. On its second mention, the word 'adjunct' had lost its charm.

Tobin raised two placating hands. 'He's saying nothing, Lionel. Just speculating.'

'Any other witnesses?' asked Vince. 'Punters?'

Duval shook his head, then qualified the gesture with, 'No, we'd only just opened. We don't attract the normal theatre crowd. We cater for a later clientele. A more adventurous punter, shall we say.' Again with the big convivial grin, topped off with a wink. 'All good dirty legal fun.'

'So I hear. Got any of it on film?' Vince asked.

Duval's grin turned into a grimace as he fixed Vince with a hard stare. 'Litigious little fucker, ain't he, Eddie?'

The club owner had himself recently made front-page news in the *People*, when a party at his Suffolk mansion had predictably enough turned into an orgy. But, more unpredictably, it was rumoured to have been filmed, with two-way mirrors and hidden cameras all over the gaff. Some fuzzy black-and-whites of a peer of the realm and a Russian diplomat being serviced by a rent boy and one of Duval's 'hostesses' had surfaced on Fleet Street. But the papers couldn't publish them – lots of arse shots but no faces.

'All good dirty legal fun,' echoed the smiling young detective, breaking off the staring competition with Duval and turning his attention to the booth where Tommy Ribbons had sat with his killers.

On the table, a candle stub was stuck in an empty wax-encrusted Mateus Rosé bottle but, like all the other candles in the joint, it hadn't been lit yet. Dark as it was, Vince reckoned the hostess must have seen Tommy Ribbons cop for the knife, but then Duval had straightened her out with a few quid to keep her mouth shut. Because that's what you do in Soho: look the other way and keep shtum. Killing a man in a Soho club was as safe a proposition for the perpetrator as using an empty back alley in a ghost town. Vince also figured, for what it was worth, and considering the 'keep shtum' policy that pervaded Soho, that Colin the doorman would have been standing by the neon-lit entrance, and therefore must have had a good look at the men.

He asked Duval, 'Where's Colin?'

'Out front, probably.'

Tobin to Vince: 'Why don't you go and fetch him. And call the incident in, whilst you're at it.'

Vince knew that Tobin wanted him out the room so he could finally pocket his envelope. He gave a slow, knowing nod to the two men, making his disapproval of the exchange clear.

Vince had been working Vice Squad, West End Central, for three months, now, and knew that envelopes were all part of the game. Like tips for the bin men at Christmas, that's how it was explained to him. But it was Christmas all year round for the Vice coppers in Soho, as the clubs, clip-joints, pimps, prostitutes and porno peddlers paid up every week. Just to ensure that they weren't hassled every week. It was a sweet deal, and Soho had been pretty much wide open since the Messina brothers (three Sicilian white-slavers who had exerted a stranglehold over vice and prostitution in the West End for a good fifteen years) got pinched and deported in 1955.

Since then, the nefarious activities of the West End vice rackets had separated into lots of little parcels. Which is just the way Detective Eddie Tobin and his cohorts liked it, because those little parcels soon turned into lots of little envelopes. The envelopes provided insurance for men like Duval, the largest player in Soho. So when a curtain was pulled around a private booth at the Peek-A-Boo Club, and a hostess administered a blow job to a visiting Unilever business man, a Chancery Lane barrister or a Westminster politician, a Scotland Yard policeman wouldn't suddenly pop his head around the curtain and say, 'Peek-a-boo!'

Vince dutifully went off to get Colin the doorman, then that call to Murder Squad. Thus he let Eddie Tobin collect his regular envelope off Duval who, as dirty as he was, was not a true villain – he was too busy legitimizing himself through buying up his own little parcels of land in the lucrative square mile of Soho.

The club's reception area was small. Black-and-white glossies of the hostesses, in bikinis and various stages of undress, were tacked to the varnished, pine-panelled walls. Behind a small counter with a cash register on it, a flight of steep, narrow stairs wound their way up through the tall building. But no sign of Colin.

There was a distant cracking sound, with enough force and surprise that Vince's eyes darted up towards the ceiling. It seemed to emanate from somewhere at the top of the building. Vince suspected a door slamming shut. He stepped over to the stairwell to investigate, noticing an axe and a cosh secreted under the counter. He pressed a light switch on the wall, but the stairs remained dark.

Climbing to the first floor he encountered two doors, both of them locked. On the next landing up he could see a light. On

the second floor, a shadeless light bulb on its last legs intermittently illuminated the windowless landing. A card inscribed
'Artist's Model' was tacked on to a door and he could hear both
the artist and the model at work. Breathless grunts from the artist,
and fake groans of pleasure from the model.

Hand gripping the rickety wooden banister, he carried on
climbing to the third floor, where the stairs then twisted up to a
narrow landing. The knackered light bulb in the hallway below
didn't have the strength to make its way up alongside him. Vince
gave an involuntary shudder and he was glad Tobin wasn't there
to see it. You never lose your fear of the dark, something deadly
hiding in its layers. He stood stock-still for a moment, waited for
his eyes to adjust and the blackness before him to dissipate, but
finally saw there was nothing on this landing, not even a door.

He cautiously climbed the narrow stairs to the next level, where
he could hear the whirring of a machine. It produced a soft but
steady hum, as he reached the landing. There was a sliver of
smoky-white light filtering through the gap under the door. The
whirr of the machine seemed to emphasize a deep silence – then,
from inside the room, came the sound of a girl screaming.

Vince tried the door handle, found it was locked. Working on
the logic that, if the rickety banisters were anything to go by, the
door should be a doddle. He focused on a spot just below the lock,
and stepped back against the wall for maximum impact. He then
lifted his right leg, pulling it back so his knee was just inches under
his chin, then shot the heel of his shoe backwards into the door.
The door splintered and cracked along the jamb, then burst open.

He stepped over the threshold and into a small room. On the
metal shelves lining it were stacked canisters, containing reels of
film. A projector sat on a tall metal table fitted with castors, as
the machine projected a beam of white light that cut through the
darkness and through a hole in the wall – down to where the
girl's screams were growing louder and more desperate.

Vince made his way towards the cavity and peered through it
to see a private cinema, containing just three rows holding about

twenty seats. Wall-to-ceiling carpeting served to insulate and deaden the sound as about ten men sat transfixedly staring up at the silver screen.

On the screen cavorted two men, either black or blacked up, their faces obscured by crazy-looking wigs and masks. Kitted out like B-movie savages, they were having brutal sex with a young white girl. She was bleach-blonde and junkie-thin, with needle tracks clearly dotted along her opaline arms. Her sun-starved skin displayed a mottled spectrum of pain in shades of black, blue, brown and yellow. Her red-rimmed eyes were vacantly doped up to the full.

The two men clearly weren't satisfied with the reaction they were getting off their zombie blonde, as they now began to punch her. Their punches weren't pulled, for there was real venom in their blows, real pain in her cries of distress. And Vince saw genuine fear trying to break through those glazed eyes, so he knew that this raping and beating wasn't just the usual pornographic play-acting. If it wasn't for the mocked-up jungle scenery – painted foliage, hanging ropes for vines, African shields and spears resting against a wall – it could have been happening live on a stage right now, and not through the filtered past of the movie screen . . .

All the stuffed envelopes in the world didn't cover this level of degeneracy, thought Vince. This wasn't one of the conventional blue movies and stag films that did the rounds of the private cinema clubs of Soho . . . He suddenly turned numb as he watched one of the men raise a knife . . .

Vince couldn't take his eyes off the screen, but he felt helpless to save the skinny girl. All he could do now was to stop the projector – but even that was too late, for her horrifying narrative had already run its course. This was just a record of it, and he was powerless to intervene as the inevitable played out before him. Nausea invaded his guts and started twisting and churning. Sweat prickled along his spine, and his whole body felt overwhelmed.

He was about to break the trance and heave the projector on to the floor, when he noticed a tall figure framed in the doorway.

The girl on the silver screen gave a final scream that trailed off into nothing.

The door slammed shut.

Then blackout.

CHAPTER 2

GOD SAVE THE QUEEN

10 May 1964. Scotland Yard.

'That's not what happened, sir.'

'Are you in dispute with me, Treadwell?'

'No, sir.'

The man sitting across the desk from him was Chief Super-intendent Ian Markham. Stiff and starched in his beribboned, inky-blue uniform, hands clasped before him, he represented authority exuding authority. Markham had an open file laid before him, and the Queen behind him. How's that for backup? thought Vince.

'You clearly *are* in dispute with me. And saying you're not just puts you further in dispute with me.'

'Sir.' Vince didn't put a 'yes' or a 'no' in front of his response, because he didn't want to risk further dispute by either agreeing that he was in dispute or denying it.

'Good. Then the case is closed,' said Markham, also closing the file to emphasize the point.

Vince imperceptibly shook his head in resignation to the fact that what was written in black and white on that report would soon be filed away as the truth. But it wasn't the truth, and he could never resign himself to the lies. He felt it burning and bubbling up inside him and just couldn't help himself blurting out, 'Eddie Tobin takes an envelope from Lionel Duval every week because he's bought and paid for and would do anything Duval wants him to, because that's where his loyalties lie.'

Markham's face was set rigid as he took stock. Then leaned forward, hands clasped again, tightening, white knuckles. 'Edward Tobin has served the Met with distinction for twenty-five years,' said Markham. 'I've no need to inform you of our disbelief concerning your judgement in this case.'

Markham unclasped his hands and leaned back, elongating his already long body against the back of the tall chair, as if stretching his authority before the young detective. He didn't stop there, but Vince had stopped listening, and focused instead on the portrait of the Queen behind him. Demure in her long black robe, she seemed to be smiling at him. She looked a little coquettish, comely and come-hither. He thought he might . . . she looked good. He wasn't giving serious thought to it, but all things considered, he would rather have been doing anything right now than be sitting opposite Markham, who was currently building up a head of steam and sounding as if he was about to erupt at any moment.

Vince stopped thinking about the Queen and focused his attention back on to the Chief Superintendent. What with Markham's thick, effulgently brilliantined and suspiciously black hair, the black-robed Queen behind him looked like an extension of his head. As if she was growing out of him? No doubt Markham was waiting for the moment when Her Majesty really did stand over him, as he knelt before her to finally have the working-class chips knocked off his shoulders with her ceremonial sword. Arise, Sir Ian, thirty years of loyal service to Queen and Country. And what of the young detective? Off with his head for servicing the Queen! The thought brought a slight smile to Vince's lips.

Not slight enough to escape Markham. 'I'm glad you think this is funny.'

'I don't, sir,' he replied, underestimating his folly with the Queen. But, after what he'd been through, he deserved a laugh.

He'd recently spent twenty-three days in a coma. The doctors were surprised at this, as the head injury had not been that severe. No lasting physical damage to the cranium, the surrounding tissue or the brain itself. A little blood draining to relieve some pressure from a 'dent on the bonnet', as the surgeon called it. And that was pretty much it from the sawbones. Four weeks of observation and further testing in the hospital, then three weeks of rest and getting his strength up at a sanatorium on the Kent coast. He'd lost weight, suffered muscle loss, felt as weak as a baby, so he had exercised in the gymnasium every day to get it back. Push-ups, press-ups, sit-ups, dumbbells, medicine ball and callisthenics.

A private Harley Street psychologist who specialized in head trauma had taken an interest in his case and volunteered to oversee his recovery. His name was Dr Hans Boehm and, as quacks go, he was straight from the Rank Organization's central casting. He reminded Vince of the professor in the Donald Duck cartoons, quack, quack! He had wild grey hair, a long beard, and spoke in a thick Viennese accent. You couldn't have made him up.

It was while talking to Boehm that Vince remembered what he had seen in the projection room, and then the figure at the door. Boehm didn't seem to judge Vince negatively, but Vince could tell that he didn't seem to believe him either. He explained to Vince how his version of events had played out in the dark, always a fertile playground for the imagination. Stripped of sight, the most powerful sensory guide, the imagination tended to run riot. *The eye is merely a lens, for it's with the brain that we see.* And just because the lens was temporarily switched off, the brain would keep on seeing – but it sees what it wants to see, no longer refracted through the lens but through the power of the imagination. With a beaming grin and in a thick Viennese accent, he reminded Vince that 'It is only in the night that things go dump, no?' Vince assured him he wasn't scared of the dark.

Boehm then adopted a more prosaic approach by asking Vince if there was any history of epilepsy in his family. Vince said there wasn't. When asked if he himself had ever been prone to blackouts, seizures or time loss, he said he hadn't. When the good doctor then inquired about any history of schizophrenia in the family, Vince felt like chinning the quack. But, realizing this would just add fuel to the fire, he solemnly and unanimously informed him that there was no such history. Dr Boehm gave Vince some pills for the sporadic headaches he was suffering and reassured him it was just his brain 'rewiring' itself after the coma. He was then given a clean bill of health.

But Vince was far from happy. Bang on the head or no bang on the head, he clearly remembered what he'd seen at the Peek-A-Boo Club on Wardour Street. In the projection room. The girl being raped and beaten on the screen. The knife held above her. The figure at the door. The man slamming the door shut. Then the big blackout.

Then, as Vince viewed it, the lies that followed. Eddie Tobin had filed his report, and everything was as it was. Tommy Ribbons corpsed out on the deck with a fuck-off carving knife through his pump (the killer nicked two days later was his brother-in-law, as it seemed Tommy had been cheating on his wife with his sister-in-law). A club hostess with the mostest from Luton not seeing a thing. Duval the proprietor not seeing a thing. Colin the unconvincing bantamweight bouncer not seeing a thing, because he was out buying pastries in Frith Street when it all happened. Oh, one thing missing: the handing over of an envelope from Duval to Tobin. But, as no one saw a thing, why waste typewriter ribbon on such details?

Then Tobin's report really did slip on to the bestseller list. After Detective Treadwell failed to return with Colin the doorman, Tobin and Duval had climbed the stairs to the fourth floor, where they found the young detective sparked out in the . . . *storage room*. Not a projection room, of course, because, according to all

21

involved, there was no projection room. Because there was no private cinema club.

As soon as Vince read Tobin's report, which was withheld from him until he was fully recuperated, he went back to the Peek-A-Boo Club. He climbed the stairs, entered the room and found a . . . *storage room*. Just mops, buckets, brooms, empty boxes. Vince wanted to get a warrant to tear the place apart, scrape off the wallpaper to reveal the fresh plaster used to cover the hole in the wall – to cover up the lies. They said no, so he went next-door to a building, also owned by Duval, and which he believed had housed the private cinema club – only to find it was a newly converted, empty office space.

And the figure framed in the doorway, the man Vince thought to have been the projectionist? No one saw him. No one knew him. He didn't exist.

And Vince's head wound? He must have got it when he fell. Tripped over something in the dark. A bump in the night.

For Dr Boehm, Eddie Tobin, Chief Superintendent Markham, and everyone else involved, what Vince experienced that night in the Peek-A-Boo just did not happen. His brain was rewiring itself and playing tricks on him. To Vince, however, it was just a big fat cover-up.

But even with the weight of evidence against him, and the facts written up and signed off in the file lying before him, Vince couldn't concede what he felt to be the truth. Just like he couldn't save the girl on the silver screen. To give in would be to say that she didn't exist. As he convalesced in the sanatorium, he painted a picture in his mind of the sad junkie life that had led to her starring role. Vince reckoned she must have suffered more than enough of not existing, or barely registering in life, and ultimately being seen as disposable. So it was left to him to keep her image alive, to conjure her up. To let her simply go would be to lose himself, lose his reason for becoming a policeman. The girl became his measure; his sense of value and belief system. And Vince knew that one day he would return to that case and prove it. Justice for the girl would prevail, and he would destroy the men who did it to her.

'Where do you stand on the current anti-establishment fad, Treadwell?'

Vince's ears pricked up. Anti-establishment? Hardly just a fad, he thought. 'Sir?'

'Have a taste for subversive humour?'

'Not that I'm aware of, sir.'

'I do wonder. I believe a television programme with Mr David Frost is popular amongst some of the younger officers in the canteen.'

'*That Was The Week That Was.*'

'Quite so.'

'I have watched it, sir.'

'Mocking Harold Macmillan and other public servants. Who's next, the Queen?!'

'Let's hope not, sir,' said Vince, smiling satirically. 'I'm much more a fan of Mr Tony Hancock and *Steptoe and Son* – and, of course, *Dixon of Dock Green*. As for the Queen, I always stand up just before the telly finishes for the night.'

Markham leaned forward on his desk, threading his hands together to make a steeple, his thumbs acting as a chin rest, the tips of his forefingers just touching the end of his nose. With his narrowed eyes locked on to Vince's, he gave him a penetrating and knowing look. Being caught in Markham's crosshairs spooked Vince enough for him to shift from cheek to cheek in his seat, and to indulge in a nervous clearing of his throat.

Markham took his own sweet authoritative time, letting a weighty silence fill the room, as if to expunge the atmosphere of the trivialities that had just passed between them, and get back on to the sure-footing of police business rather than show business.

A slight smile quivered then parted Markham's lips, and he said, almost lasciviously, 'I know what you want, Treadwell. You want Murder.'

'Yes, sir,' said Vince with a cut-glass authority to match the Chief Superintendent's tone, and the Queen's, for that matter.

Markham's furtive smile broadened once the apple had been taken, then snapped again into cold composure as he sat back in his chair. "'Course you do. Murder Squad. Who doesn't? That's not a question, it's a statement of fact. You're from Brighton, aren't you, Treadwell?'

'Sir.'

'Got something for you, then. Kill two birds with one stone. You're owed some holiday, and I think this is the time for it.'

'Sort of itching to get back to work, actually, sir. And I don't really consider Brighton a holiday destination.'

'Treadwell, been watching Mr Alan Wicker, have you?'

Vince didn't answer. Better safe than sorry. And Markham wasn't listening, anyway. He had his plans for Vince sorted out before the young detective had stepped through the door.

'It would be a dereliction of my duty, Treadwell, if I did not inform you of the hostilities felt from certain quarters towards you as a result of your accusations regarding Detective Tobin,' said Markham methodically. 'Edward Tobin leaves us in three weeks. Retirement, bungalow in Bournemouth, I believe. Good luck to him. Best keep out of his way, and let this thing blow over. Don't want any unpleasantness meanwhile. For those three weeks, you will take a well-deserved break. Some rest and relaxation, visit your family. And this,' Markham opened his desk drawer and pulled out a case file, 'should keep the grey matter ticking over.' He shunted the file across the desk.

Vince opened it.

'I know you took an interest in the case when it first came up,' Markham continued, getting up from behind his desk in readiness to usher the young detective out. 'I contacted the Superintendent in Brighton. He said they'd be happy to have you, though it's not officially being handed over to Scotland Yard. And you'd only be down there in an advisory capacity. But it's a murder case, so a step in the right direction. A foot in the door.'

Vince looked at the grisly morgue photos featuring a decapitated body. But the image that really caught his eye was a small browning mugshot taken some thirty years ago. He found himself looking at the face of Jack Regent.

With his eyes still fixed on the photo, Vince said softly, and meditatively, 'A foot in the door. Thank you, sir.'

Vince closed the file, stood up and shook Markham's hand. As he did so, he looked up at the Queen. Wham bam, thank you, Ma'am!

CHAPTER 3

BRIGHTON

Victoria Station was busy with the Whitsun bank-holiday crowds pouring down to Brighton to escape The Smoke. For Vince, Brighton held little seaside appeal or escape from the city. It was a town, but with the feel of a city. A city by the sea. The built-up tenement flats and tightly terraced rows that climbed their way up to the race hill; the white-walled Regency squares offering a facade of symmetry and order to a place that Vince knew was more like a tangled web; the two hulking hotels, the Grand and the Metropole, which sat imperiously on the seafront; the paving stones and corroding blue railings of the promenade that led you down to the beach itself.

And then the stones. Lots of them. And broken glass, tar and gnarled, desiccated seaweed that scratched you like rusted barbed wire. There were no sand dunes to play in, no soft landings in this town. To Vince, it was a city like London, just smaller. In London, if you went too far south you got depressed; in Brighton you just got wet. Seagulls ruled the air, not pigeons. Someone once said it was where the debris meets the sea – and that went for the people as well as the place. Vince's relationship with his home town was a two-fisted affair: Love and Hate.

He bought his ticket and boarded the packed train. With his second-class ticket, he sat in the first-class carriage; just a flash of the badge and the ticket clippy usually gave him the nod, like there was some sort of affinity in uniforms. Clippies and coppers, all trying to keep things running in a good orderly direction, and on time. The train was ten minutes late pulling out of the station, due to ejected drunks.

Three weeks, Markham had suggested, so Vince had packed accordingly. Two suits, five shirts, two knitted ties, three Fred Perry tennis shirts, a couple of pairs of summer slacks, a light-blue seersucker jacket, a dark-blue skinny-brimmed straw trilby and a pair of Wayfarer sunglasses for when − or if − the sun ever came out. He also threw in a couple of paperbacks, and a signed hardback copy of the book Dr Boehm had just had published, *The Conceit of the Narcissist: A Long, Lingering Look at the Dangerously One-Track Mind in the Mirror.*

Vince had cooled on this case since Markham had assigned it. He now looked at it for what it was: keeping him off the scene until Eddie Tobin had cleared his desk, collected his mantel clock, and fucked off down to Bournemouth to get some sand in his crab-paste sandwiches.

It might be a murder case but, as far as the ID of the perpetrator was concerned, there seemed to be little mystery involved. It was not so much a *Who done it?* as a *Where is he?* and here's how it had played out. Eleven weeks ago, the body of a male Caucasian in his mid-forties was washed up on Brighton beach. Wrapped in tarpaulin, it floated up smack-bang between the two piers. A major feature of the corpse was that its head and hands had been removed. And, as fingerprints and dental records were pretty much the alpha and omega for tagging stiffs, that made it next to impossible to identify the victim.

He didn't match any missing persons within the time-frame of death given by Pathology. His blood type, O positive, was as common as muck. No tattoos or real distinguishing marks. The carving knife that had been used in the massacre was wrapped in air-tight cellophane and taped to the body. There were fingerprints, or partial print traces, still on the knife. All in all, making for a nice police package. Too nice a package, Vince reckoned. And, to top it off, an anonymous caller had tipped off Scotland Yard that Jack Regent was the killer. But for every murder there's half a dozen confessors and a baker's dozen of accusers; usually telephone thrill-seekers getting their long-distance kicks.

Markham contacted the Chief Supe in Brighton, and Jack Regent was nicked. Only he wasn't, because he'd skipped town. And so had his fingerprints. It seemed there were no copies of Jack Regent's prints on record. Or, if there were, they'd disappeared. As for the mysterious anonymous phone call nailing Jack Regent for this murder, it was commonplace. Regent's status in the town was almost that of celebrity, but for all that he was enigmatic, publicity-shy and as seldom seen as Garbo. But everyone knew the name, knew the legend.

Vince opened his case and took out the Jack Regent file. Some fact, some fiction, but mostly accumulated speculation. Because, in his long criminal career, Jack Regent had only been brought to book once. A seven-year stretch for the malicious wounding of a bookie almost thirty years ago, reduced to eighteen months after he had saved a screw from a serious beating during a prison riot. And nothing else – but no surprises there. For shit, thankfully, has a downward trajectory, so there were plenty of others who had taken the fall for Jack Regent.

Vince read on and pieced together Jack's personal trajectory. Little of the early life of Jack Regent's, neé Jacques Rinieri, was known. No known documentation or records, just hearsay, and here's what it said. Born in Corsica, he came to London in his late teens, and settled in the slum area of the Seven Dials. But he then made his rep in Saffron Hill, London's Italian quarter in Clerkenwell. Charles 'Darby' Sabini and his Italian mob were the prevailing force at the time, holding sway over Soho and clubland. But their biggest racket, in fact the biggest racket during the twenties and thirties, was conducted at the racetracks.

Sabini's razor gang ran the racecourses in England. The top coppers and judges of the day were rumoured to all be in his pocket and, with the money he was making, his pockets were deep and plentiful. The racetrack rackets were like any other protection racket. If a bookie wanted to set up his 'pitch' and lay bets at the races, he had to pay someone for the privilege. Protecting the bookies and taking a percentage of their earnings could bring him in twenty grand in a day. For a big meeting like the Epsom Derby, it could go up to fifty grand. In the twenties and thirties, that was big, big money. And control of the racetracks meant you could control every street-corner bookie, spieler, betting and lay-off parlour in London.

A young Jack (or Jacques as he was still known then) was recruited by Sabini when his gang went to war with the Brummigan Boys. The rival gang from the Black Country was headed up by William Kimber, a Birmingham-based bookmaker. Young Jacques Rinieri fitted the bill: though not Italian by nationality, he had enough hot-headed Mediterranean blood coursing through his veins to find an affinity with Sabini. And Sabini liked young Jacques, saw something of himself in him. He treated him like a son and renamed him 'Jack'. And so it was that young Jack went about his work for Sabini with a diligence and enthusiasm that, along with his club foot, marked him out from the others. Jack was soon leading from the front, cutting, beating and shooting his way to a reputation of fearlessness.

The battles on the racecourses, involving gangs of one or two hundred, made a day at the races a dangerous place to be for the average punter in the late twenties. But Jack didn't just wait for the race meetings to show his supremacy; he took the fight to them. Ambushing the Brummigan Boys in their pubs, clubs, spielers, train stations or on street corners. When dead bodies started turning up, this new type of organized violence made front-page news, and questions were soon asked in Parliament. An elite group of tough coppers known as the Ghost Squad, with the authorization to fight as dirty as the gangsters themselves, was put together to crush the gangs. It all came to a head in a fierce battle at Lewes racecourse. The Sabini mob, with Jack leading the fray, beat Kimber's Brummigan Boys, but the game was over and his men were rounded up. At Lewes Assizes, forty of Sabini's men were handed heavy sentences of up to twenty years each.

But young Jack, and Darby Sabini himself, slipped under the net and moved down to Brighton. It's in Brighton that Jack further anglicized his name, deferring to the royal origin of the town by turning Rinieri into 'Regent'. Darby Sabini, wise to the last, understood the Darwinian nature of his business and, sensing Jack's growing contempt for the old-school ways, began to fear his ambition and ruthlessness and decided not to stand in his way. Sabini relinquished his penthouse suite in the Grand Hotel, and retired to the more sedate garden squares of neighbouring Hove.

Whatever mobs existed in Brighton, they were no match for Jack. They'd never seen anything like him. He soon imposed his will and took his slice of everything Brighton had to offer. And that was a lot, including gambling, thieving, fencing, protection, prostitution, pubs and clubs. The town was wide open, ready and waiting, and when the War came, Jack turned even more profit. The black market, ration cards, petrol cards, blackout smash-and-grabs, not to mention headline-grabbing bank and wages robberies. Post-war austerity soon turned into post-war prosperity and 'You've never had it so good', and no one was having it as good as Jack. With rock and roll playing on the jukebox and a packet of three in every man's back pocket, Jack invested in vending machines – slots, jukeboxes, arcades. Every time a day-tripper put a penny in a slot machine on the south coast, they also were putting a penny in Jack's pocket. He had the town sewn up, his enemies stitched up, and 'allegedly' the law in his pocket.

But, to Vince, Jack Regent wasn't just a name on a case file, or a criminal that needed catching. Vince had grown up on Albion Hill, a tough breeding ground for young tearaways, so he had lived under the spell that Jack cast over the town. Kids would sit around and swap stories in hushed tones of his daring deeds: the headline-grabbing jobs he'd pulled, the beatings he'd doled out, the killings he'd committed, and the fear that he invoked in grown men. Young Vince would listen to those whispered stories, and had once asked his mother about Jack Regent. He'd registered the fear on her face as she told him never to mention that name again. Her reluctance to talk just confirmed what Vince had heard on the streets. And therefore, filtered through the imagination of a child, Jack became omnipotent, omnipresent, a bogeyman, a hex and altogether the stuff of nightmares.

Then there was the physical twist that further set him apart and gave him a quality of otherness: *Talipes Equinovarus*, a club foot. Vince had once read up on Jack's affliction, and discovered he was in historic company. The Roman emperor Claudius, along with a list of other ailments, was club-footed. But as Roman emperors went, he wasn't as exciting to read about as his predecessor, Caligula. Then there was Joseph Goebbels, the Nazi propagandist; as well as possessing a forked tongue, he, too, was rumoured to have a club foot. But the most famous club-foot pin-up boy was Lord Byron. Vince had struggled through *Don Juan* and, whilst Byron's verse hadn't stuck in his mind, his reputation had: 'mad, bad and dangerous to know'. So bad, in fact, that the club foot was rumoured to have been a cloven hoof. Jack Regent would appreciate that, thought Vince.

Vince closed the file, deciding he'd fill in the blanks for himself.

'Here he is now, come down to help us swedes. Want a lift, guv?' called out Detective Tony Machin as he saw Vince emerge from the concourse at Brighton station. Machin was leaning against his racing-green Jaguar Mk X, parked where the taxis sat and waited.

'Don't tell me – you've given up being a copper and become a taxi driver?' Vince smiled.

'Better tips, and I get to hear what's really happening in this town.'

The two men shook hands. It had been about ten years since they'd last seen each other. They'd grown up in the same neighbourhood, but on different hills.

Machin took Vince's suitcase and put it in the back seat. 'Let's get a drink, son,' he suggested.

Machin shouldered his way into the pub, with Vince following behind him. It was a small boozer off Edward Street, just up from Brighton police station.

'Two pints please, Shirley.'

'Make one of those a club soda,' said Vince.

'What? Don't drink on duty?' Machin asked with a big grin.

'Don't drink full-stop.'

Machin stopped grinning when he realized that Vince wasn't kidding. He looked as if he'd genuinely never heard anything like it before. 'Fuck me, son, a copper that doesn't drink.' He looked around at the barmaid for verification that he wasn't imagining things. 'Hear that, Shirley?'

'Not all pissheads like you, Anthony,' said Shirley, giving Vince her customary wink and rolling out a gregarious smile. The term 'bubbly blonde' was invented for her, but she'd missed out on 'bombshell'.

Machin was a regular, so she paid him little mind, because her eyes were all over Vince Treadwell. And she liked what she saw: thick black shiny hair swept back, smooth olive skin, green-brown eyes, a strong straight nose and full lips that Shirley decided were eminently kissable, above a chin that held a dimple − like that actor she fancied, Kirk Douglas. But his dark looks gave him a touch of that other one she liked, Tony Curtis. Shirley habitually compared the pub's punters with Hollywood film stars, thus managing to turn a dingy little backstreet pub in Kemp Town into the Brown Derby in Hollywood with her, 'Ooh, a fella came in the other night, looked just like so and so . . .' All much to the annoyance of her friends, who'd turn up expecting to find at least a

Dirk Bogarde or a Terence Stamp, only to be confronted with a Norman Wisdom. Very few of those men matched up to Shirley's flights of fantastical description, but this one finally did. He was tall, and she liked them tall, just scraping six foot, with broad shoulders. A light middleweight, athletic and fast-looking under a smart light-grey three-button suit, black knitted-silk tie and crisp white shirt. Took pride in his appearance, she could tell by his footwear, for he was wearing polished black Chelsea boots. Classy, she thought. The sight of men's socks were always a turn-off.

Yeah, Shirley liked him. But she knew her true value in the looks stakes and had him sussed as an arrogant piece of work who also knew his value, and knew she didn't stand a chance with him. Not sober anyway. She resented pouring his club soda. As she pulled the pump for Machin's beer, she squeezed her shoulders together and deliberately stooped. It had the desired effect, for both Machin and Vince were instantly drawn to her cleavage; plump, flawless breasts encased in a black lacy bra, under a sheer leopard-spot print blouse.

Machin winked at Vince and said loudly, 'The beer's shit but the view's priceless.'

'But you can't see the sea from here,' she replied, with a wink.

'I'm looking at the best front in town,' said Machin, winking back.

'Cheeky bugger!' She winked at Vince.

Vince thought about joining in the winking, since it was obviously infectious – like conjunctivitis.

'He is a cheeky sod, this one!' said Shirley, her voice full of mock indignation. 'A disgrace to the boys in blue!' She looked at Vince; it was him she wanted for the conversation. There was more winking. More mock scandal, and sirens of laughter from Shirley.

Vince had heard enough now and steered his club soda over to a table by the window. He had the case file with him and flicked through it whilst he waited for Machin, who was still courting Shirley with the double-entendre shtick.

33

Machin was stocky, with cropped hair that saved him from a comb-over. No neck, tough and solid. Vince wondered if he could take him in a fight. He was shorter than Vince, but carried the kind of heft that was hard to knock down. It had always struck Vince as odd that Machin had become a copper, for while growing up, Machin had always got himself involved in the stuff that Vince had grown out of and avoided. But he'd never taken a pinch for any of it, nor picked up a record. So why not be a copper? Pay's not bad, the pension's good, and there's more than enough sidelines and backhanders to make the grief worth it. And that's exactly how Vince pegged Tony Machin.

Machin dumped himself next to Vince, his bulk reverberating through the foam and vinyl bench. He tapped his head with a forefinger and asked, 'How's the bonce?'

'Still ticking over,' Vince said, raising his glass. 'Cheers.'

'Cheers. A coma? What's that like, then, son?'

'Eminently forgettable.'

'You slipped or something, so I heard?'

Vince just nodded, not wanting to get further into the subject, whereas Machin held his beer up expectantly, halfway between the table and his mouth, wanting to get into it.

'That's right, I slipped. Lights out. Goodnight, Vienna,' said Vince, hoping to put the matter to bed. 'Can't remember a thing. No big deal.'

Machin nodded slowly, more a gesture of weighing him up than agreeing with him. 'I see, son, I see,' he said, eventually lifting the pint to his lips and taking a gulp.

Son? That grated on Vince. They were the same age, more or less, though Machin managed to look a good ten years older. On the plus side, it reduced the times Machin called him by his first name, and Vince enjoyed the distance that gave them. He recognized his own taciturn tendencies when he wasn't a hundred per cent about someone, and Machin was destined to be that someone. Vince reopened the file on the table, before Machin could use it as a beer mat.

'Mr Jack Regent,' noted Machin, in a proclamatory tone.

'Any clues?'

'He's not here. We've already looked. Not a stone unturned,' said Machin, raising a halting hand. 'And don't tell me there's a lot of stones in Brighton. We know, and that's how busy we've been with it.'

'I don't doubt that for a second. I hear the south of France, and even Corsica, are nice at this time of year.'

Machin gave a confirmatory nod to the suggestion. 'Odds on, son. Money in Swiss accounts. Enough to pay off whoever might need paying off. Spend the rest of his days sitting pretty in the sun. With the money he's made, why wouldn't he?'

Vince considered this, and it made sense. A man in the autumn of his years, getting out of the rackets to enjoy the fruits of his ill-gotten gains. But Vince hadn't come down to Brighton to toast Jack Regent's good fortune. 'Maybe Regent's not ready to retire. It's his town – got a lot invested here. I thought there might be something about the fingerprints on that knife. Could be a frame-up?'

'Frame-up?' demanded Machin, looking as if he might blow the head off his beer with a snort of derision. 'What's wrong with him just getting sloppy? Jack Regent messed up. It was bound to happen sooner or later. They get away with it for years and then they get complacent, and that's how we get 'em.'

Vince took a sip of his club soda and mulled over Machin's assessment. He wasn't buying it but conceded that, when it came to Jack Regent, he himself did have a vivid imagination. Maybe Vince was looking at it from a kid's perspective. He'd left Brighton at eighteen and never really returned. Machin had stayed, still lived and worked in the town, and knew Jack personally. To Machin, maybe he was just another villain, more successful than most but still just a villain. Fallible, not invincible. Not a young man any more.

Vince drained his club soda and asked a more sober question: 'Any clues to who the body was?'

Machin took a large gulp of his pint and shook his head. 'Not a clue, son. And we can't keep it on ice forever. He'll be going in the ground this week.'

Vince picked up the autopsy photos for a closer look. The headless and handless corpse on the white slab. The smooth hairless chest, with skin like a woman. But even dead, and his body decomposing, Vince could detect the musculature of a strong, sinewy type. He looked like an athlete, yet the report revealed that his liver showed fatty deposits, early signs of cirrhosis, and there were shadows on his lungs. A heavy drinker and smoker, then. Vince thought about the victim and, as with the girl on the silver screen, tried to give him life. A history, a story. Maybe it was because he couldn't see his face, his eyes, but he drew blanks this time. The victim remained faceless and lifeless.

'Even when you're dead, you're still not out of breath,' remarked Vince. 'And with all the gases that build up in a body buried at sea, there's more than enough to float you to the top even if you're weighed down. Pros usually stab the chest, puncture the lungs, to let all the air out, so you drop like a stone. And, let's face it, we've got to have Jack pegged as a pro, right?'

Machin nodded in agreement.

Vince ran the tip of his forefinger around the corpse in the photograph. 'No chest wounds on our boy. My guess, he was meant to be found. And planted with a knife with prints on it.'

'Only trace prints. Nothing to get too excited about, son.'

'Even so, how hard is it to wipe a knife clean? Then it's sealed and taped to the body? Whoever did this, wanted us to know who did it – or else frame someone for it.'

Machin didn't look convinced. He drained his pint and wiped his mouth with the back of his meaty hand.

Just then, the pub door swung open and a suited man lurched in. He was in his mid to late twenties, his freckled face topped off with bright ginger hair that had been dulled down with fistfuls of Brylcreem. Flushed, redder than usual for a redhead, he looked as if he'd just beaten Bannister's record by running up the hill from the station on Edward Street. He was a copper, and it was urgent. He gave Shirley, with her bawdy banter, a swerve and came straight over to Machin.

'Vince, meet Ginge, our copper-topped copper,' said Machin, giving Vince his now customary nod and a wink. 'He's a good boy, local, give you all the help you need with the new faces in town. What's up, Ginge?'

Ginge was still catching his breath as he told him, 'Bodies.'

CHAPTER 4

BODIES

Three of them. Two white men and a half-caste girl, but all reduced to the same waxy, junkie pallor. What little colour they had in their faces had left them the minute they'd taken the lethal dose of heroin. Hard to age, early twenties maybe, but they looked as if they'd already lived a lifetime – and all of it bad. Undernourished and frayed-looking, with dried foam around their mouths, vomit on their clothing. Two blood-stained syringes on the ash-smeared oatmeal carpet.

Vince bent down for a closer look. The pretty half-caste girl wore her nails long and painted letter-box red, but they were now hanging from her fingertips by bloody threads. Two nails completely off, embedded into the carpet. They looked like falsies but weren't, which meant she'd obviously tried to dig her way out of the misery and pain she suffered just before the heroin finally dragged her under.

He stood up and looked around the Kemp Town bedsit. Not even a bed, just a sit. A green vinyl sofa sagged on the floor, with yellow foam bulging out of the tears. A beaten-up leather patchwork pouffe with its kapok guts hanging out. The floor was littered with sweet and chocolate-bar wrappers. Mars bars, Bounties, Opal Fruits and Crunchies had been on the menu – junkie diet.

The main feature of the room was a big shiny hi-fi, a small stack of 45s and 33s beside it. Everything else was fixed to the walls: fireplace, central-heating radiators, empty shelves, a small green-streaked washbasin in the corner. A hundred-watt naked light bulb hung from the ceiling, to throw a brutal light on the death scene. It was like a place to shoot heroin in the comfort of not being in your own home. A horse stable but little more.

Machin was holding up a small cellophane wrap of tarry-black nuggets in some tweezers. He dropped this in a plastic evidence bag.

'What a bloody mess,' he said, handing Vince the baggie. 'Not seen this stuff before. The gear we see is usually just a dirty white powder.'

Vince inspected the nuggets. The sample had an organic purity about it, more like black Moroccan hashish. 'IDs?' he asked.

'A woman downstairs says she'd seen the bloke with the beard coming in and out, but didn't know who actually lived here. Said they made a racket, playing their music all night.'

Vince gazed down at the bloke with the beard. Not much of a beard, not much of a bloke. Looked like he weighed about eight stone. Stained drainpipe jeans, scuffed winkle-picker boots, a turtleneck jumper with holes. A vague stab at the Beatnik look, perhaps? But, by the tracks on his arms, Vince could tell he was already a seasoned junkie who'd let the fashion plate, along with everything else in his life, slide off the table.

Photos were taken of the bodies and the room. What evidence there was there was gathered. Then the three corpses on the floor were bundled on to stretchers, strapped and carted off for autopsies and toxicology reports. Simple: death by misadventure and desperation.

'The whole building belongs to a Paul DeGelb,' said Machin. 'You heard of him?'

Vince nodded. 'Slum landlord in Notting Hill. Crossed his path when I was working out of Shepherd's Bush. DeGelb probably owns the freehold, but can't shift the tenants downstairs who've been there for years. You gradually get them out by turning the place into a shit hole. Get some junkies living in the building, up all night, playing loud music, pissing the other tenants off. They soon enough sell up or leave.'

'Well, he's started buying property down here. Got some other places in the Avenues.'

Vince kneeled down to flip open the lid of the hi-fi. The long-playing 33 record on the turntable was Rachmaninoff's *Third Piano Concerto*. 'Not exactly soothing rhythms to nod out to, this. They look like they'd be more into Bob Dylan,' he observed. He then flicked through the stack of records. Some were by bands of the day, loud and electric; some were brass-band marching music; also a recording of animal noises and a recording of Donald Wolfit's selected Shakespeare monologues. A disparate collection, certainly, but all with one element in common: loud and annoying.

Vince picked up a 45 by a band called The Shakers, five quiffed youths wielding washboards, kazoos and a tea chest. Obviously they were a skiffle band. Vince recognized one of the chubby-cheeked smilers on the cover as the dead Beatnik found lying on the carpet. Vince flipped the record and checked his ID. 'Chas Starlight, he was calling himself back then,' said Vince, handing the record over to Machin. 'Not a lot of Starlight left now.'

'Dominate Records,' said Machin, reading the label. 'They must have been one of Dickie Eton's outfits.' Vince recognized the name. 'Eton lives down here,' said Machin. He clicked his fingers for recall. 'What's the name of that singer, the fella with the big lips?'

Vince gave a *how the fuck should I know* shrug and offered, 'Nat King Cole?'

'Like the Beatles.'

'The Rolling Stones?'

'That's the ones. I heard they wanted Eton to manage them and produce all their records. Eton turned them down. Shrewd move if you ask me. They won't last.'

★ ★ ★

The main incident room at Edward Street police station was all about the Kemp Town three. It was a frenzy of ringing phones and activity: coppers getting a run on where the syringes were supplied; who was out there dealing, and how much of the lethal stuff was on the street.

The heroin had been sent off to the lab for toxicology reports, but just the very raw tarriness of it told Vince that it was pure. Too pure for street consumption. It should have been cut, cut, then cut again. With quinine, laxative or talc. Whoever had supplied it didn't know what the fuck they had, or what they were doing, and neither did the three who took it. Death by misadventure it may have been, but three of them made it a headline-grabbing incident. Questions were being asked: *Does Brighton have a drug problem?* Whilst pills were frowned on, they were understood and semi-tolerated. From dodos in the morning medicine cabinets to dexies in the all-night dance halls, it seemed that in 1964 everyone needed a livener. But this was heroin . . . Blood. Fire. Needles. Nodding zombies. Oblivion. Death. No one understood it. Bad for the image of the town, even for a town that thrived on having a bad image.

So it was all being kept very much on the QT. The blessed fourth estates weren't being told it was heroin, but amphetamines, pills of some description. Because three dead in a seedy bedsit on heroin – that *was* going to put a dent in the day-tripper trade. The body on the beach was on the back burner. It had slipped out of the public's consciousness like it had slipped off the front page. No one really cared about it now, headless/handless/horrific or not. It was an old case already, left to Vince to keep it alive before it completely slipped off the dial and into a sealed file. Those kids slipping their mortal coils on hard drugs, that's what had seized the Brighton constabulary's attention now. The papers would lap it up. A sign of the times. The new scourge. The new plague! And that's where Machin was, too, downstairs giving a press conference with his Supe and the Chief Inspector.

Vince was sitting in Machin's office, drinking tea, looking at mugshots and reading the reports on the case. He'd also dug up some info on Dickie Eton, real name Neville Roper. A prodigious and precocious talent, and a millionaire before he was twenty-five. Pushy parents from Peacehaven had put their boy on the stage. A talent scout spotted him at Worthing rep, and he was signed up to the Rank Oganization. This slender hoity-toity boy was marketed at first as the new Freddie Bartholomew, and renamed 'Dickie Eton'. Lots of Little Lord Fauntleroy roles in comedies and musicals. He was also a teenage recording star with four top-ten hits.

But Rank's plans for Dickie to grow into as big a star as Dirk Bogarde never materialized. He stopped short of becoming a grown-up matinee or pop-idol stardom when he stopped growing. At five foot three inches he was never going to cut it in the big time. He stayed stunted and got bitter and twisted. But he was determined – determined to wreak revenge on all those who scoffed and saw him as a spent force.

He started working for promoter Larry Parnes as a talent spotter in the music business. Larry taught him artist management, looked on him as a son. Then he started working with the record producer, Joe Meek, and learned the production side of the business. Meek, a raging homosexual, looked on him as something a little bit more than a son.

Dickie persevered. He picked their brains. Then he picked them dry. He took their best clients and set up his own record label in Denmark Street, as Dominate Records. His trademark 'Sea of Swirl' producing style, with its swirling percussions and strings, led to many a hit with a stable of girl groups: The Heart Stoppers, The Head Spinners, The Hard-Ons, The Wolf Whistles, The Pick-Ups, The One Night Stands and The Morning Afters. And when the boys became more popular than the girls, he manufactured four-piece Mod bands: The Blues, The Bombers, The Bennies, The Dexies, The Lines, The Head Cases and The Heart Attacks. He had made his fortune.

Vince didn't find any criminal record there, or mugshots of Dickie Eton. He was, if not totally straight, then certainly undetected.

But there were plenty of Jack's associates found among the serried ranks of mugshots. And way down the list was a petty criminal called Vaughn Treadwell. His record had him pegged as a lowlife, but Vince had him pegged as his brother – older by a year. Painful reading. More often in prison than out. Not because of the severity or audacity of his crimes, but because he just kept getting caught. Pulling the same stunts now as when he was still fourteen. Chance burglaries, ill-thought-out warehouse lifts, and misjudged muggings where, chances were, he'd end up as the victim and receive a good hiding. It would be comical if it wasn't so true – and if he wasn't Vince's brother.

Then, way back up the top of the list, to the face he'd been avoiding. The real horror story, looking into the face of Jack's deeds. The man who, as a kid, had put the fear of Christ into him. He turned the pages and found a mugshot of Henry 'Redskin' Pierce. Pierce had picked up the nickname Redskin during his wrestling career, since his costume and character of choice was Red Indian. Some said he even had genuine Sioux blood in him, and others said it was because of the razor and knife cuts he'd picked up over his long and violent criminal career. They had never really healed, remaining flushed and fulsome. Against his sallow bloodless complexion, his scars looked like sets of red lipstick kisses.

It was Pierce who did Jack's bidding. It was Pierce who was the visible one. He collected. He delivered. He maimed. He sent out the message. The wrong look in a packed pub always led to the same thing, some luckless mug lurching around with half his face on the floor, asking himself what the fuck he'd done to deserve that! Nothing, was the answer, because Pierce would have done it anyway. He decided on the looks that you were giving him, even if you weren't looking at him, even if you were twenty feet away with twenty people between you and facing in the other direction, minding your own fucking business. Because he could. Because it sent out a message: 'You think I'm your worst nightmare, you should meet Jack.'

Tony Machin bowled into the office, and went straight for the filing cabinet to retrieve a quart of whisky. He poured two shots into two chipped white-enamelled tin mugs, and took what looked like a well-deserved swig.

'Did the press buy it?' asked Vince.

'Buy what?' asked Machin, distracted as he wiped his mouth with the back of his hand.

'That they OD'd on bad pills.'

'They bought it. We told them they were small-time dealers from out of town, and the pills were homemade. Said we found a chemistry set and a small press for making the pills. They'd obviously got their chemistry wrong and "paid a price for their irresponsible foolishness".'

Vince gave an approving nod. 'That should hold them.'

Machin shook his head sceptically. 'You might be able to bury this sort of stuff in London but down here – they'll be all over it. Headlines tomorrow, read all about it: "Is Brighton the new drugs capital of England? Are we out of control? Are we becoming like America? Lock up your daughters!"'

Vince laughed, but wasn't really listening. He was still studying the mugshot of Henry Pierce. One good eye staring out; one sitting there dead like a big streaky dobber.

Machin kept on with his public outcry shtick. 'Oh, and that other piece of crap they trot out every time something goes wrong in this town: "Brighton used to be such a *nice* place." Who are they kidding? It's never been a *nice* place. That's the appeal!' He then came and stood over Vince and followed his gaze. 'Henry "Redskin" Pierce. Old Crazy Horse. Forget him, son. The mad Indian's retired.'

'Is it true about him being a Red Indian?' asked Vince, looking up at Machin. 'I thought he just used to wrestle dressed up as one?'

'He did – until he almost killed a geezer. But legend has it he really has got Indian blood in him.'

Vince looked doubtful. 'I think Tonto's been speaking with forked tongue, kemo sabe.'

'Either way, he's gone back to the reservation. He's holed up in a retirement home for the blind. Lost the sight in his one good eye.'

Vince couldn't resist a smirk. 'What happened?'

'Not much. No one took it out, as much as I wish they had. He just went blind, about six months ago.'

'Maybe that eye lost the will to live after all the shit it had seen.'

'Yeah, maybe, son. Maybe,' said Machin, handing Vince a mug of whisky.

'You forget, I don't drink.'

'Oh, yeah. Hard to get my nut around that one, son – a copper who doesn't drink.' He poured Vince's into his own. 'Waste not, want not.' Machin leaned against the filing cabinet. 'Anyway, Henry Pierce is finished, out of commission. Wouldn't surprise me if someone tops him soon.' He smiled at the thought. 'Revenge for all the years of grief he'd doled out. Especially now Jack's not here to look after him.'

'I'm still going to talk to him.'

Machin frowned. 'You don't think we already have?'

Not wanting to seemingly undermine him, Vince threw him an acquiescent smile. 'I don't doubt it for a second, mate. Just to reacquaint myself, for old times' sake.'

'Be my guest. We've done everyone on Jack's payroll and, surprise, surprise, not a dicky bird. All shtum and alibi-ed up to their orchestra stalls.'

A fresh thought spiked in Vince's mind. 'How about those not on his payroll?'

Machin shot him a blank look.

'He never married, did he?' Vince continued.

Machin laughed. 'Jack? Wife, kids and all that stuff? He's not the marrying kind.' He refilled his mug. 'How about you, son?'

'Married? Not yet, no.'

'Got someone in mind?'

'Not yet, no.'

'Good-looking fella like you, all the birds fancied you.' Machin stared out the window contemplatively. 'It's not all it's cracked up to be, son.' He pointed to a framed photo resting on the windowsill, gathering dust in the fading sunlight. It was a family portrait: one wife, two kids. Say cheese. 'There's my ball and chain over there.'

Vince glanced over at the photograph. 'Nice,' was all he could come up with for the fat smiling faces in the frame.

'Jack had a bird he was keen on. A right eyeful, as it happens – not bad at all. A real looker, if you like that type of thing.'

Vince glanced around at Machin. 'What type of thing?'

'Slim ones, not a lot of meat on 'em, like a Jean Shrimpton or a Cathy McGowan.' Machin shook his head in mild disgust at the prospect of having his way with either the international model or the *Zeitgeist* pop-show presenter and self-styled Queen of Carnaby Street. 'No, son, give me a Mansfield, a Russell or even a Dors any day of the week.' Machin cupped and jiggled both his hands in front of him, as if weighing up some imaginary breasts he'd just sprouted. 'Real birds, I mean. Something you can hang your hat on.'

Vince smiled, knowing that Shirley the barmaid, with her tits spilling out of her blouse, was more the ideal ticket than Jayne Mansfield, Jane Russell or even Diana Dors.

'What's her story, then?' asked Vince.

'She runs one of Jack's clubs in Oriental Place,' Machin said. 'Place called the Blue Orchid. We had her followed for a couple of weeks, but nothing came of it.'

'What's her name?'

'Bobbie LaVita.'

'Bobbie . . . *LaVita*?'

Machin gave a bemused shrug. 'You know this town. Here everyone's a character.'

Vince repeated the name under his breath, pondering it. '*LaVita. La . . . vita. The . . . life.*'

'The what?'

'LaVita is Italian for "The Life".'

Just then, the door swung open, and Ginge swung in along with it.

'Don't you ever bleedin' knock?' Machin asked him sharply. He didn't like getting caught having a snifter at only four in the afternoon.

'Sorry, guv,' said Ginge. He then turned to Vince. 'You've got a call from a Mr Ray Dryden.'

'Thanks.' Vince stood up.

'You can take it in here,' offered Machin.

'It's OK. You're busy so I'll leave you to it,' he replied, wanting privacy for this particular call.

'I'll sort you out a desk later,' said Machin.

Vince gave him an appreciative nod and followed Ginge out the door.

Machin cleared up the evidence of booze by simply knocking it back. He then slumped into the chair that Vince had vacated, gazed at the family portrait and smiled. Then he wondered if he'd get to charver Shirley again tonight.

Ray Dryden had joined the Met along with Vince as part of the new fast-track graduate intake, and they soon became close friends. Ray read Modern Languages at university, but got caught up in detective novels and decided that was the life for him. He was smart, though not really up to the physical side of things. To make up, he had tons of enthusiasm and knew his way around research libraries, halls of records and drawers of press clippings.

He was good with names, dates, paper trails, piecing data together and thumb-tacking it on to a cork board and, to his credit, getting results. A year ago, Ray had joined the small team that ran the London bureau of Interpol.

Vince's hunch, like everyone else's, was that Jack was somewhere out of the country. Jack Regent's Corsican connection was too strong to ignore, therefore Interpol had been put on alert. Vince had put in a call to Ray as soon as he was thrown the case.

'What do you say, Ray?'

'Why the sudden air of secrecy? You don't trust our Brighton brethren?'

'London, Brighton – all the same to me.'

'The Eddie Tobin situation?'

'It's still a bad beef.'

'Don't let it get you down, Vince. It'll blow over, you'll see.'

'I don't want it to blow over, Ray. I saw a girl getting killed up on that screen.'

'Girls get killed on the screen all the time, Vince. They call them actresses.'

'This wasn't acting. This was for real, and I'm going to prove it.'

'Did you actually see her get killed? Did you see any blood?'

'No,' said Vince, almost wishing that he had, just so the vagueness of the crime would crystallize. 'And I know what you're going to say next, but I'm sure if I'd have stayed on my feet long enough, I would have.'

The silence on the phone swelled into an uncomfortable tumour of doubt and uncertainty.

'Do you believe me, Ray?'

'If you say it's so, Vince, then I'm with you – you know that. But that's another case, yeah?'

'What have you got for me?'

'What do you know about the Unione Corse?'

'Nothing.'

'They're the French equivalent of the Mafia,' said Ray Dryden. 'Corsicans but operating mainly out of Marseilles. Involved in all the usual rackets, but big in smuggling. Heroin, hash, cigarettes, gold, any other contraband they can get hold of and turn a profit on.'

'Brighton's just had three junkies turn up dead on heroin.'

'Shit! When did this happen?'

'We found them today. The stuff that killed them was so pure, it looked like it had just come off the boat.'

Ray exhaled a whistle of astonishment that acknowledged not only the tragedy but the synchronicity of the events. 'Vince, you're going to be very interested in what I've just found out. Sitting comfortably?'

Vince, knowing him like he did, knew Dryden was going to come up with the goods. Because when Ray Dryden got stuck into something, he stayed stuck in. Notepad and pen out, Vince made himself as comfortable as he could get, considering he was perched on the corner of a desk in the incident room. 'I'm all ears.'

'French cops first discovered a heroin-processing lab near Marseilles in 1937,' Ray began. 'It was a huge operation, manufacturing tons of raw opium into opium paste, then into morphine, then heroin. Some of the raw opium was brought in from Turkey, where farmers are licensed to grow opium for legal pharmaceutical drugs. The rest came in from Indochina, via the French colony out there. It's refined in Marseilles then shipped out – to the States mainly. In the thirties and forties, there was a big heroin epidemic in Harlem, New York. All the gear coming in at the time was thought to be supplied by the Unione Corse, along their opium routes, then distributed internally by the Mafia. In 1947, the Yanks discovered the first big import: seven pounds of the stuff was seized from Corsican sailors in the Brooklyn docks. Purest brand they'd seen. Anyway . . . You still there?'

Vince had let out an audible sigh at this history lesson of French villainy. He wished Ray would sharpen it up and put a point on it. But he realized that Ray was on a roll, and that he'd have to listen to the full fruits of his labour before they got to what he needed to hear.

'Ray, I'm enthralled. Pray continue.'

'The whole operation was run by the Unione Corse boss, one Paul Carbone.'

Vince jotted the name down. 'Sounds Italian?'

'Corsica's got a very mixed history and heritage. It's French, but it's an island stuck out in the Med, with the Italians, Sicilians, Greeks and Turks passing through. Lots of invasions. A real melting pot.'

'Carry on, Mr Chips.'

'Anyway, here's the thing. The French coppers uncovered a processing plant by accident. But it had already been up and running for about five years, because Carbone had protection.'

'Gangsters getting protection? There's a novel twist.'

'Yeah, and it came from way up top. During the war, the Unione Corse worked with the French Resistance. Doing what they were good at, getting in and out of places they shouldn't be and killing people. Assassinations of Gestapo officers, high-ranking collaborators, spies. They did a good job, apparently, even had medals pinned on them. Then after the war, they were used by the American CIA and the French SDESE.'

'Snappy name.'

'It's the French Intelligence service. They used the Corsicans to stop the French communists taking control of the harbour of Marseilles, which is the busiest port in the Med. Lots and lots of money involved, so the Unione Corse has big connections with the French government. I reckon they see them as the muscle, get them to do the dirty work that they can't be seen doing themselves. The pay-off, you ask? They let them get on with what they do, turn a blind eye. As long as not too much dope turns up in Paris, and most of it ends up safely in the States, they're happy.'

'Do you think Jack Regent's got anything to do with these people?'

'Do you?'

Vince weighed it up: Marseilles, Corsica, New York. It all sounded a little exotic, but why not? And anyway, there was nothing else to go on. And, like with Ray, it was the kind of intrigue that fired Vince's imagination. It was why he became a cop – seeking the bigger picture, the bigger story.

He eventually replied, 'He's Corsican, he's a criminal and three junkies have just OD'd on heroin. In my book, that's a connection. What else should I know about this Unione Corse?'

'Its members always carry the emblem of the Corsican flag with them, wearing it engraved on a piece of jewellery, like a ring or a medallion. The higher echelon members also have a tattoo. But they always have it on them somewhere. It's a badge of honour to them to never be without it.'

'What does the Corsican flag look like when it's at home?'

'It's a Moor's head. You know, the Moors?'

'Yeah, plays left back for West Ham.'

'Er, a coloured fella's head . . . North African or Arabic.'

Vince laughed. 'Yeah, thanks, Ray, I know what a Moor is. How's the glamorous world of Interpol treating you?'

'Our international police force, Vince? I haven't left my office once since I got here! The only time I see foreign climes is in the Greek or Italian place at lunchtime. Listen, I think this is good stuff. If we can build a case with—'

'*We?*' asked Vince.

'Yeah, you putting in the heavy footwork, and me the brains behind the operation. Who knows, if we put enough of a case together, we could both be out in the Mediterranean sunning ourselves.' Vince laughed, but Ray continued. 'Ah, Vincenzo, I know a wonderful restaurant in St-Tropez. And the women, the fiery temperaments, the exotic looks . . .'

'How's this for exotic? Bobbie LaVita?'

'Who's he?' asked Ray Dryden.

'He's a she.'

'Mmm, sounds promising. A date?'

'Hardly. But she's quite an eyeful apparently. She was Jack Regent's paramour.'

'Gangster molls are not my type.'

'Me neither, but I'm curious. Might be the closest I'll get . . .'

Bobbie LaVita, Bobbie LaVita, Bobbie LaVita, Bobbie LaVita, Bobbie LalalalalalalaVita . . .

The name kept running through Vince's head mambo-style as he stepped out of the station into Edward Street. It was a sunny day, not too hot, just lit up. The sun hung low in the sky, throwing a vivid light over everything.

'Detective Treadwell?'

Vince turned around sharply, and there he was.

Giving him the benefit of the doubt, he was about five foot seven inches, maybe less. Podgy with sandy hair, he looked as if he'd be bald by the time he hit forty. But that day looked at least twenty years off.

'I'm Terence. Terence Greene-John, reporter for the *Evening Argus.*'

Vince gave the cub reporter a thorough once-over: noting a brown Harris-tweed hacking jacket; burgundy V-neck jumper, probably with holes in the elbows but he couldn't see; Tattersall check shirt; green tie with small blue mallards flying all over it, and tightly knotted like a noose; faded bottle-green baggy corduroy trousers worn high with braces, exposing red socks and battered brown brogues. In fact, everything about the fellow's garb looked battered, baggy, well worn and handed down. He looked like a ruddy-faced young farmer from good stock.

'If it's about the three in Kemp Town, I don't know any more than Detective Machin already told you people.'

Terence dismissed this with a vigorous shake of his head. 'No, no, no, Mr Treadwell—'

'Detective Treadwell.'

'Yes, yes, yes, sorry sorry—'

'It's OK. What can I do for you, Mr Green . . . ?'

'Green-John,' he corrected, reaching into his jacket pocket and handing Vince his card. 'Jack Regent is the story I'm covering.'

Vince inspected the card which, on closer inspection, was not a card at all but a piece of thick, scissor-cut paper. It just had his name and a number on it in plain typewriter font. Vince inspected Terence, noting the reporter had the inky fingers of multiple ribbon changes. But the card was wrong, because he'd obviously knocked it up himself. Vince raised a doubtful eyebrow. 'You really work for the paper?'

Terence couldn't meet his gaze, instead his eyes darted downwards. Vince noticed he had exceptionally long eyelashes, like a girl's.

'To be honest, sir—'

'Honesty's always a good policy when talking to a policeman. I could easily arrest you for misrepresenting yourself and wasting my time,' he half joked. But he could see, straight off the bat, that Terence was the type that would offer up the truth before any lie.

'I'm at Cambridge, reading Classics, but I want to be a writer.' Terence paused, waited for a reply. He was obviously used to getting impressed looks or at least a 'Good for you' when he told people his career plans as a writer. None was forthcoming.

'So you go around impersonating hacks?' asked Vince.

'No no, sir,' said Terence, eyelashes fluttering anxiously. 'I'm genuinely doing an internship at the *Argus*, during the holidays. Making tea mostly. Messaging. A bit of copy-editing and some—'

'Terence, good luck with it, but I'm in rather a hurry,' said Vince, handing him back his business card and striding off down towards Lower Rock Gardens.

Thirty seconds later, Vince heard a tap-tapping sound behind him. It sounded like a drunken Gene Kelly, but it was Terence, who was wearing Blakeys in his brogues. Terence continued tap-tapping away, trying to match Vince's stride.

'Sir, sir, I can help you,' he persisted, with breathless enthusiasm. 'I'm from Brighton myself. I know you've been brought down from London on the Jack Regent case. I can help you. I know things.'

Vince stopped walking and looked round at him. 'What do you know, Terence?'

'I know what happens in this town. Maybe I . . . maybe I can be of some assistance?'

'So, tell me, what goes on in this town?'

Terence pulled a big eager grin, happy to have been asked. Then, in an instant, he became very sombre and serious. 'Well, sir, I've made rather a study of it: the history of Brighton. The people, the places, the *underworld*.'

'The underworld,' repeated Vince, savouring the word, but not as keenly as Terence, who gave it a grandiosity that only a nineteen-year-old undergraduate studying Classics could give it.

'I'm from Brighton, too, Terence. And, being a copper, I sort of make a living from it – the underworld. And sometimes getting help from the press can be construed as interference. Help from undergraduates wanting to work for the press could be construed as a downright nuisance and bloody dangerous.'

At this knock-back, Terence looked crestfallen. Vince could see his face palpably collapse under the weight of disappointment.

Vince studied his expression. He'd never seen any face quite so ridiculously honest. Every emotion and thought he had flickered across his countenance. It was a sighing mass of tics and tells, sad-eyed disappointments and dimple-cheeked excitement. He should certainly never be allowed near a poker table. Even with his retreating hairline and fogey clothes, Terence just looked like a kid who really did believe in an *underworld* of grandiose and mythic proportions.

Vince took pity, then took the mocked-up business card that was still in Terence's hand. He pocketed it and started walking away from him.

'Here's what, Terence,' he said over his shoulder. 'If I need help, I'll call you. On that you have my word, OK?'

Terence beamed with joy, his eyes lighting up like the low-slung sun in the Brighton sky.

'Thank you, sir!'

CHAPTER 5

THE SWEET LIFE

With just the establishment's name as its main selling point, Vince recced his room at the Seaview Hotel. Boats and anchors decorated the wallpaper, a ship in a bottle sat on the dressing table, and small sepia-framed prints of fishermen and their vessels adorned the walls. The bathroom continued the nautical theme: a dried-out starfish positioned on the cistern, a natural sponge in the bath, while a fresh block of classy Imperial Leather sat in a scallop's shell in the washbasin.

It was just as Vince remembered it, for he had stayed in the same room once when he was at university. A dirty weekend with a sociology student called Paula. He took off his jacket, kicked off his shoes and lay down on the springy mattress. It was so springy he thought he'd be seasick, but the bed soon subsided into calmer waters.

He laced his hands behind his head and closed his eyes. Markham's words, as Vince left his office in Scotland Yard, replayed in his head: 'Keep your head down, relax, spend some time with your family. Who knows, maybe make a case. You'll be back in a few weeks.' This case would do for a few weeks, and counting . . .

Bobbie LaVita, Bobbie LaVita, Bobbie LaVita . . .

The name. The moll. The Blue Orchid club in Oriental Place. What did she look like? Vince smiled to himself and thought about his intended ports of call. She would be the first. On the way to the club, he could call in on his brother, Vaughn. And tomorrow the big one, the monster from his past, Henry 'Redskin' Pierce.

Vince stood up to draw the curtains, so he could get some proper sleep. He hadn't heard the big bang, but when he got to the window he was greeted with a view of Armageddon. Khrushchev and LBJ had finally thrown their toys out the pram and sent them rocketing into the firmament. An atomic bomb had gone off and was blasting the sky red and orange. Vince smiled at this nonsense but it really did look more like the end of the world than just the end of a day. He stood and watched as the Earth set its sun.

Vince left the Seaview at 9.00 p.m. He walked along Marine Parade to the Aquarium, crossed over by the Palace Pier, and headed along the prom to be nearer the sea. True to bank-holiday form, a balmy night had been seasonally usurped and blown away by cold gusts of wind and storm clouds. The sea tore at the beach before it and sucked it into its belly, greedily reclaiming the stones, seaweed, cuttlefish and tin cans, fish-and-chip paper and French letters. And then threw them back up again.

The revving, stopping, starting and spitting of small engines, as Vespas and Lambrettas in red, white and blue, festooned with lights and mirrors, wove in and out of the traffic. Astride them sat young men kitted up in Italian-tailored three-button suits and US Army-surplus fishtail Parkers. The scooter in front of the pack carried a girl whose hair was cut in a short Jean Seberg crop. She had heavy panda eye make-up, and wore a short sequined dress that looked as if it had been fashioned from tinfoil. Her skinny, goose-bumped arms were wrapped around her boyfriend. In an Ivy League striped boating blazer and a Paisley cravat, he looked as though he was wearing almost as much eyeliner as her, but Vince thought they looked good weaving in and out of the traffic, like Gregory Peck and Audrey Hepburn in the 1953 film, *Roman Holiday*.

The seafront was gridlocked with drinkers spilling out of the pubs, a disgruntled queue of clubbers awaiting entry to Sherry's dance hall. The boys and the girls moved in packs, the girls linking arms and discharging choruses of catcalls and shrill laughter at the boys who were circling around them, showing off, swaggering and swearing.

Then, somewhere in the distance, the breaking of glass and a gap in the laughter that let in a scream of pain. In a pub down on the seafront, smart-suited Mods had just met and locked horns with leather-jacketed, battle-ready Rockers. Both were vying over the pub jukebox and the soundtrack to their night ahead. Otis Redding versus Gene Vincent, their fortunes would be decided over hurled beer glasses and upturned tables.

Margate and Southend last year had been just a taster for the Mods and Rockers. Battle lines had been drawn, and Brighton was now the theatre. Headlines were ready to roll. And so were the police. A wail of sirens and two Black Marias manoeuvred their way on to the pavement and down the tarmac ramp to the pub on the lower front. Truncheons were drawn and, if the truth be known, the boys in blue were as ready and eager for a tear-up as the Mods and the Rockers themselves. Vince felt detached from the milieu and the mêlée. No allegiances either way, he carried on with his walk.

Ten minutes later, he was in Waterloo Street, outside the address Machin had given him for his brother. A basement flat boasting a never-swept entrance littered with cigarette butts, crisp packets and other debris that had blown down from street level. No lights on as Vince knocked on the door.

It was a door that looked as if it hadn't always waited politely for an answer. Cops raiding, creditors collecting, bailiffs seizing. Vince thought about making the same kind of entry: one strategically placed kick would break the door's cheap lock. Instead, he took out his notepad to write down the phone number of his hotel and a direct line to the station, and slipped it under the door. He didn't expect to receive a call.

Ten minutes later, Vince was in Oriental Place. Another base-ment, but of a different class. He stood in front of a varnished, oak-panelled door replete with spyhole and a big brass doorbell. Over the door a sign scripted in blue neon tubing: *The Blue Orchid*. Vince rang the bell and the door was opened by a gorilla in a tux and a toupee. Or maybe his hairline was naturally simian. Either way, it looked as if it was sliding down his face.

The gorilla attempted something akin to a smile and grunted, 'Welcome.'

Vince handed over ten shillings entrance fee to the bored-looking brunette reading a paperback at the cash register, and entered the club.

Like all these gaffs, it was bigger than the outside gave it credit for. It was the usual lounge set-up: a long bar at one end of the room, about fifteen tables, with a small dance floor and a stage. Framed photos of movie stars hung on the walls: Jean Harlow, Joan Crawford, Bogart and Bacall. The Blue Orchid had plumped for movie-set night-club glamour, with zebra-striped banquettes and bar stools, and lots of potted palm trees dotted around the joint.

Four stooping waiters in little white bolero tuxes and black bow-ties were mooching around. The place was otherwise dead. Three men occupied stools at the bar; their faces didn't register with Vince. A lone couple sat at a table near the stage.

On the stage was a three-piece, playing jazz slow and low. The band consisted of a silver-haired, sleepy-looking drummer stroking the skins with his brushes, a hollow-chested codger lean-ing against a double bass for support, and an alto sax that hardly felt a breath from its goatee-bearded player. Just background stuff, the music hardly registered.

Vince went up to the bar and ordered a club soda with Angostura bitters and a twist of lime – his version of a livener. He looked over at the couple who sat by the stage. The girl was about twenty, twenty-two, the man about mid-forties. He was paying her the kind of hands-on, drooling attentiveness that marked her out as the secretary, not the wife. And not Bobbie LaVita either. Even with Jack in the wind, no one could be that droolingly stupid.

Vince was about to ask the barman where he might find Miss LaVita, when the lights dimmed. The rheumy-eyed drummer woke up, ditched his brushes, picked up the sticks, hit a rim shot and went on a roll. The double bass stiffened up and got well and truly plucked; while the alto sax wiped his face and blew a genuine blast of hot air.

And there she was, Bobbie LaVita.

Platinum blonde, worn in a short asymmetric bob cut, its sharp short fringe slanting down to the left. Like a bleached-out Clara Bow with a modernist twist. Slender, a gamine quality about her. Big brown eyes, heavy on the mascara that emphasized long black lashes and accentuated the feline shape of her eyes and light on the lipstick that was a shade of pale. She wore a crushed turquoise-silk gown, again asymmetrical, sweeping down from neck to armpit so as to expose one arm and cover the other. It worked the same way with the legs, one exposed almost to the hip, the other fully covered. She was in her early twenties – but no more than twenty-five he guessed.

Over her left breast, she wore a brooch with silver plumes and a spray of diamonds. It depicted a bird of some description, but could easily have been a dragon or a phoenix. She held a cigarette in one hand, smooth slender fingers tipped with dark nail varnish. The other hand, swinging at her side, clutched a pair of silver-strapped shoes. Otherwise, Bobbie LaVita was barefoot.

The place itself looked thirty years out of date, the song she was singing was ten years out of date, but the singer herself seemed right up to date. She looked as if she didn't belong there but, then again, thought Vince, she would have looked out of place in Sherry's among the boys and girls her own age. But on Jack Regent's arm? No, that didn't fit either.

Vince told the bartender that he'd like to buy Ms LaVita a drink. The barman gave him a look that said, 'For the sake of your own health, steer clear.' And if Vince hadn't received the message, he backed it up with words: 'For the sake of your own health, mate, steer clear.'

Vince flashed his badge.

'Tread . . . *what*?'

'Treadwell.'

She laughed.

'What's so funny?'

'Oh, nothing,' she said with a playful smile, not letting him in on the joke. Then she repeated, 'Tread . . . *well*.'

He was sitting with Bobbie LaVita in the corner booth furthest from the bar. She pulled a cigarette out of her pack, then offered one to Vince.

'I don't smoke.'

'Good for you,' she said, then glanced down at a book of matches in the cut-crystal ashtray. Vince took his cue and lit her cigarette. The light illuminated her face, a face that was just about as perfect as he might want it to be. The eyes were flawless in shape and proportion. The lips were fuller than they originally seemed on stage, the pale lipstick playing down their natural poutiness. A small shallow dimple adorned the chin.

She was undoubtedly a beauty. He knew the face, had seen it before. His mind scrolled back, but nothing came up. He tried his old trick of attributing a movie star to her. Was she a . . . Sophia Loren? Darken the hair, put a few pounds on . . . Or maybe she was an . . . Audrey Hepburn? He gave up, knowing he'd been wrong about this kind of shorthand before; and some faces just don't match the movie-star photo fit. Yet he felt sure he'd seen her somewhere before.

'You look like that actor,' she said.

Vince smiled. She obviously liked to play the same game as him.

61

'Yeah? Which one?'

She pursed and parted her lips, made a clicking noise against the roof of her mouth with her tongue. The answer was already on the tip of it. 'Victor Mature?' she offered up.

Vince smiled. Like him, she obviously played the game badly. He didn't look anything like that brawny actor.

'I watched *Samson and Delilah* on the TV last night.' Her eyes narrowed in examination of his features. 'Must be the nose, sort of Roman.'

'Don't tell Vic that. I think Samson was Jewish.'

'It was rather corny, so I wasn't paying much attention.' She stopped smiling and a short sigh announced that playtime was over. 'I'm assuming you're here to ask me questions about . . . that *thing* on the beach?'

'That *thing?*'

'You know what I mean.'

'I know what you mean. The murder.'

'I thought that was done and dusted. All you fellows assume Mr Regent did it.'

'By "all you fellows", I'm assuming you mean the Brighton police.'

She looked quizzical. 'You are a policeman?'

Vince nodded. 'Scotland Yard, not Edward Street.'

'Scotland Yard? Is that supposed to impress me?'

Vince smiled. He was kind of hoping it would. 'Not really, Miss LaVita. I'm just saying I'm new to the case. I have no predisposed views regarding Mr Regent's guilt or innocence, either way. We're trying to find him to help us with our inquiries.'

'Oh, yes, you *are* a policeman. Only they can talk like that.'

Her accent was hard to place. A little clipped and done with such precision, Vince suspected maybe she was trying too hard at it, and pitching it above her station.

'That's why I joined the force – the hip lingo,' he said.

She suppressed a laugh, conceded a smile, re-reviewed him.

'I'll be straight with you, Miss LaVita. He's our main suspect until we can prove otherwise.'

'So what can I do for you, Detective Treadwell?'

Vince pulled out his notebook and showed her an image he'd drawn, a good likeness copied from an encyclopedia.

'That's the Moor's head, which is the emblem on the Corsican flag. Did Jack wear any jewellery that had this on it, such as a ring, a medallion?'

Bobbie inspected the drawing. 'No, but he did always say that his role model was Napoleon.'

'Napoleon?'

'Napoleon Bonaparte was Corsican. Jack's keen on history, but you're not, obviously.'

'History? It's the nightmare I've yet to wake up from.'

She threw him a querying look.

'A famous writer said that, or something like it.'

'I was just kidding about Napoleon, Detective.'

Vince gave her an acquiescent smile, but didn't think she really was kidding. Most gangsters were tinpot despots running their little fiefdoms fuelled on massive egos and Napoleon complexes. And, whilst Jack wasn't known for a diminutive stature, Vince reckoned the club foot must have given his psyche a good kicking over the years.

'Did he have any tattoos?'

She frowned. 'Tattoos?'

Vince replied, facetiously, 'Yeah, inky markings, snakes coiled around daggers, eulogies to dead mothers, odes to girlfriends.'

'Thank you, Detective, but I know what they are. And he had none that I noticed.'

'And you *would* have noticed?'

'We weren't that close.'

'Really? I thought you were about as close as two people could get.'

Bobbie dragged on her cigarette and blew out a plume of smoke that suggested either she was bored or that he should back off. 'From my intimate knowledge, I never saw any tattoos. But, then again, there's intimacy, and there's intimacy. And if I was that intimate, why would I be telling someone whom I wasn't that intimate with?'

'Because it's a murder investigation and I'm a policeman,' he said, as a reminder to himself as much as to her.

'Well, maybe we should get more intimate, then I might tell you.' She searched his face for embarrassment.

None was forthcoming, as Vince held her gaze, his slightly hooded eyes expressing a world-weariness that suggested he'd heard it all before. He put his notebook away and glanced around the room. Two punters had left the bar. The couple sitting by the stage were now locking lips – that Bed & Breakfast was clearly beckoning.

'Did Mr Regent talk about his family, Miss LaVita?'

'No.'

'Then what do you know about them?'

She shrugged to signify *nothing*.

'I'm sure the officers you spoke to made you fully aware that withholding information is—'

'I'm not withholding anything, officer. And if I sound a little obtuse, it's not deliberate. These last few weeks have been very difficult, very difficult indeed.'

Vince wasn't buying her last line, as her delivery seemed devoid of the emotions that usually went with such a statement: the tears and the quaking voice of an innocent caught up in the maelstrom of a murder investigation. Her response sounded too lawyer-rehearsed and cross-examination ready.

But still Vince was compelled to give the stock answer: 'Yes, I'm sure it has been, and I won't take up too much more of your time. We just need to find out the truth, so—'

'I'm answering your questions as truthfully as possible. You asked me if he talked about his family, and I said no. You asked me what I knew about his family, but I know nothing about them, because we never talked about them. So I assumed he didn't have any.'

'Everybody has a family, Miss LaVita, whether we like it or not.'

'You'd be surprised.'

'And in the time you spent together, you never thought to ask more about his family?'

'No. And he didn't ask about mine.'

'What did you talk about, then?'

'What's that got to do with anything?'

'Just curious.'

'Far more interesting things.'

'Oh, that's right,' he said derisively. 'Big weighty subjects like history? And there's such a lot of it, must have kept him amused for hours.'

She eyed him contemptuously, then pinched a piece of tobacco from her tongue.

'You said history was a favourite, Miss LaVita?' he pressed.

'So I did.'

'Just not each other's.'

'For a lot of people, Detective, families are rather like your writer chap's description of history: a nightmare I've yet to wake up from.'

Vince twigged the bitterness in her voice. There obviously *was* a history.

'So, in lieu of any family, it's safe to assume that you were, or are, the closest person to him?'

'You think I know where he is?'

'I think someone does.'

'And, if I knew, you think I'd tell you?'

Vince gave a noncommittal shrug.

'You're wrong. I wouldn't.'

'Maybe. But someone, anonymously, has already told us something. That's why we're after him.'

'You think I'm the anonymous someone?'

His shrug was less noncommittal this time around.

She tensed, straightening her back. Her whole face became defensive, eyes narrowed, her bottom jaw jutting slightly. 'And why would I do something like that?' she said, tightening the clip in her voice.

'Well, look what happened in that film you watched last night. Samson fell head over heels with Delilah. Delilah found out all his secrets, cut his hair, took his strength. Then the whole shebang fell in about their ears. I forget my Bible stories, can't remember why she did it. Maybe you could fill me in?'

'Like I said, Detective, I wasn't paying that much attention.'

'To get him out of her hair, perhaps?'

'You're right,' she said. 'You look nothing like Victor Mature.'

'And I don't think you're the anonymous someone.' Vince gave her a warm smile, followed by a cold fact: 'You wouldn't be sitting here now if you were. You'd be dead.'

On hearing this, her eyes flicked downwards and she stubbed out her cigarette. As she crushed the lipstick-smeared butt into the glass ashtray, Vince registered her unease. He reached into his jacket pocket and took out his card and a steel Sheaffer ballpoint pen, wrote down his phone number, and rested the card on the rim of the ashtray. 'If you think of anything that might help, here's my number. I won't take up any more of your time, Miss LaVita.'

She picked up his card and gave it a quick glance, then smiled and announced, 'Bobbie. Call me Bobbie.'

'Thanks, I will. Because you really don't look like a LaVita.'

'How many have you met?'

'You're the first.'

'Then you've got nothing to compare me with,' she said, her smile widening, accentuating the high cheekbones that cradled those perfectly poised green-brown eyes. 'We're rare birds, we LaVitas.'

Vince felt happy to see her smile. Rows of strong white teeth, cheeks that dimpled, eyes that lit up. She'd look good in the sunshine, he thought. It would seem more natural to her than the night, the gloom of a nightclub, or the persona of the sultry torch singer. He still thought the name LaVita was as much paste as the diamonds on her brooch which, at close quarters, featured either a peacock or a phoenix.

She pulled another cigarette from the packet. This time, Vince lit it for her without a prompt. She shielded the flame unnecessarily. It was about contact, and Vince flinched when he felt her hand touch his. The tiny jolt alerted her. Her eyes widened as she took him in. Every little movement, magnified, measured, significant. Every gesture becoming stupidly big.

'Can I call you Vincent, or are there rules against calling policemen by their first names?'

'I get called worse.'

'Like what?'

'Vinnie, or Vin.'

'How about Vince?'

'I can live with that. And I do.'

'But you introduced yourself as Vincent.'

'I live in hope.'

'Then that's what I shall call you.'

He *wanted* her to call him that, and the realization made him uncomfortable. Of course, he didn't trust her, and her sudden 'intimacy' was probably all a flirtatious routine to throw him off the scent. And that deceit made him feel uncomfortable, though it shouldn't have. Because he operated in a world where deceit was a cloth worn close to the skin.

There's only so long you can sit in a booth in silence without resorting to smoking or saying something you might regret; so he stood up and broke things off.

'Where are you going, Vincent?' she asked, giving him a play-ful smile that verged on mockery.

The way she used his proper name made him feel like a kid. 'Busy day tomorrow,' he explained.

Busy day tomorrow? He felt an internal wince at that statement. It dripped 'gauche' and undid all the ironic, sardonic and snappy repartee that had gone before, in his attempt to bury the plod-ding copper spiel.

'That's a pity, because I know of a good party tonight.'

He smiled. A reprieve: she'd thrown him a line. 'Not tonight, Josephine. Napoleon might not like it.'

There was another internal wince; but cheap as it was, the wisecrack worked. He'd wiped that playful smile off her face and brought it all back into check.

He'd brought Jack back into the equation. Her lover. His quarry.

CHAPTER 6

THE MODERNISTS

Heading towards Hove, and away from the bank-holiday crowds, Vince and Bobbie walked along the promenade to the party. He hadn't needed a lot of convincing. It was a good opportunity to find out more about Jack Regent.

The coast road was now alive with packs of Mods, who revved and rode their scooters, three or four astride, straddling the lanes and stopping normal traffic. A gang of Rockers tore past in the opposite direction as Triumphs, BSAs, Nortons and Royal Enfields gunned their heavy engines and burned up the tarmac. In their brief passing, insults were thrown either way. The ever-present sound of sirens just behind them reminded these opposing forces who held the real power in the town tonight – even though it was a tenuous hold. On the main drag running from Marine Parade to the West Pier, packs of Mods promenaded and pea-cocked: sleek, sharp à la mode urbanites with their faces alert, glowing and glowering, searching for the enemy. That meant any-one in leathers and with greased-backed hair, who they viewed as rural, uncouth, dated and definitely not *them*. While for *them* the weekend was about hitting the dance halls, popping pills, putting on a performance, having a tear-up, making the newspapers and getting your picture taken. And sex, lots of sex. On the beach, in B&Bs, in public bogs, in back alleys, in the backs of broken-into cars, underneath the arches, underneath tables, on top of tables! Sex and violence threaded through the air like electrified wire. It was all set to go off like a bank-holiday firework display, burning up the night sky with its petrified chorus of alarms, sirens and flashing blue lights. It was undeniably a good time to be young because, as far as sex and violence went, the young were so undeniably good at it.

Vince stuck close to Bobbie, who nevertheless seemed fearless and completely impervious to it all. Vince noticed that, as much as she gleaned turning of heads and wide-eyed admiration from the oncoming traffic of males on the street, her beauty didn't attract the usual wolf whistles, statements of intent or the comments that young men are likely to make when they travel in predatory packs. Instead they'd approach within a certain distance, and then give respectful smiles and nods, and almost doffs of their proverbial caps. Or maybe it was because of himself. When in protective mode, Vince's dark good looks just got darker. They'd linked arms since leaving the club, and Vince was aware he was walking with his chest thrust out, his jaw set firm and his eyes cautiously in command. His present mien undoubtedly sent out its own warning signals.

'I believe that once you stop learning, you die. When you stop asking questions, the big important questions, you die,' declared Bobbie LaVita. 'Because you lose your purpose in life. Is that why you became a detective, just so you could ask lots of questions?' He didn't get time to answer before she continued. 'But the thing is, Vincent, you're asking all the wrong questions. You're not looking at the bigger picture. You involve yourself in a mystery but it's just a sideshow. It's not the main event. You're not engaging yourself in the main event, or the big questions. You're being sidetracked by matters of inconsequence.'

'I don't see a man turning up on the beach minus his head and hands as particularly inconsequential. And I'm sure his family don't, either.'

'I'm sorry about the man, too, and it is very sad. But that's not what I'm talking about, Vincent.'

Bobbie looked up to the heavens and shook her head as if in incredulity at the prosaic nature of her companion; making it clear that she was working on a higher plane of consciousness than the flat-footed copper who plodded diligently alongside her.

And this was pretty much how it played out between them on the fifteen-minute hike towards the party. Bobbie LaVita had talked – a lot – and she had successfully bobbed and weaved and deflected all his questions about the case.

She covered a gamut of kooky-bird themes, flitting from an A-to-Z of Astrology to Zen Buddhism. She appraised him of her love affair with the arts, all the arts, riffing on poetry, mainly French and some of the American Beat stuff. She told him how she admired the Existentialist *and* the Situationists. But it was music that held her greatest devotion, letting slip that she was signed up to a major record company, Dominate Records, had already cut a 45, and was set to go into the studio and record a 33 with no less than Dickie Eton producing. And – bingo! – Vince now had a connection between the music producer/impresario Dickie Eton and the gangster/boyfriend Jack Regent. When he asked her about Eton, she became cagey and dodged the bullet. Instead, she asked him what star sign he was, and what had really made him become a cop. Vince claimed he liked the badge because it had a star on it. That was his best shot at both astrology and being kooky.

The party was at Third Avenue, another basement. There were four Avenues in total, not including a Grand Avenue. They were all lined with tall ash-coloured brick town houses that descended from the main drag of Church Road to the seafront.

As Vince made his way down the steps with Bobbie, he thought of Terence, the young Classics undergraduate and wannabe writer, with his scholarly romantic ideas of an Underworld. From Hades to Brighton basements. The smell of reefer hit him even before the door opened.

As they made their way along the narrow hallway lined with joint-toking West Indians in straw trilbies and knitted shirts, Bobbie was greeted like she probably always wanted to be – like a star. A sea of red-eyed, smiling faces parted and all nodded their respects to Jack Regent's girl.

The place's official title was the Beach Bottle club – or the BBC for short. Four walls trapping smoke and sweat, and loud music pumping out of huge stacked-up speakers. Murals on the walls: a sunny Caribbean scene peopled with elastic-limbed islanders dancing and smiling under palm trees. Clouds of reefer smoke hung in the air like incense, and the crowd moved with the kind of swampy rhythm that only potent ganja produces. They weren't so much dancing to the music as dancing *in* the music. White girls hanging off the necks of black guys, while white guys in three-button tight-fitting Italian-cut suits stood around eyeing up the alluringly aloof black girls. The white boys did their own little dance, with their arms up tight by their chests as if they were going into a fight, and feet shifting as if they were grinding out cigarette butts. The music system blasted out Jamaican Blue Beat, American Soul. The Miracles, Prince Buster, Carla Thomas, The Mar-Keys, Major Lance, Curtis Mayfield and The Impressions.

There was a homemade bar in one corner, with optics on the wall behind – all of them serving different shades of rum. Only rum. Two bins were chock-full of ice and bottles of Red Stripe. A gorgeous black girl, with straight bleached hair piled up in a beehive, was busily serving the drinks.

Vince saw a man enter the room and prop himself up against the bar, and decided he recognized the face. It was pinched and gaunt under a skinny-brimmed trilby, while its owner was stick-thin and failed to fill out his flashy houndstooth-check suit. Spider's nickname was obvious and soon apparent to anyone around him, from the skeletal frame and the fast-moving limbs. He held a brown bottle in each hand, one a bottle of Red Stripe, the other a phial of pills; swigging beer out of the one and dealing dexies out of the other. If Spider had truly lived up to his sobriquet, he could have worked even faster, using all eight limbs to either open the other bottles that he kept retrieving from his pocket or to bank the constant flow of cash. The besuited, buttoned-up Mods had ceased their uptight twisting and were now gathered at the bar to hand over the notes, before tuning up on blues, dexies and purple hearts. Spider was the medicine man they'd all been eagerly waiting for, to loosen them up and get their party started properly.

Spider's malicious features had already come up on the list of known Regent associates, where it easily fitted in. Jack Regent had been rumoured to be manufacturing amphetamine pills at a farmhouse somewhere in the Sussex countryside, in a big operation said to be supplying most of the South, and also making inroads up North. Mods regularly visited clubs in Soho like the Scene, the Flamingo, the Marquee, La Discothèque and the Twisted Wheel in Manchester, where they played American Soul and R&B. They wanted to dance all night if they could and fuelled by this gear, they certainly could.

Vince glanced around to see that Bobbie was now in possession of a big fat joint. She stood in the midst of a crowd enveloped in smoke and loud with laughter. One of the men he seemed to recognize: a handsome, square-jawed Harry Belafonte lookalike. Vince could have sworn he'd seen him somewhere before, but couldn't precisely put his finger on it. An old collar maybe? Looking at Bobbie and the handsome fellow laughing it up together, as they enjoyed the cordiality of a shared joint, Vince felt a distinct twinge of . . . *jealousy*?

He shook off the inappropriate thought, and returned his attention to the bar, instantly realizing that Spider was gone.

Because Spider had gone running as fast as his skinny legs would carry him. He was already out of the basement flat and ringing the front door of the building above. As Spider was buzzed in, Vince came darting out the basement after him. At the top of the stairs he scoped the street. No sign of Spider, but there was a telephone box about fifty yards up the road.

'You should see this. I'm sorry, I know I shouldn't say that, but you should see it. This is out of sight. It's wild!' The voice spoke in a mid-Atlantic showbiz drawl. 'She's a real looker this one, and so is he.' There was a gasp. 'Oh lord, it's enormous!' Another gasp. 'Oh my, carrying that thing around would ruin the cut of your trousers, it really would! It's a sight to behold, Henry. Sorry, I know I shouldn't say that, but it really is!' The voice spilled over into high-pitched giggles.

The man commenting was in his early thirties. He remained stick thin not from malnourishment or from any chemical metabolism, like Spider, but through vanity. And he also was small. Size-wise, there really wasn't a lot to him. But there was a lot on him, for what he lost in stature he made up for with his dazzling panoply of duds. Kitted out in as vivid a collection of clothing as could be assembled on such a meagre and unpromising canvas, he was from head to toe a dandy. A regular Regency fop or a pint-sized Beau Brummel. The hair worn in a high bouffant was centre-parted and kept in place with lashings of hairspray. He had a white collarless shirt with ruffles spilling down the front; a purple satin flared frockcoat with pleats, darts and bows; drainpipe trousers in crushed black velvet; and shod in a pair of black patent-leather Beatle boots equipped with stacked Cuban heels that elevated this five-foot three-inch peacock to a level slightly above laughing-stock. With rings on his fingers and no doubt bells on his toes, the Sartorialist in question was Dickie Eton.

He was sitting in the dark, peering through the viewing side of a two-way mirror, as an orgy took place in the next room.

The man he was commenting to was Henry Pierce, seated next to him. Time had played its tricks, of course, but Pierce was the same giant, lethal block of a man he had always been. His scars had weathered slightly, melding in with the more natural lines on his face, but were still brutal reminders of the man he once was. The hair, however, was still unnaturally and refulgently as black as boot polish. He sat there impassively, like granite, behind his small, round blacked-out glasses, as Dickie Eton yelped, guffawed, giggled and talked him through what was occurring in the room next-door.

At a knock on the door, Pierce tapped his heavy white stick on the floor.

Spider entered.

Vince made his way back to the party, and straight over to Bobbie. He'd been gone ten minutes, and she hadn't missed him. She introduced him to the Harry Belafonte lookalike as a fellow musician, then she drifted off somewhere. Belafonte smiled and offered Vince the joint. Ignoring it, Vince clicked his fingers three times and, in rapid recall, pointed at him and said, 'I know you. You played at Ronnie Scott's last year.'

The handsome Harry took a long draw on the skinny marijuana joint he was holding, then nodded his head and smiled, 'Sheeet, Ronnie's, that's right, man. I've played that joint.'

He was a Yank.

'You were on the bill with Dave Brubeck. Alto sax?'

'You've got me, baby. First time I played with Dave in London. Laid down some good shit, if memory serves. You enjoy it?'

'I loved it. You tore the place up that night,' said Vince, casually reaching into his pocket and flashing his badge. 'I'd like to catch you again sometime, so if you value your work visa, you'll split. Now.'

Handsome Harry stopped smiling, chipped the joint, gave Vince an appreciative salute for the tip, and split as recommended.

Bobbie drifted back over to Vince in a haze of smoke. 'Let's dance,' she said, her diction slowed by the pungent, multi-papered hash joint that she kept waving around like a magic wand.

'I think we should go,' he said.

'You're not having a good time?'

'You're forgetting something. I'm a copper. I could nick every-one in here. I could even nick you.'

She wrapped her arms around his neck, stoned white girl style, more for support than anything else. Her eyelids were at half mast, yet when he looked into her eyes he saw them light up, her pupils dilating and contracting, in and out. Her head lolled back and she erupted into a peal of laughter; then stopped it as suddenly as she started. Her face rolled towards him as she said, 'You won't, will you, Vincent? You wouldn't put me in jail?' Her voice was slurred, but managed to sound teasing and coquettish. And al-together incredible.

No answer from Vince, now too busy admiring those hypnotic green-brown eyes. Someone next to them lit up an even bigger joint than the one Bobbie was holding. It crackled and spat like a firework and, even in the smoke-filled gloom, it threw light on to her face. Her eyes widened, till Vince could see his own reflec-tion in them. The sheer proximity made him feel good.

'Let's go,' said Vince again, hands around her waist, guiding her out of the crowd and into the fresh night air.

Just as they hit the pavement, three panda cars and a paddy wagon pulled up. No warning sirens. Ginge was bang on time and, as always, in a hurry. Flushed red and raring to go, he was the first out of the car. He then looked more than a little surprised to see Vince propping up Jack Regent's girl.

Vince gave him the nod and said, 'Enjoy yourself, Ginge. You've got pills, marijuana, hash and booze being sold down there. A real good collar. Run a check on a fellow named Spider, about five foot ten inches and skinny—'

'I know him.'

'He was the one dealing the pills.'

'Gotcha, guv.' Ginge raced down into the basement, with six uniforms following him.

Bobbie was now stoned out of her box. The lit-up Sophia Loren eyes were fast losing their glow and turning red and tired-looking. But for her the night wasn't over. She declared she had a craving for a 'Nickerbrorrahrrrrrrorlywithasherrryontop', and kept giggling and slurring, her tongue lolling around redundantly in her mouth and failing to baton out the words. And her legs weren't feeling too clever, either.

What she had a craving for, it seemed, was a Knickerbocker Glory with a cherry on top; and she knew a Wimpy bar in East Street that served them. Vince tried to explain that it wouldn't be open at this time of night, but she kept insisting. Vince tried to remind himself that this wasn't a date, and that he was a copper, and that, with her tongue loosened up by the copious amounts of reefer, this was a good opportunity to get more information out of her.

On the promenade, the sea air worked its magic and sobered her up. Vince tried his best to keep up with her as she performed an Isadora Duncan routine, running ahead, then jumping and dancing around him. To grab her attention he asked, 'What's with the surname, LaVita?'

Bobbie stopped dancing immediately. She didn't like this line of questioning and could sense the cynicism in his tone. Understandably, while on Jack's arm she never got pulled up about anything, however silly. She could have called herself Helen of Troy and no one would have dared bat an eyelid.

'Was it you who called the police, party pooper?'

'I am the police, remember?'

She threw him a playfully alarmed look and said, 'Then I'd better answer your question, Detective, before you lock me up. It's Roberta.'

'That makes sense. It's the LaVita bit I'm curious about. Are you Italian?'

'Maybe.'

'You'd surely know, wouldn't you?'

'Not necessarily.'

Vince gave a resigned shrug. 'LaVita it is, then.'

They walked in silence for a few moments, then she announced, 'It's Drinkwater. Roberta Drinkwater.'

Vince stopped in his tracks and put a hand archly to his ear. 'Drink . . . *what*?'

'You heard.'

'If you don't mind me saying, Miss *Drinkwater*, you've got some nerve taking the mickey out of *my* name.'

She laughed. 'I know. *Tread-well* and *Drink-water*, they do have a certain ring to them. That's why I'm having second thoughts about marrying you, Mr Treadwell. It would be out of the frying pan into the fire.'

Vince didn't take the hint of flirtation too seriously, as she was stoned.

'And anyway, I'm looking for something more exotic. Like a Rockefeller or a Getty.'

That remark he did take seriously. He was about to tell her she was keeping the wrong company to run into those boys, but stuck with the affinity in their names instead, 'Treadwell and Drinkwater, they're not names, they're instructions. Could be worse, though. Could be Roberta Guinnessisgoodforyou.'

She laughed. 'Or Vincent Anappleadaykeepsthedoctoraway.'

'So what made you settle on LaVita?'

'Have you seen *La Dolce Vita*? It's my favourite film.'

He had. Fellini's Eternal City rendered godless, with Anita Ekberg dancing in the Trevi Fountain. It made sense: the look, the gown, the shoes in hand. All now done as a cheeky seaside parody.

'Also I was in a hurry to get away from Drinkwater. Anyway, what's in a name? I can always change it again.'

'Life could get very confusing,' he said. 'You wouldn't know who you are.'

'Do *you* know who you are?'

'I like to think so.'

'But you changed your name, too. You went from Vincent to Detective.'

'It's a job title, not a name.'

'And are you always the detective?' she asked as she sidled up to him, hooking her arm in his. He didn't answer.

They walked down from the lawns on to the promenade. The tide was out, revealing the wet sand. On a beach full of hard stones the sand looked exotic, and almost erotic, like soft forbidden flesh only glimpsed under the cover of night. And as he gazed out at its moonlit iridescence, his memory rolled back to the long summers of his youth, when the tide was right out, and he could almost feel again the wet sand squeezing between his toes.

About twenty yards ahead stood a man leaning on the railings, looking out to sea. He looked like a tramp, with layers of shabby clothes, and a length of string keeping his trousers up. Yellow hair clumped like straw; a beard covering his face as freely as moss. In scabby hands he held up a copy of the *Evening Argus*, and he was reading the obituaries out loud. His voice sounded haunted and sad, as if he'd known every dead person intimately.

Vince felt Bobbie draw closer. 'He's here every night,' she whispered. 'Always the same routine.'

They were about to make a detour round him when his head turned sharply in their direction. The tramp had looked so caught up in his eulogy that they didn't even think he'd notice them. Bobbie wanted to keep walking, but Vince stopped, because he recognized the man. Even though the face was one of those that had become unrecognizable, weatherbeaten features blunted like the stones washed over on the beach. But he still had two distinctive features. One side of his nose was bulbous, with a red-veined whisky river running through it, the other side was withered and fleshless, so it seemed hardly there. But what really marked him out was what was written there. Scrawled on his forehead in blue biro were the words: *I AM DEAD.*

Bobbie said softly, 'Why would anyone do that to himself?' Vince knew the answer, because he'd witnessed it first-hand. But this wasn't the time to enlighten her.

The tramp stared at them vacantly with glazed eyes. He lowered the newspaper and spoke in a raspy, barely audible voice. 'Never be without . . . never be without . . .'

Bobbie asked Vince, 'Do you have any money?'

Vince nodded. He took out a ten-shilling note and offered it to the derelict. The offer was accepted, and a scabby hand grabbed the note. He then lifted the newspaper again and returned to delivering his eulogies. 'Elizabeth Creighton, loving daughter of Ethel and Peter Creighton, died peacefully on . . .'

Vince and Bobbie walked on.

'What did he say?'

Vince shrugged. 'Who knows. Best ask the sea.'

'That was good of you, to give him that much money. I was thinking of just enough for a cup of tea.'

'He looked like he could use something stronger. A lot stronger.'

They made their way past the angel statue that divides Brighton from Hove. The crowds were coming out of the pubs and clubs and dance halls. Things could get lively now. And a stoned blonde turning cartwheels could prove a hazard. Vince stuck closer to Bobbie as they passed the pub on the seafront, between the two piers, where the Mods had clashed with the Rockers earlier. It had portholes for windows and a 'seafaring' wooden facade that jutted out like the bow of a boat about to set out to sea.

There were about thirty boys and girls milling outside. They were dancing around to Major Lance being played on a plastic portable record player, and clearly well tuned up on pills, speeding the night away. Bobbie wanted to join them, but Vince saw the looks some of the girls were giving her. Under all that make-up were hard little faces, hailing from Shepherd's Bush, as tough and territorial as any of the boys. Vince steered Bobbie away, but she saw something else taking her fancy, and spun away from him.

A small bonfire was dying all alone on the beach, and that's where Bobbie was now heading. Still barefoot, she skipped over the shingle, which didn't seem to bother her. Vince followed obediently and laid down his jacket for Bobbie to stretch out on it, her eyes closed as if *moonbathing* on the beach.

He sat down beside her and stared at the crackling embers of the dying fire. 'Are you originally from Brighton?' he asked.

When Bobbie's eyes opened, the redness had disappeared – seemingly cleansed under the blue light of the moon.

'No, a small village in the New Forest. Before he retired, my father was the local GP, and my mother taught at the local school. We lived in a house just outside the village, surrounded by woods and fields. Father used to grow all his own vegetables. My mother kept horses, so my brother and I were riding almost as soon as we could walk. We had two dogs, a pair of black Labradors.'

Vince nodded solemnly, then commented, 'It sounds . . . idyllic?'

Bobbie sat up and wrapped her arms protectively around her knees. She hadn't noticed the question mark in his tone.

'It really was. I was lucky to have such parents. Those were the happiest times of my life, I think.'

Vince retrieved his jacket and draped it around her shoulders. 'Why did you come to Brighton, then? Why not London? That's usually the first port of call.'

'I did live in London for a few years. But there's something about the sea, I guess. I just felt drawn to it.'

'How do they feel about you being with Jack Regent?'

'Who?'

'Your parents.'

The dreamy melancholy look she had worn whilst talking about her childhood was suddenly transformed into a challenging glare. It was accompanied by a snide, pointed reply. 'Oh dear, you really are a policeman, aren't you? Really just can't help yourself.'

This broke the spell of the moonlight and the music, and brought Vince sharply back into focus. 'Well, Jack Regent isn't exactly ideal son-in-law material. Just wondering how two such pillars of the community might feel about their daughter shack-ing up with a known killer.'

The clipped tones intensified, becoming positively haughty, and playing the class card for all it was worth. 'My parents are educated people, Mr Treadwell. They were both born and bred in London, and they met at Cambridge. Just because they now reside in the provinces doesn't mean they hold provincial view-points. They want me to experience life and make the most of my talent.'

'So where does Jack Regent fit in with your talent?'

She didn't answer.

'I guess he knows a lot of useful people. Like Dickie Eton?'

She sounded not so much angry as petulant. 'What have you got against Dickie? And where's the proof that Jack kills people? You don't know him . . . Those are just rumours that people put around. People can't kill people and get away with it.'

'Not in the land of horses munching in the stable and a pair of black Labs pissing on the vegetable patch, no.'

Now she was angry. She stood up suddenly, threw his jacket off her shoulders, and said, 'Fuck off!'

It was the first time he'd heard her swear, and he decided she was good at it.

'I want to go home,' she said.

'Where is that exactly?' Vince asked, standing up. 'The New Forest?'

And then the soundtrack changed. The music was drowned out by the sound of engines. Heavy engines from ton-up motorbikes making their way down the ramp towards the neat-suited and desert-booted sharpshooters listening to their sweet soul music. Not to Eddie Cochran – and that was the problem.

Vince stood up when he heard the first glass smashing. He was about to say 'Let's get out of here' when already they were on him.

It was happening so fast that Vince couldn't really get a line on them. They were indistinct danger, but he reckoned there were three of them. Not Mods, not Rockers, not even kids. The way they moved, they looked like professional muscle, looked like they knew what they were doing. The first that came at him wielded a cosh.

He swung, Vince ducked it, and threw his first punch. It connected, right in the gut, winding Cosh Boy, doubling him up. Attendant screams from Bobbie on the sidelines. Vince swung up again, and his fist smashed Cosh Boy on the jaw. He could feel teeth give way, and then Cosh Boy was down. Vince followed it through and stamped on his head. Cosh Boy was effectively done.

Then came number two, who was shorter, stockier and fireplug fast. Vince couldn't see his face because his head was down and aimed like a bullet into his stomach. The bull-like charge put Vince on his back, and Stocky was immediately on top of him. Vince knew that one blow from the man's balled fist would be like an anvil dropping on him, so the Queensberry Rules were quickly ditched. Vince put his right hand up to Stocky's face and gouged his eye. Stocky grabbed at Vince's hand and reeled backwards. Vince slid his left hand down to his attacker's crotch and squeezed hard. On this fresh assault Stocky discharged a squeal. Stocky now had some painful choices to make, as Vince's thumb pitilessly worked away at his eye socket. He rolled away, grabbing simultaneously at his aching balls – both pairs of them.

The screams from Bobbie grew louder. Vince looked up to see number three, a tall skinny fellow with crinkly blond hair, had grabbed hold of her and had a knife to her throat.

Vince shouted, more in hope than expectation, 'Drop the knife and let her go!'

The skinny man smirked and tightened his grip on her.

Stocky got up and started to go over towards Skinny. Vince pounced, tackling him around the legs and propelling him to the ground. Unfortunately for him, Stocky fell forward into the bonfire. With Vince now on top of him, his face was forced down into the burning cinders. Stocky screamed, he choked, he burned. Vince lifted the man's face out of the glowing embers, and registered that it was a mess. Red, blistered and powdered in grey ash, red-hot pebbles stuck to his face and blackened like leaches.

Bobbie screamed even louder. The blond skinny fellow meanwhile assumed the facial expression of a scream, but nothing came out.

'Let her go!' yelled Vince, with higher expectations this time around.

Skinny stood transfixed, with the knife still at Bobbie's throat, but Vince could sense that his stomach for the fight was waning.

'Per . . . per . . . please . . .' coughed and spluttered Stocky, through lips that looked as if they'd been freshly gummed together.

Skinny finally had enough. He let go of Bobbie but kept hold of the knife. One out of two was not bad, thought Vince, standing up.

Bobbie ran over to him. She stood staring down at Stocky, who was still writhing on the hot stones in voiceless pain. She then slowly backed away.

Vince's eyes were totally fixed on Bobbie, who couldn't seem to look away from him. He moved towards her and she stopped retreating. Her expression gradually changed, her repulsion at the sight of the burnt man melting away. She now wore the hint of a smile, but not a smile born of gratitude. It was something more base than that. There was even something cruel about the twist of her lips . . .

Then came a roar, and Vince was knocked to the ground.

Armed with chains and axe handles, the leather-clad Rockers had got the better of the Mods, who clearly didn't go in for any bulky concealed weaponry ruining the fine lines of their whistles. In the tear-up stakes, they could be assessed as style over content. But they had the numbers on their side, and now about fifty fellow Mods, armed with broken deckchair struts, were driving the marauding Rocker hordes into the sea.

As one Mod wag was heard exclaiming, 'Greasy fuckers could use a wash!'

And there was Vince, smack bang in the middle of the mêlée. Looking more like a Mod than a Rocker, his side was picked for him as a quiff redolent of engine oil butted him in the face, with a cry of "Ave some of that, you fuckin' ponce!'

Vince went down, rolled over and prepared to take a kicking. Staying down was his plan, until the cavalry arrived. He was right in the middle of it, and didn't fancy fighting his way out of it. Skinny, Stocky and Cosh Boy had taken it out of him. But he thought of Bobbie, found an opening in the scrimmage, and staggered to his feet. Saved by the bell, just then: the wailing of sirens and the familiar voices of coppers. As the battlefield thinned out before the boys in blue, Vince smiled, glad to see them.

Shame he didn't see the truncheon that cracked into the back of his head.

CHAPTER 7

ART

The next morning, Vince woke up to find himself in a cell. First thing he saw, groggily, was the laughing face of Tony Machin. Ginge stood behind him, holding a mug of tea.

'So which are you, then, a Mod or a Rocker?' asked Machin.

'A Mocker,' Vince replied. 'What time is it?'

'Just gone nine.'

Vince tried to sit up, feeling not so much a 'twinge' in his ribs as a sustained 'twang'. But he was nevertheless sure nothing was broken. He took it slowly and shifted himself sufficiently to lean against the wall, whereupon Ginge handed him the mug of tea. Vince looked around for his jacket, then remembered that the last time he saw it, it was wrapped around . . . 'Bobbie? The girl?'

Machin and Ginge quickly exchanged a surreptitious look.

But Vince wasn't that groggy, and they weren't that quick. He could see how Ginge was taking his cue from Machin. 'Don't worry, guv,' said Ginge, 'we picked her up near the pier and took her home. Bit shaken up, but fine.'

Machin gave Vince a knowing look, then one of his customary winks. 'What did I say, eh? Quite a looker, Miss LaVita? Did you get anywhere, son?'

Vince wasn't playing along. 'I'll need her address. She's got my jacket, keys, wallet, badge.'

'No problem there. So what do you think of her?'

'You tell me. You've had her under surveillance. Find anything?'

'No, son, nothing. She just went on with her routine. Singing classes three times a week, otherwise shopping and going to her club.'

'Did you check her bank-account records?'

'Give us some credit, son, 'course we did. No big money movements in or out, and she hasn't left town since the body showed up. Apart from the known faces that go to that club, of which there are markedly few now, she hasn't had any contact with Jack's associates. Unless you already knew she was with Jack, you wouldn't guess that she had anything to do with him. Tell you the truth, son, she didn't seem much bothered that Jack isn't around.'

An involuntary smile flickered across Vince's lips, which he quickly disguised as a grimace of pain. He stood up, very slowly. 'Where's the stocky fella?'

'What stocky fella?'

'I got jumped, there were three of them, not Mods, not Rockers either. They were specifically after me. Tooled up with coshes and knives. Two got away. But the stocky one, about five foot seven, mid-thirties, pumped up like a body builder, he wasn't going anywhere apart from hospital.'

This drew blank stares. Ginge said, 'We pulled up about thirty of them. Got them all downstairs in the other cells, if you want to take a look.'

'How many in hospital?'

'Four got taken in,' said Ginge. 'No real damage, just minor injuries.'

Machin shook his head in disappointment. 'Shame about that, the fucking hooligans.'

Vince was getting impatient. 'This wasn't a minor injury. You'd know it if you saw him. His face was badly burned.'

'*Burned*?' Machin screwed up his own face. 'What happened?'

'They had a knife to Bobbie's throat.' Vince corrected himself. 'I mean Miss LaVita's throat.'

It was too late. Machin's eyebrows arched themselves accusingly, as he said, 'So *Bobbie*, is it? What were you doing with her at that time of night, anyway?' He winked, inevitably. 'Spot of overtime?'

'I went to the Blue Orchid. Then she invited me to a party. You know I was at the party, since I called it in.'

Machin gave a slow, considered nod. 'So how come you set fire to this geezer's face?'

Vince realized he was finding himself on the wrong end of a questioning session. 'I didn't set fire to his face. There was a bonfire on the beach, and he fell into it.'

Machin winked again in a further display of chummy knowingness. Violent drunks, wife beaters, kiddie fiddlers, loudmouths and shtum artists who needed their tongues loosening, they had all been known to take a 'fall' on Machin's watch.

Vince could see that Machin thought he was getting the measure of him, a man cut from the same cloth. Vince was equally sure they weren't. But he had no inclination to get the man's back up by disputing the point. 'How about Spider?' he asked, instead.

Further shakes of the head from Ginge. 'No good, guv. We did have an address for him, but his landlady claimed he did a bunk a month ago. Owed her three weeks' rent.'

Vince felt the lump on the back of his head start to throb.

Vince was sitting at his desk, where they'd found him an office in the basement. Mops and buckets had been its last occupants. A small wired window partly painted over in green gloss to match the surrounding walls. He kept the door standing open, or else he'd have felt as if he was still in the cell.

He was currently thumbing his way through two hefty tomes of mugshots, on the lookout for the three thugs on the beach. Passing resemblances, so far, but nothing to hang your hat on. And, after a while, these tense-faced mugs staring out at him all looked the same anyway. So where was Burnt Face now? Vince made some calls to local hospitals throughout the Sussex area, but no one had been admitted suffering wounds of that description. Then he tried further afield: London hospitals, specialist burns units, private clinics. But, again no joy, just assurances that they'd get in touch if anyone fitting his description was admitted. By the time Vince put the phone down, he was half hoping no one would call him back, because he was half hoping that it all had never happened. He looked at his watch, found it was just gone 10 a.m.

He went and picked up the car he'd been allotted: a two-door Triumph Herald, remembering the smirk on Machin's face as he handed him the keys to the 'little run-around' as he described it. He regretted it wasn't a standard police vehicle, but it was all they had available in the carpool. Vince knew how unclaimed stolen or abandoned cars were kept for a while in the carpool before being either compacted or sold off at auction. And this sluggish little heap of rattling rust was clearly one of them. Still, he counted himself lucky, he wasn't allotted the Messerschmitt bubble car that had taken a severe hit and been left wallowing in a puddle of oil.

Adelaide Crescent adjoined Palmeira Square, and faced directly on to the seafront. Tall white town houses lined its well-kept undulating lawns. Most of the houses had been converted into flats, but had all kept their facades of Regency grandeur. The house Vince was looking for was without a doubt the grandest in the entire crescent, like the jewel in the crown. A baluster-walled drive led up to the building that faced directly out to sea, adding to its fortified appearance. It seemed like a fitting place for Jack Regent, the Corsican, to reside.

Vince repeatedly pressed the doorbell on the glossy black front door. No response, so he was about to walk away, when suddenly he heard Bobbie's voice. It came through a small tannoy hidden in the corner of the portico. 'Speak into the bell,' she instructed. Vince noticed now that the black casing housing the doorbell itself was perforated like the mouthpiece of a phone. 'It's me, Vince . . . Detective Vincent Treadwell.' A long pause – long enough for Vince to think he was being ignored – then, 'The door's open. Stairs to the top floor. The lift's not working.'

He pushed the heavy black door open, and noticed there was no lock. The lobby had a chequered marble floor and a staircase that coiled up around the redundant, old-fashioned gated lift. Vince climbed the stairs to the top floor. On each of the three levels were four doors leading, Vince assumed, to four different apartments. They looked freshly painted as if they had just been converted. On the top floor there was just one door, and his jacket was hanging on the doorknob. Vince slipped it on, checked the pockets for his wallet, badge and hotel keys – all present. He then knocked on the door. Ten seconds later, it cracked open as far as the fastened security chain would let it. A glimpse of Bobbie LaVita appeared and, from what was available to him, he could see there was no welcome on her face. He could sense that the door was ready to slam shut at any moment.

'Thanks for the jacket.'

'You're welcome,' she said tensely and, predictably enough, the door began to close.

Foot thrust in fast. 'Hold it . . . can I come in?'

'No. Move your foot.'

'I need to ask you some quest—'

'I said no. I've answered all the questions. Both to Detective Machin and to you. I don't have to answer any more.'

With his foot still in the door, Vince stepped up the officious tone. 'I need to talk to you, Miss LaVita. If that means getting a warrant—'

'Then *remove* your foot.'

'You won't slam the door?'

'I won't slam the door.'

Vince did as asked, and stepped back. She slammed the door. Vince mouthed 'Shit' to himself, and was about to walk away when he heard, 'Go on, then. Talk, and make it fast.'

'Did you recognize that man last night?'

'After what happened to him last night, I doubt even his mother would.'

'Have you seen them hanging around Jack?'

'No,' she replied irritably. 'Why are you asking *me*?'

'Maybe you took me to that party just to set me up.'

There was no reply, just the faint sound of what might be derisive laughter.

'You work your charm on me,' he continued. 'You aim to get me stoned, boozed up, then down on the beach to get the shit beaten out of me – maybe worse.'

'You don't drink, you don't smoke pot and, from what I saw, you can more than handle yourself. Not much of a plan of mine, Detective. And they held a knife to *my* throat, remember. Jack wouldn't do that, and he wouldn't let anyone else do it.'

Vince had a new thought. 'Maybe it wasn't me they were after. Maybe I just happened to be in the way . . .'

There was silence after that. A chord had been struck. Just the one he wanted. Now she was scared.

He called out, 'Miss LaVita,' but there was no reply. He was about to bang on the door, when he heard the chain sliding across. The door opened and there she was, wearing a white towelling robe that was too big. The J.R. monogram on the breast pocket explained that. She wasn't wearing any make-up, her skin looked fresh and young. She looked good, even better than he remembered, and he prided himself on having a good memory.

'Come in,' she said.

Vince gave her a small appreciative smile, and stepped over the threshold. The class evident in the lobby extended itself up into her flat, or 'apartment', as she called it. And the word apartment seemed more appropriate. It was huge, and the main room had the hand of an interior designer about it: exquisite opulence, Regency flamboyance, art on the walls that ranged from the old masters to the moderns. Pride of place, above the white marble fireplace, was an abstract oil on canvas, in muddied grey and swirling red mist, but not abstract enough to disguise the foreground figure of a sinewy but powerful wolf at the head of a baying pack. And not too abstract to see that the pack leader represented Jack Regent himself.

A Louis XIV couch and chairs. A walnut and tortoiseshell armoire, a weighty-looking ebonised bureau with ornate ormolu decorations depicting exotic birds and dragonflies from the aesthetic period. There wasn't a flat surface in the place that missed the opportunity to contain something exquisite and expensive, like those Meissen and Sèvre figures in fine porcelain and Lalique frosted-glass bowls. A glass-domed skeleton clock – obviously a horological masterpiece – sat on the marble mantelpiece. The sun streamed in through the tall mullioned windows, throwing light over walls covered in red-striped Regency-style wallpaper. On every wall, huge baroque gilt-framed mirrors, adorned with swags and cherubs, stretched up to the lofty ceiling. It was a room of mirrors that gave the already large room infinite space, but ultimately trapped you, since you couldn't escape the sight of yourself.

Vince waded across a thick blue carpet and sat himself down on a red velvet sofa, which was shaped like a woman's pouting lips ready to plant a big kiss. It was the only real piece of kitsch in the room and, to the untrained eye, the only item looking as if it didn't belong in the Victoria and Albert Museum.

'Can I get you a drink, Detective Treadwell?' she asked haughtily, obviously feeling in her element now, sensing how impressed her guest was with the living arrangements. Her arched eyebrows seemed to point him out as a parochial plod sitting uncomfortably on a Dali-designed sofa, amongst antiques and art and an opulence altogether out of reach of his puny public-sector pay packet. 'A nice cup of tea, perhaps?'

'No, thank you,' he said politely. He needed answers, not arguments. Last night he had got caught up in her act, letting her play him for a mug. This time he would play it differently.

She sat down on the chaise longue opposite, her feet curling up beside her.

'Nice place,' he remarked.

Bobbie took a cigarette from the large Asprey's silver cigarette box resting on a marble coffee table. She lit up with a silver table lighter shaped and detailed like a pineapple, but, about the size of an apple, it looked as though it weighed a ton. She glanced around the huge room as if taking it in for the first time, blasé because it all came so effortlessly to her, as if she was to the manor born. She took a long drag of her cigarette, then, with a pinkie finger cocked high, pinched a piece of imaginary tobacco off the tip of her tongue. An unnecessary gesture she must have seen in a movie, because the cigarette was filter-tipped, but it looked very damn sexy, thought Vince. She then plumed out the smoke with a bored sigh, and wearily asked, 'Why would those men want to hurt me?'

Vince waited until she did him the honour of actually looking at him, then said, 'Maybe they work for Jack. And he thinks you made the call that set him up?'

'Didn't we go through this last night?'

'Maybe I was proven wrong last night. Maybe you were tired of him, bored with him, scared of him. Either way, you wanted out, and you know Jack's not the type of man to take rejection lightly.'

Her eyes narrowed and held him in a dissecting gaze. Then, in mock legalese, she gave her summary. 'And I put it to you, Detective Treadwell, that your motives are personal. You want this to be true so I can be a damsel in distress and you can cast yourself in the role of my knight in shining armour. You want me to have betrayed Jack, because you don't want me to love him. Because, let's face it, Detective, you want me for yourself.'

Vince felt a sudden and pressing need to do something with his hands. He took a strip of Wrigley's spearmint chewing gum out of his pocket, carefully released it from its paper sheath and foil wrapper and popped it in his mouth. She was right. Sitting there, stripped of her make-up, and naked – as he imagined – under that soft towelling robe, he realized he did want her for himself.

He suppressed the thought, stood up and went over to the mantelpiece to inspect the skeleton clock under its glass dome. All those little cogs, levers and gears working flawlessly away. He then checked the time, because he didn't have all day. 'You know, Miss LaVita, I'm making it up as I go along – just like you.' No reply. Vince looked around to see her flicking ash into the heavy crystal ashtray. 'The other flats in this building, are they empty?'

'That's right,' she said.

'And this one is Jack's place?'

'The whole building is. It's not in his name but, then again, nothing is. In fact, Jack is officially of no fixed abode. Even before he flew the coop.'

'I admire his taste.'

She smiled. 'How do you know it's not *my* taste?'

'The Gallic influence. It's like a scaled-down version of the Palace of Versailles, or a French tart's boudoir.' He then added quickly, 'And you're not French.'

Her smile vanished. 'Neither is Jack. He's Corsican. He's very particular about that fact.'

'Your contribution, my guess, is this,' he gestured to the red lip couch he'd been sitting on. 'Mae West's lips? By Salvador Dali, right?'

She nodded and looked surprised.

'When I was reading Law at university, I used to sit in on the Art History lectures.' He knew he'd thrown her with this revelation. He'd unsettled her on her Louis XIV chaise longue and wiped the smugness off her face. She had him pegged as a flat-footed prole, and why not? Last night he'd given her precious little reason to think otherwise. He had just listened to her life story without offering any of his own.

Vince looked at the painting of the wolf and gave it a dismissive shrug, then went over to another painting hanging to the side of the mantelpiece. It was a small portrait of a smiling, moustachioed man in a blue uniform, circa 1880s.

'He's looking happy and relaxed, but notice how he's hiding his hands. If the painter could do hands properly, he would have painted them. Hands are a common weakness in artists, because they're so hard to get right. And hiding them is his "Tell". You know what a Tell is?'

Bobbie looked at her own hands, and flared her fingers. Long, elegant, slender, soft and smooth fingers. She let them relax, but the rest of her remained tense. She smiled a rather sad little smile, and said, 'I've been around enough gamblers and chancers to become familiar with the term.'

Vince had spotted her Tell on the beach last night, and was sure he'd have found out more had they not been interrupted by the Three Stooges. He sensed there was a lot more to her story than the picture she'd painted of a rural childhood idyll.

He was straight in. 'That Jack might want you dead doesn't worry you?'

From art to brutality. She looked startled by the sudden change of subject.

'It doesn't,' she said, 'because it's not true. Jack wouldn't hurt me.'

'Not even if his own life depended on it? Or he suspected you'd set him up for a fall?' She didn't answer, and he continued. 'You shared a home together, a life together?'

'Only for six months.'

'Six months, six weeks, six hours – he let you into his life, so he must have trusted you with things. And told you things he wouldn't tell anyone else?'

'He didn't.' She frowned. 'And I think you should leave now.'

'He'll do anything to stay out of jail and you'd be deluded to think otherwise. The truth is that Jack Regent is a cold-blooded—'

'How dare you!' she shouted, and sprang to her feet. 'You think you know Jack? You know nothing! As smart as you think you are, Detective, you're just bumbling around in the dark.'

They stood staring at each other for what seemed to Vince like quite a few minutes, as he tried to assemble a defence for himself. He ended up looking away from her because, however much he thought he knew about Jack Regent, he knew that Bobbie had him bang to rights. When he turned back to her, she had sat down again. Lighting another cigarette, her hands trembled.

He muttered 'Thanks' by way of a goodbye, and made his way to the door.

Bobbie unfurled her legs from under her and stood up to see him out. 'What were you hoping to learn here today that you didn't know already?'

'To tell you the truth, Miss LaVita,' he said with a shrug, 'I really don't know.'

Bobbie let out an audible sigh, then said, 'Follow me.' She stepped briskly back into the living room.

Vince followed her as she headed over to the far side of the room, approaching a wood-panelled wall where yet more paintings hung. She slipped her hand behind one of them, and pressed something, whereupon a section of the wall opened up like a door.

A secret door? A hiding place? Was Jack in there?

Vince smiled at the thought, but went over to take a look. A mechanical skylight cranked open to reveal a room beyond. It was a study or library lined with books from floor to ceiling. It contained an antique mahogany desk with a well-used green leather writing surface, and a brass Anglepoise light on top, also a red leather chesterfield sofa and a matching armchair. Vince stepped over the threshold and went to inspect the book-lined shelves.

It was quite a collection. No paperback penny dreadfuls, or cheap romances or hardboiled thrillers. Instead there was philosophy, western and eastern; liturgy and religious matters; fine art and antiques. And lots of French writers: Baudelaire, Balzac, Diderot, Dumas, Gide, Rimbaud, Rousseau; and the contemporaries such as Camus, Sartre and Genet. And then there were the histories. War mainly. Napoleon, the home-town boy, Corsica, not Brighton, was well represented in large volumes; conquering more shelf space than those other glorious tooled-up globe trotters: Alexandra, Attila and Genghis.

Bobbie joined him and picked out a book randomly. It was Genet's *Our Lady of the Flowers*. 'Jack spent hours in here. This was his private place. We all need one, don't we?'

Before Vince answered, he reviewed the angles: Jack Regent, the cultured criminal in his lair, surrounded by beauty while indulging a thirst for knowledge. It fitted a profile but then, again, just because you surround yourself with this stuff doesn't mean it rubs off on you. Take Lionel Duval for instance: a mock Tudor mansion apparently stuffed with art and uniform sets of hand-tooled leather-bound books. It was unlikely that any of them had ever been opened, never mind read. They were bought by the yard to present a facade of intellect and respectability. But Jack's library was different, carefully hidden away and out of sight. The books well thumbed, and obviously read.

Vince glanced around at Bobbie as she replaced the volume on the shelf. She was right, Jack wouldn't sully her with his business. She was up on the walls with the art, and on the shelves with the books. The guilty pleasure, the weakness. He needed her. He wouldn't hurt her.

'You're right, we do all need our little private places. Many men make do with garden sheds.' He went over to the desk and started opening drawers.

'What are you doing?' she asked.

'When Machin searched the flat, did he take a look in here?'

'No.'

'Did he even know about it?'

'No.'

All the drawers were completely empty, except the last one contained a lone paper clip that was bent out of shape. It looked as if it was laughing at him.

'It's just books in here. Nothing more, nothing less.'

'I should get some of our men over to take the place apart.'

As if calling his bluff, she said, 'Be my guest.'

Vince believed her, though. If there were any clues to Jack's whereabouts here, they'd already been cleared out. He'd seen enough and walked out. Bobbie closed the door and the secret room disappeared.

'So, Vincent, when are you going back to London?'

'I'll be around for another week or so.'

'Good. That means you can buy me that Knickerbocker Glory we didn't have last night.' She opened the door for him and Vince stepped out into the hallway. 'Where are you off to now?' she asked.

'To see my brother, Vaughn.'

'Can hardly be the same Vaughn I know, who's small and skinny with an acne-scarred face and—'

'Yeah, that's him.' He cut her short, not wanting to hear any more about his brother's inadequacies.

Her smile twisted. 'But you're nothing like him.'

Vince looked wary. 'It has been noted.'

'He's scum. Junkie scum.'

CHAPTER 8

ALBION HILL

He was standing amongst the collected debris littering the entrance to Vaughn's basement flat. But just because it was ankle deep didn't mean Vaughn wasn't at home. It just meant Vaughn didn't care.

Vince knocked on the door. No response. Eye pressed to the keyhole, he saw a window wide open, a net curtain fluttering, and a foot making a hasty exit. Vince put his own foot to the door, kicking it hard, and it flew open. A dingy hallway with a bedroom to the left. An unmade mattress, some scattered clothes, a set of dumbbells on the floor. The living room was a dark dungeon of damp: black-speckled magnolia chip wallpaper, and mismatched sticks of furniture. A roll of linoleum chucked on the floor and peeling Formica made for an unconvincing kitchen. On further inspection, there were signs of a woman's touch. A framed photo of a married couple standing with a shy little girl, the child wincing as if almost trying to hide herself from the camera's unrelenting gaze. One hand had dragged a lock of her hair into her mouth to obscure half of her face. Next to it stood a bunch of posies in a jam jar, making an attempt to jolly the place up.

So this was the girl Bobbie had told him about just before he left her apartment. The same girl Bobbie had given a job to, working in the cloakroom of the Blue Orchid Club. Because she felt sorry for her. Because it was dark there. Because in the darkness of the cloakroom you couldn't see the purple birthmark that blighted half of an otherwise pretty face. She wore her wispy mousy hair like Veronica Lake. A long fringe covering one side of her face. For Veronica it was a sexy trade mark that provided her with a look. For the girl with the wine stained skin, it was a mask, a veil.

Vaughn had started hanging around the cloakroom, paying the girl attention, until Bobbie had banned him from the club after he was caught snorting speed in the gents. The girl had left only a week later. Bobbie said that she suspected Vaughn had introduced her to drugs. Vince didn't argue the point.

The back window was still open and Vaughn had made his escape. Vince wasn't too troubled; he knew he'd catch up with his brother soon.

Vince was now standing at his mother's grave. He knelt down and cleared away the leaves and bracken, and laid down a modest bunch of flowers he had bought. At just eighteen, Vince's mother had boarded the ferry from Ireland and crossed the water to England, and had ended up in Brighton. Her first job there was waitressing in the restaurant at Hanningtons, which was Brighton's most prestigious department store. It was a popular hang-out for 'the racing fraternity' of bookmakers and gamblers, and it was there that she first met Lenny Treadwell. He was then working for his uncle, who was a bookmaker, but Lenny had big plans. He wanted to become a 'face' in Brighton, not remain a bookie's runner and driver. That was how he came to hang about in the shadow of men like Henry Pierce and the Jack Regent mob, who had the money, prestige and power he craved.

Besides a nice smile, there was an innate honesty about her, and maybe that's what attracted Lenny, since it was something he would never possess. They started going out, and he looked good in his suit. He was a handsome charmer, and a degenerate gambler, and with that comes optimism but seldom a sense of reality. Lenny fancied himself at the tables and reckoned he had a good nose for a nag but, as his uncle had always warned him, the only way to make a small fortune as a gambler is to start with a large one.

She really liked him, no matter what her friends said about him, so one thing led to another and soon she was pregnant. Lenny wasn't ready for this, still had his dream of the big score. He wanted her to visit a woman he knew of who got rid of such problems. She showed a steely determination and resolutely refused. They got married in the registry office and moved into a tiny terraced house on Albion Hill. There, Vaughn was born and, like most families on Albion Hill, they struggled. Whatever Lenny had dreamed of soon went out the window. And so did his luck at the tables, the races and the dogs. He couldn't seem to back a winner, ended up throwing dud betting slips in the air like confetti. And that's how he developed a gambler's Tell – he started weeping uncontrollably and everywhere. Not a good look to possess amongst the hard cases he was wont to run with. As well as the belly-up gambling, he took the plug out of the jug and started drinking, crying into his cups. He started skimming money off his uncle who, after giving him a good talking to, eventually gave him a good hiding then the sack. Lenny developed the shakes, needed to swallow a quart of Scotch before he could leave the house. He started placing bets he couldn't afford and writing cheques he couldn't cover. When his own money was exhausted, he pawned the modest pieces of jewellery his wife's mother had bequeathed her. Finally he started borrowing from the only people who would still lend to him. The wrong people. The Jack Regent mob.

When Vince came along a year later, things just got worse. Earning whatever she could from cleaning jobs, his mother had long since given up on her husband, after it became clear he couldn't provide for his family. The writing was on the wall when Lenny fell behind with repayments to Jack Regent's shylocks. That was when Lenny skipped town, never to be seen again, leaving Vince barely a year old, and Vaughn only two. Their mother kept her boys above the breadline only by working her fingers to the bone. Cleaning in the mornings, pulling pints in the evenings, both jobs she hated, but she did them because she had to.

The boys living on Albion Hill fought regularly with the boys of Carlton Hill. Occasionally they would join up to fight the James Street boys. Who, in turn, would join up with them to fight the boys from the estates in Moulsecoomb and Whitehawk. Vince marked himself out as a fearless fighter. Tall for his age, strong, game and fast, he was a natural-born scrapper endowed with a precision and powerful punch. And he was smart, too, passing his Eleven Plus exam despite himself. Even while attending grammar school, he carried on running with the boys of Albion Hill. As they got older, and further into their teens, the gang fights became more vicious, more organized, the gang became a mob and Vince became a natural leader. And it looked as if he was heading the same way as them, crime, time, more crime and always more time.

When Vince became old enough to learn that his father had skipped town because he was in debt to Jack Regent, the childhood awe he'd harboured began to turn into teenage resentment. But it wasn't that act alone that focused him on Jack Regent and shaped his future.

Billy 'the Schnozz' Riley was eighteen, and living with his mother four doors up from Vince. He was a braggart and a bully with a screw loose; and that loose screw made his tongue flap and talk himself up, and eventually dig himself a hole. It had been a Saturday afternoon, and hot. Most of the families were out on the street, the women gossiping and smoking, the men struggling back from the pubs, the kids fighting a losing battle with gravity as they chased footballs that kept rolling down the hill. Their playtime activities summed up the neighbourhood: a constant uphill struggle.

The big black car had no trouble rolling up the hill, however. Vince couldn't remember the make of it, not a Rolls-Royce but with the same kind of pedigree and prestige to make heads turn as it glided up Albion Hill. It came to a halt outside Billy the Schnozz's house.

The driver, thickset and bull-necked, sprang out the car and dutifully opened the back door. Out stepped Henry Pierce, while another man stayed inside, his face obscured by a low-slung panama hat and black wraparound sunglasses. What little of his face was visible was shrouded in thick smoke from a bespoke blended cigarette. The kids murmured his name as if he was the bogeyman made flesh.

'Heard he's got a crippled foot,' one boy whispered, his tone so hushed that his mate asked him to repeat it. But the boy didn't dare speak louder, for fear his voice would penetrate the black car and reach the ears of Jack Regent.

Pierce cracked his knuckles and took a cursory look around him, not to check that no one was watching, but to make sure everyone *was* watching. And everyone was, for a crowd had already gathered. Pierce strolled up to Billy's door. He didn't bother knocking, just kicked it off its hinges and entered. Meanwhile, the driver waited on the kerb, eyeing the crowd for any dissent or potential rescuers. He needn't even have bothered; there were no candidates for either role.

A minute later, and Billy the Schnozz exited via a top-floor window. A closed window. Loud gasps from the crowd. Women looked away, girls started crying; the boys' faces lit up as if they were watching a firework display, as shards of glass exploded into the air and Billy hit the pavement with a bone-buckling thud.

Vince noticed two beat coppers appear at the top of the hill, from where they had a good view of what was happening. When they saw who was in the black car, they quickly turned and walked away.

It should have been all over for Billy. But Jack needed his *coup de grâce*. He needed to put his signature on this violence. With one hand, Pierce hauled Billy up on to his knees by clasping a handful of his hair. Pierce then reached into an inside pocket, and everyone thought they knew what was coming next. Because everyone knew what Henry Pierce usually kept in there: the knife, the razor or the ice pick. Instead, Pierce pulled out a . . . *pen*? The sight of this drew unexpected gasps from his audience, like a magician pulling a rabbit out of a hat. Pierce was given to poetic flourishes in his frequent acts of violence, so in his hands, the slim steel Sheaffer ballpoint pen still managed to look like a weapon, glinting lethally in the sunlight. Pierce gripped Billy's hair tighter, pulled his head back and inscribed *I AM DEAD* on his forehead.

He then told Billy, 'You'll wear this on you for the rest of your days, boy! If the rain washes it off, you run straight home and write it back on. Never be without, boy. Never be without!'

When the inscription on the forehead was completed, the writing was already on the wall as to where the pen would end up next. Pierce thrust the pen up into Billy's nostril, through the bone, the cartilage, until the blunt end of it emerged, bloodied, just above the bridge of his nose. What saved Billy from getting his brain skewered was also the reason for his nickname, 'the Schnozz'. That was the considerable size and length of his nose, against the relative dimensions of the pen.

Pierce wiped the pen clean on Billy's shirt-tail, climbed back into the car, and it was gone. An ambulance was called, which collected Billy and carted him off. The boys laughed at his fate, but Vince didn't join in. In broad daylight, right under everyone's gaze, Billy the Schnozz had been destroyed. And no one had lifted a finger to help him, not even the law. It had all clearly been orchestrated and sanctioned by one man, but there were no repercussions and no questions asked. Vince thought long and hard that night. It wasn't just the horror of the act that affected him, it was the power behind it. The power that one man could exert over others. And Vince didn't ever want to be one of those *others*. An innate sense of justice had stirred in him, without him fully understanding it. At first he thought he was weak, so he kept his tears to himself and laughed along with the *others* when it was talked about the following day. But he'd changed.

He put childish things behind him, stopped hanging out with the pack that trawled the streets, knuckled down and got on with his school work, listened to his teachers with fresh ears. Achieving top grades, he went to Durham University to read Law and get as far away from Albion Hill and the memory of that hot summer's day. But as the old adage goes: you can take the boy out of Albion Hill, but you can't take Albion Hill out of the boy. And now Vince was back to finish the job.

CHAPTER 9

A DAY AT THE RACES

As Vince parked his car outside the Seaview Hotel, he found Terence Greene-John sitting on the steps, waiting for him. Terence rose to his feet grinning with Boy Scout enthusiasm. 'I got your address from Detective Machin. Hope you don't mind?'

Vince certainly did mind. He could just imagine Machin getting the measure of Terence, sussing him out as a potential pain in the arse and sending him around to the Seaview.

'Did he now? That was nice of him,' said Vince, making his way past him while searching his pockets for his room key. 'What can I do for you, Terence?'

'I appreciate you're busy, Detective Treadwell, but I thought I might be able to help.'

'How so?'

'It's Brighton races today. Might be some interesting people there.'

Vince stopped searching for his keys and looked at the young would-be hack in a new light. It was a useful light. An informative light. Vince smiled at him and Terence smiled back.

Vince's next port of call was meant to be the Sunnyside Retirement Home, to visit Henry Pierce. But he realized Terence was right: Brighton races was where the action would be today. And Pierce would be caught up in it because, retired or not retired, blind or not blind, villainy always loves the races. It gives them a chance to spend their illicitly earned cash. Clean it, launder it, wash away its sins in the bookie's satchel.

At eleven years old, Vince knew all about the Brighton races. He had found himself a Saturday job as a 'bucket boy', which meant going around the betting ring, wiping the chalked-up odds off the bookies' boards between races. He did it so fast that he soon put the other bucket boys out of business. Not only fast on his feet and swift with a wet sponge, Vince was good with num-bers. Soon the bookies trusted him enough to run bets around the ring with other bookies. They didn't even have to write them down for him, since he could hold complicated lay-off bets – with all their mathematical intricacies – in his head, three or four at a time. He looked like a natural for becoming a bookie himself.

Brighton races would never be confused with 'glorious' Goodwood or Royal Ascot. It was all about the lumpen prole-tariat having a laugh and a day out. Grizzled punters studying *Sporting Life*; flash young men with their dates, hoping to pay for a good night out on their winnings; gangsters and clergymen all mixing it up – and all of them taking their chances against that old enemy: the bookies.

Vince stood in the grandstand, surveying the scene before him through a pair of binoculars. The course was packed, and the bookies were doing a thriving business, taking bets and throwing notes and coins into their battered, painted satchels. Tic-tac men standing high on upturned crates, flailing their arms about in that secret semaphore used to manipulate the odds and move money around the betting ring. The action was as fast and furious as a stock exchange in a trading frenzy.

Vince had already recognized some 'faces' from London. There was Benny Blake, small, compact, dark and sharp-suited, with a ready smile disguising the fact that he had been certified insane several times. Next to him stood Albert Dimes, the Frith Street bookmaker, who was boss of the Italian mob from Clerkenwell and overseer of Billy Hill's rackets.

But the number-one pitch in the bookies' ring was reserved for Sammy Bellman. A heavy-set, broad-shouldered man, he looked the part in an off-white linen suit, brown fedora and gold-rimmed glasses with a clip-on sun visor. For all his natty attire, Sammy B was a known shtarker who purportedly wasn't afraid of anyone. Apart, of course, from the man who would take a cut of whatever he would earn today – Jack Regent.

Vince's binoculars then picked out the Bartlett brothers, Victor and Terry, two of the top 'knocker boys' in town. The knocker boys were Brighton's indigenous racket, mainly due to its large antiques trade. Teams would go out all over the country, usually in pairs, knocking on doors and advertising themselves as: *'Surveyors and purchasers of fine art and antiques, offering the best prices, and free insurance valuations for furniture, silver, jewellery, paintings, ceramics and objets d'art'*. That's what it said on their card, anyway. But once the unsuspecting homeowner had answered their knock, heard the patter and invited them across the threshold, they were subject to a fast-talking conman charisma that would empty their house of its valuables and leave them both breathless and pot-less. The knocker boys were like alchemists working in reverse. Things that seemed worth their weight in gold soon got reassessed as base metal; furniture by Chippendale was suddenly overtaken by an infestation of woodworm that might infect the whole house if it wasn't swiftly removed; paintings by Dutch masters became apprentice pieces at best, if not outright forgeries; Fabergé eggs hatched little more than a few pounds after being denounced as the baubles they really were. Thus the knocker boys made it clear that they were doing the householders a favour by relieving them of their worthless possessions. Some of them came from Romany stock, and couldn't either read or write, but they could certainly tell quality antiques when they saw them. And if the knocker boys couldn't convince the householder to part with his treasures, no problem, for the place had been cased. Either they or their colleagues would return at a later date – and this time they wouldn't be knocking on the front door in broad daylight, but jemmying open a window in the middle of the night. So it came as no surprise to Vince to see the Bartlett brothers were talking to a bald man in a long camelhair coat, who went by the name of Murray the Head, or Murray of Mayfair, or even Murray of St-Tropez. These last two sobriquets came from the places he had worked, either as cat burglar or sleight-of-hand thief. The first one, 'The Head', was most frequently used and the most obvious: for his head was noticeably large and cue-ball bald. But it wasn't white, however, but deeply tanned. In that regard more St-Tropez than Mayfair.

There was a nudge at Vince's elbow, and he turned to see Terence standing at his side, holding two bottles of Coca-Cola with straws in them. Vince accepted one. 'Cheers.'

Terence pointed excitedly. 'That's Sammy Bellman in the white suit.'

Vince sucked on the straw, sluiced the fizzy liquid around his mouth, gulped it down, burped, then said, 'Tell me something I don't know, ace.'

Terence cleared his throat and elaborated. 'Sammy Bellman, forty-three, bookmaker. Jack Regent's bookmaker. Has pitches at all the top southern courses and runs most of Mr Regent's gambling interests, on and off the track.' Vince noted his respect-ful enunciation of the name 'Mr Regent'. Terence continued: 'Bellman runs all his betting activities and a lay-off operation; which lays off bets with bookies all over the country. He also runs Jack's private casino, the Brunswick Sporting Club.'

Despite himself, Vince liked what he was hearing: this was good information, and better than any Machin had furnished. He was surprised Terence had it. As a reward, he threw Terence a bone and divulged some information of his own. He began by point-ing out Bellman's position on the bookies' number-one pitch.

'What does that tell you, Terence?'

Terence's brow creased; he was giving it serious thought.

Vince then pointed to Johnny Price, in the second row of bookies. Standing beside him were Benny Blake and 'Italian' Albert Dimes.

'Those men there are supposedly in the same league as Regent. In fact, some might say that, because they're from London, they're in a bigger league than Regent. But the truth is they have to share London with three or four other mobs. Would you rather have just a slice of a big pie, or the whole of a smaller pie? I know what I'd prefer – but then I don't like other people touching my food.'

Terence nodded in recognition of the economics, and the fact that Jack Regent was more than happy with his lot. Besides, Jack, like Vince, wasn't the kind of man to share.

Vince continued. 'So the fact that Sammy Bellman is still holding on to the number-one pitch tells us . . . ?'

'That Jack is still a force to be reckoned with?'

'Exactly. Because Sammy Bellman, on his own, couldn't hold off men like Blake and Dimes. There just isn't that kind of muscle in the town – only Jack Regent. Now, Terence, tell me about the Brunswick Sporting Club. What's the score there?'

Terence, back on home turf, explained confidently, 'It's in Brunswick Square and it occupies a whole house, meaning four floors and a basement. High-stakes poker, blackjack, chemin de fer, baccarat, roulette, a craps table – you name it. It's a full house casino, apparently, a very slick operation. Lots of high rollers from London come down to play, on gambling junkets with their rooms paid for at the Metropole and the Grand.'

'I never reckoned you for a high roller, Terence.'

Terence laughed. 'No, God, no. I couldn't even get in.'

'Then how come you know so much about it, ace?'

'Told you I knew things,' said Terence, obviously pleased with himself.

'Then keep on telling.'

'Through a friend of a friend at university. He was going out with a girl he met at the Slade school, who used to model for the students. Very shapely. Very . . . *sexy*. She had a job in the club as a cocktail waitress. She told him all about the place. She gave it up after a few weeks, thought it was all a bit too . . . well, some of the men used to want more than just drinks off her. And Mr Regent scared her. She didn't like being anywhere around him . . .'

Vince thought about Bobbie. Why did she stay with him? Why wasn't she scared, too?

'There's a password to get in,' continued Terence.

'You know what it is?'

'She said they change it every few weeks.'

Vince took another swig of Coke and considered his earnest young sidekick. He was bright, smart and obviously a sponge when it came to any information regarding his beloved *underworld*. Vince decided he'd better pay the Brunswick Sporting Club a visit.

'The Indian! The Indian!' Terence was now yanking Vince's elbow.

'Take it easy!' said Vince, as he raised the binoculars to his eyes. Henry 'Redskin' Pierce was currently making his way over to Sammy Bellman's pitch. He held a distinctive white stick as he tapped his way through the crowd. Vince noted that it wasn't the usual slim cane that blind people use as a form of antenna, but a solid white stick looking heavy and gnarled; as if fashioned from bone or ivory, or had been ripped straight from a tree. In the wrong hands – like Pierce's hands – it looked as if it might make an effective weapon. Pierce forged a path before him, as the bodies in his way quickly dispersed. Behind him – not leading the way as you'd expect – followed his driver and companion, Spider. Amphetamine-freak thin, his long, sinewy body kept twisting this way and that as his bony head gazed around him; soaking up the respect and fear that eddied in his boss's wake. No doubt emboldened by Pierce's patronage, the skinny spiv wore a lairy bottle-green tonic suit and a pork-pie hat.

No such clown clothes for Henry Pierce, though. Funereal as ever, he was enveloped in black from top to toe. With his inky-black hair, the black-on-black shirt and tie combination, a black suit, heavy black brogues, the entire ensemble was sheathed in a black Crombie overcoat with a black felt collar. The only thing that wasn't black was the white stick; and, of course, his skin with its sickly pallor. Otherwise monochromic, but for one tiny detail of colour: the gold tie clip containing a blood-red cabochon in its centre. It was the same outfit he always wore: there was no inconsistency about Pierce; he stuck to his guns and to his garb. He wasn't in the business of subtlety. Only in the business of scaring people. There was no guise of respectability about Henry Pierce. He was what he was, and you had to admire his honesty. He was bad. He was *good* at being bad. He didn't go for redeeming features. There were no shades of grey. He wore black.

Pierce exchanged a few words with Sammy B, who handed over a roll of notes out of his satchel. Pierce pocketed the money as he turned away.

It was Vince's turn to yank Terence by the arm, 'Come on, let's go,' he instructed, and headed down towards the betting ring.

They made their way over to Sammy B's pitch. No sign of Pierce by now. But he was a man you'd have difficulty missing, and Vince recognized the head above the crowd before he heard the tapping of the heavy stick. A path opened up before Pierce like the Red Sea, and Vince felt the tide of people getting out of his path. Vince followed quickly in his slipstream while Terence followed in Vince's.

Pierce still leading, with Spider in his shadow, they made their way through the atrium of the grandstand, and up the stairs to the upper tier, then along the corridor to one of the private boxes. Vince and Terence still tailed them at a careful distance.

With large windows set in the partitions of the private boxes, they were not that private, and Vince could see all he needed to. Henry Pierce was now sitting at a table, talking to a very fat man while Spider stood sentry at the door.

The fat one was still picking over the remnants of the 'catch of the day' that lay before him. He'd been feasting on shellfish, and you could tell that eating was a serious business for him. His shirtsleeves were rolled up so that he could set about his work unencumbered, while his chubby fingers glistened with grease. His cherub-cheeked face was almost featureless due to the excess weight he was carrying, and the full head of golden-blond hair looked downy, almost transparent on top of it.

'Who's the big baby with the bib?' asked Vince.

Terence chuckled. 'That's Max Vogel. He's an antique dealer with a shop in the Lanes. I gather he's not too bothered about the provenance of items he deals in, if you get my drift. His nickname is "Treble Dutch", partly because he's of Dutch extraction and partly—'

'Yeah, I get the picture,' said Vince, studying the man who sat with Henry 'Redskin' Pierce. The way they were positioned struck him as interesting, for Pierce who, being taller, would normally tower above Vogel, sat strangely hunched up, as if making himself look smaller. It was Vogel, also, who was doing most of the talking, without bothering to give Pierce a glance as he continued picking the last vestiges of meat from a lobster claw he was holding. Without being able to hear a word, or even lip-read, Vince interpreted a lot from their conversation. Vogel clearly held the power between the two of them, and whenever Pierce did start to talk, Vogel felt free to interrupt and talk over him. Then Pierce would clam up again, listening intently as Vogel delivered instructions or counsel.

'What else do you know about Vogel?' asked Vince, still watching the two men.

'Nothing really.'

Vince frowned, and as if thinking out loud, murmured, 'He wasn't on any list of known Jack Regent associates. Machin never mentioned him, either, yet here he is sitting . . .'

Terence gave a contemptuous little laugh. 'Well, you know what they say about the Brighton police force.'

Vince stared at Terence. 'What exactly do they say?'

'They're the best money can buy.' Terence now laughed nervously.

When Vince didn't respond, Terence stopped laughing. He looked down at his shoes, convinced he'd put his size-eight brown brogues right in it and overstepped the mark.

But he hadn't, for Vince already knew this. He also knew the rest of the saying: 'Best police force you can buy – if you can't afford the Met.' He gave Terence half a smile. 'That's slander, Terence, outright *slander*.'

Vince focused his attention back on Vogel and Pierce. After using the finger bowl, Vogel grabbed the napkin and pulled it from his collar, revealing a red polka-dot bow tie underneath. Pierce then stood up and the two men shook hands. Whatever business they were conducting was now concluded. Pierce stepped out of the private box to rejoin Spider, leaving Vogel alone to peruse the dessert menu.

Vince grabbed Terence, who was gazing at Pierce in awe as he moved towards them. 'Go hang around Sammy Bellman's pitch, see what happens.'

'Where are *you* going?'

'To play blind man's bluff with Henry Pierce.'

Terence looked at Vince in wide-eyed awe. 'Be careful, Vince. He . . . hurts people.' Then, as Vince walked away, he hissed to him, 'Vince! By the way, it's buff. Blind man's buff!'

Vince turned around and smiled. 'Not the way I play it.'

CHAPTER 10

REDSKIN

Henry Pierce was smiling, his head arrogantly cocked as he steamed ahead, seemingly buoyed up and confident after his confab with Max Vogel. Shouldering his way into the bar, as big as he was, he made himself seem bigger, as if he was holding a pair of medicine balls, one under each arm. His stick swung freely, beating a path before him. He took his place at the counter, which was previously three other people's places in the packed bar. Having looked up at who had come muscling in, they wisely and swiftly got out of his way. Spider stood next to him and ordered two bottles of brown ale. Spider poured the ale into a glass for his boss, and Pierce emptied it in two gulps. Wiping the foam from his mouth with the back of a big vein-streaked hand, he put the glass back on the bar, upside down. It was a warning, a sign: a piece of bar-room semiotics that alerted anyone in the immediate vicinity that violence was pending.

With one shoe on the brass foot rail, and one planted well back on the floor, Pierce gripped the edge of the bar as if he was either about to tear it off or push it into the wall. He looked straight ahead of him, so that if he was able to see, he would have seen himself looking straight back in the mirror, and in a booming voice announced: 'I'll have it with any man here!'

Silence. The kind of pin-dropping silence that is deafening. A silence that reverberated like the beating of a bass drum. Conversations collapsed under a weight of fear, jokes dried up and nervous laughter petered out. Henry Pierce had just offered the whole bar out, and no one wanted in. Spider smirked around the room, confident of being on the winning side, even though to a betting man (and surely everyone in the bar *was* a betting man), the odds of one blind man against a good one hundred were stacked against him – like a hundred to one? There were no takers. No one even dared meet the blind man's gaze. And that's a little fact worth repeating: the *blind man*'s gaze. Heads were bowed, shoes were closely inspected. The racing form was being examined with a close-up, paper-rustling intensity.

Satisfied they now held sway over everyone, and happy with the ambience of fear they had created in the room, Pierce and Spider could now enjoy their drinks.

Then they heard the footsteps behind them. Even on the drink-sodden swamp of a carpet in the public bar, they could still be heard. That's how quiet it was.

And then they heard: 'I'll have it.'

Under the black cover of Pierce's tightly fitting Crombie coat, Vince detected a rippling as the knots of muscle in the man's back contorted until his neck almost disappeared, and his head bowed under a tidal wave of indignation and rage.

Spider's mouth hung open like a dumb waiter. As he stood there, accommodatingly slack-jawed, Vince thought this might be a good time to chin him. An adroit left hook would send him flying across the bar, and his jaw off its hinges.

Spider looked up at Pierce for guidance.

Pierce had turned slowly to gauge where the voice of this fucking liberty-taker had emanated from.

'Say that again?'

'Tell the blind man there what I'm holding in my hand, Spider.'

Spider stared at the Metropolitan Police badge Vince held up, and then took a closer look at Vince himself. An excitable expression came over his gauntly spiteful features. 'Look who it isn't . . .' Spider let that hang in the air, and slowly nodded at Vince in recognition.

Pierce's head slowly turned and dipped in the direction of Spider, as he spoke in a voice higher-pitched than his large frame would give credence to. 'Speak up, boy. Half-spoken words avail a blind man of nothing.' Pierce's own words were not half spoken. They were fully formed and overripe and clearly pronounced. It was plain by now that he was putting on a performance, but this was what Henry Pierce was all about. From the wrestling ring to the bar room, he was a natural performer, and the act was all about erudition – a calculating intelligence that belied the mindless violence that permeated a brutal body.

Pierce continued to Spider: 'Tell me, boy, clearly and concisely. Who do you see?'

Spider, still smirking, said, 'I see Vincent Treadwell – Vaughn the spawn's brother, the London copper.' Spider's face then twisted into a smirk and he began to giggle. That giggle had been carefully worked on, thought Vince. It was pure Richard Widmark playing Tommy Udo, the psychopath gangster, in the film whose title temporarily escaped him. Spider was playing for the cameras right now, another little movie gangster in a flashy suit.

Pierce's head straightened and he faced Vince directly. Vince turned away from him and looked at Spider. Vince's heavy dark brows knitted as he fixed him with his dark brown eyes, his dilating black pupils seeming to take up the entire expanse of his eyes. And everything else about him got darker, more threatening. 'Tell your *boy* to go, Pierce.'

The giggles dried up and the smirk slid off Spider's face. Even standing under the protective wing of Henry Pierce, he knew he was now only a flinch, a frown or an ill-thought utterance away from a fucking good hiding.

Pierce gave him the prompt, 'You heard the man, *boy*.'

The slighted Spider sidled off the stage, leaving the two principals alone with each other.

117

Pierce leaned forward, sniffed the air around the young detective, smiled and said, 'The prodigal has returned.'

Vince stood stock-still, looking into the black discs of Pierce's glasses. He couldn't see his eyes. 'Is this performance part of your famous Red Indian shtick, Mr Pierce?'

'It's no shtick, boy. It's in my blood. My grandfather was a full-blooded Sioux. Warrior, tracker and buffalo hunter, he could sniff out his prey a mile away.'

'Not a lot of buffalo here in Brighton.'

Pierce pulled a grin that showed buckled rows of grey teeth. 'You're not wrong there, boy. You're not wrong. He came to these shores with the Buffalo Bill show in 1897. They were playing just outside Manchester, when he made the fatal mistake that most men make at least once in their life. He fell for a slip, a Salford girl of Hungarian extraction. Funny old world, crooked old planet. Made their way down to Brighton. But you're right, not a lot of buffalo in Brighton. He ended up working the fairgrounds and sewing fishing nets. Drank himself to death: they're bad with the firewater, the redskins. As for me dressing up as a brave for the wrestling, that was all just a bit of sport.'

'Sport?' Vince raised a doubtful eyebrow at this. 'I heard you killed a man in the ring. Not very sporting?'

Pierce let out a breath carrying a satisfied 'Ahhh,' then recalled, with some vigour, 'Leo "the Lion" Lomax was his name.' He smiled at the memory, then tapped his cane on the bar twice, calling out to the terrified barman, 'Two bottles of brown ale!' The bottles were at his elbow in an instant, and Vince assumed the second bottle was for him.

'Leo was a fine specimen of a man,' continued Pierce. 'Big thick mane of blond hair, billed as the housewives' favourite. You know, when I started out in the ring, I was considered the goodie. But I had a gift, you see – showmanship. I was a natural performer. And then the promoters didn't want me to be the goodie, because in the wrestling game the goodie is the baddie. You know why?'

Vince shook his head, then remembered that it 'availed a blind man nothing' so he piped up, 'No, I don't.'

'Because the goodie doesn't draw the crowd. It's the baddie they come to see.'

Vince inquired: 'So what was Leo, a goodie?'

'Correct, but he was a bad goodie. He was bad at being good. And you'll have to excuse my language, but he was a right cunt. And that aspect of him came across to the audience. They all knew it, and they used to call him it. They used to shout it out at him. They used to climb into the ring and tell him so. All the promoters and other wrestlers knew it, too. In fact, the only person who didn't know it was Leo himself. Which just goes to show you what a right cunt he was.'

He paused for a quick swallow. 'Anyway, one night at Hoxton Baths, I was due to fight Leo Lomax. I comes out in my full regalia: headdress, warpaint, buckskins and me tomahawk tucked in me trunks. And the crowd is cheering. Even old women and kids, they're cheering their heads off. Tomahawk in hand, I starts doing me war dance. Me squaw at the time, Rita, a real looker if you like that sort of thing, she takes my headdress off, and I'm dancing around the ring and the audience is loving it. Lapping me up they was. And *I'm* supposed to be the baddie!'

Pierce pulled a big grin, but it soon faded as the memory rolled on out, and he then gave a remorseful shake his head.

'Then Leo comes out. Oh dear, there were boos. You've never heard boos like it. Deafening boos. They're booing the *goodie*. Anyway, Leo doesn't like it. He's not happy, not happy at all. And the reason he's not happy isn't strictly on account of the boos, because they'd stopped booing by the time he'd got into the ring; and started spitting and throwing coins, and door keys and car keys. No, he's not happy on account of everyone shouting out "Cunt" at him. He's angry, he's humiliated, he's enraged, then he's only gone and chinned Rita, my squaw. He'd taken umbrage at her, you see, on account that she'd already told him what she thought of him, and what everyone thought of him, in the dressing room. And she'd led the chant of calling him that as he made his way into the ring. Well, I wasn't having that, was I? My Rita? My lovely Rita? No, I wasn't having that. So I scalped him.'

Vince looked around him to check it was still 1964. Then he checked to make sure he'd heard right. 'You *scalped* him?'

'Scalped him,' said Pierce with a blunt nod. 'Done him with a right-hander first. Lifted him up by his greasy pompadour, took out me tomahawk, and started chopping away at his forehead. From ear to ear. Lucky for me, Leo had such a fine head of hair on him, and he wore it long for them days. So there was plenty to get hold of. Me tomahawk was a bit blunt, so I couldn't get a clean cut. And what with Leo still being alive when I took his scalp . . . well, not the best circumstances for both of us. But, when the job was done, I had enough of old Leo in me hands to hold up to the crowd. At first the crowd thought it was all part of the act. They was very encouraging of it. Then they saw the blood, lots of blood. I can't stress just how much blood there was. Bleeding on to the canvas, comatose from the shock, the sympathies of the crowd had now shifted in his favour. In a big way, I'd have to say. Leo was quite the hero again. He really was the *goodie*. So, in many ways, I did him a favour. Not that he'd ever admit it, the ungrateful cunt. He died four years later. Put his head in the oven. Still, that's show business for you.'

Pierce picked up his glass and guzzled thirstily.

Vince's mind scrolled back through the annals of gruesome stories he'd heard over the years, to check if he'd heard of anything even comparable. Nothing came to mind. Nothing quite so gruesome, quite so *public*.

Pierce put his empty glass on the bar with a thud that drew a line under the good old days.

'But that's enough about me,' he said. 'How about you, Vincent? Have you grown into a tall handsome man? Have you fulfilled your potential?'

Vince looked up at Pierce and watched a long, scaly purple tongue – looking like a piece of rotten meat – slip lizard-like out of his mouth and work its way around those dry old lips. There was a predatory smile on his newly moistened mouth which made Vince's skin crawl. And it was *meant* to make his skin crawl. The soft touch of a woman, the curves of a woman, the scent, the chitter, the chatter, the gentle and fairer sex, these weren't for Henry Pierce. For Pierce to be with a woman – a slip – would just seem queer. And yet he wasn't queer, either. He didn't get it up any more for the boys than he did for the girls. He didn't get it up for anyone. To get it up would be to admit that there was blood flowing through his veins. The 'predatory' Pierce was just more shock shtick. It fitted the outfit he was wearing, the voice he was doing: it was all part of the act. Like he said, it was showbiz, and he was above all a performer.

'Cat got your tongue, boy?'

'I'm going to need to ask you some questions, Mr Pierce.'

'What questions?'

'About the body on the beach. And Jack Regent.'

'Me, I'm a blind man, retired. I know nothing about nothing, officer.'

'You're too modest, Mr Pierce. A man about town like you, who's a friend of Jack Regent, you must know lots of things.'

Pierce gave a knowing nod. 'The body on the beach, you say? I heard he died with a smile on his face. When you find it, do tell.' Pierce sniffed the air again, then said, 'I like you, boy. Full of piss and vinegar, as the Yanks say.'

'I'm glad you like me, because you're going to spend some time with me. To discuss your whereabouts. Tomorrow, nine-thirty, Edward Street. If you're not there I'll come and find you.'

Vince turned his back on Pierce and walked away.

Pierce bellowed, 'You wanna know my whereabouts, copper? Ask your brother.'

Vince stopped walking.

'He was my chauffeur around about that time. I had a little uniform and cap made for him, to cover his bald spot.' Pierce laughed loudly, encouraging those around him to join in.

Vince felt the blood drain from his face, his stomach churn, not through the shock of it but the *obviousness* of it. Vaughn was made to measure for Henry Pierce: small, scared and pliant.

'And a nice pair of kid gloves, too, so his hands wouldn't chafe on the steering wheel and gearstick. Oh, he did look a picture.' Pierce was really playing to the gallery now, whipping up the audience response. The crowd joined in eagerly, not because it was funny, but because it was the safest thing to do. And Henry Pierce playing Widow Twankey was always preferable to him playing Attila the Hun. Christmas had come early for the men in his immediate vicinity, because to have Pierce laughing lowered the odds of him randomly glassing someone, or putting an ice pick into your groin.

Spider had sidled back under his protective wing, and reverted to the Richard Widmark/Tommy Udo giggle.

All eyes were on Vince as he turned around when his tormentor continued.

'Detective Treadwell, don't you want to know what Vaughn's been up to whilst he's been squiring me about? Don't you want to know what *she's* been playing at? Oh, she is a real cup of tea, that one!'

More laughter; Spider cranked up the Tommy Udo.

Vince was livid. He could feel the balance slipping away, the police badge melting in his hand. Time to take back control. He strode over to Pierce, snatched the heavy stick out of his hand and, swift as you like, before Pierce even knew what was happening, he jabbed the gnarled end into Spider's groin. Three times in succession: *one*, Spider bent over, winded; *two*, Spider let out a guttural groan; *three*, Spider dropped to his bony knees. And another one for luck . . . Vince went to smash the cane into the nape of Spider's neck. But, in a trice, Pierce had unclenched his fist and caught the descending finial in the palm of his hand. His fingers wrapped themselves around the contested cane. Vince had hold of one end, Pierce was holding the other.

The audience hushed. Like Vince, it awaited Pierce's next move.

Pierce dipped his head towards the floor, where his sidekick was squirming at his feet. Spider wasn't doing his Richard Widmark/Tommy Udo bit any more. He was doing his doubled-up and whimpering-in-pain bit. Pierce considered Spider as if just a minor embarrassment, then redirected his attention to the young detective.

Vince still gripped the cane. He didn't want to let go, partly because he was worried what Pierce might do with it, and partly because it gave him a strange buzz. So he continued to clutch the lightning rod that kept him plugged into Pierce, plugged into a childhood fear of this monster of his past. Until the buzz faded, the surge subsided – and he wasn't scared anymore.

Pierce emitted a low, thoughtful growl in his throat, then said, 'Mine, I believe.'

Vince considered this suggestion, like handing over a loaded gun. 'Yours, I believe.' Finally he let go of the stick.

Henry Pierce held the retrieved cane ambiguously, neither as crutch nor cudgel. Straightening his back, he extended himself to his full height.

'Edward Street police station,' said Vince calmly. 'Nine-thirty. I'll see you there, Mr Pierce.'

But, before Vince could turn away, Pierce suddenly upped the ante in the madness stakes. He fell to his knees, arms outstretched like he'd just been felled by a sniper's bullet, yelling, 'Police brutality! Can I get a witness? Can I get a witness?'

All eyes were on Vince, who was trying to ignore the madman on the floor.

'Hear ye! Hear ye! Hear ye! Can I get a witness here?'

As Vince turned away, he felt a shooting pain in his head, and an incipient surge of nausea. It gathered apace and washed over him. It came on him so quickly, he feared he'd been stuck with a syringe and shot through with bad medicine. Vince attributed this to Pierce: he'd allowed himself to get involved, to get tangled up in his web of madness. But tomorrow would be his day. 'Nine-thirty. I'll be waiting. So don't make me come looking for you.' He strode out of the bar, and could hear Henry Pierce laughing behind him.

Vince swung straight into the gents' toilet, headed into a cubicle, kicked the seat off the bowl and puked up.

CHAPTER 11

THE ORACLE

Back in the betting ring, Vince spotted Terence dutifully standing by Sammy Bellman's pitch. He looked as inconspicuous as a man who had been told by the police to stand next to a bookie and watch what occurs. Sammy B and the people around him obviously viewed him with suspicion, and just then Terence was approached by Sammy B's tic-tac man. 'Long George' Silverman was in his late fifties and, as the nickname suggested, he was tall: a good six foot plus something ridiculous. Height was a great advantage for a tic-tac man, enabling him to loom high above the crowds and see all the action occurring in the betting ring. Long George wore big black-rimmed glasses that magnified his eyes to clownish proportions. In fact his entire face had a comic appearance: big, fleshy and bulbous, as if designed not to be taken seriously. He'd obviously been sent over by Sammy B, to get the SP on this suspicious-looking fellow hanging about. Vince watched as Long George struck up a conversation with Terence who obviously wasn't furnishing him with the right answers, because the long fellow started prodding him in the chest with a pointed finger, backed up with accusations.

Vince stepped in. 'Gentlemen.' He whipped out his badge.

Long George studied it, then gestured at Terence, saying, 'This man has no cause to be here. He has no cause at all! He's loitering without intent of having a bet. Not one wager has he made. We're just trying to earn an honest living.'

Terence protested: 'It's a free country.'

'The bloody young farshtinkener! It's only free because men like me fought for it! For the freedom to get on with our business without being bothered by loiterers.'

Vince gave a conciliatory smile and announced, 'He's with me.'

'Him? No disrespect, officer, but he looks too small to be a bogey.'

'He's not. He's just a friend.'

Long George stared at Vince, a glimmer of recognition lighting up his big brown eyes. 'Mmm, I reckon I know that face.'

Vince smiled. 'Detective Treadwell, Vince Treadwell.'

'Ach, boobalah! I knew I recognized that face!'

Long George cupped Vince's face in his large fleshy hands, shook it from side to side in disbelief, slapped both cheeks, twice, then gathered the reddened cheeks up in pinches and shook it from side to side again. It was a show of affection. It was a very painful show of affection that Vince wished would stop. But it was all so genuine that he didn't have the heart to tell Long George. After a back-breaking bear hug, the pain stopped.

'So how are you, Long George?'

'Ach, still a million shy of becoming a millionaire. Much I care!'

Vincent knew, however, that Long George's use of the word 'Much' meant the opposite to most other people's use of the word.

'Terence, I want you to meet Long George Silverman.'

Long George grabbed up Terence's hand and began to shake the life out of it. 'Why didn't you just say you were a friend of young Vincent?'

Vince intervened. 'You got a tip for me, Long George?'

'You're much too smart to bet on the gee-gees, so what's the game here, Vincent? Why was your man here posted beside Sammy's pitch?'

'I thought Jack Regent might turn up to keep an eye on Sammy, what with all this London muscle knocking around today.'

'No one's going to move Sammy from the number-one pitch.'

'So where is he, Long George?'

'From what I hear, he's in the wind. But, ach, what do I know?'

'In this town? You know *everything*.'

'Would I kibbitz you, boobalah?' Long George looked around as if for eavesdroppers, then leaned in surreptitiously. 'Listen up, you wanna tip? I've got a tip for you, Vincent. The Oracle. It's running in the last race. It's a sure thing, so bet the house. But do me a favour, and don't bet with Sammy. We're doing our money!'

Vince smiled at the way Long George was changing the subject by throwing him a tip. If only all lines of questioning were this profitable, he reflected. 'Don't worry, Long George, I know my racing etiquette, I won't bite the hand that feeds me. Oh, one last thing,' he said, trying to sound casual, 'how can I get into the Brunswick Sporting Club?'

Long George gave several slow, thoughtful nods, as if he was waiting to hear more from the copper before he answered.

Vince responded, all smiles and congeniality. 'I've got some holiday pay due, and Tony Machin told me that club was the right place to lose it.' Vince noticed how the mention of Machin's name put the long fellow at ease.

'Ah, Machin, yes. Surprised not to see *him* here today, being a degenerate gambler and frequent visitor to the tables. 'Tis a pity for him, and blessing for us, that he always leaves his luck at home. Let's hope, for your sake, that you're not of the same luckless disposition.'

Vince felt a tug at his sleeve. He'd almost forgotten about Terence, who rose on tiptoe and whispered in Vince's ear, 'The password?'

Vince favoured him with the kind of conspiratorial nod that he knew he would appreciate.

Long George shook his head. 'What's with your boy here? He's all whispers and secret squirrels. Doesn't he know we're all friends around here?'

'He's asking about the password to get into the club.'

'The *password*?' Long George's fleshy face screwed up as he examined Terence more carefully. Then he leaned towards Vince conspiratorially and murmured, 'Swordfish.'

'Swordfish?'

Long George gave a solemn nod and repeated, 'Swordfish.' After that revelation, he gave a curiously Germanic click of his heels, about-faced and headed back to Sammy Bellman's betting pitch.

As Vince turned towards the line of bookies, in the distance he caught sight of his brother Vaughn studying the runners and odds chalked up on the boards.

'Wait here,' he said to Terence, and began picking his way through the crowd. As soon as Vaughn spotted him making his way over, he took to his heels. Vince uttered a heavy-hearted sigh, and gave chase.

Vaughn's usual luck held out, all of it bad, as ever. While he scrambled up the steps leading to the exit, someone trod heavily on his foot. Vaughn carried on scrambling away with one shoe still trapped under the man's foot. Vince spotted the abandoned footwear lying on the ground and snatched it up, then grabbed Vaughn himself at the rear of the stand.

Doubled over and wheezing heavily, Vaughn took a couple of minutes to straighten up. Automatically he then pulled a crumpled pack of Craven A out of his pocket, sparked up and inhaled a long, deep drag. He coughed and hawked, then through a shaky exhalation of smoke asked reproachfully, 'What are you doing here?'

'I think you forgot something.' Vince handed him the shoe. 'Why are you always running away from me?'

Vaughn's eyes darted everywhere except towards his brother, and eventually settled on his feet, where he slipped his slip-ons back on.

'I've just been talking to Henry Pierce,' Vince continued.

Vaughn redoubled the attention focused on his feet. Vince followed his brother's gaze down to his slip-on/slip-off shoes. Not the most sensible footwear for a burglar, quick-getaway artist and leg-it merchant like Vaughn.

'Look at me, Vaughn. Pierce says you used to drive for him. Is that true?'

The apple never falls far from the tree, so the maxim goes. And, as maxims go, in Vaughn's case this was spot on. The man began to sob, like his father would have done years before him, and in much the same circumstances and much the same locale. The betting ring, the dog track, the card school, the spieler, anywhere that money and luck were inextricably linked, rather than a demand for hard work, skill or brains. Vaughn's luck, like his father's before him, had all run out.

'I needed the money,' Vaughn sobbed.

Vince handed him the handkerchief from his top pocket. 'Then why didn't you come to me?'

'*You* – my kid brother?' He gave a bitter laugh. 'I can look after myself.'

Vince felt exasperated. 'How the hell does getting involved with Regent, Pierce and the rest of them count as looking after yourself!'

'You don't have to live here,' Vaughn protested. 'You want to turn a pound in this town, you gotta work with them. *Fucksake*, they run everything!'

'You ever thought about getting yourself a job?'

Vaughn blew his nose into the handkerchief. Vince suddenly grabbed his arm. He rolled up his brother's sleeve to reveal the bony white limb. It looked almost transparent, the blue veins so pronounced they looked as if they'd been piped on by a cake decorator. No track marks, yet.

'How long you been on the gear?'

'What gear?'

'Vaughn the Junkie, that's what I've heard. And I believe it, so don't lie to me, Vaughn.'

Vaughn grabbed back his arm and pulled down the sleeve. 'I don't shoot. I just smoke it.' A defiant smirk crossed his face as he tried to rustle up the bravado to put some distance between himself and his policeman brother. 'You don't get it, man. It's cool. It's jazz. It's *Bird*.'

Vince didn't even sneer. 'It's a mug's game, and smoking it don't make it any better. It's just the start, Vaughn. You can't beat that stuff. It's bigger than you and it *will* get you. Just ask those three they found in Kemp Town how . . .' Vince's voice trailed off and he shook his head, more at his own ineffectuality than at his brother's plight. He could see his words were useless, were merely falling on deaf ears, and, if he wasn't careful, his brother would soon be a lost soul mired in the haze of the 'nod' that all junkies perpetually craved.

'You know anything about that business?'

'They were out-of-towners, so how would I know them?'

'Because you share the same hobby.'

Vaughn again stared at his shoes. There were more questions Vince might have asked him about the Kemp Town deaths, and the body on the beach. But he didn't have the stomach for it now. So he kept it simple: 'You been winning today?'

Vaughn gave a noncommittal shrug, but then confirmed his losing status by asking, 'You couldn't lend us a few quid? I'm a bit shickered at the moment.'

Vince had lost count of how much his brother was already into him for, so he didn't bother mentioning it. 'How much do you need?'

Vaughn lowered his gaze and inspected his footwear again. 'A pony?'

Vince pulled out his wallet. He didn't need a deerstalker and a meerschaum pipe to deduce that the money was most likely destined for the bookie's satchel. But equally, it could have been any number of bad luck scenarios, from shylock repayments, to back rent, to hocked belongings. And now there was a new one added to the list – scoring junk. Vince extracted all the notes he had on him: a fiver and two ones. 'That's all I've got right now.'

Vaughn snatched the money eagerly out of his hand. 'I'll get it right back to you.'

'The Oracle. Go back it.'

Vaughn's head shot up. 'It's fifteen to one.'

'Trust me, and you can buy your girlfriend something pretty.'

'How d'you know about her?'

'I was at your flat, remember? Unless you've started wearing lipstick, it looks like you've got yourself a girl.'

Vaughn gave a cautious shrug. Normally he'd be boastful about being able to snag himself a girl, so his hesitant reaction merely confirmed what Bobbie had told Vince earlier.

'You'd better get going, if you want to get on to it at that price.'

Vaughn shuffled off as fast as the loose shoes would carry him. 'I'll pay you back, I promise!'

'Keep it,' Vince replied. 'Buy yourself some decent shoes.' He stood, watching Vaughn disappear into the crowd. Then, to no one in particular, or maybe to the ghost of his brother, he said softly, 'Then you'll be able to run faster.'

CHAPTER 12

SWORDFISH

Vince entered the Seaview Hotel. The lady at the desk informed him there was one call for him, Ray Dryden, who said to get back to him ASAP. There was no mail for him, but his wife was waiting for him in the lounge.

Vince stepped into the lounge, and there she was. His 'wife', Bobbie LaVita, was on the sofa by the bay window, while the bartender fetched her a brandy. She smiled at the man as he took away an empty glass. Five French cigarette butts sat in the ashtray, their white filters smeared with her coral lipstick.

Bobbie was wearing a short light-blue skirt with a matching tunic-style jacket with a black border round the collar, done up with six brass buttons. It looked expensive, Chanel perhaps. A navy-blue, patent-leather clutch bag, with a gold clasp in the form of a woman's hand, rested by her side. Her long slim legs were curled under her. It seemed to be a position she favoured. As with a cat, there was never any hesitation about making herself comfortable; she just did it. A pair of elegant black slip-on shoes with low heels and silver buckles lay discarded on the floor. Her hair, worn a touch higher, looked as if it had been backcombed and sprayed. She was fragrant, and her face was made up, powdered and pale. The eyes were framed by black eyeliner, with little ticks in the corners that gave the almond-shaped eyes more emphasis. It looked heavier than she had worn it before, the black lines seeming not so crisp. The eyes had been redone, and with a not so steady hand, because she had been crying.

'I'm sorry,' she said, as she unfolded her legs and slipped her feet into her shoes to make room for him on the sofa. 'I didn't know what to say when that lady at the desk asked who I was, a strange woman turning up at your hotel. Saying "Your wife" sounded more respectable.'

He gave an appreciative nod, then followed through with an uncertain smile. 'But a wife turning up at my hotel in tears, I'm not too sure how respectable that is.'

'I'm sorry.'

'Don't be.'

'It's nice to know, though.'

'What is?'

'That you wouldn't want your wife to cry.'

'I didn't say that. I just said I wouldn't want her turning up at my hotel.'

She saw that he was joking and managed a smile, too.

'If I may ask why you've been crying?'

'Can we go somewhere more private?'

Vince nodded and suggested, 'My room?'

Bobbie collected her cigarettes and lighter off the table, stood up and followed him out of the lounge.

Up in his room, Bobbie had flipped off her shoes and plonked herself down in the armchair, in what Vince could only take to be her default sitting position: legs curled under her.

He pulled down his suitcase that had been stashed on top of the wardrobe and put it on the bed, then opened it up and took out a small brown phial containing his pills.

She looked at Vince as he popped a pill. 'What are those?' she asked.

Vince swallowed the pill without water, then read out the label, stumbling over the pronunciation, 'Recal . . . dro . . . lycine. They're for headaches.'

She frowned. 'What kind of headaches?'

'The kind of headaches you get when you've been in a coma for three weeks.'

'*Three weeks?*' Bobbie's eyes widened. 'Are you . . . fully recovered?'

'Apart from the headaches, and a little nausea – but they told me those'll just pass,' replied Vince, looking down at the bottle of pills. He leaned back against the chest of drawers, flipped the bottle of pills from hand to hand, and smiled. 'The doc said some people undergo a complete personality change after emerging from a coma. All the things they used to like, they have no more interest in – books, movies, food, women. They almost get two lives for the price of one, as well as a bang on the head.'

'How about you? Did you get two lives?'

'I don't know. I like the same movies, same food. And I still can't play the piano, so I guess I got lucky – or unlucky. It depends on what you thought of your life before.'

'How about your taste in women, has that changed?'

'No, I still like them old and ugly.'

She laughed. 'How did it happen – the coma, not your taste in ugly old women?'

Vince took a deep breath and sighed. 'I don't know.'

'How come?'

'It's a moot point. Some people say I must have fallen some-how and hit my head.'

'What do *you* say?'

'I say I can't remember.' Determined. 'But I will.'

Bobbie just nodded, seeing that he didn't want to take this con-versation any further. Vince threw the bottle of pills back into the case, and sat down on the corner of the bed. 'So why the tears?'

She composed herself briefly, then said, 'Henry Pierce.' She knew that name alone was enough to get his full attention.

It did. Vince straightened up. 'What about him?'

'I got a call from him at the flat, about an hour ago. Henry has never phoned there before. Even when Jack was around, he would never call. Jack wouldn't allow it. Like I said, Jack kept his business and personal life very separate. He kept me very separate.'

'But Jack's not here now,' said Vince, looking squarely into eyes that were still red-rimmed from tears. 'The rules have changed, whether you like it or not.'

Bobbie nodded, conceded the point, and let out a fearful little sigh. 'He's never liked me,' she said.

'Henry never liked anyone.'

'Apart from Jack.'

Vince arched his eyebrows and moved his head from side to side, weighing up that claim, but clearly feeling doubt. 'Henry Pierce *fears* Jack. There's a world of difference.'

'Either way, he despises my intrusion on Jack. There's something else, too.' Bobbie picked up her cigarettes. 'May I?' Vince nodded and handed her the small glass ashtray from his bedside table. She lit up a cigarette and took a long, thoughtful drag. 'I was the one who blinded Henry – did you know that?' She stared solidly at Vince. It was a dramatic statement, delivered with dramatic intent and poise. The cigarette struck Vince as a prop to provide theatrical flourish. But he had heard a lot worse, and coolly instructed her to carry on.

'That's what Jack told me,' she continued, 'by way of a joke.'

'A joke, eh? What made him come up with that particular side-splitter?'

A small laugh rocked her head back. 'Henry went blind soon after he met me. It was my first night on stage, and Jack brought Henry round to the club with some other men.'

'Who were the other men?'

'They were from out of town.'

'Apart from Jack, any Frenchmen amongst them?'

She creased her brow quizzically. 'French?'

'Just a lead we're following. Doesn't matter. Go on.'

135

'I was introduced to them but I can't remember. They all sort of looked the same.'

'Strangers to choir practice?'

'Exactly. They looked like the kind of men Jack would be doing business with. Apart from Dickie Eton . . . no one looks quite like Dickie.'

'Yeah, so I hear.'

'Jack brought Dickie down to hear me sing, and I joined them at their table after my set. Jack then introduced me to Henry Pierce. He stood up, like a real gentleman, took my hand and kissed it. He scared me. But, then again, that's his job. He looked at the brooch I was wearing—'

'The brooch you wore last night?'

She nodded. 'He asked if he could hold it. I thought that was odd. I remember Jack just gave me a little smile like I was dealing with a child who should be indulged. So I took the brooch off and handed it to him, but he hardly looked at it. To be honest, I thought he was looking at my tits. I told Jack this, and he laughed, said I had nothing to worry about. Told me Henry had no interest in such things.'

'The brooch is paste, right?'

'I brought it with me.' She picked up the clutch bag by her side, unhooked the little gold hand, and took out the brooch.

Vince stepped over to her and inspected it. The little bird with outstretched wings was a phoenix rising from a spray of diamanté cut stone that represented the fire. It was cheaply cast costume jewellery of no real intrinsic value. Vince handed her back the brooch and sat back down on the corner of the bed.

Then he said, 'I don't think he was out to steal it.'

She looked at the brooch, assessing it. 'No, I guess not. It just struck me as odd.'

'Why do you even wear it? Jack could get you all the diamonds you want.'

She threw him a sharp look and curtly replied, 'You think I'm a gold digger?'

He looked again at the brooch, which she was turning over in her hand, caressing it as if it held the power of a magic amulet. 'Just curious,' he said.

'I've had it for years.'

'Well, that brooch, nice as it is, is pretty worthless. And, unless you pinched it from the tomb of Tutankhamun, there's nothing to be scared of.' Vince saw that she wasn't following his lead and laughing it off. 'Sentimental value, uh?'

'Not really,' said Bobbie. 'But the dress is. It belonged to my mother. It had a tear in it when I got it, so I bought the brooch to cover it.'

'*Belonged* to your mother?'

Bobbie looked uncomfortable, her eyes darting downwards. She put the brooch back in her bag and snapped the little gold hand clasp shut. 'My mother passed away . . . two years ago if you must know.'

'I'm sorry.' Seeing the bereavement was still fresh for her, he left a solemn little pause before he said, 'Let's get back to what happened tonight.'

'Like I said, Henry called me at the flat. He wanted to come round, to talk to me privately. Wanted to know about you.'

'What did you tell him?'

'Nothing. Because I know nothing. And anyway it's none of his business.'

'His driver, Spider, saw us together at the party you took me to. I'm assuming he told Pierce. He knows who I am now. Before he called you, I met up with him at the races. We had a slight *altercation*.'

'What happened?' she asked.

'Nothing much. But it makes sense that Pierce would want to know what your movements are, who you're seeing, who you're talking to. You're the boss's girl, after all.' Vince stood up and went over to the chest of drawers, opened them in turn and took out the few items he'd neatly folded inside, and transferred

them to his suitcase. 'It was probably Pierce's men who jumped me last night.'

'I'm not anyone's girl,' she said firmly, crushing her cigarette into the ashtray. 'What are you doing?'

'What does it look like? I'm packing.'

'Where are you going?'

'Always fancied an open-top sports car driving around Europe. Italy, south of France, Monte Carlo . . .'

'Isn't the south of France a little too rich for a policeman's pay packet?'

'A policeman who got hit on the head and put into a coma gets compensation. And I've also got holiday back pay. Haven't taken one in four years – too busy being a copper and trying to build a career. I'm pretty well fixed for dosh.'

'So you're running out on me?'

'I was never *in* with you to run out on you. If that makes sense. Even if it doesn't, it does to me. This case is a waste of time. Brick walls and dead ends is all I've run up against. And that's not good for headaches. Everyone knows Jack did the murder, but Jack's not here. Someone may run into him at some time, but not in Brighton, not now. Truth is, I was sent down here to recuperate, and to be out of the way of another case I was working on. But my superintendent, knowing me to be the industrious ambitious type, threw me the Jack case. Well, I'm done with it now. And if I'm going to take in some sea air, I'd rather be lying on sand not stones, and eating calamari not chips. Can I be honest with you, Miss Drinkwater?'

Bobbie's eyes narrowed on hearing her real name. 'Go ahead, Mr Treadwell.'

'You're worried about Henry Pierce, right?' She nodded. 'Well, you've got every right to be,' he said. 'Pierce is a dangerous man who works for another more dangerous man, who controls lots of other little dangerous men. You got yourself into this mess and you'll have to get yourself out.'

Bobbie uncurled her legs, and slipped her feet into her shoes.

'I don't know what you saw in Jack,' he continued. 'Was it the power, the glamour or just middle-class kicks?' She still didn't answer. Irritated, Vince threw the last of his shirts into his suitcase and said, 'Let me tell you about Jack Regent, and what he's really about. Last night, the man on the beach . . .'

Vince was going to tell her the story of Billy the Schnozz. And how it came to pass that he'd gone from a vainglorious braggart to a broken shell of a man looking thirty years older than he really was, with a death sentence scrawled on his forehead, and reading the obituaries to the sea. But he couldn't, because it was too suffused with the past. A world he wanted to distance himself from. He just wanted to get in his car and drive away, feel the sun on his face and foreign accents in his ears. He was sick of Brighton. And, anyway, what did he care about the company she kept? The men she shared her bed with? *What did he care?* Too much. And he knew it.

'Forget it. My advice is leave town. Go back to the New Forest and the two black Labradors in the garden.'

'I don't want to leave. Why should I? I've got my club and—'

Vince cut in, hard. 'If it's your club keeping you here, forget it. Because everyone else has, so why shouldn't you? It's dead now. Here's the news: you were never the main attraction, the star turn. It was Jack they came to see. He pulled in the crowd. And now he's gone, so have they. Way I see it, you've got two choices, Miss Drinkwater: leave town and rack it up to experience, like a true actress; or wait for the next psycho to come along and fill Jack's crippled boots, and then cosy up to him—'

Before he could finish, Bobbie was on her feet and had slapped him. Hard. He didn't move. She slapped him again. Harder. With his torched cheek, he still didn't move. She went for the hat-trick; he grabbed her hand mid-slap and held it in the air.

'You lie with dogs, you get fleas. Don't take it out on me,' he said, pushing her back into the chair.

Her breath turned loud and juddery as a delta of tears rippled out of her.

Vince stood there, rooted to the floor, feeling like an awkward bully – even though she was the one who had done the slapping, and he was the one with the torched cheek. It was the parting shot he'd had in his sights since the first time he'd set eyes on her, yet it gave little satisfaction. He went back to his case and zipped it up, ready to leave. He looked around at the sobbing girl. The tears seemed real enough. No method acting here. She was, if anything, attempting to suppress the tears, but was failing miserably. Her slender frame quivered like a just plucked bow. If left alone, she looked as if she would be sobbing her heart out on the floor.

A small voice: 'I'm scared.'

With an enervated sigh, he said, 'Go see Machin.'

'I don't trust him.'

Vince couldn't argue with that. He sat down again on the corner of the bed. Elbows on knees, head bowed, hands running through his hair, exasperated and exhausted with it all. 'So what do you want me to do about it? '

'I don't want to be alone tonight.'

He stopped running his hands through his hair and looked up towards her. 'You can't stay here. I'll drop you back home. You'll have to—'

'I'm sorry I slapped you.'

'It's OK. Not the first time it's happened.'

'And not the last, I imagine.'

Vince smiled. 'No, you're probably right there.'

She looked up at him with eyes that meant it, and said, 'I trust you, Vincent.'

Ten minutes later they were getting into the Triumph Herald. Before they set off, Vince was struck by a new thought. A new player. 'What do you know about Max Vogel?'

'The antique dealer?'

Vince nodded.

'I know Jack did business with him.'

'Fencing the antiques the knocker boys got hold of?'

'Vogel's in the antiques game, so I guess so. But, more than that, I know that Jack respected him.'

'How do you mean?'

She shrugged uncertainly, but was working on that most formidable of intuitions: female. 'Vogel wasn't just another lackey. I think Jack trusted him with certain things that he wouldn't trust other people with.'

'Like what?'

She gave another speculative shrug. 'Money?'

Treble Dutch began to make sense to Vince. Jack was undoubtedly rich but, as Bobbie pointed out about the flat, he possessed very little that was actually in his name. He relied on and trusted others to honour business agreements that were not backed up on paper. They were, of course, backed up by fear, more potent a guarantee than any contract could provide. No small print, just big pain if the contract was broken. That made it easy for Jack to disappear into the wind, relying on a network of off-shore accounts holding Jack's untraceable money. No doubt about it, Jack would need men like Max Vogel.

Vince twirled the key in the ignition, started the engine, then turned to Bobbie. 'Before we head back to your place, I want to stop off somewhere first.'

'Swordfish.'

'Swordfish?' repeated the fuzzy electric voice over the intercom.

'That's right, *Swordfish*,' replied Vince. He was standing in the vestibule of a four-storey Regency town house in Brunswick Square.

Vince thought he heard some chuckling in the background as he said the fabled password. He looked over at Bobbie seated in the car, fixing her hair in the rear-view mirror. Hair done, she looked over at him and waved. He smiled, waved back, then was buzzed in.

Vince scoped the rooms of the Brunswick Sporting Club. The layout was just as Terence described. Wall-to-wall red carpet. A full-on full-service casino. Tables offering roulette, craps, blackjack, stud and four-card poker, chemmy. A caged *caissier's* desk. Pretty young waitresses in revealing little numbers ferried drinks from the bar to the tables. In another room, big-hit slot machines lined the walls; the slots only accepted tokens that needed to be cashed with the *caissier* in the event of a jackpot. The Brunswick Sporting Club was clearly doing cracking business.

It was the usual casino crowd: a handful of hopefuls who thought they could beat the house; and, if cuts of suits and the quality of wristwatches were anything to go by, a smattering of punters with serious money. But they all had one thing in common: the gambler's mindset – optimism and cynicism held in one hand. And, like all people who chase money through games of chance, the air they breathed was malodorous with jaded desperation. No clocks on the walls, no timely reminders that their luck was up.

A big fleshy hand was laid on his shoulder. 'Ach! Such mischief! I heard about the kerfuffle at the races! Are you pots!?'

Vince turned around. 'What are you talking about, Long George?'

Long George leaned into him, eyes bulging under the magnification of his heavy-rimmed glasses, and said, 'Henry Pierce. Crazy Horse! Big Chief Mashigina himself! Much I care for the man, but you ruffled his feathers. And when Big Chief Mashigina has his feathers ruffled, we all feel the flap. I thought you was a good boy. What was the cause? What was the cause?'

'There was cause, Long George. There was definitely cause . . .'

Vince was about to reassure him that he was 'a good boy' and reveal what 'the cause' was, when he suddenly spotted Machin at a card table. He was sitting between two Chinamen, playing black-jack and looking for all the world as if he was going belly-up.

Vince made his excuses to Long George, since he wasn't there for the local colour. He was in a hurry, and went straight over to Machin.

Machin threw in his cards from another bad hand. As he lifted a large Scotch to his lips, he saw Vince coming over. Machin nervously shuffled a small amount of chips in his hand then stood up and made his way over to meet Vince.

'I'm doing my bollocks tonight, son, so don't give me any grief or your holier-than-fucking-thou Scotland Yard shit either,' began Machin, pre-empting and cutting off at the pass. 'Look around, son. Unless being a mug punter is a crime, this is a victimless crime scene. And, another thing, it would be up and running somewhere anyway. Just smaller rooms and more of them. This way it's more contained.'

The Brighton copper obviously had his excuses and justifications well rehearsed for such an event as getting caught gambling in an illegal casino. Vince gave him a blank-eyed, couldn't-give-a-fuck look and said, 'Buy you a drink?'

Machin nodded, and Vince sniffed the air. The Brighton copper stank of booze. A good three or four hours' saturation of single malt had made his face and breath fume. They now made their way to the bar.

'You should have said you were working undercover,' said Vince.

'Would you have believed me?'

'Don't be fucking silly. How you do your money is your business. Why you want to put it in Jack's pocket is also your business. But, then again, it probably comes back to you with interest.'

At the bar, Machin ordered. 'Scotch. Large one. Dash of water. No ice. And tomato juice for the lady.'

Vince smiled. Being teetotal, he was used to the gags. Being teetotal in the world he operated in, he might just as well have worn a tutu. Because all coppers drank, the incident rooms on any given Monday morning, in any given city, were a swamp of hung-over coppers, slowed down and slumped over desks while soaking up the weekend's bacchanalia with bacon sarnies and golfing stories. But Machin was poisoned, polluted, pickled with the stuff. Vince wondered how he did it. Then he saw how he did it. A scab of white powder was lodged in the corner of Machin's nose. He'd clearly been balancing out the booze by tuning up in the gents' with a toot of amphetamine. He was now speeding, edgy, tapping his fingers on the bar as though he was playing an invisible miniature piano.

Vince asked him: 'How much d'you make out of this place? What's your graft?'

'Not as much as you greedy cunts in Soho.'

'Not me, *son*.'

Machin smiled smugly. 'No, you're Mr Vinnie-fucking-clean-face.'

Vince kept shtum at that. The London-to-Brighton jungle drums had obviously been beating out his song, as 'clean face' was Tobin's nickname for him.

Machin took a slug of his drink, rubbed his nose, tap-tap-tapped his tune on the bar. The speed had made his nose run, and stalactites of white powder, carried in an aspic of snot, edged down across his sweaty top lip, only to be hoovered back up again. It was like watching some repellent sea creature retracting its antennae.

Vince leaned against the bar, keeping his eyes off Machin and his yo-yoing amphetamine snot stream. But he could still feel the man's hot alcohol-fuelled breath on him.

'You don't think I've got friends in the Met? I've got friends in the Met, son. I hear things. The Peek-A-Boo Club . . .'

Vince tensed up.

'. . . You didn't have a warrant to search the place. Never mind go around kicking doors in . . .'

And then it was on him, again, the searing pain in his head. Vince knew he couldn't neck any more pills – doctor's orders, two a day, max. He looked around the room for a distraction, hoping to hit upon something to move him out of the narrative of nausea he was trapped in. His eye fell on Long George, the smiling pit boss, checking the tables, making sure the games ran smoothly; making sure all the cash kept running uphill to his boss Sammy Bellman; who in turn kept it flowing at a good, orderly pace towards his boss, Jack Regent.

'You know your problem, son? You take it too personally. That's why I didn't tell you about your brother being – what shall we say? – Henry's *stick man*. And a junkie. But you found out for yourself, so I hear. Been causing right commotions, police brutality. I mean, Treadwell, in a public bar of all places? We all have to loosen tongues every now and again, soften them up a little. But you, you're university educated. Your lot are supposed to be our fucking betters!'

Vince's headache torqued. He leaned more heavily on the bar.

'You can't go around upsetting the apple cart,' continued Machin, straightening up and wiping his typhoid gob with the back of his fat hand. 'So do yourself a favour, and relax, take it easy, take a couple of weeks off, then piss off back to London.'

Vince turned sharply around to Machin and spat out the words, 'Shut the fuck up and tell me about Max Vogel.'

Machin did as instructed and shut the fuck up, and looked alarmed. It wasn't being told to shut the fuck up that brought the alarm to Machin's face; it was the name Max Vogel. It unnerved him. It meant something. Drunk, unguarded, his face gave it all away. If he were to return to the tables and play cards wearing that kind of face, he'd lose his house, his pension and his fat wife. Machin mopped his brow with a red napkin plucked from the bar, but he couldn't wipe the big fat gambler's 'Tell' off his face. He knocked back the last of his drink.

'Fuck off, Vinnie,' said Machin with a sudden smile of cama-raderie. 'It's my night off.' He put his drained glass down on the bar and staggered off.

Vince watched him take his seat at the blackjack table. Machin now looked pissed off, a bad loser. Couldn't take his luck, or his drink. Vince didn't follow him to the table, since he'd heard all he needed.

Vince left the Brunswick Sporting Club. He needed the fresh mid-May air that still held a chill. The headache mellowed; no longer a searing pain, it now beat at a manageable thrum. As he made his way downstairs, he thought about the pain intervals, which were getting closer and closer together. But he dismissed the problem – it wouldn't always be like this. This was Brighton, the past. Bad memories. Bad juju. Dr Boehm had told him how the brain protects itself against bad memories, puts up a fight when they try to break through. And then there was Vaughn. Always a source of pain, but it seemed that he'd surpassed himself this visit. Vince knew that he would finally have to cut him out of his life. Back in London it would be different, with fresh cases, fresh faces. There he could again be the cool, detached, objective detective going diligently about his business. Vince smiled at the thought: it had a ring to it.

As he reached the bottom of the stairs, he heard the car horn. He stepped outside and saw Bobbie sitting in the car. Two men stood over her, tapping on the window and telling her to open up. She looked scared. The men were in their early twenties, and they were both wearing houndstooth-check suits. Vince thought he might have recognised them from the Beach Bottle club the night before.

Vince strode towards the car. Bobbie still looked scared, started shaking her head as if to warn him. It was a trap. Emerging from the basements behind him were about ten of them. They were tooled up, carrying coshes, bottles, switchblades and chains. Vince was going for his badge when he felt a blow to the back of his head. He swung around and saw them lined up against him, and he knew he was fucked, badge or no badge. A cosh swung towards his head, and Vince ducked it. Another quickly followed and crashed into his shoulder blade. He rode with the blow, and rode with the pain that came along with it. He knew that if he went down he was double and treble fucked; he was never getting up again.

They moved around him, encircling him, all in their late teens and early twenties. And, like the two by the car, they were dressed in houndstooth-check suits. All cut from the same cloth and sharing the same tailor as Henry Pierce's driver, Spider. Used to hunting in a pack, they moved in unison, their eyes wide and wild. They wore vicious smiles on their expectant faces. They were getting ready to go in for the kill.

Vince needed a tool, something more threatening than just the bluntness of fists. He reached into his jacket and pulled out a . . . *pen*. It was a slim, stainless-steel Sheaffer pen. Vince knew from experience that, wielded in the right hands, the pen could prove as mighty as the sword; and right now Vince's hands were the right hands. He moved it fast, jabbing all around him. In the dark, it did the trick. The houndstooth mob must have thought it was a knife, a stiletto, because they gave it a respect it didn't deserve: stepping back, widening the circle, allowing gaps for Vince to make his escape.

Again, like the night before, Vince heard Bobbie's scream. She pressed down on the car horn. She even tried getting out of the car to help Vince, but the two hounds beside the car wouldn't let her.

There were just too many of them, and he knew he was going to get cut. The baying hounds could smell blood. After assessing the danger of the shiv in Vince's hand, they were moving in again, six, seven, maybe more. Lights had been turned on in the square, so the hounds had to make their move now. The knives were coming in, and Vince felt one slash at his back. He felt a chain wrap around his leg, yanking him off balance. Then, he saw two thick, fleshy hands brace one of the hounds, lift him up by his shoulders off the ground and throw him on to the bonnet of a parked car, where he lay like a broken hood ornament. It was Long George doing the throwing.

The Long Fellow reached into his jacket pocket and pulled out a cosh, then began hammering away on the heads of the hounds like he was playing a drum kit. Vince joined in. He stuck one in the throat with the pen, and the fellow fell away, choking. A chain swung around Vince's head, but he ducked it, and it thrashed across Long George's back.

'ACH! Kacka-de-hoiser!' shouted the Long Fellow, as he grabbed the hound up in his arms and threw him down into a basement.

Vince instantly grabbed another who had a broken bottle in his hand. Two fast jabs to the face, then he twisted his arm around and made him drop the jagged bottle. A knee to the face crunched the hound's nose, another dislodged his teeth, then Vince lifted his head by a hank of hair and dispatched him with a ferocious right hook.

Vince turned just in time to catch sight of a bottle Catherine-wheeling its way towards his head. He ducked it – it smashed against a wall. Vince had turned around to grab the propellant, a goofy-toothed kid with another bottle in his hand, when . . .

BANG! BANG!

Vince, Long George and the remaining hounds still on their feet all froze like a photograph. Then checked themselves for bullet holes. Then all looked around in unison, and saw the heavy-set figure of Sammy Bellman holding a small gun, a Beretta. He'd fired the gun into the air, so the *bang-bang* was actually more like the *crack-crack* of a starting pistol. But no one was about to question the authenticity of the weapon in Sammy Bellman's hand.

'Any more for any more?' he asked with a dark growl.

The hounds looked at each other, wised up quickly and shook their heads.

'Thanks,' said Vince, nodding at Sammy B in his tux. He looked around at Bobbie, in the car, and saw that the two hounds previously standing over it were now running down to the seafront to make their escape.

'Ach! What took you? And where's that piece of shit, Machin? He's a policeman, for the love of God!'

'Too drunk to be of any use,' said Sammy B.

Vince went to cuff one of the hounds.

'Easy, copper,' warned the shtarker bookie, now pointing the gun at Vince. Sammy looked at one of the hounds, a swarthy-looking kid who might have been the leader; probably because he looked like a younger version of Sammy. 'You know who I am?'

'Mr Sammy Bellman,' the swarthy kid intoned respectfully.

'Then you should know, if we ever see you around here again, you'll get worse – a lot worse. You understand?'

Leaving nothing to chance, to a man the hounds made like nodding dogs and muttered servile yes-es.

'Now, get out of here!' barked Sammy, the top dog. They started to leave, but Vince grabbed the husky kid by the shoulder and said, 'Sorry, Sammy, they're not going anywhere.'

'Then catch 'em yourself,' said Sammy B. 'Because I'm not doing it for you.' Vince looked at the gun; it wasn't raised in his direction, but it was held firmly enough in Sammy B's hand to mean business. Vince gave an understanding nod to the Beretta-toting bookmaker, let go of the husky one, and gestured for the hounds to take off. And they did: hightailing it down to the seafront to lick their wounds.

Sammy B pocketed the gun. 'We were just doing you a favour, and I'm not in the habit of doing the law any favours. Long George here says you were all right, so that was all right by me. But don't push it, policeman. We've just saved your bacon, so some gratitude wouldn't go amiss.'

Just then, Bobbie joined them and stood by Vincent's arm.

At the sight of this, Long George and Sammy B exchanged troubled looks.

CHAPTER 13

LA DOLCE VITA

Vince fixed Bobbie a large brandy. She was curled up on the sofa. The surreal Salvador Dali sofa that was shaped like Mae West's lips, which really didn't seem that surreal now. Vince handed her the tumbler of brandy.

She sat up and took it. 'Thank you,' she said, in a voice that still held a tremble.

Vince sat down on the sofa, too. The room seemed smaller now, not so grand. They sat in silence for a minute, till Vince broke it with, 'Have you seen that mob before?'

Bobbie shrugged a shrug that, even for a shrug, was pretty indolent and evasive. He excused her. She'd popped a Valium.

'Well, *I* have,' said Vince vigorously, trying to up the energy levels in the room and give the situation the sense of emergency it deserved. 'I spotted a couple of them at the Beach Bottle Club you took me to last night. They look like they might knock around with Spider . . . Henry Pierce's driver.'

'I know who he is,' she said. Her voice was slowed-down and smeared due to the sedative she'd taken.

'So what does that tell you, Bobbie?' Vince stared at her, but he didn't need an answer. He saw that she knew that the rules had changed. Without Jack around, she was in danger.

She sat up straight, took a deep breath to alert herself, then stood and said, in a clear firm voice, 'I'll be right back.' She walked out the room and disappeared into the hallway.

Vince fixed himself a soda water with a dash of lime. Settling back on the sofa, he felt a twinge of pain in his shoulder where the cosh had made contact – and he was still carrying the lump on the back of his head from the previous night. He shook his head and forced out an ironic little laugh. He was sent down to assist with inquiries, but his primary purpose here had been to take in the sea air and relax!

Bobbie returned, holding a blue leather-bound photo album. She sat next to Vince, with the album resting on her lap. The volume was worn, tatty and well-thumbed, its ribbed spine coming away from the covers. She opened it up and starting turning the pages. Photos of the large house in the New Forest. Photos of the family in the garden, with fields and trees stretching beyond the mossy-green wooden fences. The mother, with a refined, kind face, serving the two young children lunch on a long wooden table. The father, in rolled-up shirtsleeves digging about in the garden, two black Labradors foraging in the background. The young girl playing on the swing with her young brother. The living room, spacious, book-lined, country-style furniture. Father at his partners' desk in the large study, obviously going through his paperwork. Mother in her favourite armchair, reading . . .

And so they went on, snapshots of happy lives in a happy place. Bobbie turned over the card pages without saying a word, leaving Vince to fill in the story. Like she had, previously.

Eventually, Vince pointed at one photo. 'Your mother and father? They're a good-looking couple. What are their names?'

Bobbie ignored that, or at least seemed not to hear him, and carried on looking at the photos in silence.

Vince tried again and pointed at a picture of the little boy standing next to the little girl, in their Sunday best, heading off to church. 'Is that you and your brother?'

Again, no answer.

Vince stopped looking at the photos and turned his attention instead to Bobbie. Her face was rapt, almost trance-like, in studying the subject before her. She slowly turned the pages, as if seeing what was on them for the first time. These photos were taking her somewhere almost mystical that seemed beyond memory good or bad.

'It's customary, when being shown family snaps, to be put in the picture a bit,' he said, trying to make light of it. No response, still. 'Bobbie, aren't you going to tell me who they are?'

Without changing her facial expression, she said, 'I don't know who they are.'

She closed the album. The world inside it was gone. And she took a deep breath. Then told him who she was . . .

. . . She was an orphan raised in institutions until the age of seven when she was first fostered out. Even at that tender age, her sullenness and an innate sense of tragedy conspired against her. She didn't smile, kept her head in books, and wouldn't play cutesy with the hopeful parents looking to adopt. There were three sets of foster parents in all, but only one she really remembered. And not because of any paternal love. She was eleven when the man, her new 'father', first came into her room to comfort her after a night fright.

Bobbie had experienced the same nightmare as far back as she could remember: death climbing the stairs. The footsteps slowly making their way up the steps leading to her room. She sees it, hears it and feels it now, those heavy footfalls stopping outside the door, and the doorknob turning. But she always wakes up before he enters.

She'd read up on dreams, including the old chestnut about falling from a great height, and if you hit the ground you never wake up. For Bobbie it was something similar: if the door opened and *it* came into the room, she knew she would never wake up.

That night the dream played out as usual, the footsteps on the stairs, slowly making their way up; the turning of the doorknob and herself waking up screaming, drenched in sweat. She must have screamed aloud this time because the doorknob turned and her father came through the door. He sat on the bed, kind, gentle, comforting. Then he stripped himself naked and slipped into bed with her. Roberta, as she was then called, never suffered the nightmare again. The new one had begun. The door had opened and *it* had walked through. And this time she was awake. And this time she was dead. Once, sometimes twice a week, the father made his visits to her room. Did the mother know? Probably, but it was never spoken of. From eleven to fourteen the father would come to her. He told her to close her eyes, but she didn't need telling. They were squeezed shut in the hope that nothing could penetrate her corpse-like body.

Then he was struck down by a stroke: a stroke of good fortune for her. At fifteen Roberta ran away. But not until *she* had crept into *his* room. He was lying there one morning, after sucking down his breakfast through a straw, silent and supine, his eyes like one of those creepy paintings that followed you around the room. He could see what was coming: she made sure he saw what was coming, as she slowly pulled back the sheets and stuck a pair of scissors into his scrotum.

She then ran away to London, and into the arms of the first boy who showed her any interest. A young man from Clapham South. A wannabe villain, a gonnabe drunk and, if they married, a probable wife beater.

They married in a registry office. Paste sandwiches at the pub for a reception. The honeymoon at a Butlin's holiday camp in Skegness. Roberta didn't know where Skegness was when the boy first proposed it. It didn't sound very exotic, but it did sound very far away. In Scotland, perhaps? Far away from the dingy two rooms they'd moved into in Battersea. But Skegness really wasn't that far away; and really nowhere near far enough away from the dingy rooms in Battersea.

It rained – and the gags poured down about that being a bonus, because you never want to leave your room on your honeymoon. But Roberta wanted to leave that room. The boy drank all day at the bar with some fellow soaks, and didn't make love to her at night. She was so alone.

Back at the dingy two rooms in Battersea, the blows came down hard and heavy, as the boy sank into his cups. Drenching his fears and inadequacy with booze, he'd never done right by Roberta, either in the bedroom or in the bank account. He just wasn't up to it, and Roberta even thought he might be a queer. This boy just wasn't set up for life, and certainly not for his chosen profession as a thief. He was one of life's patsies and maybe a pansy, yet he really wanted to be a thief, a villain. It was his ambition, but never his calling. One night in the pub, a mate gave him a shooter to look after. Instead of hiding it away, he walked around the flat with it tucked in his waistband, admiring himself in the mirror with it. He thought he looked the business, thought it put a couple of inches on him. It scared her, so she made him hide it until his mate returned for it, though he never did. He had another gun and picked up a seven for shooting someone with it.

On a warehouse job, he took his usual position as the look-out. Not smart enough for breaking and entering or strong enough for the lifting. Just the looking. He didn't spot the two plain-clothes coppers coming out of the pub across the street. But they clocked him all right: furtive, nervous and looking for all the world like a look-out. He got pinched.

That was Roberta's cue to leave. During visiting time in the Scrubs, he advised her to start a new life. She needed no prompting; her bags were already packed and sitting in the car outside. The car belonged to a dashing young racing driver she'd met in a nightclub. He turned out to be a getaway driver, and got nicked while speeding away from a pay-roll job in Leatherhead. He got a six-year stretch. She wasn't going to wait for him either.

She then answered an ad in the London *Evening News* for 'models required' and ended up with a job at the Raymond

Revue Bar. Standing there stock-still and starkers, save for some 'arty' head gear. If a draught blew in and her nipples stood to attention, she had to leave the stage. But she met some interesting people and soon found a flat share in Earls Court with two other girls working at the Revue Bar. They were actresses training at the Webber Douglas Academy of Drama. They saw the gig as life experience (purely *still* life was the joke) and a quick way to make money and get an equity card. They liked young Roberta and took her under their wing, and suggested she change her name to Bobbie as a stage name, because all the world's a stage. And, with her looks, maybe she should try her hand at acting and apply to drama school.

For the two and a half years of the flat share in Earls Court, Bobbie was the perfectly pliant Pygmalion student. She absorbed the two middle-class girls, soaked up their mannerisms, their RP accents, their affectations – of which they were legion, and all of them aspirational. They had a serious game plan: it was Hollywood or bust for these two stargazers. Each determined to be a tour de force! Not force to tour, treading the boards in half-empty reps around the country, with the indignity of shared changing rooms and damp digs. If Hollywood didn't beckon in three years, they were determined to marry, and marry well. Bobbie read what they read, Shakespeare; Shaw; Chekhov; the Greeks – Aeschylus, Sophocles, Euripides; Ibsen; Tennessee Williams; *Tatler*, *Vogue*, *Harper's Bazaar*, *Debretts*. They took her to the theatre, and to the art-house cinema they were all watching at the time. The French New Wave: Charbol's *Le Beau Serge*; Truffaut's *400 Blows*; Goddard's *A bout de soufflé*. The Italian Neo-realism: Rossellini's *Rome, Open City*; De Sica's *Bicycle Thieves*. But it was Fellini's *La Dolce Vita*, that was her epiphany. Anita Ekberg, shoeless, strapless, godless, dancing in the Trevi Fountain. In that moment, that image on the silver screen, all her dreams crystallized. Bobbie saw the sweet life she knew she had always wanted . . .

* * *

'And the photo album?' asked Vince.

'I found it in a jumble sale, in an old box of stuff. I had no photos of my own, so . . . I was twelve at the time, just after the bastard started . . . 'tucking me in' as he called it. I used to hide it under my bed, then look at it after he left. Then I found myself looking at it all the time. I pretended they were my family. I told myself that my foster parents were just looking after me for a few days, and soon my real parents in the photo album would come and pick me up and take me back home, and the nightmare would be over. That's how I got through it. I knew every inch of that garden, what the house looked like, what my room looked like. I imagined stables, the names of the dogs; my father's job, GP; my mother, a teacher; my brother . . .'

Vince broke her reverie by taking the album and putting it on the coffee table. 'Maybe it's time to put it away now?'

'It's the only thing that kept me going. The only thing that stopped me from killing myself.'

'But it's the past. And it's not real.'

She turned sharply towards him, with a defiant edge. 'It was real to me.'

Vince didn't argue, and he didn't have any answers for her either. It meant reaching into a realm he knew little about. He could help her by getting practical, though. He got up and went over to a large ebonized ormolu bureau, which looked as if it weighed a ton. It didn't, in fact, but it was heavy enough. He dragged it over to the front door.

'What are you doing?'

'The days of not having a lock on your door are over,' he said, sliding it against the door. 'You said that Pierce was always polite and courteous to you, right?'

She nodded.

'Well, he's not that way now, which tells me Jack's gone and he's not coming back. And whatever privileges you enjoyed, they're over. And this place' – his hand led her eye around the room, which was stuffed with art and antiques – 'is up for grabs. And you've got to leave town.'

'Where will I go?'

'Come on, Bobbie, we've been through this – you're not little Miss New Forest. You're the babe that's been out the woods for a long time.'

Bobbie managed a small laugh. She stood up and walked over to him.

'It's the first time you've called me by my first name.'

'Well, it's the first time you've been straight with me.'

'The first time I've been straight with anyone in a long time.'

'Not even Jack?'

'He doesn't know what I've just told you. No one does.'

'Why me?'

They were only inches apart. Vince's hands reached out to her. She took them and their fingers laced together. He could smell the sweet brandy scent of her breath, filtered through her lipstick. He'd always loved the smell of lipstick.

'I thought you were going to kiss me after I slapped you in your hotel.'

'Is that why you slapped me?'

She nodded. 'Corny, uh?'

'You've been watching too many movies.'

'I've been wanting to kiss you since—'

He cut her dead with a kiss.

They lay in each other's arms, under silk sheets, and under the silk canopy of an Emperor-sized four-poster bed. It was a French antique that could have been lifted from the Palace of Versailles and, knowing Jack's dealings with the shadier side of the antiques business, it may well have been. The ambience of the room was redolent with Jack's touch, his sense of grandeur, bombast and Napoleonic ego.

Vince, wide awake, studied Bobbie with her eyes closed, the hint of a contented smile on her face; the tears and fears seemingly vanished. She was as strong a contender for the definition of 'beautiful' as he had come across. But not all his. In this room he couldn't forget the previous occupant of the bed, under the silk canopy and sheets. The king usurped? He wasn't sure, not yet.

Her eyes opened, aware of his gaze. 'Penny for your thoughts?' she asked in a sleepy, sing-song voice.

'What brought you down to Brighton?'

'It's where my mother was from, I think.' Her hand moved across his chest, tracing his musculature.

'She lived down here?'

'I think so. But I'm a foundling.'

Vince lifted himself up to get a better look at the foundling, the first one he'd ever met outside the pages of *Tom Jones*. With elbow on pillow, head propped in hand, with his free one he traced her profile. She gave him a playful nip when his forefinger reached her lips.

'Ouch. Where were you found?'

'On the steps of a church.'

'In a basket?'

She kissed his finger better, held his hand to her breast and said, 'No. I was wrapped in my mother's dress – or what I assumed was my mother's dress.'

'The turquoise one?'

Bobbie yawned, and repeated lazily, 'The turquoise one.'

The full meaning of Bobbie's sentimental attachment to the slightly worn and faded dress, with a tear hidden by a brooch, was clear to Vince now. 'What church?' he asked.

'I don't know. I was moved about a lot and the records got lost.'

'Then how do you know your mother was from Brighton?'

'I don't, not really. I was like you, a detective. I was given the dress to keep, and it has a label in it, "Penelope of Brighton". So I came down to Brighton to find her. I put in some ads in the personals of the *Evening Argus*. No luck. But I did find out there'd

been a dressmaker with a shop called Penelope of Brighton. But she'd died years ago, and the shop died with her. Then it was all dead ends.'

'So you gave up?'

Bobbie sensed the slight reproving tone in his voice. 'Aren't *you* giving up?'

'But I'm not looking for my mother.'

'She did a pretty good job of losing me. I don't want to hunt her down. It's not my job. I think about her, and when I do she looks just like me. I think she must have had the same luck as me, as a kid. It couldn't have been easy for her. She wasn't being callous. She was young, made a mistake, and did what she thought was right. She wanted the best for me, wanted me to live in a nice house in—'

'A village in the New Forest, with two black Labradors?'

'You're mocking me, Vincent.'

'No, I'm not. But you've been dealt your cards, so nothing you can do about it. You just have to get on with it. All this hiding in fantasy, behind movie-star names . . . doesn't seem right.'

'So what's *your* story?

'Nothing like yours, but it wasn't happy families either. My old man left us when we were still crawling, and my mother worked herself to an early grave raising us.'

'You and your brother, not exactly peas in the pod?'

'Not exactly. But, like I said, that was the card that was dealt and I got on with it. Why did you stay in Brighton?'

'You're changing the subject. You don't like talking about your family?'

'There's only Vaughn left, so no, I don't. And now you've changed the subject. And I find the subject, meaning you, end-lessly fascinating.'

'I'm tired.'

'Me too. But I'm going to keep asking it until you answer me.'

'You're being a policeman.'

'A compromised one.'

She smiled. 'Does your authority extend to my bed, Detective Treadwell?'

He pulled the silk sheets over both their heads and said, 'Only if I'm working undercover.'

She laughed and then pulled the sheets back down. 'That's corny.'

'Then tell me, why did you stay in Brighton?'

'The sea.'

'Not Jack?'

She shook her head, then in a sing-song voice she intoned: '*The sea, the sea, the sea . . .*' until her words faded and her eyes closed. The Valium she had taken earlier must have kicked in, because they stayed closed. He lay on his back, and he could hear her breathing, the steady peaceful rhythm of slumber. The pain in his shoulder was still there, but he knew he'd soon lose it in languid sleep. He closed his eyes.

. . . The door would be open. Never locked. Never an intruder. Who would dare? The feet adjusting on the black and white marble floor, the acoustics in the hallway unforgiving. Every piece of grit and spec of dust under leather registered. A pin drop was like a tree falling, he thought. You could do a dance . . . that reminded him of an act he once saw, two tap-dancing spades throwing down sand on the stage, the noise they made, a right fucking racket . . . the sandman . . . he was the sandman. Past the broken lift. Padding his way to the staircase. The hand on the ornate gilt banister, steadying himself, cherubs and satyrs smiling at you from every fucking cornice. Regulating his breathing so as not to be heard. But the noises in his head were so loud, terrible acoustics . . . Undeterred, he climbed until he reached the top floor. The hand on the doorknob, turning slowly, knowing it wasn't locked, knowing it was never locked, who would dare? Who would fuckin' dare?

★　★　★

160

She screamed. Sat bolt upright and tried to open her heavy eyes struggling against the cobwebs of sleep that had glued her lids shut, trapping her, wanting to keep her locked in the darkness of the nightmare. She suddenly felt hands on her. Her eyes opened to find Vince holding her.

'What's wrong?' he asked.

Breathless, panting: 'The door . . . the man at the door!'

He gathered her up. She fought against him, with gulping sobs, but eventually yielding and resting in his arms until the sobs subsided.

'There's no one there,' said Vince. 'It's just a bad dream.'

'I felt . . . I felt him in the room.'

'Who was in the room?' She didn't answer. 'Your father?' Again no answer. 'Jack?'

It's not that she didn't know, because it was always the same man. It's just that she felt foolish. She'd given up on her act, and now she felt the rest of her was slipping away, too. The parts of her she didn't want anyone to see. Reporting your fears and your weaknesses is one thing, but to have people witness first-hand what you've reported is another matter entirely. She wasn't ready, not yet, not with *him*. She felt too vulnerable, like a child in his arms. And being a child in a man's arms was never a happy place for her to be. She untangled herself from him and, with a determined voice, said, 'He was in the room.'

Vince threw back the sheets and went to investigate the bad dream. He grabbed a towel from a chair and wrapped it around his waist, went through the flat's main hallway and into the living room. And there it was. The heavy, ebonized ormolu bureau was away from the door, almost ostentatiously so, sitting in the centre of the room. The front door itself was wide open.

Vince ran down the stairs, hand on the banister to steady himself. Within seconds he was down all four flights of stairs and in the entrance hall, the marble floor cold under his feet. The street door was wide open. He ran out into the middle of the road, looking for signs of life. Looking and listening for a heavy foot on the pavement, or the fading lights of a speeding car disappearing out of view. He saw nothing, heard nothing: it was strangely quiet, like a history of silence had mounted up. As if nothing had trodden the street or driven along the road in years. He felt as if he had stepped out into reality, still holding the fantasy of Bobbie's nightmare, and under the radiance of the street lamps realized that it didn't exist. But the reality before him couldn't explain the heavy bureau sitting in the middle of the room.

He looked over at the crocus-lined lawn that occupied the centre of the crescent, where a woman was taking her dog out for an emergency visit. The dog was a small grey terrier, she was a large middle-aged brunette. She looked over at him, quickly grabbed up the dog and ran back into her house. Vince looked down and saw the towel had slipped from his waist while running down the stairs. He was naked.

CHAPTER 14

UNIONE CORSE

Vince arrived at Edward Street police station at 8.30 a.m. Outside, well-groomed, clipped-voiced reporters were holding microphones, talking to the cameras. They had an energy and sense of emergency about them that told him this wasn't about the Kemp Town junkies. This was today's news.

He walked through to the incident room. All eyes were on him, he thought. He interpreted the looks he was getting from the coppers, right down to the tea lady making her morning rounds, as knowledge of his guilt. He *had* compromised the case by his behaviour with Bobbie.

'Morning, guv,' said Ginge sitting at his desk, his face darting up from the paperwork in front of him. 'You got two calls.' He picked up his pad. 'Some fella called Terence, said you'd know him. And Ray Dryden rang twenty minutes ago, said it was urgent. And the guv's been trying to contact you. We've got two more bodies.'

'Heroin?' Ginge gave a solemn nod. Vince appreciated the copper-topped copper's customary springy self; it helped wipe away his paranoia. He looked around the office with fresh eyes, found no one was looking at him. They were engrossed in their work: making calls, pulling files, clipping mugshots on to cork boards. Vince knocked on Machin's door. He heard a cough, a clearing of the throat, and what sounded like gob descending into a waste-paper basket, that was followed by a gruff, 'Come in.'

Vince opened the door and entered. Machin sat at his desk, a pile of paperwork in front him, knocking back a live Pepto-Bismol that was still fizzing away in a tall glass. Rough as guts and thoroughly poisoned, Machin looked at Vince through hooded, bloodshot eyes. They greeted each other with sheepish nods, both carrying a burden of guilt they couldn't shake off from the previous night. Like the cold war, with its mutually assured destruction, it had a harmonious effect. Neither of them tried to scramble on to the moral high ground; they just cracked on with the business at hand.

'You heard?'

'Two more dead on heroin,' confirmed Vince, closing the door behind him.

'Terminus Road, by the station. Males about the same age. Same deal. Same gear.'

Vince thought the name of the road was apt, as he slumped into the chair opposite Machin.

Machin leaned back in his own chair. 'I tried calling you at the hotel. Where were you?'

Vince rubbed his brow with his thumb and forefinger, as if he was soothing a hangover. His hand meanwhile formed a visor on his forehead, shading his expression from Machin's prying gaze. 'I was out,' he replied in a tired voice.

'I heard you got jumped last night,' said Machin. 'Long George said it was just some kids, that right?' Vince gave a jaded nod. Machin shook his head in disgust. 'The little bastards, they've been causing havoc all this bank holiday. Mods, Rockers, fucking hooligans the lot of them. We're calling in more coppers from the surrounding counties for the rest of the weekend. That said, it's been kicking off all over the place: Clacton, Southend, Hastings.'

Machin picked up a biro from his desk as if to start work, and stared at the blank sheets of paper that needed filling. He bit the

tip of the biro, then threw it down. 'Listen, son, about last night
. . . about your brother, I was out of order. I get a few drinks inside
me and start flapping my lip.'

'Forget it, I'd have found out anyway, one way or another,' said
Vince.

'Maybe I should have told you about him earlier . . .'

'No one likes to be the bearer of bad news, and when it comes
to Vaughn that's all there is.' Keen to change the subject Vince
pointed to the window and said, 'You've got quite a press pack
outside. They baying for blood yet?'

Machin reached under his pile of papers and pulled out an
edition of the *Evening Argus*, which he handed to Vince. The paper
was open at page four. The rioting Mods and Rockers, with their
generational moral panic, had managed to kick it off the front
page. The headline read: *'Police Helpless in the Face of the Deadly
Plague Sweeping Brighton!'*

Vince picked up the paper. 'Mind if I take this?'

Machin, without looking up, replied, 'Be my guest.'

Vince stood up, walked over to open the door, and then timed
to perfection his throwaway afterthought – and the real reason he
was there. 'Oh, yeah, another thing. I mentioned him last night,
but what have you got on Max Vogel?'

Machin took a cigarette out of the packet lying on the desk,
picked up a box of matches and fished about for a live one
amongst the dead littering the box. His hands shook, but Vince
gave him the benefit of the doubt and put it down to the booze.
Machin found a live match and lit up his cigarette. He sucked
down the smoke, studied the tip of the cigarette, then blew the
smoke on to it so that it glowed. 'Vogel? Antique dealer. Got a
shop in the Lanes. Why you so interested in him?'

Vince gave a slack shrug, carrying on the game of nonchalance
they were both engaged in. 'Nothing much but, like I said, I saw
him with Pierce at the races.'

'Lots of people go to the races, son. Who else did you see?'

'All the usual faces. Tell me, is Murray the Head still the best fourth-floor man in the business?'

'Was he at the races?'

Vince nodded. 'Had a nice suntan on him.'

'You know Murray, he likes to holiday on the Riviera, Monte Carlo, anywhere there's rich women with big tom staying in big hotels with slack security. Word is he's just come back from a job, south of France. That movie star Zsa Zsa Gabor had her jewellery pinched. Made all the papers.'

'Yeah, I read about it. That was the Head?'

Machin smiled and shrugged. 'That's the rumour.'

'He couldn't have just been after her autograph?'

Machin laughed, a little too hearty for a man with his hangover, and also a little too hearty for Vince's liking. Vince wasn't going to let him off the hook. 'The Head fence any of his stuff with Vogel, down here?'

'I doubt it,' said Machin, no longer laughing. 'The Head doesn't pull jobs here in the town – not rich enough pickings for him. But, more importantly, his old mum still lives here. And, to her, Murray's still a good Jewish boy at heart.'

'Vogel interests me, talking to Pierce like that.'

'It's a small town, son. People run into each other and they talk. No law against that.'

'They didn't run into each other, because Pierce sought him out. But they did talk, for about twenty minutes. Vogel looked like he had a lot to say, and Pierce did a lot of listening.'

Machin looked up at him and announced solidly, 'If a country house gets turned over, Brighton's the first place they look. And we do a regular sweep of all the dealers in the town. Nothing on Vogel, but I'll run a check for you.'

'Thanks. But you're right, it's probably nothing,' said Vince placatingly and continued through the door.

Machin stubbed out his cigarette, picked up his pen, and put his head down for some work. Vince thought of Machin in the Brunswick Sporting Club – toiling away at the tables, regularly losing, feeding Sammy Bellman's gambling house and fattening Jack's coffers – meant nothing; he probably had an account at one of Jack's whorehouses for when his amphetamine jags led him astray from the fat wife. But Vogel meant something to him. And it was proof, if proof were needed, that Machin was dirty. He was protecting Max Vogel, therefore Jack's bank.

Vince smiled and closed the door behind him.

Vince picked up the phone and dialled the number. He was seated at his desk in the basement, staring at a window that was painted over in green. Behind it he could hear the constant trickle of water. The view behind the green paint had to be a brick wall with blocked guttering and waste water cascading down it. The view summed up this case, he thought.

'Ray Dryden,' responded the energetic voice down the line.

'What do you say, Ray?'

'Vincenzo! Hold on a second.' The rustle of papers. 'Sitting comfortably?'

'How could I not? This office they've assigned me is the lap of luxury.'

'Remember what I told you about the Unione Corse?'

'Yeah, the French mob. Heroin distribution.'

'OK, now, I ran a check on your boy, Jacques Rinieri. In 1961, New York City, one Antoine Rinieri, Corsican, worked out of Marseilles. Very close with Paul Carbone, the boss of the Marseilles faction of the Unione Corse. French Interpol had been trailing Antoine Rinieri for a couple of months, because he'd been doing a lot of travelling of late. Especially out in Bangkok, Laos and Vietnam, where there are big French colonies. Anyway, they'd linked up with the FBI, because he'd made a couple of trips to the US. The FBI found him in a place called Pleasant Avenue, in East Harlem – or Italian Harlem as it's known in New York City. He was picked up with two hundred and sixty thousand dollars on him. When the Yanks collared him, they realized the money was from a drugs deal. Pleasant Avenue is the district where the Mob distributes heroin. They interrogated Rinieri, but got nothing, not a word. The Corsicans are tough, don't open their mouths, don't cut deals. They won't admit to anything, especially being part of the Unione Corse.'

'What happened to him?'

'They banged him up for six months, then they deported him back to France. The thing that really got up the Yanks' noses, is that in the end they couldn't actually connect the two hundred and sixty grand with a drug deal, so Uncle Sam had to pay the frog back his money – with the six months' interest on top!'

'You think Jack and Antoine, they're related?

'The Unione Corse are clannish, they work only with their close family.'

'Like the Mafia?'

'Very similar MO,' said Ray Dryden, 'but even more tightly knit. We're talking about brothers, cousins, blood relations. I checked: Antoine Rinieri had four brothers. One served with distinction in the French Resistance and became a schoolteacher, one got killed in a motorcycle accident just after the war. Two other brothers we have no names for: seemed to have disappeared off the dial. When did your boy come to England?'

'In the twenties, when he could only have been about fifteen, sixteen.' Vince could almost hear Ray's brain ticking over.

'Maybe he had to leave Corsica,' said Ray after considered thought. 'For centuries that island has been invaded, raped and pillaged. There're two things Corsicans know, and one is how to hold a grudge.'

'What's the other?'

'Revenge. It's in their blood. They've got Moorish blood running through them, which means they're a warrior race. He could have got in a feud with someone, and England was as good a place as any to come to. From what I've read up on Jack Regent, he's a resourceful fellow, could do what he does anywhere: Corsica,

Marseilles, New York, London, Brighton. Like I say, Vince, it's in his blood. You can't escape your blood.'

Vince wrapped up the conversation, agreeing they'd be in touch as soon as one of them found out more. Vince thought again about the young Jack, and the bloody feud that might have brought him to these shores, and the two of them together. From the parched hills of Corsica to the damp hills of Albion. He could imagine the insult, something about his club foot; and Jack responding how he always would – with violence. *You can't escape your blood.*

The phone rang. It was Ginge to tell him that Henry Pierce had turned up for his interview.

CHAPTER 15

BIG CHIEF MASHIGINA

Vince headed through to the interview room. He'd pulled Henry Pierce's form sheet on the way and was giving it a read. The weighty tome was ring-bound and bulging with a cornucopia of crime and violence that he had mostly got away with.

Machin was waiting for Vince outside the interview room. He was pacing up and down, his yellow-stained fingers holding the hot, wet butt of a cigarette that was smoked down to the ink. He looked nervous.

'Is he in there?' asked Vince.

Machin stubbed out his cigarette into the sandpit of the knee-high cylindrical ashtray. 'Ready and waiting. No brief with him. How do you want to play it, son?'

Vince replied firmly, 'Just do me a favour. Don't call me "son" in front of him.'

Machin gave a brief nod and they entered.

Pierce was sitting at the table. His hands rested in front of him on the top of the gnarled white stick. The small room made his huge bulk just look bigger. In his customary black garb, all slightly faded and cruddy up close, he looked as if he belonged on a plinth in the middle of some roundabout in central London.

Sitting on the desk in its pearl-grey leatherette case was a Grundig TK20 reel-to-reel tape recorder.

Machin spoke first. 'Mr Pierce, I'm with Detective Vin—'

'I know who you're with.' Pierce sniffed the air. 'Piss and vinegar.'

Vince and Machin exchanged glances, then sat down.

Vince: 'Seeing as you've not brought a solicitor with you, Mr Pierce, we've decided it might be best to tape this interview.'

Pierce considered this, running the tip of his tongue around his liver-coloured lips, eventually uttering 'That's a new one on me, copper, and I'm no stranger to this particular establishment. But if *you* think it's for the best . . .'

'Considering you're blind, and can't make out or sign a written statement, it's a precaution I thought we should take.'

'Well then, Detective Treadwell, I best make sure I'm in fine voice for my recording debut.' Pierce cleared his throat theatrically and then started to sing 'Mister Sandman'.

Vince knew the song. It was loud and clear, piercingly so. And he knew that the Sandman was capable of bringing nightmares – like last night – as well as dreams.

Pierce: 'You recognize the tune, do you?'

Vince reached over to the Grundig TK20 and pressed *record*.

Pierce reached over, found the *off* switch, and pressed it.

Machin smirked.

Vince looked slightly confused. Then pressed *record*.

Pierce pressed *off*.

Audible sniggers from Machin.

Vince moved to press *record* again, then froze with his finger hovering over the red button.

Pierce pursed his lips, then relaxed.

Vince rested his hand on the table, satisfied with what he'd seen.

Pierce: 'I want to talk to you, Detective Treadwell, on your own.'

Machin stopped smirking, looked concerned. Then he piped up, 'I'm afraid there has to be a another officer present at—'

Pierce cut in: 'Then arrest me and charge me with something. Otherwise I'm going to get up and walk out of here, unless I get my needs met.'

Vince considered Pierce. A record of violence, intimidation and madness. But capable of putting together a sane sentence. And a real cunning lurking beneath. Vince turned to Machin, who was looking intently at Pierce, and said, 'I think we can accommodate Mr Pierce.'

Machin didn't like this. This was his police station, his rules, and he wasn't moving or accommodating anyone.

Pierce turned his head and *looked* at Machin.

Machin laughed, making a joke of it. 'It's like you can see right through me, Henry.' He mock-shivered as if he was spooked. No one laughed, and he stopped chuckling. But he couldn't stop being spooked. 'I'll be outside if you need me,' he said to Vince, as he left the room.

Pierce smiled. 'Ah, we can all breathe easy now that cunt's gone.'

Vince wanted to agree, but didn't. 'Sorry about your boy, Spider. That was rash of me.' Not a nod, a shrug, or even an involuntary twitch. The apology didn't register with Pierce, because the violent incident meant nothing to a man who dealt in violent incidents.

'So tell me, Detective, what's on your mind?'

'First of all, I want to know the whereabouts of Jack Regent, and how a body turned up on the beach.'

Pierce tapped his stick on the floor and beat out, 'No no no no no no!' He stopped tapping the stick then said, 'Your mind. The contents of *your mind*. Not what you want to know. If you don't already know it, it's not on your mind.'

Vince knew this was too good to be true: Pierce was back with Big Chief Mashigina. Vince knew he wasn't interested in what was on his mind. Pierce was a performer, a stage-hogging psychopath. Sounding off and giving coppers the run-around had been elevated to an art form in his hands. So let him perform, let him talk, thought Vince. Loosen him up and he might let something slip without knowing it.

'OK, Henry, I'm curious. Why's Jack the boss, and not you?'

Pierce didn't answer, he treated the question as though it was a trap. Which it was.

Vince then continued. 'You're tough, resourceful and people are scared of you. You've got all the qualities to be the boss.'

Pierce smiled again. There was a slight wobble of the head, some clearing of the throat.

'Jack had seen me wrestle. He knew me by reputation before we actually met. And, of course, I knew Jack, knew him by reputation, too. And I knew that he'd moved down here with old man Sabini. After me seven in Broadmoor, Jack offered me some work. I didn't say yes, didn't say no. Kept me options open. Before the war you see, Brighton was wide open. There was a few faces floating about – one horrible piece of work in particular. Scottish he was, had bright red hair, stuck out like a sore thumb. Forget his name. Fancied himself, though . . .' Pierce cocked his head to one side, reliving the story.

Vince thought about turning on the tape-recorder, but knew the Red Indian would sniff him out.

'We was playing cards in a club, one of Sammy Bellman's places. The Scotsman's there, talking himself up. He'd been winning all night. We all thought he was lucky. He *was* lucky, until Jack walked in and sat opposite him. He was about eye-level with Jack, and I think that was his first mistake. Jack don't like anyone looking at him. They played a bit, with everyone hoping the Scotsman's luck would hold. It didn't. He kept on winning, taking Jack's money, but I knew what was gonna happen – on the cards, as they say. No one gave a fuck about the Scotsman now; he was finished. The Dying Scotsman coming in right on time. When it happened it was quick. You can usually tell when someone is gonna do someone. They give off warning signals, can be anything: nostrils flaring, lips twitching, ears burning, anything. Not Jack. No grace notes from him. He just did it, like turning off a light. I don't know who actually did turn off the light, but when it got turned back on again, the gaff was empty. Just the Scotsman lying over the table, in a pool of his own blood. Throat cut. And that's the night I decided to throw my lot in with Jack. I knew my place. You see, Jack just had that something extra, that certain quality. A quality that he either had in abundance, or a quality he didn't have at all. He either was, or he wasn't.'

Confusion warped Vince's brow. He waited for an explanation. None came. So he prompted, 'Jack was . . . ?'

Pierce's brow wrinkled in equal confusion. He was confused that the young detective had needed to ask. Because to him it was obvious; it needed no further explanation. Pierce leaned in and said, '. . . Or wasn't.'

'Was or wasn't what?'

'God. Or godless.'

Vince took a deep breath and considered this. It seemed that Pierce, like Pascal and his wager, was covering his bets by throwing his lot in with Jack. Vince moved on to a more secular plain. 'Tell me about Max Vogel.'

'Fat antique dealer.'

'What were you doing with him yesterday at the races?'

Unflinching monotone: 'I've moved into a retirement home. Small room, so I'm selling the contents of my previous abode. Moving in the circles I've moved in over the years, I've picked up some interesting trinkets. And now I'm retired and stretching into the autumn of my life, I could sorely use the money.'

Vince considered Pierce's overly considered and out-of-sorts sensible reply. 'You asked me what I was thinking, Henry . . .'

'I'd dearly like to know. Now we're alone' – he pulled a grey-toothed grin – 'together at last.'

'I think you set Jack up. I think Max Vogel is Jack's financier. And I think you've got something going with Max Vogel.'

Pierce, without flinching, replied, 'Sacrilege. I know my place. I'm strictly number two.' Shaking his head in disappointment. 'Weren't you listening, boy? Didn't my little story about the Scotsman tell you anything?'

'That's the whole problem. It told me what you wanted it to tell me. And let's not forget what happened in the wrestling ring.

You were number two then, and you were supposed to lose against Leo the Lion. Then you scalped him instead. Maybe you got sick of playing second fiddle.'

Pierce put his left hand on the table, gnarled vein-streaked fingers spread out like dead coral. 'You're your father's boy.'

Vince knew he mustn't bite. Let a man like Pierce get inside your head and he'll wreak havoc.

'Back to Jack.'

'Your father. Lenny.'

'Jack.'

'Don't you want to talk about your old dad? It's important a man knows where he comes from, because it will tell him where he's going.'

'My father? I never really had the pleasure. You probably knew him better than I did. I hear he got in with the wrong crowd. He owed Jack. So he skipped town. It's no secret, and you know that. He was a two-bob drunk and a gambler.'

'You were there at the races, and I hear you were at the Brunswick. Like a gamble, do you, boy? Games of chance, easy money, just like your old dad?'

'I don't drink. I don't gamble. I was looking for you. You're on the wind-up now, Pierce. Forget it. You can't touch me. Lenny Treadwell's just a name on a birth certificate, who means nothing to me.'

Pierce gave a smile of satisfaction, as if he had the measure of the young detective. 'Fancy yourself, eh, boy? Full of piss and vinegar you are.' He then took off his glasses. The good eye fixed on Vince. His dry old lips smiling.

Vince adjusted to the new face in front of him.

Pierce leaned in, and hissed, 'Did you fuck her?'

Vince pressed *record*. 'I've got nothing to hide, Pierce.'

Pierce pressed *stop*. 'The slip. Did you fuck her?'

Vince pressed *record*. 'Gimme a name, Pierce.'

Pierce pressed *stop*. 'Bobbie Lalalala – whatever the fuck she calls herself.'

Vince pressed *record*. 'For the record, Mr Pierce asked if I quote, fucked, un-quote, Miss Bobbie LaVita. I categorically state for the record that I did not.'

Pierce pressed *stop*. 'My advice, leave town now. Before you do.'

Vince went to press *record*. 'She told me you wanted to see her. And, while we're at it, the men on the beach and the houndstooth mob, your boys, I take it?'

Pierce pressed *stop*. 'You don't know what you're messing with, boy. This thing is bigger than you'll ever know.' Pierce pointed a finger straight up to the ceiling. 'This goes right to the top.'

'Corruption?'

'More than you could ever know!'

Vince went to press *record* . . .

Smash. The white stick was upended and put through the tape-recorder.

Pierce was up on his feet. Black glasses back on his face.

Machin swung the door open, and Pierce was gone.

Vince sat in his office, drinking a nice strong cup of tea and collecting his thoughts. In front of him was the spool of tape he'd retrieved from the broken machine. '*I've got nothing to hide, Pierce . . . For the record, Mr Pierce asked if I quote, fucked, unquote, Miss Bobbie LaVita. I categorically state for the record that I did not.*'

He hadn't lied either. Once he and Bobbie had got into bed – Jack's bed – it didn't feel right. The weight of Jack hanging over them crushed the moment. They knew the moment would come, but not then.

Vince looked down at the newspaper on his desk: '*Deadly Plague Sweeping Brighton*'. It was a dramatic headline, biblical, mythical. He picked up the phone and called his favourite student.

CHAPTER 16

TREBLE DUTCH

Terence had been waiting on the corner of Market Street, at the entrance to Brighton's famous Lanes, for a good ten minutes before Vince turned up. Terence, ever eager, wanted to know what the caper was and how he could help. Vince filled him in as they weaved their way through the narrow Lanes, a cobbled maze of twisting and turning alleyways, lined with low-slung jewellery shops, silversmiths, curiosity, objet d'art and pawn shops with 'Best Prices Offered' boards swinging gently in the spring breeze. Bill Sykes wouldn't have looked out of place selling his stolen swag to Fagin somewhere in this old rookery that used to house fishermen.

Outside Max Vogel's antiques shop sat a Rolls-Royce, a *purple* one. The driver, smartly dressed in a light grey chauffeur's uniform with gold brocade spilling down the front and a leather cap, was leaning against the car looking self-conscious and reading a news-paper. Despite the garish colour of the car, what drew Vince's eye was the number plate: D E 1. A private number plate. Dickie Eton's private number plate?

The chauffeur quickly jettisoned his newspaper into the passenger-side window, and straightened up ready for duty. And out of the shop he stepped.

'That's Dickie Eton!' announced an animated Terence, gesturing at the cartoonish figure strutting across the pavement ahead of them.

'So I see,' said Vince, not taking his eyes off the pint-sized, preening pop mogul. He lived up to expectation. If the driver provided a sartorial appetizer, a taste of things to come, the man he ferried around was undoubtedly the main course: a flambé of over-fettled fashion. The velvet cape he wore even matched the colour of the car. The chauffeur opened the back door for his liege, and the louche Svengali stepped up to it, stepped in and purred away in the gliding Roller.

Vince looked around at Terence, who stood there in his 'rumpled farmer' duds. 'I hope you picked up some tips. Now wait here,' said Vince, about to step into the shop itself.

'Can't I come with you?'

'No, Terence, you can't.'

Terence switched from wide-eyed excitement at the prospect to a furrowed look of disappointment. Knowing the young scribe to be the excitable and facially volatile type, Vince didn't pay that too much attention as he instructed him to wait in the pub opposite.

The bell above the shop door alerted an assistant to Vince's presence. He sprang out from behind a brown velvet curtain which separated the main shop from what Vince assumed to be the back office. He was an effete-looking man in his thirties, stick-thin with a cascade of blond curls. A pair of gold-rimmed pince-nez style spectacles hung limply from a long, rose-gold Albert chain around his neck.

'May I help you, sir?' The sprightly assistant's alert smile exposed twin rows of small, precise teeth.

Vince returned the smile. 'I'm hoping you might,' he said, gazing around the shop. It contained three large glass-covered counters chock-full of gold jewellery, while the glass cabinets on the walls were stocked with silver Corinthian-column candle-sticks, cruet sets and planished goblets. It was clear that Max 'Treble Dutch' Vogel dealt only in high-end goods.

'I'm looking for something rather specific.' Vince reached into his jacket pocket and pulled out his notebook, tore out a leaf of paper and handed it to the effete assistant. The man retrieved the half-rimmed spectacles hanging on his hollow chest and fixed them on the tip of his long thin nose, before inspecting Vince's drawing of the Moor's head.

'Mmmm,' hummed the assistant, obviously having nothing like this in stock, but canny enough not to lose business over it. 'Curious – a cameo of some description?'

He was about to open the glass counter cabinet containing a cushion of assorted cameos, when Vince explained, 'It's a Moor's head, from the Corsican flag.' Nothing registered on those effete features, so Vince smiled and continued in a sparkly, flirtatious tone, 'Perhaps Mr Vogel may be able to help? I believe he's an expert on Corsican antiquities. I would be most grateful.'

This was obviously news to the assistant, but he wasn't about to deny it. 'One moment, sir,' and he disappeared behind the brown curtain. Five minutes later, his dainty head popped back around the curtain. 'This way if you will, sir.'

Vince slipped behind the counter, then behind the curtain, and followed him through to Vogel's private sanctum. The man knocked on the door, and a clear-cut voice responded: 'Come in.' The assistant opened the door and Vince entered.

Max Vogel sat at his desk, eating. It looked almost the same culinary set-up as at the races, only not quite such gargantuan portions. A platter of a dozen discarded oyster shells lay before him, and the crusts of four crabmeat sandwiches sat on a white plate nearby. There was a saltiness in the air that you could almost taste, and the room stank of fish.

The whale man was smiling. 'Forgive me, sir, I've been lunching. Please take a seat.'

Vince sat down in an antique bow-backed chair. 'I'm sorry to disturb you, Mr Vogel.'

'No, no, I'm quite done,' he replied with a sated smile.

Vince scoped the office: shelves with silver items stacked high; a huge safe, about the size of a refrigerator, took up a corner of the room; a pair of weighing scales sat on top of it. The shelves behind Vogel were lined with reference books and antiques guides.

Vogel gestured, with a flourish of his fat hand, for the assistant to take the mollusc platter away. He did so, and exited.

'Seafood, a weakness. Oysters especially. From English's restaurant, the finest in the land.'

'I know the place, but I didn't know they did deliveries.'

'I enjoy my food, as you can probably tell, sir, and am not given over to the tiresome etiquette of communal dining. So I dine alone. Just as I bathe alone.'

Vince nodded, trying to shake off the image of the fat man at his ablutions.

'And I do not enjoy watching others. After all, "'twas a brave man who first swallowed an oyster",' Vogel said with a chuckle. 'But my dining habits are not what you are here for.' He lifted the drawing of the Moor's head off his desk and studied it. 'Corsican, you say?'

Vince nodded.

'Whoever told you I was an expert on Corsican artefacts is mistaken. Beyond certain Napoleonic items, I am a layman. But I do have a contact up in town who may be of service to you, and that's the reason you are now sitting before me, Mr . . . ?'

'Treadwell.' Vince reached inside his jacket pocket and showed him his badge. 'Detective Vincent Treadwell of Scotland Yard.' An imperceptible smile crossed Vince's lips, as he never got tired of reciting that in full.

Vogel drew back, opened-mouthed and enlightened. 'Ah, so the item you are looking for has been stolen, and you believe it has ended up in Brighton. Well, sir, I have a very good standing with the local constabulary who deal with such matters, and I shall endeavour to keep my eyes peeled.'

Vince contemplated the whale man, and concluded that he wouldn't look out of place with a fez on his head in some back-street bazaar in the Kasbah, drinking tarry cups of coffee and smoking a bubbling baccy-packed hookah. Vince imagined he might suffer from gout and have a dozen passports stashed away in a drawer. The heavy gold signet ring on his pinkie finger featured a heraldic crest depicting some kind of bird. Vince wondered if it held any significance, maybe his family crest, or was just purchased over the counter as a mere affectation. Antique dealers drew from all parts of the world, in the hunt for that object of desire that would turn the greatest profit. It was a business with many shades and classes – and most of them with as potted a provenance as the goods they dealt in.

'I'm here investigating "the body on the beach" case.'

Vogel sat back in his chair, put his hands across his gut, and his fingertips together as if joining them in prayer. 'A gruesome business. Reminds me of "the body in the trunk" crime of a few years back. The perpetrator of that crime lived not three doors away from here, in the Lanes. Before your time, I assume?' Vogel screwed his face up, amused. 'I must say, Detective Treadwell, I do find it amusing, if not exciting, to have you sitting here, sir. Am I a suspect?'

'No. Our chief suspect is Mr Jack Regent.'

'Ah, we reach the meat of the matter. The Corsican! To which the Moor's head, the symbol on the Corsican flag, is pertaining?'

'You know him, I take it?'

'You come to my business armed with a sketch of a Moor's head, so you strike me as a man who has done his research. All very clever, albeit rather overly melodramatic.'

'Well, if you're going to be melodramatic, you might as well be overly so.'

'First class, Detective, first class!' Vogel gave a full-lunged laugh, that subsided into a rosy-cheeked chuckle. 'I know Mr Regent, just as many people know Mr Regent. It's no secret that he is a powerfully pervasive presence in this town. A man not to be trifled with.'

'Do you do much business with him?'

'No.'

'May I speak bluntly?'

'You strike me as a man who will do so, anyway, with or without my permission.'

'I don't believe you.'

Vogel narrowed his already impossibly narrow eyes. 'Trust, I reckon, has never played a big part in the law. 'Tis proof you need.'

'Henry Pierce, and your little powwow at the races?'

Vogel arched a downy-gold eyebrow in surprise. 'Me, sir?'

'You, sir.'

Vogel nodded slowly, his jowls juddering and his chins – of which Vince counted three that rested on top of a solid goitre – rolling around like choppy waters. When he stopped nodding, there was still movement, involuntary reverberations as the rest of his face took moments to settle. Then he finally said, 'If Henry Pierce decides to grace you with his company and converse with you, you have very little say in the matter. To put it bluntly, sir, one is hijacked, seized, enslaved, ensnared and, if I may be so bold, fucked!'

Vince laughed. 'Yes, I know what you're saying about Pierce, and normally I'd agree. But it struck me that you were doing most of the talking, and Pierce most of the listening.'

'Have you been – what's the vernacular? – tailing me?'

'No, him.'

'And what do you deduce from that exchange, an exchange that you couldn't possibly have overheard, and it is questionable that you could have actually witnessed?'

'Oh, I saw, and I deduce that you're not telling me the truth. You indeed work for Jack Regent. You receive the antiques and

jewellery that certain associates of Mr Regent, by hook or by crook, procure.'

Vogel's eyes bulged with indignation. '*Receive* and *procure*,' he spat out, like ejecting a bad oyster. 'Those are two words I have no truck with! Two words that in my line of business are considered an anathema!'

'It gets worse.'

Vogel clasped his hands together tight, bracing himself for the worst, the blood squeezed from his knuckles turning them white. 'Not in my office, it doesn't.'

'We could go down to *my* office and, believe me, that is a lot worse.'

'I have lawyers who will skewer you over your unsubstantiated slander.'

Vince gave him an affable smile. 'Oh, Mr Vogel, I don't think it will come to that.'

Vogel untangled his fingers from that tense and tightly knotted prayer position, and slipped his right hand under the desk. 'You strike me as a clever young man. Not the usual pedestrian patter I would expect from a public servant. And pertinacious, too. That you are, sir, pertinacious!'

Vince remained smiling. 'I'm like a limpet once I find something worth hanging on to. I'm sure you'll appreciate the mollusc analogy.'

'If you must know, Mr Pierce has moved out of his home into a residential home for the blind, and has some items he wished to be appraised and valued.'

'Yeah, he told me,' said Vince, with one eye watching Vogel's hand slowly disappearing out of view under the desk. 'You're not getting over-melodramatic, and about to pull a gun on me?'

Before Vogel could answer, the effete assistant, alerted by the buzzer secreted under the desk, was at the door with a knock and a swishy entrance.

'Cheesecake!' Vogel ordered.

The assistant nodded and exited, closing the door behind him.

'Cheesecake? Is that a secret password?' Vogel threw him an irritated look. 'I only ask because I've heard some other funny ones lately.'

'I'd ask you to stay but, as I've already told you, I dine alone. It would not be an experience you'd enjoy watching.'

'Shame. I like cheesecake almost as much as I like swordfish.' Vogel's narrow eyes redoubled their scrutiny. 'A seafood lover such as your good self, Mr Vogel, would surely appreciate that fare, especially when caught locally.'

'Hardly indigenous to these waters.'

'The big fish? No, I imagine it migrates to the warmer waters of Corsica, or Marseilles, whenever things get too hot around here.'

Vogel, knowing the young detective wasn't going to let him off the hook, threw him a line. 'I have been known to frequent a certain club, in a certain square, for a certain game of poker. Just as I have been known to frequent the sport of kings. A weakness of mine, yes, but hardly a crime.'

'If the premises are unlicensed for gaming, then, yes, it is a crime.'

Vogel offered up his hands in mock surrender as if for Vince to slap on the cuffs. 'Do your worst, officer.'

'Oh, I think we can do better than that, Mr Vogel.'

'Very good, sir. Well, now you have it. That is where I know Henry Pierce from. That is where I know Jack Regent from.'

'I'm guessing that you handle more than gambling chips at the Brunswick Sporting Club. A lot more than crooked antiques. You're Jack Regent's financier, investor, bag man, call it what you will.'

Vogel did not flinch at this. There were no shocked reverberations and flesh-quakes. He sat perfectly still and said, 'What brings you to this conclusion?

Vince leaned forward, elbows on the desk, hands clasped together, giving Vogel a browbeating stare. 'When I saw you talking to Pierce, he did everything but get on his knees to you. You had him eating out of your hand.'

A single knock at the door and the effete assistant entered with a large white cake box and placed it before Vogel, and then left. Vogel opened the box, dipped his hand in, grabbed a handful of cheesecake and shovelled it into his mouth. He then fixed Vince with a baleful glare.

Vince met it with a relaxed smile. 'Like I said, eating out of your hand.'

Vogel ignored him and guzzled more fistfuls of cake. Through the glut of cheesecake, he said, 'I did . . . warn you . . . Detective . . . Treadwell.'

'I'm just glad you didn't order the soup.'

Vogel took a big swallow that Vince was convinced could be heard across town, and said, 'Well, sir, if you don't like it . . .'

Vince stood up and made his way to the door. 'Oh, one last thing. I saw Dickie Eton leaving the shop. May I ask what business you have with him?'

Vogel gave a wearisome sigh, licked the cheesecake off his fingers, twisted around in his chair, pulled down a slim reference book from the shelf and plopped on the desk. 'Page forty-seven.'

Vince went over to the desk, picked the book up and flicked through to page forty-seven. Vogel, a greasy thumb in his mouth, smiled when he saw that Vince had found the right page, and the fat man said, 'Shocking, don't you think?' Vince had seen worse. A lot worse. Working vice in Soho, you did, but never on such finely struck pieces of enamelled jewellery, silver snuffboxes or paintings. It was a reference book of antique pornographic and erotic art.

Vogel continued, 'Mr Eton does have exotic tastes. Some of these pieces have come on the market through a private source, and Mr Eton wants me to appraise and authenticate them for him.'

Vince's eye fell upon one piece in particular, an oil on canvas, that took his interest and seemed familiar: two black men raping a white girl. The painting wasn't impressionistic; it was blunt, brutal, photographic and pornographic. Looking at it, Vince was back in Soho, in the projection room: the white light, the silver screen, the junkie-thin blonde with the knife to her throat. Vince put the book on the table. 'Is this for sale?' he asked, pointing at the picture.

Vogel looked at the illustration, 'I believe it is. You have excellent taste. This is the most expensive item in the collection, and the one piece that Mr Eton is prepared to go to the limit for. It's by Jacob Radlington, 1747 to 1789, and an artist of the Royal Academy.'

Vogel leaned back in his chair, spreading his hands across the great expanse of his waistline. He looked ruminative and relaxed now, within his field of knowledge, hostilities temporarily assuaged. 'A tragic figure, Radlington fell foul of John Barleycorn. Ended up living in squalor in Deptford, reduced to hawking his wares around the taverns he frequented, sometimes exchanging them for just the price of a drink. Tell me, sir, do you know much about art?'

Vince smiled at the thought of his conversation with Bobbie about the painting of the French soldier. 'I have a friend who works at Sotheby's auction house, who tells me just enough to impress the girls with, should the need arise. But not really.'

Vogel met the detective's honesty with a hearty laugh. 'I see, very good, sir. Very good. Well, as you can imagine, Radlington's original landscapes, with their subtle play on light and nature, held little interest for his new boozy public. So he turned to a baser art form: no other word for it but pornography. Note the shackles on the Negroes' ankles. This was painted at the height of the slave trade. A "trade" that was a blight on humanity, when man's morality was at its lowest. This image of Negroes raping a white girl exploited the white man's basest instincts and fears of the day. In other words, if they were set free or to break their shackles, this would be the inevitable result. The oppressor becoming the oppressed? The artist played on his clientele's prejudices, anxiety and stupidity.'

'I'm afraid not a lot has changed in two hundred years, then,' said Vince, still not looking up from the painting reproduced on the page.

'Indeed not, sir. Note, if you will, the hint of ecstasy playing on the girl's lips, which panders to the baser male instincts. It suggests that the woman is enjoying it; that all women enjoy it. Remember, when we view a painting, we are never strictly impartial or objective observers. Ultimately we put ourselves somewhere inside the picture. And this painting, no matter how unpleasant, does as all works of art do: it gives the viewer several choices. Note that the shackles on their ankles are not broken, so these slaves have not escaped. No, sir, this painting could only have been painted by a white man, and not just because of the formal European aesthetics of the brushwork, but because of its very warped out-look. He puts us in the picture, all right, and asks us who we are. Are you one of the Negroes raping the woman? Or are you the master of these Negroes, somewhere just out of view, but sanc-tioning the rape for one's own perverse gratification? And that's what makes it truly pornographic, and therefore of little value to the legitimate art world – only to a certain type of collector.'

Vogel had assumed a wistful expression, as if saddened to look at this image. 'As for the painter of this aberrational eyesore, what a terrible existence. He was a fine and gifted artist; like all great artists, a man who was truly touched by the hand of God. His brushwork and the use of light in his landscapes are exquisite, and yet he was reduced to this. Driven there by his addictions and despair.'

'They're usually one and the same thing.' Vogel nodded in silent agreement and put the book back on the shelf. 'Like I said, not a lot has changed in two hundred years.'

'I take it, Detective, you are talking about those three young people who died in Kemp Town?'

'That I am.'

Vince searched Vogel's face for clues, for signs of guilt perhaps, but nothing jumped out at him. The man's face bore the impartial protocol of sadness, and a sense of bewilderment for their fate. Much as there had been for Jacob Radlington's squandered talent and ruined life.

'Yes, a shocking business,' said Vogel. 'But you're right, Detective, nothing is new in this world, and we learn little as we stumble blindly through life.'

On that jolly note, Vince decided to head for the door. 'Well, I hope you get a good price for your client, Mr Vogel.'

'Detective, may I turn the tables on you and ask a question?'

'Be my guest.'

'Do you know who you are?' asked Vogel.

Vince tensed up. 'How do you mean?'

'Do you know who you are in that painting? Where *you* stand in the picture, Mr Treadwell?'

'Detective Treadwell.'

'Sorry, Detective.'

'Yes, I'm standing at the door. And I'm about to tear it down and then put an end to it all.' Vince swung the door open and exited.

CHAPTER 17

KNOCK, KNOCK

Terence was dutifully at his post in the pub opposite as Vince walked in.

'What happened?' Terence asked, with a half-sunk pint of cider in his hand.

Vince sat down at the table, his mind not on the question but on the painting Vogel had just revealed. From the shop to the pub, Vince had weighed up the art-history lecture, and found he agreed with Vogel's critique of both the painter and the human condition. He broke out of his reverie and put a question of his own, more to himself than to Terence. 'If Vogel is Jack's money man, and Jack is on the run, it's safe to assume that Jack's going to need him more than ever now, right?'

'Er, right.'

Vince stood up, hit by two new thoughts. Jack's library – why conceal it if it didn't hold something that he didn't want anyone to know about? The other thought, best kept quiet for now – Murray the Head.

'Terence, d'you drive?'

'Yes. And no.'

Vince rolled his eyes. 'Which one is it?'

'I can drive, but I don't have a licence.'

'But you can drive?'

'But I don't have a licence.'

Vince gave him a manful slap on the back. 'I didn't hear the last bit, so here's what I want you to do. I want you to stay here and keep your eyes peeled on Vogel's activities.' Vince took out his notepad and scribbled down Bobbie's phone number, tore out the leaf and put it on the table. He then took out his car keys and dropped them on top of the piece of paper. 'If he leaves, I want you to follow him.'

'Tail him?' Terence asked excitedly.

'Yes, tail him. Then call me at this number and I'll meet you, OK?'

'Where are you going?'

'We're switching roles. You get to do the fun stuff. I'm going to the library to stick my head in some books.'

Vince took a taxi to Adelaide Crescent. The street-entrance door was locked, no surprise, since he'd told Bobbie to call a locksmith and get it fixed. He rang the bell, Bobbie answered and he was buzzed in.

She answered the door of the flat, still clad in the white-towelling dressing gown with the initials JR over the breast pocket. There was an awkwardness between them: they didn't embrace or kiss. Their relationship now occupied that charged hinterland of expectation and awkwardness. Vince followed her into the kitchen, where she made them some coffee. He sat down at the kitchen table and told her about his visit to Vogel. Then asked her if she knew whether Jack was involved in pornography.

Turning away from him, she said, 'I thought you were finished with the case.'

'There's something else. Sit down.'

Bobbie did as she was told. She could sense that he was troubled, and said, 'I trusted you. You can trust me.'

He did. He took a deep breath, and then told her about Soho, about Duval, Eddie Tobin, the private cinema, what he saw on the silver screen, about the man who entered the projection room, the coma that she already knew about and why he was sent down here. He laid out the whole deal.

When he was done, she took a deep, thoughtful breath, then said, 'These films – I know Jack wouldn't get involved in anything like that.'

'Can you be so sure? After everything you know about him?'

'Jack wouldn't hurt a woman.'

'He already takes a cut from every pimp and whorehouse in town. Wouldn't hurt a woman – do you know how naïve that sounds?'

'Maybe so, but what you saw in Soho is different, just . . . just evil. I just know he wouldn't.'

Vince didn't have time to argue the point. He stood up. 'I need to make a call, then I need to look in Jack's library.'

'Why?'

'To see what his tastes in art are like.'

She sighed, then gave him the nod.

Vince gave her an appreciative smile, then went into the living room to make the phone call. 'Ray, it's Vince.'

'Vince, how are you?'

'Any news?'

'I've sent the mugshot of Regent over to Interpol in Marseilles. It's an old photo but, assuming he's not been home in a few years, it may still do the trick.'

'Good. Ray, I need a favour: Eddie Tobin's address.'

There was a tense questioning silence before Ray finally put the question, 'Why?'

'I came across a connection, Max Vogel, an antique dealer down here. He's tied in somehow with Regent, maybe his money man. He deals in pornographic art.'

'I don't know much about art, but I know what I like.' Ray laughed.

'You wouldn't like these. Vogel showed me a book that had a painting in it that was up for sale. Private seller – wouldn't tell me who it was. It's by an artist called Jacob Radlington: two black slaves raping a white girl. A blonde white girl. It's very similar to what I saw in Duval's place.'

'A painting?'

Vince replied impatiently, 'No, Ray, on the screen!'

Ray Dryden caught the edge in Vince's voice. 'OK, OK, I'm with you. How old is the painting?'

'1780s.'

Ray Dryden let a very sceptical silence swell, before he said, 'I heard there were Mods and Rockers rucking on the beach in Brighton, so are you going to make a connection with the Bayeux Tapestry?'

'I don't believe in coincidences in police work, and neither do you.'

'Vince, you were told to stay away from Tobin, from the whole thing. That's why they sent you down there, you know that.'

'You gonna help me out or what?

'Listen, Vince, you told me what you saw, and I believe you. But don't muddy the waters, blot your copybook or piss on your chips, for that matter! If you can just find Jack Regent and we can tie him in with the Unione Corse heroin connection, you'll be doing yourself and your career a big favour. Don't get side-tracked by the Soho thing.'

'Ray, I'm not getting sidetracked. Like I said, I don't believe in coincidences. I believe that it's all connected and we just have to work it out.'

There was another protracted and uncertain silence. Followed by a swift decision: 'Consider it done. But if you do find him, not a word about me.'

'You have to ask?'

'And promise me nothing will happen to him.'

Vince heard genuine concern in Ray's voice and repeated, 'You have to ask?'

★ ★ ★

Wincing in discomfort, Vaughn Treadwell stood in the concourse of Brighton train station, holding a bunch of wizened daffodils wrapped in newspaper, and admiring his new shoes. The flowers were wizened because he'd bought them cheap off a barrow. He himself was wincing because the new shoes were too small. They were the last pair of their style in the shop, and the woman had assured him that they would 'give'. Vaughn had fallen in love with them the minute he'd set his beady little mincers on them. Italian loafers, they were the kind of shoes Cary Grant would wear, without socks; or Frank and the boys when playing at the Sands in Vegas. Soft brown-suede loafers with tassels. Class. He'd bought them with his winnings at the races. It made them even sweeter.

Vaughn looked up at the board announcing departures and arrivals. The slats flapped over to reveal that the train he was waiting for was running an hour late. A voice over the public-address system confirmed this. Vince looked down at the flowers, which didn't appear to have an hour left in them. He knew a place close by, and he knew the stuff they peddled was good. Good as in it was not the bad stuff that was currently doing the rounds and killing people. He knew that for a fact. He'd been good, he thought; he'd promised the girl he wouldn't indulge, not without her at least. They had made a pact. *Together* they could control it, look out for each other. It brought them closer. It brought them into soft focus. They needed the warmth that flowed through them whenever they were on it; it gave them comfort, solace. He looked up at the station clock. He had time, he reckoned. All the time in the world.

Vince was on his knees. Half the books in the concealed library were on the floor with him. The books were already arranged in order of subject. He took each book and carefully flicked through it, hoping that something would jump out at him. Or, better, that there might be some information written on a piece of paper hidden between the pages. Art took precedence over Literature, while Geography and Travel took precedence over History, Politics and Philosophy. He thought Jack might have the whole story here in the books spread out across the library, encompassing a whole range of subjects, coded and unbreakable.

He picked up a reference book on British artists of the Royal Academy, all alphabetically listed with a short précis of their lives and works. He found the reference for Jacob Radlington. High praise for his landscapes and portraits. No mention of his not-so-legit works, his rapes, orgies, sodomies, paedophilia and the such. And a clear reference to him dying impoverished as an addicted opium user. And yet Vogel, who seemed so well read on the artist, had made no reference to the De Quinceyan route Radlington had gone down. Was it maybe too close to the bone for him?

Bobbie dutifully brought him in cups of tea every fifteen minutes. Laid them down on the floor, then stood by the door for a few moments, watching him go about his work, making his notes, cross-referencing, looking up different subjects. To Bobbie it appeared like detective work. She enjoyed watching him, as it was somehow soothing and reassuring: a man with purpose and intelligence diligently and methodically carrying out his duty. He had a look of intense concentration about him. She'd made him six cups of tea so far, but three had gone un-drunk and cold, so caught up was he in his work. She was just wondering how long he'd continue kneeling there, when the phone rang.

She went into the front room and answered it. But before she could even ask who it was, Vince had grabbed the phone from her.

'Terence?'

CHAPTER 18

FRESH HELL

The taxi dropped Vince off at the entrance to Shoreham harbour. Waiting for him in the car park was Terence, leaning up against the Triumph Herald. The first thing Terence did when he saw Vince was apologize – he'd creased the front bumper while getting out of a parking space. Vince gave the damage a quick once-over. Nothing major or really to worry about, especially when it was a company car.

'Where's Vogel?' he asked.

'He went into a warehouse over by pier three.'

As they walked towards the pier, Terence filled him in. Vogel had shut up his shop and left in a hurry at around 4.30, walked around to East Street and got in his car, a brown and beige Bentley, then drove straight to the harbour.

They reached the warehouses, three of them terraced together, each was as big as an aeroplane hangar, with a corrugated sheet-metal front painted green. They were windowless apart from the warehouse in the centre, which had a small round window, almost like a porthole, set in the top of the facade. Terence pointed this middle one out as the warehouse Vogel had entered. His Bentley was parked outside. A sign over the door, in flaking black paint, bore the legend: Tartarus Storage Ltd.

'Now what?' asked Terence.

Vince noted that Terence's voice sounded a little smudged. He sniffed the air and turned towards him. 'Have you been drinking?' Terence looked guilty, and if not pie-eyed, certainly red-eyed. Vince shook his head at his own negligence. 'My fault. I shouldn't have left a writer alone in a pub.' He then turned his attention to the warehouse and said, 'We do what all good coppers do, and what accounts for ninety per cent of our work. We wait.'

They strolled back to the car, got inside and waited. In the distance, a freight ship was docking. Terence, emboldened by booze, wanted Vince to tell him some more about the case.

Vince figured he owed Terence that much and he was beginning to trust him, so he told him about Ray Dryden at Interpol and the possible Corsican connection. Terence, his mind fired, didn't take long to put the heroin connection together. Vince didn't verify or deny this. Terence also laid out how easy it would be for Jack to come in and out of the country – being a professional smuggler – and pointed out that Shoreham airport was just up the road, with private planes taking off all the time.

Terence wanted to scribble it all down in his pad, but Vince told him that right now it was all up in the air, up for grabs and, most importantly, off the record. But he promised that, if the story broke, Terence would be the one to break it. It would be a story Duncan Webb at the *People* would give his eye-teeth for.

It was an hour before Vogel emerged from the warehouse. He then walked around to the docking area where a ship was being unloaded.

'Terence, you wait here,' said Vince, getting out of the car.

'Why can't I come?' asked Terence, in a disgruntled tone.

Vince looked around at the cub reporter. It was the first time he'd seen him looking anything but receptive, excited or awed. Terence, vexed, continued, 'I mean, you know, I've been doing a lot of waiting . . . sitting around. You didn't let me go to the

Brunswick Sporting Club, and I was the one who told you about it. Gave you the lead, as it were.'

Vince scrutinized the young hack. Was this his first stab at defiance, or simply the drink talking? Terence's brow was creased and he was wearing a clown's frown, obviously more petulance than anger. Vince gave him an encouraging smile. 'What did I say earlier? Waiting is ninety per cent of the work. You're doing a stellar job, but just think about it. If I'm seen palling around with the press, no one will ever tell me anything. You're not supposed to be here, Terence. You're my back-up man, so don't under-estimate that role.'

Terence deliberated for a good ten seconds, then nodded in recognition of his role.

Vince trowelled it on. 'You're my secret weapon, Terence. You're more of a secret agent than a copper.'

'Vince, I'm not a kid. Or an idiot.'

Vince opened the door and stepped out of the car.

A team of stevedores was securing the main container ready to be fitted on to a haulage lorry for the short distance to the ware-house, to be unloaded. The whole procedure should have taken about an hour − until Vince decide to intervene.

'Mr Vogel!' he called out.

Vogel looked around and saw him approaching. His face couldn't hide his displeasure at seeing the detective. 'I take it this is no coincidence.'

Vince was now standing alongside Max Vogel and one of the tough-looking stevedores. 'I can't lie. What's in the container?'

'Who are youse, pal?' barked the stevedore in a broad Glasgow accent, by way of the Gorbals. The Scots seadog wore a string vest that showed off his tattooed torso and arms, with muscle lashed around him like knotted rope. He'd obviously been eating his spinach.

Vince reached into his pocket and badged him.

Popeye looked at the badge. 'Scotland Yard? Then you got no authority here. I've got my own badge, pal. Any problems, you call me first.'

Vogel chipped in, 'Mr Charmers is right, it's none of your business. And you have no authority here.'

On hearing the surname, Vince eyed the scowling Charmers. Never was a name more ill-fitting. He was all hard edges; with his jutting jaw and hook-nose he looked like a giant's bottle opener. His body was lavishly decorated with tattoos featuring flamenco dancers and hula-hula girls that gyrated with lascivious intent at each flex of a pec or a biceps. As pretty as they were, they weren't as eye-catching as the vicious-looking cargo hook that was looped into his belt.

Knowing he couldn't out-scowl this stevedore, Vince gave him a smile and turned his attention back to Vogel. 'It's a simple question. What's in the container?'

'I do a lot of business exporting to America, Detective Treadwell,' replied Vogel. 'The Americans are very keen on antique furniture, no matter what the quality.'

'May I?' asked Vince, pointing at the manifest in Charmers' hand.

Vogel gave a reluctant nod to Charmers to give it up. Matching Vogel's reluctance, the man did so.

Vince checked it out. 'This cargo's from France. Calais.'

'I shall pick off the best pieces, then the rest will end up in America.'

'French furniture?'

'Yes, of varying quality,' said Vogel, trying to muffle this admission with an embarrassed cough.

'Let's crack one open. I'd like to see.'

'You imagine Mr Regent is hiding inside?' protested Vogel, pointing at the container still on the ship.

'I leave nothing up to the imagination, Mr Vogel. Unload it and open it, or I'll have the whole lot impounded and coppers taking it apart stick by stick.'

Vogel, furious, speechless, gave Charmers the nod.

'Need any help?' came the panting voice jogging up behind them.

Vince fixed the young hack with a baleful stare and, through gritted teeth, answered Vogel's questioning look with a pissed-off, 'He's with me.'

Vogel gave Terence the once-over, and once was all it took for him to conclude: 'He doesn't look like a policeman.'

Vince saw there no disputing that point. 'No, he doesn't much.'

The girl felt sad. She thought that Vaughn would be meeting her at the station. He'd promised her a taxi ride home. She hadn't packed much in her suitcase, since she'd only been away for a week. But her mother was worried that she wasn't eating properly – she looked so thin and drawn – and had insisted she take some food with her. Mother had packed her case with pots of jam, tins of corned beef, Spam and other victuals. She'd had to haul the heavy case on and off a bus, then dragged it down their street. She felt sad when she entered the basement, stood amid the grime that had blown in off the street and settled. She made an effort to sweep it daily, but it was a losing battle since the basement just seemed to attract debris. And now, as she entered the dank gloom of the flat, she felt like crying. There's no place like home, and this crepuscular flophouse was never like a home. She'd done her best to pretty the place up since she'd moved in a month ago, but all her hard work had been undone in the six days she'd gone away. It was a mess.

She was about to unpack when she heard a knock on the door. She thought about how she'd react, knowing she certainly wouldn't fall into Vaughn's arms as if happy to see him. She didn't want to seem too needy, even though she knew she was. The truth was, she felt at ease with Vaughn, because for the first time she felt equal to someone. When they were alone together, they could pretend – pretend everything was just so. And whenever they were on the stuff, they felt better. She was reluctant to try it at first, since one heard such terrible things. But Vaughn had told her it would be OK if they only smoked it. And he was right, it made her feel warm, it made her feel whole, it made her forget. She'd heard such terrible stories about it, but surely she wasn't addicted to it. True, she had been a little testy with her mother, ill at ease, so she did wonder if she'd come back to Brighton early so she could take some more. But it wasn't a habit; no, she was sure of that. And anyway, she and Vaughn were going to leave Brighton soon. She wanted them to make a fresh start, maybe start a family. But right now it was just a bit of fun over the summer. They first took it after the pills Vaughn had got hold of for them to go out dancing with. It was the first time she'd been out dancing with boys and girls of her own age. The pills gave her energy, brought her out of herself, made her feel confident, made her feel *normal*. She had danced all night. It was the first time she had let her hair down, literally, since she became aware that she was different, since she was a child and had first been stared at in the classroom. Vaughn had given her this happiness, given her this magic. She ran to the door, knowing she would fall into his arms. She knew she wanted to feel warm again. She knew she wanted more . . .

She opened the door. It was all wrong. A figure filled the door frame, blocking out what little sunlight did manage to penetrate the basement. Where Vaughn's apologetic little eyes should have been, there was a black expanse. A blood-red ruby stickpin was stuck in the black tie. She followed the tie up to the knot and, with her head leaning back at full tilt, she looked up to see the smiling, scarred face of Henry Pierce.

'Hello, my dear.'

'I told you to wait in the car!' Vince growled, his finger prodding firmly into Terence's chest; so firmly that Terence was forced against the wall. They had just entered the container, after standing in silence for about twenty minutes, while waiting for it to be unloaded on to the dock. Terence had tried to talk to Vince, tried to apologize, but Vince was having none of it and merely told him to shut up. It wasn't that Terence had disobeyed an order, for he was a civilian, and insubordination was a trait that Vince possessed enough of to forgive in others; it was just that, by sticking his face up alongside Vince's, he'd now put himself in the firing line.

Terence had blown his own cover and, in some ways, his usefulness, and Vince was forced to lie for him. With a crowbar in hand, Vince started opening the wooden crates to check the contents. Terence helped out, and they worked in silence.

Half an hour later, straw and newspaper packing was strewn all over the floor of the container. They'd checked every box, to find it was just what Vogel had said it was – French furniture. Flashy stuff: gilt-framed mirrors, stripy silk-upholstered white-wood salon chairs, heavy black-lacquered oriental-influenced bureaus, bow-fronted chests of drawers, bookcases and screens. The only thing of real interest was the fact that Vince recognized some of the pieces from Bobbie's apartment. Which again connected Vogel with Jack. But it was a tenuous link; Vogel dealt in furniture. Jack owned some of it – big deal, so what? Vince had meanwhile checked every stick of furniture, looking in every drawer of every bureau, desk and chest of drawers. Anywhere you could conceal contraband heroin, and he'd come up with a big fat nothing.

The last box contained ceramic figurines with the cross-sword Meissen mark on the base. There were about a dozen of them, worth on their own a small fortune. Especially if they contained pure heroin. Vince figured these were definitely Vogel's fakes. And if they weren't, he was in trouble. But it was worth the risk. He removed all the straw packing from the box, and threw it to the ground. Then he started rooting around among the broken figurines inside it.

'Er . . . why did you do that, Vince?'

'Because Vogel's lying. He told me most of this stuff was fake – or reproduction, as he put it. But he's selling it as the real McCoy, which is strictly illegal. That part I believe.' Vince bent down closer to inspect the damage. 'So why would you offer up the truth about an illegal venture to a copper?' Terence shook his head. 'To cover up the real lie. Vogel's throwing us a herring, and it's as red as . . .' Vince stuck his finger in his mouth, having cut himself on a shard of broken porcelain '. . . red as blood.' He stood up, looking at his handiwork, while stemming the blood from his finger with his tongue.

'What fresh hell is this!'

Vince and Terence looked up from the box of broken figurines to see Max Vogel standing at the entrance of the walk-in container. His fat hands were then in his mouth, up to the knuckles, his eyes bulging. He looked as if he was about to start eating himself. The container felt as though it was being hit by a small earthquake as he dropped to his knees.

Vince turned to Terence and, in a voice deader than the deadest of deadpans, said, 'Whoopsy-daisy, looks like they were real.'

Vince parked his car at the bottom of Waterloo Street, and made his way to Vaughn's flat. Once Max Vogel had struggled up off the floor of the container, and dried his tears, then ceased his threats to sue Vince and Scotland Yard for every penny they possessed, he told Vince that Machin was on the phone and wanted to talk with him urgently.

So there was Vince, stepping under the police tape, heading down the stairs and into the gloom of his brother's basement flop. Which was now a crime scene.

And there she was. The girl. On the floor. Dead. A depressed, bent syringe hanging out of her arm. Blood oozing from her nose, foam around her mouth. Eyes wide open in horror. It was the same MO as the other dead junkies. Six in all, now. The only thing really marking her out as different was the blemish she'd tried to cover up all her adult life with a Veronica Lake peekaboo hairstyle. The birthmark on her face.

'Welcome to shit street, clean face.' Machin emerged from the kitchen into the living room, Ginge, as ever, following a few paces behind him. Machin wore a malicious expression: the gloves were off now between them. It was war, open hostilities.

That didn't bother Vince; he'd been expecting it.

'I thought you should see this, son, before you go back to where you fucking belong.'

Vince, eyes on the girl, asked, 'Is this Vaughn's girlfriend?'

'Max Vogel called me. He said you were harassing him. Searching a cargo of his without a warrant. What the fuck's all that about? Is that the way you do things in the Met? 'Course, you've got form for that, sticking your nose into places you shouldn't. I reckon you've gone rogue on us, Treadwell. What d'you reckon, Ginge – reckon he's gone rogue on us?'

Ginge, without much enthusiasm, replied, 'Guv.'

'You didn't answer my question,' said Vince. 'Is this Vaughn's girl?'

Machin looked down at the girl, as if noticing her for the first time. 'Who knows, poor cow. If she is, it makes sense. Not much to look at, either. A right face-ache.'

Machin went back into the kitchen and returned with a paper bag. He emptied the contents on to a side table. The same gear that had killed the others. Wrapped in cellophane, it was about the size of a big fist. A big fat fist that packed a killer blow.

'We found this behind there.' Machin pointed to an old brown sideboard. 'We got an anonymous tip that your brother's the dealer. He's the one putting it out on the streets. He's responsible for the deaths of six people.'

Vince, with his eyes still on the girl, gave Machin a swift nod. He wasn't agreeing with him; the nod was just a receipt for the goods, the assessment. Which Machin had delivered as if it was fact. Vince wasn't buying it. Not yet, anyway. Not because Vaughn was his brother, but just because good coppers don't do that. Such supposition and speculation had not yet turned into stone-cold facts – no matter how bad it looked.

Vince bent down to take a closer look at the body, and began some real detective work. She was wearing a knitted jacket and matching skirt. Cheap but giving her a smart appearance. Her arm with the syringe in it had the jacket sleeve carefully rolled up. On closer inspection, it wasn't. It was pulled up unevenly, hurriedly and forcefully. There was a small tear at the seam which looked fresh from where the sleeve had been yanked up. He looked at her shoes: black, small heel, buckle, again formal. It all looked wrong, her being in her Sunday best. She looked like a secretary in an insurance company or fresh out the typing pool. If she was going to do junk, she wouldn't be dressed so formally. She'd have got herself nice and comfortable for the big nod. At least have kicked off her shoes, even taking into account the filthy carpet. And, most important, the bared arm was clean, baby smooth. No track marks. No history of sticking needles in herself. The suitcase in the room revealed that she'd just got back from somewhere, or was about to go somewhere. The contents of the case would tell them, through being fresh or worn clothes. But Vince doubted he would get a chance to check the contents.

Either way, it all looked rushed and wrong. She'd been unwittingly caught out.

Vince stood up and gave it a shot, already knowing he didn't stand a chance. 'I want to come to the morgue with you, to check her body for bruising and signs of a struggle.'

Machin laughed incredulously. 'Whhhhat!' He swung around to Ginge, pulled a face to emphasize that he couldn't believe what he was hearing. Ginge, not twigging that he was part of a double act, or else just pricked by his conscience, didn't join in with the incredulity; he merely shrugged and looked away.

Machin's face hardened. He stepped over the dead girl, stuck his face right into Vince's. 'You have to be fucking joking, Treadwell! This isn't your case, this isn't even your town any more. You were sent down here because you weren't wanted up there. You were sent down here to chase shadows. And, by the sounds of it, you've fucked that up, too. We're being billed for that broken crockery.' He pointed at the girl. 'This is real stuff, Treadwell. You're not in Soho now, with your imaginary crimes. Driving everyone fuckin' mad. Accusing good men of cover-ups. You're out your coma now, and this is the real fuckin' world. This is a real body, a real crime, real police business. And you're not wanted. And if you go anywhere near your brother, try to warn him, try to get him out of town, or try to help him in any way, shape or form, we'll know and we'll throw the book, the shelves, the fuckin' house at you!'

Vince knew that Machin wanted him to take a pop at him, chin him, give him his best shot. Because it would add to his woes. Vinnie 'clean face' Treadwell, loose cannon, rogue Old Bill. And Vince was sorely tempted. So he closed his eyes and rode the torrent out. And Machin carried on, wave after wave of pure, driven vitriol. Vince could feel Machin's breath on him: cigarettes, stale booze, *fresh* booze, salt and vinegar. It was making him feel sick.

'Jesus Christ!' bellowed Machin, stepping back, his back heel treading on the dead girl's hand. A sickening, wincing sound as a rigor-mortic finger snapped like a brittle twig.

'Easy, guv!' said Ginge, opening his mouth for the first time, before guiding his boss off the girl's hand.

'You fucking *freak*, Treadwell!' shouted Machin, whipping out a white handkerchief from his top pocket and wiping Vince's blood off his black brogues.

Vince looked down at his hand, which was bleeding. He'd dug his forefinger nail into the cut thumb he'd received from Vogel's smashed porcelain figures. He abruptly turned his back on them and walked out of there.

As he left, Machin shouted out, 'You're finished, Treadwell! Fucking finished!'

CHAPTER 19

POOR COW

Vince got into his car and drove to Adelaide Crescent. During the short drive, he tried to think about his brother. He tried to get worked up, sad, angry, heartbroken, whatever meaningful emotions you're supposed to have when your brother is accused of being responsible for the deaths of six people. But he couldn't. Vaughn was his brother, but in name only, it seemed. He had somehow slipped away from him. Vaughn's fate now seemed sealed, the logical conclusion to his life. It had been on the cards for years that this scenario would finally play out: Vince would have to confront his brother as a copper.

He parked up outside Bobbie's place and killed the engine. Then he clenched his fist and smashed it down on the steering wheel. Something came loose, either a bone in his hand or something in the steering column, he didn't care which. A new thought had struck him: how he had messed up and played right into their hands. It all felt like a set-up. Like he was being painted into a picture, by a greater hand at work, and he couldn't see his place in it. He felt as if he was banging his head against a brick wall – or, in this case, his hand on a steering wheel.

Vince glanced into the rear-view mirror just in time to catch sight of Bobbie walking up the street towards him. She was dressed formally, like the dead girl, but her outfit was the real thing. Expensively tailored Pierre Cardin, Yves St Laurent, the best that money could buy. Bobbie presented a stark contrast to the dead girl, one that divided the world up into its harsh component parts: the winners and the losers, the haves and the have-nots, the glamour pusses and the poor cows. The living and the dead.

Bobbie wore large black sunglasses that seemed to cover half her face like a mask. Her stride was brisk and he watched as she walked past, the clip of her heel gathering pace. She was obviously in a hurry. Her head down, she looked distracted as she ghosted past, so didn't spot him sitting in the car. Vince got out and called to her. She glanced around at him, unsmiling, then carried on walking.

Vince loped along the street to catch up with her. Even walking by her side, she still didn't look at him. From what was available to him of her face, he could tell she wasn't pleased to see him. Her lips were pursed and angry.

He grabbed her arm and stopped her walking. 'Tell me what's wrong?'

She grabbed her arm back and told him, 'Your brother. That's what's wrong!'

'You've heard?'

'I got a phone call ten minutes ago. I've been asked to go to the morgue to identify Wendy.'

Vince didn't recognize the name but knew it was the dead girl. 'I've just seen her.'

'They want me to identify her before they tell her mother what's happened.'

'Why you?'

'They found my number in her address book. It was circled,' said Bobbie, her voice still with a lacerating edge. 'She didn't have many friends, and it seems my number took pride of place. I'd told her she could call me if she needed help, if she needed a friend.'

'I'm sorry, Bobbie.'

'I'm sorry for you, too. For having a brother like . . .' her voice trailed off. She felt uneasy that the hatred she now felt for the man who had killed the girl could so easily transfer to his brother. 'Well, you can't pick your family, can you?' she rationalized. 'A bad deal all round, wouldn't you say?'

Vince agreed, but didn't say anything. Then he was hit by an idea. 'I need a favour.'

'What?' Bobbie was in no mood to be doing favours for any man.

'I want you to check if there's any bruising on her arms, or anywhere else on her body.' Bobbie looked confused. 'She'll be lying on a gurney, with a sheet over her body.' She searched his face for any sign that he was joking. Realizing it was no joke, she shook her head in disbelief. 'Vince, how am I supposed to do that? Don't they have rules for this kind of thing?'

'I'd go myself but, for obvious reasons, they don't want me anywhere near this new case. Or near Brighton for that matter. Machin's made it very clear that I'm not welcome.'

'What are you looking for?'

'Signs that she had the drug forced on her.'

'If you're trying to help your brother get away, then you'll rot in hell with him.'

Vince recoiled at the strong words that packed a vicious punch. He took a deep breath. 'Me and Vaughn aren't close, never were. To be honest, I think he hates me. And I think he's been heading for a long stretch all his life. It was bound to catch up with him. If he's guilty, then so be it. I hope he gets what's coming to him. But I don't think she injected that heroin herself. In fact, I don't think she's ever injected heroin in her life. And I don't think Vaughn did it either. And the reason I think he wouldn't is because he hasn't got it in him. And, to be more prosaic, he's never had a girlfriend before, not a real one, so killing the one girl he could find wouldn't be an option.'

Vince couldn't see Bobbie's eyes, but her jaw was set tight, defiant, fixed. Her lips were thinly drawn as her voice jabbed at him again. 'I'm going to have to stand alongside her poor old widowed mother. Her daughter was all she had. And everyone else seems to agree she wasn't much, but I liked her. Think about that too, whilst you're at it.'

Vince, on the ropes, just nodded. He knew he only had a stock answer for her, but she deserved more.

'I'll do what you want,' she said in a detached tone. 'Marks on her arms, you say?'

'Bruising anywhere.'

Bobbie gave him a curt nod and walked off.

'I'll call you.'

She carried on walking.

'Bobbie, I'm sorry.'

She stopped and turned around. 'Her name was Wendy . . . Wendy Hamilton. I think it's a nice name. Don't you?'

Yes, it was a nice name, he thought. It had a dignity about it. A dignity denied her in death.

'She deserved better, Vincent.'

Vince watched as she disappeared around the corner, then he uttered, 'The dead ones usually do.'

Vince stood in the phone box at the top of Palmeira Square. He dialled the operator, asking to be put through to Ray Dryden. In the time it took, Vince thought about his brother Vaughn. If he had a duty to, would he send his own flesh and blood to jail for the rest of his life, or worse? He didn't know, but he knew he now had to get to him before Machin did, to find out the truth. But what if the truth wasn't what he wanted to hear?

'Putting you through now, caller.'

Saved by the bell. The call clicked into place and broke off his dilemma.

'Ray Dryden.'

'Ray, it's me, Vince.'

'Hey, Vinnie boy, how's it going?'

'It's been better.'

'What's up?'

'I'll tell you later. Any news on Eddie Tobin?'

'I called your office, the number you gave me, got put through to a DC Marks. He said you'd gone back to London.'

That made sense, as DC Marks was Ginge. 'Forget that. Eddie Tobin?'

'He's in your neck of the woods.'

'What are you talking about?'

'I got his home number off Mickey Brice. You know him?'

'Brice of Vice, as the poem goes.'

'That's the fella. Brice and Tobin worked on the Messina brothers' case. I know his son, who works in admin at West End Central. He put me in touch. I told Brice that an ex-copper I know wanted to get back in touch with him because he was having a golf weekend—' *Beep-beep-beep.*

The pips went. Vince poured the last of his change into the slot, to keep the call alive. 'Make it quick, Ray, I'm on a meter here.'

'OK, Brice said that Tobin had bought a bungalow in Bournemouth. Nice place, swimming pool, the works. Didn't have the actual address, but he did have his number. I got his wife on the blower. Nice woman, very chatty – too chatty for Tobin's tastes, I imagine. She said that Eddie couldn't make it this weekend, as he was going down to Brighton on business. Even told me his hotel. The Grand.'

'Did she say what business?'

'No, she was too pissed off that he wasn't taking her with him! He's probably got a bird stashed away down there, or is taking one with him for a dirty weekend. What do you reckon?'

'Yeah, lots of dirty weekends in this town. Lots of coincidences, too.'

'Sounds like a pretty good one to me, Vince. This way you can bump into him, accidentally on purpose, without getting in trouble.'

'Yeah, pretty good.' Vince smiled to himself, then his voice dripped irony. 'And God forbid I should get in trouble.'

'What's going on down there, Vince—' *Beep-beep-beep.*

Saved by the bell again. 'I've gotta go, Ray. I'll call you.'

The phone went dead. Vince put the receiver back in its cradle, and backed out of the phone booth, with a righteous smile on his face.

CHAPTER 20

THE HEAD

The blood-red sun was dying in the sky, fading, falling and bleeding into the sea. Vince reached into the glove compartment and took out his sunglasses. He also took his hat off the back seat and put it on, snapping down the brim to obscure as much of his face as possible. If he'd had a false beard, he would have stuck that on too. He really didn't want to bump into Eddie Tobin in the lobby. He got out of the car, crossed the busy road, weaving through the traffic towards the hotel.

The Grand Hotel sat on the seafront, between the Palace and West piers, and it was as grand as it got in Brighton. Its white facade shimmering in the sun, looking out across the English Channel and maybe wishing it was on the other side, it wouldn't have looked out of place in any grand Mediterranean resort. As he approached the hotel, he thought this would have been a perfect gig for Terence, with his trusting face and nondescript demeanour, if only he hadn't now blown his cover. After the debacle on the dock, Vince had dropped Terence off at a bus stop without saying another word. Terence wisely kept his mouth shut, but Vince thought he detected a tear as Terence stepped out of the car.

Luckily, there was enough human traffic going in and out of the hotel for him to easily meld in. The lobby was busy: a wedding party, a bar-mitzvah and bank-holiday punters with enough money to stay at the best and enjoy caviar with their chips.

'Yes, sir?' said the girl behind the desk, wearing a fixed smile and too much make-up.

Vince talked fast. 'Hello to you. I'm here to meet a Mr Edward Tobin and I believe he's staying in the hotel.'

She looked at the register. 'He's not booked in yet, sir.'

'Has he not? Mmm.' Vince checked his watch with a troubled expression. 'He's late. I do hope he won't miss our appointment. He'd be so disappointed. Tell me, I forget, what room is he booked in to?'

'Penthouse suite.'

Penthouse suite? Not at all Tobin's style. And, at their prices, not within his pension plan either. 'He should have been here an hour ago,' said Vince looking flustered, while giving further examination to his watch.

'When he arrives, shall I tell him you called, Mr . . . ?' asked the receptionist.

'That would be fine. The penthouse suite, you say?'

'Yes, sir. What's your name again, sir?' she asked, picking up a pen to write it down.

'Shamus Shallanfalander.'

'Shal . . . ? Sorry sir, I didn't get that.' She looked up again to find Vince was gone.

'Swordfish.'

'Swordfish?' responded the voice. Even with only two syllables, four floors, and the intercom static between them, Vince could tell it was the Long Fellow, as he was buzzed into the Brunswick Sporting Club. Long George was waiting for him at the top of the stairs. He wanted a word in private and looked concerned.

'Boobalah!'

'Long George, I need a favour.'

Long George threw an avuncular arm around the young detective. 'What's all the tumult? I hear you've been making a nuisance of yourself. Treble Dutch Vogel?'

'That's the least of it. You heard about Vaughn?'

A mixture of sadness and disgust assembled itself on the tall fellow's face. 'It's a bad, bad business. That filth, that kaka-da-hoysen! I've always kept my mouth shut about your brother, out of respect for your mother. But he's got two character traits that go hand in hand: he's weak and he's foolish. If he's mixed up with that game, he deserves what he gets. There, I've said my piece!'

'And I agree. But there's big money in that game, Long George, so a lot of people get involved. A *lot*.'

Long George looked away. 'Much I know of such things!'

'I know you don't, but you know people who are involved. The gear that killed those three in Kemp Town and the others, it's still out there, Long George. My feeling is there's going to be a lot more of it still out there, too.' Long George shook his head in disgust. His conscience pricked, nevertheless. Vince knew how to play him. 'And who's dying but kids? You've got daughters, grandchildren.'

'They'd never touch that filth!' Long George was full of indignant rage at such a thought. 'And if they did, I'd cut their hands off!'

'There's big money in it, Long George. Bigger than in any other racket you care to mention. You think Jack Regent would pass that up?'

Long George knew the answer. His big, magnified eyes looked sad and tired. He sat down on the stairs with a wearisome sigh, as if dizzy from a world that was moving a little too fast for him. Vince sat down next to him, whereupon Long George's big eyes narrowed, instantly suspicious. Suddenly remembering that he was talking to a copper, and not to the kid who used to run bets for him at the races. 'Where's this leading? What do you want off me?'

'Murray the Head.'

Long George turned and put both of his big hands on Vince's shoulders, as if he was going to shake some sense into him. 'Murray? You fucking mashigina! He'd have nothing to do with this! He's a good, honest, respectable thief!' It was all said without an inch of irony.

'I know, I know,' said Vince reassuringly, while recoiling from the tall man's grip and wriggling himself free of those huge hands. 'I want to ask the Head a favour. It's on the up and up. I don't know him, but if *you* introduced us, he'll listen. Trust me, Long George.'

Ten minutes later, at the very top of the building, Vince sat at a card table in the private room reserved for the big games involving the high rollers. Murray the Head was seated opposite him. He was immaculate in an electric-blue, double-breasted suit, creases pressed razor sharp, an inch of perfectly folded white silk handkerchief poking out of the breast pocket, which matched his shirt; and a blue silk tie with hand-painted red dice detail. Always with the good-quality schmutter. Vince would lay odds that everything was monogrammed, too, from his socks to his handkerchief.

The Head lit a Pall Mall cigarette with a fluted gold Ronson lighter, then started the conversation. 'Any friend of Long George, whilst not automatically a friend of mine, I certainly consider worth some of my time.'

His voice was a product of careful adaptation: he was able to shift it around depending on the company he was keeping, between the penthouse and the pavement, and all of the social and class levels in between. Murray the Head swam with the tide of money and usually washed up in Bond Street auction houses, Belgravia town houses and Mayfair jewellers. The voice was as necessary a tool of his trade as a plunger was to a plumber. He used it to blend in with his environment, case it, then plunder it. He was as adroit at the sleight-of-hand and swift-of-tongue con as he was at scaling the rooftops and cracking safes.

Vince eyed the bald head, tanned and glimmering, then said, 'I was hoping you could do me a favour.'

Murray, matter-of-factly: 'What is it?'

The room was warm; the radiators must have been turned right up, because Vince was sweating. He felt it beading on his top lip. He shifted uncomfortably in his chair as he said, 'It's a job.'

'Can you be more specific?'

'It's a painting.'

'Does it belong to you?'

'If it did, I wouldn't be sitting here with you.'

The Head cogitated for the fat end of thirty seconds. He was never one to lead a conversation, especially an incriminating one, especially with a copper. He pulled back his chair and instructed Vince to stand up.

Vince did as he was told, whereupon the Head bent down on one knee and his well-manicured hands frisked him from sock to collar. It was a professional job.

'Now empty your pockets.'

Vince emptied his pocket paraphernalia on to the card table: wallet, cash, separate wallet for the police badge and car keys. The Head inspected the contents.

Vince, with his arms outspread, couldn't help but smile at the novel reversal of roles. 'Shouldn't I be doing this to you?'

'Carry on asking people to take property that doesn't belong to you, and you might have to get used to it, Detective.'

'What are you looking for, a tape?'

'You'd be surprised. These are dangerous times. They just popped a US President on his home turf. Then you got your H-bombs, Fidel Castro, cold wars . . . and some very good friends of mine have just been sent down for thirty years apiece. So excuse me if I seem a little paranoid when talking to a policeman about performing a robbery.'

Vince knew the friends he was referring to were the train robbers, but he didn't want to start getting into names.

'Did I ever tell you about the time I was approached by a Russian fellow in the Pillars of Hercules public house, and he asked me to obtain some very sensitive information on national security?'

It wasn't a question because they both knew the answer, and besides they'd never met each other before. But Vince played along in the spirit of cordiality, since he'd never met a seasoned villain who didn't have a good yarn to tell. 'No, Murray, you never did.'

'A certain Tory politician got caught with his trousers down in the company of some brass. Nothing unusual there, but what was unusual is that he'd filmed it. For posterity, I can only imagine. But the brass was also having it off with this Russian fellow, a diplomat who was sidelining for the KGB. He knew about the film and wanted it. And he was prepared to pay top rouble for it. The Russki taped our whole conversation with a device secreted in a Swan Vesta matchbox. Unbelievable what they can get up to these days. Whatever next, you have to ask yourself.'

Vince knew he was talking about the Profumo case, but again didn't want to start getting into names.

Satisfied Vince wasn't a cut-price James Bond, the Head sat down again as if nothing had happened. He then reached into his breast pocket and pulled out the white silk handkerchief with a flourish. 'You're schvitzing like a kipper,' he said, offering it to Vince.

Vince eyed the handkerchief as though it was too good to mop sweat with. The Head gave him a slight smile, and nod of encouragement. Vince took it and did the necessary. 'It's certainly warm in here.'

'I like the heat.'

'I imagined it would be monogrammed,' said Vince, inspecting the silk handkerchief before handing it back to the Head.

'Why would I want to put my name over everything?' he said, putting it back in his breast pocket. 'Like I said, any friend of Long George's. So tell me about it.'

Vince then laid out the caper. He described the painting and where he thought it was stashed. But he left out certain specifics like names, and why a policeman would be stealing a painting, and what he was going to do with it. And, to the Head's professional credit, he never asked. The Head just listened, weighing up the proposition.

'Mmm. It doesn't seem like that tough a job. Lock might pose a problem, but nothing you yourself couldn't handle. Why don't you do it yourself?'

Vince, appealing to his professional vanity, replied, 'I'm not a pro and I don't want to take any chances. If the painting's in the room, I want it here in my hand. And I know you're the best person to put it there.'

'That's about as true as a true thing gets,' said the Head, with a solid smile on his face. 'Shouldn't be a problem. The security, the locks, a piece of cake. And I'm already well acquainted with the layout of penthouse suites at the Grand.'

'I bet you are.'

The Head placed one tanned hand on the green-baize card table. He inspected his nails, obviously admiring them. They looked as if they meant more to him than the two rocks he was wearing, one on each pinkie finger, and they gleamed almost as much.

'So, my young detective friend, I know what I'm gonna steal. I know how I'm gonna steal it. All I gotta know now is why I'm gonna steal it.'

'I need the painting because—'

'Dat dat dat.' The Head held up a halting palm. 'Why you need the painting is none of my concern. My concern is, why should I get it for *you* of all people?'

Vince nodded in appreciation of the thief's concerns. 'Zsa Zsa Gabor ring any bells?'

'She's an actress – and not a very good one, at that. But nice to look at, all the same.'

'Yeah, and now she's light of a suite of diamonds, lifted from a hotel on the Riviera. Nice tan you've got there, Murray.'

The Head smiled, cat and mouse. 'Maybe some diamonds did come my way when I was on the Riviera, I really couldn't say. And, more importantly, neither can you.'

'I have a pal works for Interpol, name's Dryden. Ray Dryden. I can remove your name from the Zsa Zsa Gabor caper.'

'My name's not on the Zsa Zsa Gabor caper.'

Vince smiled, didn't say a word. Didn't have to. They both knew the Head's name was only a phone call away. 'But it's not all bad news, Murray. If your name comes up again, I'll make sure, as long as no one gets hurt and it's all covered by the insurance, you'll get another pass. *And*, furthermore, any money from the painting, you can have.'

'How much?'

'The man who wants to buy it is ready to go all the way. *You* negotiate it.'

The Head weighed this up. 'So, essentially you're giving me a tip about a painting that I can keep after you've done what you need to do with it?'

'Correct.'

'And you don't want it?'

'Correct.'

'Or any of the profit I make from it?'

'Correct.'

'And, more importantly, I'll have a man in Interpol watching my back should such an occasion arise?'

'Correct.'

'So, should such an occasion arise and I was to get pinched over a piece of work, hypothetically, of course, because we both know that such an occasion would not arise, I'd get a pass?'

'Correct.'

'Mmm, money in the bank,' he crooned contentedly. He then narrowed his eyes and refocused on Vince. 'What exactly do *you* get out of it?'

Vince's mouth slipped into a knowing smile. 'I've got a hunch that if the shoe was on the other foot, you wouldn't tell me, would you, Murray?'

'Correct.'

Vince and Murray the Head were sitting in Vince's car outside the Grand. Eddie Tobin had booked into the hotel twenty minutes ago. Vince had already concluded that they needed a decoy. The Head concurred and provided one, the statuesque redhead Vince had seen at his side at the races: Valerie the Volcano. Her reputation and the gags were plentiful and obvious: when she blew, you knew about it. Not far off six foot in her stockinged feet, with flame-red hair, she was stunning in a sexually unmanageable way. No one could handle Valerie, simply too hot. Of Scottish extraction and male distraction, born and bred under the sound of Bow bells and wolf whistles. Fiery, feisty, full-lipped, long-lashed with cheekbones that just didn't give up. Broad of shoulder and beam, providing an hour-glass figure you'd happily spend your finest sixty minutes watching, and fortified with biblical bosoms that heaved and hoed with every breathless coo and sigh, the Volcano oozed sex and heat. But she was the Vesuvius you could not mount – because she was the property of Murray the Head.

The Head had tamed her, taught her and cultivated her with diamonds, furs and the good life. She was his muse, his benchmark for taste. He wouldn't steal anything unless the Volcano could carry it off. And carry it off she did, with stolen jewels stashed away in her backcombed beehive, her heaving cleavage, or places too sweet and sweaty to mention, as she sashayed her way through various airports, customs stops and Checkpoint Charlies.

Ten minutes after Eddie Tobin had checked into the hotel, she stepped out of the car and into her position at the hotel bar. The way the Head and Vince figured it, Tobin, who liked a drink and was probably having his whole stay here paid for, would mosey on down to the bar before dinner. There the Volcano, the Venus flytrap, would be waiting to snag him up in conversation and promises, and keep him enthralled for as long as it took to let the Head get into his room, search the place and procure the painting. Back in the bar, Tobin, thinking he was on for a night of rapture and eruption with the Volcano, would then receive a slap across the chops and hear, *'What kind of girl do you take me for?'* ringing in his ears with indignant rage as he watched her shimmy out of the bar and straight into the arms of the Head, exiting the hotel with the painting concealed about his person.

The Head checked his platinum Cartier Tank watch. 'Meet me at midnight in the Brunswick,' he said, eyes still on his watch.

Vince checked his own watch, neither platinum nor Cartier, and not stolen. It was only 8.30 p.m. 'Will it take that long?'

'Maybe, maybe not. Either way, midnight's got a nice ring to it. Better than quarter past ten.'

Vince watched the Head saunter over to the Grand Hotel, then rotate out of view through the revolving door.

Vaughn was happy, or as happy as any man walking in tight shoes could be. His suede, tasselled loafers were on his feet and his wizened flowers were in his hand, and his head and body oozed the comfort and concord that only Chasing the Dragon could provide. He reckoned that he'd missed meeting Wendy at the station, but he still had a few quid in his pocket, so he put it to good use. Instead of walking on his throbbing feet or catching a bus, he got into a cab and headed home to Waterloo Street.

On the ride home, he thought firstly about his new shoes. He'd stuff the loafers with damp newspaper overnight, which would loosen them up and take away the pain. Then he thought about an excuse to fob his girl off with, as to why he'd missed meeting her train. Easygoing, gullible or trusting as she was, she'd swallow any reason he thought up. So he soon went back to thinking about his shoes.

As the cab swung into Waterloo Street, he noticed a small crowd gathered near his flat, so he asked the driver to slow down. As the cab eased past the basement flat, he saw two uniformed coppers posted at the entrance to the steps, and a black vehicle parked right outside. He'd seen these before: black and ominous allowing enough room for one fully outstretched passenger in the rear for a ride you didn't want to take: destination the morgue.

Vaughn froze in the back seat, as stiff as a corpse himself, as the rigor mortis of a grim realization set in. When the cabbie asked where he wanted dropping off, Vaughn, his mind racing but going nowhere, chose as far away as his remaining funds would take him.

CHAPTER 21

A NAKED GIRL AND A GUN

Vince took out the spare key that Bobbie had given him and twirled it in the lock, but the door was already open. He stepped into the vestibule, checked the newly replaced lock, and saw that it was on the latch. Sensing something was wrong, Vince bolted up the stairs to Bobbie's apartment. Quietening his breath, he tried the door handle, found it was locked. He therefore unlocked it and stepped cautiously over the threshold. The room was in total darkness, the heavy curtains drawn.

Vince carefully closed the door behind him, found the light switch beside the door and threw it. He headed through to the living room, then jumped back as his heart jackknifed. Bobbie stood before him with a gun gripped in both hands. She was naked.

Vince's first reaction was to put his hands up, as the gun was solidly trained on him. Her legs were slightly apart for better balance, as if she was about to fire off a shot. As guns went it was big, and it looked huge in her delicate hands.

Voice hushed, he tried, 'Bobbie . . . ?'

No reply. She stood transfixed, didn't move.

He looked into her eyes: they were wide open, intently focused. He took a half step to the side. They stayed focused, but not on him; instead on the spot he had just vacated. He carried on side-stepping, as silent as a crab on wet sand, until he was now over to the side of her, but about five feet away. Still she didn't move. Her eyes remained wide, too wide, their natural almond shape disfigured into unblinking saucers. Her body was unflinching, as if caught in a trance, witnessing a ghost in her sights. As Vince edged towards her, he realized she was in the grip of some terrible nightmare.

His first thought was not to wake her, having heard that you must never wake a sleepwalker, since the shock might kill them. He'd also heard that if you dream about falling from a tall building and you hit the deck, you never wake up. He didn't believe that; it was just a piece of nocturnal nonsense that some dozy chump had dreamed up – for how could anyone live to tell the tale? All the same, he wasn't going to take the chance.

His second thought was to get the gun out of her hand. He'd heard they fired bullets that could kill you – that he knew for a fact! Two more paces and he was by her side. He could feel her breath on his cheek, like short bursts of warm exhaust. He put his arm gently around her waist. She smelled sweet, almost sickly sweet, reminded him of—

'*Ahhhh!*' She let out a scream. It was genuinely piercing, because it was only about an inch from his ear. He grabbed both her hands and shook the gun out of them, gathered her up, eyes following where the gun was landing and keeping them out of the way of its muzzle. The gun landed where he wanted it to: on a heavy floor cushion by her side. It did a bounce, a little somersault, then flopped on to the heavy Persian rug. A satisfactorily soft landing, with no sudden jolts and no bullets discharged.

Vince held Bobbie tightly. Her eyes were now closed, her face scrunched up as if to make sure they stayed that way. There was fight in her body, but Vince wouldn't allow it freedom to express itself. He held her tight and close, overwhelmed by the desire to protect her. He whispered softly in her ear, 'It's OK, it's OK, baby, it's OK, it's me, baby, it's me . . .'

He didn't know if these words would soothe or anger her, considering the way they had left things that same afternoon. He needn't have worried, though, for she wrapped herself around him so tight that her feet were almost lifted off the floor. He carried her over to the pouting Mae West red-lip sofa. She was entwined around him. She wouldn't let go. And he didn't want her to. Her hair was damp, her body glistened with a sheen of sweat; it was as if she had just stepped out of the shower. But her scent wasn't fresh; it was sweet, ripe, syrupy and sickly all at the same time. That was a smell he knew he would never forget, a smell that would be on constant recall. On her arms and around her body she had elongated red marks like tiger stripes, where she must have tossed and turned as the nightmare twisted and tightened its hold, the silk sheets wrapping around her like ropes, fettering her to the four-poster bed until she finally broke free . . .

And then the gun . . . *the gun?*

On the sofa she gripped him tightly, till it felt as though she was welded underneath him. He grabbed her hair, pulled back her head, tugging her face away from his chest, and softly he licked her lips. Eyes still closed, she smiled, yet her mouth looked twisted, deceitful, arrogant. Vince had known this was going to happen from the moment he'd lit her cigarette in the Blue Orchid. As their hands touched, they had flinched, as a charge passed between them, alerting them both to the inevitable. And here they were now, both naked, as she wrapped herself around him.

His hands gripped her hair. She bit into his lip. He pulled his mouth away from hers so he could study her face as they built up a rhythm. He wanted to look at her. Observe her. Soak up every moment. Have it seared visually in his memory like a painting, and not just the physical sensations coursing through his body: her face, her breasts, her hips, that smooth damp belly, the mound of her vagina pushing into his crotch. The way he held her, dominating her, seemed brutal but she was complicit, eyes still closed, as if asleep, but so wide awake, so very alive. Vince closed his own eyes, put his mouth back to hers, felt the scrape of teeth as they found each other, melded together and came.

Vince stood naked in the living room. The gun was in his hand. It was a Smith & Wesson, a big heavy black thing. It was jammed up and rusted, hadn't been oiled or used for an age, so he couldn't even tell if it was loaded. He didn't like guns. Didn't like the feel of them or what they did. He carried it over to the big black bureau, opened a drawer and put it inside.

He then padded back into the bedroom and slipped under the sheets alongside Bobbie. She was fully awake: arms outstretched behind her, gripping the struts of the headboard, a sated smile transforming her face. The bad dream was vanquished, the memory of what they'd just done still fresh.

'The gun – is that the one your husband was given to look after?'

She didn't look at him, but said languidly, 'Don't say that.'

'Say what?'

'Husband.'

'Well, you are still married.'

'What is the statute of limitations on that?'

'There isn't. There's only death and divorce.'

She smiled and said, 'I'll look into the latter.'

'Keep messing with guns, you'll be looking at the former. Is it loaded?'

'I've never used it.'

'Don't try. If it is loaded, it'll blow up in your face. Want to tell me about it?'

'The gun? I don't know anything about—'

'The dream.'

'Oh, the nightmare.'

'The nightmare.'

'The usual,' she sighed, closing her eyes. She was obviously used to it and bored with it. It held no surprises for her now. It was just tiring – truly tiring – and no longer terrifying. Or that's what she told herself, unconvincingly, whenever she awoke from it. Dismissing it thus helped to take the power out of it.

'Who was climbing the stairs this time, Jack or your father?'

Her eyes opened and, still looking up at the stripy canopy, she pointedly said, 'Stepfather.'

'Sorry, stepfather. Well . . . ?'

She thought about it, then turned to him. 'You.'

'*Me?*'

'Well, you were the one who walked through the door.'

'I'm your nightmare?'

'No. My dreamboat.' Bobbie leaned forward and bit him on the nose, then pretended to kiss it better. She sat up, reached over to the bedside table, and fished a cigarette out of the packet that lay in a heavy crystal ashtray along with her lighter. With the curtains open, there was enough moonlight for Vince to examine her body: svelte, flawless, taut skin, nipples like bullets, no unsightly bulges or ripples. She then glanced around and caught him looking. She smiled, confident in her nakedness, knowing she looked good, knowing she didn't have to grab at the sheets to cover herself. She lit up the cigarette, took the heavy crystal ashtray and rested it on Vince's chest. Bobbie took a long drag of the cigarette, lay back and exhaled slowly, sending a jet of smoke up into the canopy. 'To be honest,' she said reflectively, 'I don't know who it was, because I woke up. I always wake up.'

'Do you always sleepwalk?'

'Sometimes.' She then creased her brow, as if puzzled by her own actions. 'But it's the first time I've woken up with a gun in my hand. I forgot I even had it. Jack didn't know about it, and he certainly wouldn't have been happy about it. He didn't keep a gun in the house in case the place was searched.' She took another long draw of the cigarette and blew out three perfectly formed smoke rings to join the gathering fog above them.

Vince watched them float up and smiled. He'd never seen a girl do that before; it was considered a boy's trick. The smoke hung

227

in the airless room, swirling around, encircling them. It gave the bed, the room, the moment, an ethereal feel.

Staring up at those clouds of smoke, Bobbie said, 'They say that if you dream you're falling from a great height, say Beachy Head, and if in your dream you hit the ground, you never wake up. Although, how the hell would they know that?'

Vince smiled. *Great minds* . . . 'More pertinently,' he said, 'I heard that if you shoot people who walk through doors, you swing for it.'

'But I was asleep.'

'Technically you were, but by the time the police arrived, there was a good chance you'd be awake.'

'Sleepwalking, that's a good alibi. I'll remember that one.' She kissed him. 'I wouldn't shoot you. You're far too gorgeous.' She stubbed out the half-smoked cigarette, took the crystal ashtray and put it back on the bedside table and lay back next to him. Her fingertips glided over the smooth firmness of his chest and shoulders, over the defined ridges of his biceps. She could feel him tense as her hand passed over him, as she had known all men react when touched: chest out, stomach in. She smiled at their predictable vanity, and settled her head on his chest.

'Did you see the girl, Wendy?' asked Vince solemnly.

Bobbie let out a slow, sad sigh. 'I saw her. And your friend Machin was there. He made some snide comments about you, so I've got the feeling he knows about us.'

'I guarantee he does,' Vince said, without any surprise. 'He's probably had me followed ever since I got here. Tell me about Wendy, though.'

'It was horrible. Machin wouldn't let me touch her and, to be honest, I'm glad. I don't think I even could have. I'm sorry.'

'It's OK.'

'Do you know what was so horrible about it?'

'I saw her, Bobbie. I know what you mean.'

'No, you don't. They'd obviously cleaned her up, brushed her hair, tried to make . . . to make her look presentable, I suppose.

What was so horrible was that she looked as if she belonged there. She seemed at peace – like she was always meant to be dead.'

Vince withdrew his arm from around Bobbie's shoulder. The luminous markers on his watch told him it was ten past midnight. 'Shit!' he said, throwing back the sheets and springing out of bed.

'Where are you going?'

He ran out to the living room where his discarded clothes lay. Bobbie sat up and called out, 'Vincent!'

'Got an appointment with Murray the Head!' he said, pulling on his trousers.

'The Head?!'

'Yeah, you know him?'

'Of course! I know his girlfriend, too!'

'The Volcano?!'

Vince was almost dressed when Bobbie came into the living room. She sat on the arm of a chair and watched him slide his broad shoulders into his jacket, then said, 'Valerie, she's quite a character.'

Vince looked around and noticed she was wearing Jack's mono-grammed towelling robe. That nettled him. He wondered why she still wore it, did it still hold his smell? Did it remind her of him? Bring him closer to her?

'Why are you seeing Murray?' she asked.

Vince headed for the front door. 'I'll tell you when I get back. I won't be long.' He turned around and looked at her, unable to hide his irritation. 'That robe, it looks ugly on you.'

She frowned, then glanced down at the big embroidered initials, *JR*, as if noticing them for the first time. She had unthink-ingly grabbed it off the back of the bedroom door where it hung. But she understood his irritation, knowing how she would have felt the same if the shoe was on the other foot.

CHAPTER 22

THE VOLCANO

'Swordfish!'

'Ahhch! Enough! We've changed the password!' replied the static voice of Long George, over the intercom.

Vince cursed under his breath then growled impatiently, 'I've got no time for this, Long George. Let me in!'

'A clue. We're still keeping it fishy, but we're going Kosher!'

'Er . . . spring mops? Salted herrings? Lox?'

Crackling over the intercom, as Long George laughed. 'Gefilte fish, you schmendrick! The new password is Gefilte—'

'*Gefilte fish!*'

Vince entered the top-floor room to find Murray the Head sitting at a card table. No surprise there. What was surprising was what he was doing. His right hand was spread out on the green baize, while his left hand held a small brush with which the Head was carefully painting his nails. A bottle of clear nail varnish sat next to an emery board, which in turn sat next to a small pile of powdered nail.

'You're late,' said the Head, not looking up from his paint job.

Un-fucking-believable, thought Vince as he watched the Head deep in concentration. 'Sorry, Murray. What colour is that?'

'It's transparent,' he replied, glancing up at Vince to administer an admonishing look. 'What do you take me for?' Vince's return expression was that of a blank canvas. The Head focused back on the job 'at hand'. 'Just puts a nice shine on them. You can tell a lot about a man from his hands, Detective.'

'Yeah, I know. And I can also tell you haven't done an honest day's work in your life. Whilst we're talking about paint jobs, you got it?'

'Wouldn't be sitting here, if I didn't.'

Vince gave the room a cursory scope, but saw nothing that looked like the purloined painting. 'Where is it?'

'Sit down. What's your rush?'

Vince sat down at the table, his back to the door. Not his favourite position in these circumstances, but it was the only available chair.

The Head admired his handiwork, then daintily put the brush back in its pot and screwed it securely shut. He blew the nail powder off the table. Fanned his hands up in front of his face, puckered his lips and dried his nails with a steady stream of breath.

'Everything go OK?'

'Like a dream. Your mark, Tobin, went to the bar, Valerie sashayed over, worked her magic and kept the mug tied up for an hour. She let the poetry happen, had him eating out of her hand: marriage proposals, foreign travel, breakfast at Tiffany's. He was falling all over himself to impress, claimed he was connected to a big player in Soho with friends in show business, movie business, music business. Name of Duval – you know him?'

'You know that I know him, Murray.'

'You didn't tell me Tobin was an ex-copper.'

'You didn't ask. I'm surprised he blabbed.'

'When the Volcano works a fella, they blab, they give her their whole life story. They volunteer information they didn't even know they had, just to smell the air around her, get lost in her eyes, dream about those lips and stare at those tits.'

'I bet. Are you going to put a full point on the end of all this?'

'My point is, I don't want to get in bad with the bogies. I want to be in *good* with the bogies. That's why I did what I did, Detective Treadwell.'

'Eddie Tobin's retired. He now does some muscle work for Duval. He's as much used to you as a back pocket in a sock. Me? I'm still gainfully in Her Majesty's constabulary.'

'But not in good standing, I hear.'

'What do you hear?'

'That you were sent down to Brighton because of some discrepancies in something that may or may not have occurred.'

Vince weighed up how much the Head knew. And realized the most important thing, he didn't know the truth. So he played it cooler than a big old bowl of gazpacho.

'That's what the painting's for – to put me back in good standing. Good standing better than ever. Do you have it or not?'

The Head contemplated the young detective. Whatever he saw there, it must have passed muster, because he called out, 'Valerie!'

Vince heard the door open, and glanced around to see the Volcano framed in the doorway. A curvaceous peg in a square hole.

'How are you, sweetie?'

'I'm good, Valerie,' said Vince, while doing what she wanted, what her presence and figure demanded: giving her the once-over – twice! There was a costume change since he had seen her last. She had become more demure since her date with Tobin. That outfit had been borderline obscene: a black, sheer spray-on job with strategically placed embroidered fig-leaf details – Vince counted three of them. This outfit was tame in comparison: a clinging emerald-green gown to go with her eyes and set alight the flame-red hair; with a neckline that swooped, swooped, then swooped some more; and when the swooping was done, just for the hell of it, swooped again. If the painting was concealed about her person, he didn't know where, or even dare to think.

Vince ventured, 'So . . . where's it stashed?'

'Frisk me and find out.'

Vince looked back to the Head for counsel.

The Head gave the Volcano the nod. Before Vince could look around, a freckled and fleshy arm wrapped itself around his shoulder, her wrist holding a diamond, emerald and ruby bracelet, her flawless fingers docking some serious rocks that wouldn't have looked out of place on a movie star . . . say, Zsa Zsa Gabor? She placed a rolled-up canvas on the table. Vince smelled her cocktail breath on him as she leaned in and nuzzled his neck. She worked her way around to his ears and sniffed him some more. Vince kept on looking at the Head, who was smiling not winningly but knowingly, showing his full set of smoker's ivory-coloured teeth.

The Volcano purred, 'Mmm . . . Chanel No. 5. Had you down more as a Guerlain man. Reminds me of a certain little lady I know. One Bobbie LaVita.'

Vince kept looking at the Head, who kept smiling and show-ing him his teeth.

'Bobbie sends her regards,' said Vince.

The Volcano moved around and sat on the table, blocking Vince's view of the Head. 'She's a sweetie, too. I had the hots for her myself. She doesn't play, though. And Murray is so old-fashioned that way, aren't you, baby?'

The disembodied voice of the Head came through: 'I don't mind you dyking off, baby plum, just as long as I'm in the room when it happens.' He leaned around the fleshpot partition, winked at Vince and announced, 'She likes you. Valerie the Volcano and Bobbie LaVita? Now that's a picture worth painting. Better than the shit I just lifted.'

The Volcano, not taking her eyes off Vince, who in turn couldn't take his eyes off her cleavage, because it was parked right in front of him, licked her cherry-red lips and said, 'That can be arranged, Murray. How about you, gorgeous?'

Vince sat as far back in his chair as possible without causing offence. He didn't nod, because it would have been like a fly nosing into the Venus trap; he'd never get out. 'Is this the per-missive society I've been reading about?' he asked.

The Volcano gave a chesty, breast-juddering laugh. 'I like him, Murray!' she said, running her fingers through Vince's black hair. 'He looks like Tony Curtis.' Her finger then traced his profile, running down his smooth forehead, his nose, flicking his bottom lip, then moving around the dimple that sat in the centre of his chin. 'Or is he more of a Kirk Douglas?'

Vince, far from impervious to the Volcano's ample charms, was getting hot under the collar. He did a nervous clearing of his throat, and said, 'Sounds like I'm in *Spartacus*, whoever I am.'

Vince heard a slap, flat palm against satin. Valerie jolted, sat bolt upright, twisted around to the Head and glared. 'Murray!' He'd just slapped the ample yet delectable derrière that was spilling over on to his side of the table.

'You're embarrassing the boy, sugar plum.'

The Volcano took it for what it was: her cue to dismount the table. Vince took it for what it was: playtime was over, back to business. The Head had stopped smiling and fixed Vince with a firm but benevolent gaze. 'You're playing with fire, my young friend.'

'Tobin's no trouble, Murray. Let me handle him.'

'I'm not talking about Tobin. I'm talking about Jack. He likes that girl, likes her a lot.'

'Did he tell you that?'

'Yeah, downstairs, five minutes ago.'

Vince's heart jumped into his mouth. The Head wasn't smiling.

'Murray, don't tease the boy,' said the Volcano.

'I like the boy, baby plum. I'm just doing him a favour. Giving him the SP.'

With his heart out of his mouth and back in its designated spot, Vince said, 'Thanks for your concern. I was working on the theory known as "out of sight out of mind".'

The Head sucked at his teeth. 'Some theory. I hope it works for you. Anyways, it's your business. And our business is concluded. I've done my part, just need to make sure you keep up your end of the deal.' The Head reached into the inside pocket of his jacket and took out a box of Swan Vesta matches and put it carefully on the table.

Vince frowned. Then he cracked a wide smile, devoid of mirth, indicating just disbelief and a question: 'You're fucking kidding me?'

'Would I kid you?' Murray said, sliding open the sleeve of the yellow box. Inside were matches – or, on closer inspection, a plastic facade of matches.

Vince leaned forward for a closer inspection.

The Head dipped in a freshly varnished finger and something clicked into place, and the device started . . .

'. . . A certain Tory politician got caught with his trousers down in company with some brass. Nothing unusual there. What was unusual is that he'd filmed it. For posterity, I can only imagine. But the brass was also having it off with the Russian fellow, a diplomat who was sidelining for the KGB. He knew about the film and wanted it. And he was prepared to pay top rouble for it. The Russki taped our whole conversation in a device secreted in a Swan Vesta matchbox . . .'

Vince had heard enough, and the Head switched the device off.

'Bang to rights, I'd say if I was criminally minded. Which I am. Did I neglect to mention that I picked the Russian's pocket after our little tête-à-tête? Well, I couldn't have him walking around with my voice in a matchbox, could I? Never know whose hands it might fall into. You just can't trust people these days. Just in case you're wondering, I didn't get that film for the Russki. I'll be a monkey's uncle before I start doing dirty work for the commies. I'm a free-market patriot at heart.'

'That's good to hear, Murray,' replied a distracted Vince, more worried now about his own localized predicament than international affairs. 'You didn't trust me?' he asked.

'Don't take it personal. I don't trust anyone.'

'I trusted *you*, Murray.'

'And that's your problem, kid. You trust too much. Should have frisked me.'

Vince reached over to pick up the Swan Vesta box – not going for the fast grab, but fast enough to feel a muzzle of cold steel at the nape of his neck. He realized that the Volcano was now behind him holding a gun.

'The Head painting his nails, and the Volcano with a shooter,' observed Vince. 'What a turn up.'

'We're nothing if not different down here,' she said.

'Second time I've had a gun pulled on me by a woman today. The first one was naked.'

'That can be arranged, sweetie.'

'What do you want, Murray?'

The Head weighed it up, then nonchalantly replied, 'What we all want in this life: some peace of mind. So I'm just showing you the little insurance policy I took out, which will pay for that little peace of mind. Just in case you experience a sudden case of the uncorruptibles and forget that this little caper ever took place.'

'I won't forget. You have my word.'

The Volcano ran a playful finger through Vince's hair and said, 'I believe him, sugar.'

The Head's eyes narrowed in judgement, then he quickly concluded, 'Me too, babycakes.' He pocketed the Swan Vesta box.

'We done?' asked Vince.

'And dusted.'

Vince felt the cold muzzle of the gun withdraw. He collected the rolled-up canvas from the table. 'Like I said, when I'm finished with this, Murray, you get to keep the painting. I'll drop it off with Long George.'

'Forget it. I don't like the painting. More importantly, the Volcano doesn't like it – thinks it's sordid. And she's a broad-minded woman.'

'Very.'

Vince stood up and made for the exit. The Volcano was already at the door and opened it for him, saying, 'Take care, sweetie, and give my regards to Bobbie LaVita.' Before he could reply, she puckered up her plump red lips and planted a big fat kiss full on his mouth.

CHAPTER 23

ROOM SERVICE

Vince had parked outside the Grand Hotel. Back in the car, he'd unrolled the canvas and was now looking at the painting. Up close, full size, and in the flesh, as it were. Vince's thoughts on the painting were the same as Max Vogel's: it made his skin crawl. But his disgust wasn't born out of a cold analytical critique; it was because he knew where it came from and where it was going. And what it had inspired. He'd seen it made flesh, screaming up at him from the silver screen, begging for mercy, for help, for *his* help. And he'd been unable to give it. On reflection, that's what disgusted him the most, because he too had became a voyeur – just another man watching her demise.

He rolled the painting up roughly, not caring if it incurred any damage, and stashed it under his seat. He was about to get out of the car when he saw a cab pull up, and Tobin stepping out with a woman. Vince realized that Tobin hadn't yet discovered that the painting was missing.

After the Volcano had left him, he must have gone in search of a replacement. She was obviously a brass, and a cheap one at that. The Volcano had evidently set off something in Tobin, something that needed to be sated. Unable to have the real thing, he'd settle for an out-of-the-bottle redhead, a second-rate parody who looked as if she spent most of her time in the bottle, too. Her hair was not so much a beehive as a bird's nest, and the heavy make-up covering up a hard life looked as if it had been trowelled on during a power cut. And, to add to her considerable woes, Tobin was now at her elbow, pulling her out of the cab, pushing her up the steps, and dragging her rapidly through the hotel lobby. He didn't see Vince sitting in the car because Vince had ducked down, just in case. But there was no need for that. Tobin kept his head bowed, his hat pulled down, collar up. He wasn't proud of his companion and wanted to get her up to his room with the minimum amount of attention.

Vince made his way into the hotel lobby just in time to see Tobin yanking his companion into the lift. Poor thing wasn't even getting a nightcap in the bar. Vince pulled a wicked grin and, with a spring in his step, headed briskly back to his car and retrieved his camera from the glove compartment.

Five minutes later, he was standing outside Tobin's room, with his Leica M2 ready in his hand. Vince put his ear to the door and heard voices. High-pitched and whiny, the brass was running through her available services: what she would do, what she wouldn't do, and what she might do if the price was right. Everything sounded negotiable: even the stuff she said she definitely would not do sounded as if it might be done for the appropriate money. Either way, whatever Tobin was planning hadn't started yet.

Satisfied that they were both in a state of undress, Vince rapped on the door and pulled out of the hat a last-minute, ill-conceived and improvised voice; not much different from his normal one, just pitched a couple of octaves higher and suffused in subservience: 'Room service, courtesy of Mr Eton.'

Vince heard Tobin's muttered swearing, but didn't hear him questioning the courtesy of his host. And if Vince had any lingering doubts about the deal taking place, they were now fully confirmed.

'At this time of night?' Tobin demanded.

'Oh, it's no trouble, sir. Mr Eton said we were to take care of your every need, and he thought you and your lady wife would enjoy a nightcap.'

There was a cackle of laughter from the brass, then Tobin responded with, 'I don't want it!'

'It's free, sir. Free champagne,' said Vince, getting further into his role and settling into his new voice which was becoming foreign, fruity and a little Peter Lorre. Vince heard the girl protesting that she wanted the free champagne. He rather suspected she *needed* the free champagne. Still with his ear to the door, Vince heard Tobin cursing under his breath.

The door opened, offering a perfect snap. Cecil Beaton couldn't have hoped for a better composition. Foreground: Tobin stood framed in the doorway, late fifties, ex-muscle gone flabby, his midriff hanging over a hotel towel. Background: the brass sprawling on the about-to-be-pummelled bed in red bra and panties, sucking on a cigarette and reeking of toilet water.

Vince stood back, saying 'Cheese' and took the shot.

Tobin slammed the door shut. Vince heard the brass asking what was wrong, whereupon Tobin told her to 'Shut the fuck up!'

Vince called out, 'Eddie, we need to talk.'

A muffled voice could be heard, the brass's. Tobin had now obviously shut her up with his hand. Then twenty seconds later came his vexed tones: 'I'm warning you, Treadwell, get out of here or I'm calling Tony Machin. I've got friends in this town, more than you do, you little prick!'

'I don't doubt it for a second, Eddie. You're a very likeable fella. Very likeable and pliable, so you're bound to make friends. Be my guest, call Machin. Let's have it all on the up and up. Think about it, Eddie. You think I took the photo just to stick your ugly mug on the wall next to Brigitte Bardot? What would the real Mrs Tobin think when it comes out that you've been entertaining two-bob brasses?'

'Bleedin' cheek . . .' came a high-pitched protest, soon muffled.

Tobin threatened, 'I've got a gun, Treadwell. What do you want?'

'Relax, Eddie. I'm not interested in your love life. It's the painting I'm interested in. The painting that I've got.'

Vince heard Tobin scrambling about in a panic, looking under the bed, he suspected. Then another 'Shut the fuck up' to the sadly put-upon brass. Then a compilation of curses followed by a baying mantra of: '*Fuck! fuck! fuck!*'

'Stand back from the door, Treadwell!'

Vince stood back obediently, thinking Tobin was going to do something stupid, like fire the gun. The door opened and the brass was propelled out, clutching her clothes.

'What the bleedin' hell's going on?!'

Vince badged her silently.

'I'm a good girl, I am. Just trying to earn a living.'

He pocketed his badge and said, 'You're OK.'

'I've never been treated like this.'

'That I doubt. You been paid?'

She nodded.

'Then you've had a result, so vamoose.'

She 'vamoosed' down the hall, disappearing around the corner to where the not so private dressing room of the lift awaited.

'OK, Treadwell, what d'you want?'

'Only to talk. Then you get the painting back.'

Silence.

Vince knocked on the door. 'Eddie?'

'Meet me downstairs in the bar.'

'Be better in private.'

'In the bar, Treadwell!'

'OK, nice and public. What are you drinking these days, Eddie? Still too much?'

'I wouldn't accept a drink from you, you poncified little prick!'

Vince waited in a corner booth. A drained Club soda bottle sat on a doily on the glass-topped table in front of him. Three huge crystal chandeliers lit the place up a little too brightly for his liking. There were only about twenty people scattered around the bar, and all out of earshot. Mostly couples, he decided. Nice place to take a date.

His own date entered the bar. Tobin was wearing a fresh suit and a well-worn scowl. He clocked Vince but didn't come straight over. Still the copper, he scoped the bar, checking all the angles before going into a situation – any situation. And casing the place for a quick getaway if things didn't turn out right for him. Finally satisfied that he knew the layout, he came over to the table and sat opposite Vince.

Tobin's face was red and tense, blood pressure popping. He kept his hands on his lap, ready to ball them into fists. Or reach for his gun if he had to, which Vince was sure was tucked into his waistband. Everything about the way he sat was defensive, but ready to attack at a moment's notice.

'That's a novelty.'

'What is?'

'The gun you're carrying. I thought it was just women who carried guns in this town.'

Tobin gave a slow, measured nod. 'Always with the smart mouth, eh, Treadwell?'

'Did you make your call?'

'What call?'

'You took your time, so did you call your paymaster, Lionel Duval?'

No reaction from the ex-copper.

'Sure you don't want a drink, Eddie? I hear they do a good cocktail. A redhead I know told me about that.'

Tobin's already slitty eyes narrowed even more. His face reddened up further. Vince could see the humiliation seeping in and settling. Tobin balled his fists and spat out, 'Who was that bitch – your girlfriend?'

'My girlfriend? What would I be doing with a girlfriend, Eddie? I thought you reckoned that everyone who goes to university is a queer.'

'I do!' barked Tobin,

'Calm down, Eddie.'

Tobin's blood pressure now looked as though it was going through the roof. He was actually purple, his boozy face lit up with a firework display of exploding capillaries.

'If I ever catch up with her, I'll smash her to pieces!'

'You'd never get mistaken for David Niven, would you, Eddie?' With Tobin a shade of puce now, Vince thought he should get off the humiliation caused by the Volcano. 'Let's talk business. The painting.'

Tobin nodded and took several deep, calming breaths. His face cooling down through the cardiovascular colour chart to something resembling ruddy. As he took control of his temper, a smugness crawled across his face and he creased his mouth into a smirk. 'Think you're holding all the aces, don't you, Treadwell?'

'No, just a painting that I know belongs to Lionel Duval. One that portrays an image very similar to the one I saw screened in the private cinema of his club. The one I reported, and the one you said didn't exist. Let me refresh your memory; it was not exactly *Spring in Park Lane*.'

'I read your report, Treadwell,' said Tobin. 'Two spades raping and beating a blonde junkie, if I recall.'

'That's right. There seems to be a theme emerging as to Mr Duval's taste in art, don't you think, Eddie?'

But Tobin wasn't listening. His attention was distracted, looking over Vince's shoulder. Vince followed his gaze and saw a tall, slim-built man in his mid-twenties. He was wearing a brass-button, double-breasted blazer, an open-neck shirt with a polka-dot silk Windsor knotted around his long neck. He wore pristine white slacks, sockless with blue canvas deck shoes, and looked as if he'd just stepped off a yacht in the Med. He was also deeply tanned, with short, neatly groomed and brilliantined curly hair. He walked straight up to the table with a graceful measured stride, smiled a pleasing toothpaste smile, and said to Tobin, 'Mr Eton's ready to receive you now.'

Tobin gave a blunt nod.

Vince recognized the handsome lad, but last time he was wearing boots, a peaked cap and a grey uniform with gold brocade. It was Dickie Eton's chauffeur. Vince stared at the chauffeur, but he didn't look back at him. Eddie Tobin stood up.

'Where you going, Eddie?'

'You want to know the truth, and Dickie Eton wants his painting. So let's go.'

Tobin undid his jacket to reveal the gun tucked in his waistband. Vince didn't know if the chauffeur was dressed heavy too, but it was clear Vince was going for a ride.

CHAPTER 24

ROCK & ROLL

The purple Rolls-Royce made its way noiselessly to Dickie Eton's mansion. They glided through the town and up to Dyke Road, an area long described as the Beverly Hills of Brighton. The further up the hill you got, the plusher the houses got. Gated mock-Tudor mansions with sweeping gravel drives, faux-French chateaux hidden behind elaborate topiary, neo-classical Palladian parodies, 1930s-style deco with life-sized plastic pink flamingos artificially feasting on manicured lawns, and sixties modernist bunkers in steel and glass, hunkering down next to small moated castles.

Eddie Tobin sat up front with the chauffeur, who had introduced himself to Vince as Nick Soroya. He was a softly spoken young man who seemed more than happy to chat away while Eddie Tobin contented himself with just sitting there looking stupid and violent. Nick Soroya explained that he had been working for Dickie Eton for three years. He himself used to be a crooner who was once signed to Dominate Records, Dickie Eton's label. But his career never took off (he hinted that certain indiscretions had come to light that ill qualified him for his target audience), so Dickie offered him a job as his driver. Nick Soroya proudly told Vince that Dickie Eton was paying for him to go to secretarial school, after which he would then be qualified to attend to Mr Eton's personal affairs.

Nick Soroya was singing Dickie Eton's praises just as enthusiastically as he had once sung his own bubblegum pop tunes. He said that Dickie really looked after his artists, even the ones who didn't make the grade and reach the heady heights in the fickle world of the hit parade. Vince could tell he was doing a pre-emptive PR job on the midget music mogul.

Vince then piped up and pointed out that not all of Dickie Eton's 'artists' got this treatment. Take Chas Starlight, the skiffle artist, for instance – dead in a seedy bedsit while on bad heroin. At this unpleasant little disclosure, Eddie Tobin made some ursine growling noise. Nick Soroya, however, politely ignored it, and went about his task of manoeuvring the car up the drive to Dickie Eton's house. The car slowed to a stop, the window rolled down and Nick Soroya tapped in a code on the sidepost that opened the gates. They continued on through.

Dickie Eton's contribution to the eclectic mix of moneyed piles lining Dyke Road was an audacious assortment within itself: Gothic Hollywood baroque with a twist of pre-eruption Pompeii could best describe it, about twice the size of its nearest neighbour, or rival. The front lawn contained a water feature as a centrepiece: a Trevi-esque fountain that seemed to equal its Roman counterpart in dimension. Vince thought suddenly of Bobbie.

There were about fifteen well-appointed cars parked alongside the sweep of the gravel drive. They themselves parked and piled out. Nick Soroya led the way, with Tobin tailing Vince, his paw indiscreetly hugging the butt of the gun in his waistband. They forwent the grand arch of the front door, and took the tradesmen's side entrance. Through the large kitchen with shiny copper pots hanging from hooks, and along a red-carpeted hallway. Lots of oil paintings on the walls, but these were just fillers. Merely for decoration, not the private collection, and therefore they were all seemingly kosher. But, still, the themes and subject matter: naked flesh in classical settings or bloody battle scenes, all edged towards the kind of art Dickie Eton obviously preferred: sex and death.

Ahead of them, a party was in progress in one of the rooms. There was laughter that seemed both raucous and furtive. Strange music was playing: sitars, Moogs; swirling, distorted sounds. The meaty whiff of cannabis smoke filled the air. Vince peeked through a partially open door at the far end of the hallway, and spotted naked flesh – lots of it.

'Looks like I'm a little over-dressed for the party,' he remarked.

Nick Soroya blocked his further view and pointed to some side stairs. 'This way,' he said, with his easy congeniality, but one that Vince thought hid a darker purpose. He looked around at Eddie Tobin. His hand was still on the butt of the gun.

They went up the stairs and along an unlit corridor until they reached an ancient-looking dark-oak door. The seemingly medieval theme of this part of the house, or certainly this particular floor, was augmented by two staunch-looking suits of armour standing sentry outside the arched door. They were about the same size, though one was a little more battered and looked sorely in need of a polish. Nick Soroya knocked on the door, and a reedy voice on the other side beckoned them in.

Dickie Eton was seated at a large mahogany partners' desk. Dressed in purple silk pyjamas with gold trim, and a pair of buckled black-velvet slippers (his feet were up on the desk), he was barking instructions down the phone. It was clearly a business call, a music-business call.

'. . . Listen Mardell, if she can't be bothered to rehearse, then I can't be bothered to book recording time . . . Fuck her, she's a minor talent with nice tits is all she is, Mardell. They're ten a penny . . .' Vince noted that Dickie Eton's showbiz voice was pitched somewhere between Brighton and Brooklyn.

Nick Soroya gave Vince a smile and gestured for him to sit down in the high-backed chair that was placed in front of the desk. Vince sat down. Eddie Tobin took a seat to one side, by the window.

'Fix our guests a drink, Nick,' said Eton in between 'yeah yeah yeahs' to Mardell, his subordinate on the other end of the line.

'I'll take a Coke,' said Vince to the subordinate. Nick Soroya gave him an accommodating nod.

Eddie Tobin gave a low-muttered curse at this sober request. 'I'll have a Scotch,' he said, looking at Vince and shaking his head in disgust. 'No ice, no water, *straight*.' Vince smiled at Tobin and threw him a wink. Eddie Tobin, straining to contain his rage, cracked his knuckles.

The room was a wood-panelled, study-type affair, done out like a gentleman's club, which seemed surprisingly conservative considering the house's owner. The only tell-tale signs of Rock & Roll were some framed gold and platinum records on the walls, along with similarly framed photos of Dickie shaking hands with just about everyone. There was a fully stocked bar in one corner of the room, and a Wurlitzer jukebox in another. Nick Soroya fixed the drinks and brought them over with his easy-on-the-eye courteous smile, then wafted back over to the bar, where he perched on a stool drinking a tall cocktail.

Dickie Eton dropped the phone into its cradle. 'Jesus Christ, these people!' he complained, swinging his feet down off the table. 'Sorry about that, but I get calls at the most inconvenient times. It's the Americans usually; they never know what time it is here. They assume it's *their* time all over the world. Well, why not, they've got the bomb!' Eton picked up the frosted block of knobbly glass that held his whisky. It looked too big for him. In fact, as Vince studied him, he realized that everything looked too big for the man: the chair he was sitting in, the desk he sat at, the phone he had just talked into. It should all have been scaled down slightly to fit the owner.

But, as Vince was taking Dickie Eton in, the imp-like impresario was doing likewise in return. 'Ah, Detective Treadwell, we meet at last,' he said, with a satisfied and fatalistic sigh. 'I heard I might be getting a visit from you' – he clicked his fingers for recall – 'about the Chas Stardust thing . . . ?'

'Starlight, I think he called himself,' Vince corrected.

'Quite. Do you think he was being ironic there? Because I'll be damned if I can remember him, and I certainly know a star when I meet one.' Eton made a dismissive flourish of his floppy little hand, which was weighed down by the chunky rings he was wearing. 'I should never have signed them, since there was no one in the group I wanted to fuck. And I'm really not that fussy, so if *I* don't want to fuck them, why should anyone else? No, Detective, a rare mistake on my part, and of course they bombed. I guessed ages ago that Skiffle was dead, and now we all know it's for real.' Eton smiled and raised his glass again, 'Well, let's toast his memory. Cheers, Detective.'

Vince took a sizeable swig of his Coke and put it down on the desk. 'I think we both know what I'm here for. I take it you took a call from Lionel Duval, after your gun-toting sidekick here phoned him.'

'Smart mouth,' sneered Tobin, no longer growling, but looking surprisingly smug and self-satisfied, even verging on amused.

'God, that man. Never a simple transaction with Lionel, always intrigue,' said Eton. 'Like that painting I wanted to buy off him, what could be simpler than two dear old friends trading a painting for some cash. And yet here you are.'

'"Dear old friends"?'

'You didn't know that? Oh, Lionel and I go back a long time. Soho, Denmark Street, when we were both making our way in the business. Lionel used to book some of my acts for his clubs – his legit clubs.'

'Before he got into dirty movies?'

There was a quick exchange of glances between Tobin and Eton. Eton's face then lit up as he replied, 'Well, there's no denying it, Detective, you're right. What you saw that night is exactly what you saw.'

Dickie Eton gazed squarely at Vince, yet Vince didn't flinch. He didn't even bother to look around at Tobin and shout, 'I knew it!' Because he'd known it all along, there was no victory here for him. There was, in fact, a sense of loss. Because a part of him wished he had imagined it all, then the poor skinny blonde girl would still be alive. If Eton was looking for a strong reaction, he wasn't getting one.

So the midget music mogul inspected his rings, and continued. 'As for "dirty", Detective, it's all a matter of taste. Like with music, all tastes need catering for, wouldn't you say?'

'No, I wouldn't.'

Dickie Eton's pinched, almost feminine lips shaped themselves into a dry, derisive little smile. 'I didn't suppose you would. Well, myself and Lionel share similar tastes. The film business is a private little enterprise we run for friends with like-minded proclivities. Oh, you'd be surprised, there's a real mixed bag of them. Some showbiz chums, naturally, while in politics there's a couple of *very* upfront backbenchers. Also a lawyer, a smattering of the landed gentry or peers of the realm, a society dentist and an eminent Harley Street doctor. He's a psychologist, in fact. I could go on.'

Vince digested this information with an audible gulp, then again looked around at Tobin. The slitty eyes still burned into him, but he hadn't touched his drink and Eddie Tobin was usually a glass-guzzling booze hound. His ex-partner in Vice didn't seem such a figure of fun now. Also the gun tucked in his waistband wasn't just a prop any more; it seemed very real, stuffed with bullets and ready to be fired. Worse still, Tobin looked as if he was itching to use it.

Vince couldn't see Nick Soroya without craning his neck, but he guessed he was still sitting at the bar, in the gloom behind him. It made him uncomfortable not being able to see the chauffeur. Failed crooner followed by secretarial school hardly marked him out as anything to fear, but behind those pretty-boy good looks lurked cold danger. So much was evident in eyes that were chillingly detached from the warm smile he habitually wore.

Vince had been freshly weighing up these two men for a good reason. He was sure one of them was going to kill him.

'Oh,' continued Eton, 'one other person I haven't mentioned in our little enterprise is your old friend, I believe, Henry Pierce. He takes care of security at this end of things, makes sure everyone does as they're told and keeps their mouth shut.'

Vince froze over at this information, though his killer wasn't in the room – yet. Keeping it casual, he asked, 'Where is Pierce, then, at the party downstairs?'

Dickie Eton let out a yelp of derision that turned into a cackle of laughter. 'That's just off-the-scale funny! Henry wouldn't approve of the parties I have – not unless he could make money out of it. Oh, no no no, Detective Treadwell, you don't invite a man like Henry Pierce to an orgy. No one would get it up! No no no no, Detective, we don't need Henry here – not yet anyway.'

The 'yet anyway' worried Vince, but he focused on the business at hand. 'What happens to the girls in the films?'

Dickie Eton smiled. 'What do you *think* happens?'

'I don't know, because I missed the very ending. I was clocked on the head. I'm assuming the one who clocked me was the projectionist.' Vince looked around at Eddie Tobin for confirmation.

Tobin smiled, and rolled out some little nods that suggested Vince had it about right.

'If I told you those girls went home, if not happy, then certainly well paid, would you believe me?'

'That's not what I saw. I saw a knife.'

'A prop?'

Vince dismissed that with a humourless laugh. 'I wasn't watching something by Fellini. It was real degenerate filth and the knife was no prop.' Vince glanced again at Tobin. 'I've been right about everything so far, eh, Eddie?'

Tobin smirked. 'That's right, champ, a real smartarse – and look where it's got you.' Tobin cracked some knuckles and turned to Dickie Eton. 'Come on, let's get it over with.'

'Patience, Eddie, patience,' drawled Eton, who was obviously savouring his role.

Vince heard the sound of a straw sucking up the dregs of a cocktail behind him. Knowing the answer, he asked anyway. 'Get what over with?'

'Oh, I think Mr Tobin has some things he wants to say before . . .'

Vince watched Dickie Eton as he let the outcome of his sentence hang, but he already knew the end. Eton was clearly enjoying himself. He liked having Tobin at his side with a gun. It wasn't enough for Dickie Eton to be rich and successful – he wanted the danger, the underbelly, the intrigue that came with dealing with gangsters and bent ex-coppers. His heavy glass hung limply from his hand as he inspected the rings on his fingers.

Vince weighed up his options. Tobin was sat about eight feet away. Judging by his posture, he was relaxed, at ease with himself, and certainly thought he was in control of the situation. Never a quick draw, Vince reckoned he could have the gun off the man before he knew what hit him. Then there was Nick Soroya sitting at the bar behind him. Vince couldn't see him, and that scared him. He scoped the desk for a weapon – a letter opener, a pair of scissors, a paperweight – but there was nothing. With just a phone and some papers, it looked unnaturally uncluttered. Tobin had probably warned Dickie Eton over the phone. The only real weapon was the heavy crystal glass now held limply in the midget music mogul's hand.

'Remember one thing,' said Vince, trying to sound as unmoved by his predicament as possible. 'I still have your painting.'

'You got nothing!' blurted Tobin.

Vince eyeballed Eton. 'It's a painting which indicates that you and Duval have sick tastes. I could make a connection, easy.'

Dickie Eton's response was one of comprehensive casualness, the kind you'd expect from a man padding about his palatial home in his pyjamas. 'I have to concur with Mr Eddie. You have nothing. And this conversation is hopelessly pointless. I feel like a pussy cat toying with a half-dead bird he's brought into the house. Because, you see my friend, you may have my painting . . . but you only have *half* the picture.'

Dickie Eton looked pleased with his summation of the scenario, and Vince believed what he said.

'And this, Detective, is where I leave you. I have guests to attend to.' On that note, Dickie Eton drained his glass and stood up. As much as he could stand up – because to get off the chair there was an element of jumping down before there was any standing up. Vince's eyes were on the crystal glass – the weapon? Dickie Eton put it down with a thud, and padded over to the door.

Tobin went to stand up . . .

Vince sprang to his feet to grab the glass off the desk, then send it smashing into the side of Tobin's head, then retrieve the shooter from the ex-copper's expanding waistband, and make his escape. That was the plan he'd set irretrievably into action.

But instead he found himself on his knees on the floor.

As soon as Vince had stood up, his legs had just buckled under him. His head spun, and it felt as if his eyes were somersaulting around his head. He could feel himself melting as the carpet became quicksand, and a sensation of limblessness made it impossible to get up. The sound of laughter cascaded around him. Vince felt hands grip him under where his arms should be, and he was lifted up and dumped back into his seat. He felt like a baby in a high chair, all head and ineffectual body. Vince looked up to see a giggling Dickie Eton disappearing through the door, with a languidly amused Nick Soroya in tow.

Vince focused on the fizzing Mickey Finn in front of him on the desk – the drugged glass of Coca-Cola. The fear he'd been feeling had somehow overridden the effects of the drugged drink as it set about disabling him. It seemed his head was still working, but his body had retired. In fact, it felt . . . *dead*. And Vince suspected that, with Dickie Eton now out of the room, his head would soon be joining the rest of him.

Tobin now sat on a corner of the desk, with a big shit-shovelling grin on his face. He, it seemed, had no qualms about playing the big kitty toying with the little bird.

'You're a smart boy, Treadwell. I could tell, the minute the little fella started talking, that you started thinking: "Why's he telling me all this? Why's he putting himself in the frame?" Yeah,

Treadwell, smart boy like you already knows the answer; because dead men don't talk.'

'That's why you never made Murder Squad, Eddie. They do talk. They tell you all sorts of things, if you look close enough.'

'I never made Murder Squad because there wasn't any money in it. A dead loss, you could say.'

'Oh, yeah, the envelopes.'

'Not any more, now I'm a partner in *this* little caper.'

'Going up in the world, Eddie, or down in the gutter?'

'We're gonna kill you, Treadwell. And we're gonna get away with it. And I'm now gonna tell you why.'

Vince couldn't move, felt as if he was encased in lead. His brain was ticking over and his mouth still seemed to be doing the business, even though his lips, and even his eyelids felt sluggish. He felt as though he'd been shot through with some huge dose of local anaesthetic. 'What was in the drink?'

'It's the same stuff we dose the girls with.' Tobin smiled. 'They can see it coming, but they can't do anything about it. It's all in the eyes, you see. The director, he always goes for close-ups of their faces just before they get it. That's what the perverts really like, the fear in the women's eyes.'

Tobin took a slow smug stroll around to the other side of the desk, and sat down in the chair Dickie Eton had vacated. Physically the desk *fitted* him better – but it didn't *suit* him. His prole face still had him pegged as the heavy sitting in the boss's chair. 'Smart mouth, Treadwell. You fuckin' little know-it-all.'

'From what I've just heard off the Mighty Atom, I got *most* of it right,' replied Vince.

'Ha! You know nothing!'

'I've been hearing that a lot lately. Go on then, Eddie, educate me.'

Eddie Tobin sat back in the chair. 'You remember Tommy Ribbons, dead on the floor, right?'

Vince nodded, or gave what he thought might be an approximation of a nod, with his new disembodied body.

'You were asked to get the doorman?'

The sight of Eddie Tobin savouring the moment grated, so Vince decided to spoil it for him and speed things up. 'I went to the front of the club. He wasn't there. I heard a noise upstairs, a door slamming shut. So I went upstairs to check. It was dark. I heard a girl screaming from inside a room, top floor. Door was locked. I kicked it open and went inside. Shelves, stacks of film canisters. A table in the centre of the room, movie projector sitting on it, showing a movie. A private cinema. About twenty fellas sitting watching stag films. No big deal, they're all over Soho. But this was different . . .'

Eddie Tobin pulled a grin when he saw the disgust on Vince's face. 'Yeah, I've seen that one,' said Tobin. 'Two spades togged-up like Zulus raping and beating a junkie blonde.'

Vince continued, 'I heard something, turned around, saw a man standing in the doorway. Tall fella. Not the doorman. The projectionist I assumed. Then I wake up in the hospital with a headache, and your report in front of me – telling me I made it all up. Then I end up here and, bingo, I find out I'm right on the button.'

'You don't remember anything else?'

Vince shrugged, or at least thought he did, because he wasn't sure his shoulders were working.

'The man in the room, you're right, he was the projectionist,' said Tobin, leaning forward across the desk, as if he wanted to get a closer look at something being held under glass. Then he announced, 'You killed him, Treadwell.'

What stopped Vince from falling to the floor, but this time in howls of incredulous laughter, rather than as a result of his spiked drink, was Tobin's expression. There was something there that transcended a bent copper's thin-lipped, slitty-eyed dishonesty. And if it was meant to be a joke, he was playing it straight.

'Go on,' said Vince.

Eddie Tobin sat back in Dickie Eton's chair, no longer triumphant. This moment was bigger than his victory over Vince. 'Me and Duval went looking for you when you didn't come back,' said

Tobin. 'We went upstairs, saw the door was open to the projection room. Blood on the floor, lots of it. The projectionist was
starfished on the floor. You were kneeling over him, pounding his
face to a pulp. Smashing him to pieces. I called out, told you to
stop. You were killing him. *Killing him*. You turned around and saw
us. Then you just carried on pounding the shit out of him. You
wouldn't stop. Duval had the cosh in his hand that he keeps
stashed under the counter. I took it out of his hand because he
was useless from shock. And, bang, got you on the top of the head,
hard enough to put out an elephant. But you carried on.'

Tobin sucked at his teeth at the memory of it, then continued,
'You knew what you were doing, Treadwell – head shots direct to
the temple. All bruised and battered, brains like mush, until he was
dead. Tongue lolling out his mouth, he was smashed to pieces. You
killed him, Treadwell. You *slaughtered* him. Duval was puking. Me,
I just stood there. You know, like a rabbit in the headlights. Never
seen anything like it. Then you stood up, turned around. Duval
was out the door, screaming like a fucking girl, with tears in his
eyes. And he's been about a bit, seen a few things. Me too.
Nothing like this, though. It was your face, Treadwell . . . you were
smiling. You stood up and then you fell over. The whacks I gave
you must have got through that thick skull of yours. A delayed
reaction. You had this look on you . . . I've never seen nothing
like it. Twisted it was. Pure evil.'

Vince stood up, fast. Then fell right down again, just as fast. It
was the information, the shock shooting through his body which
had got him up. A reaction, a spasm. But, once up, his body just
didn't know how to cope, so it sent him straight back down again.
He squeezed his eyes shut, then reopened them to see Tobin's
shoes just inches from his face. Brown wingtips, cracked and over-
polished, crud on the welt that smelled like dried dog shit. The
shoes shuffled off out of view. Vince was grabbed by the lapels and
heaved up, and dumped back into his chair. Breathless through the
exertion of lifting the young detective, Tobin rested himself on the
corner of the desk.

'I'll give you the whole deal, Treadwell. You like movies, don't you? Well, now you're starring in one. You're on *Candid Camera*. The whole thing was filmed, because Duval had a hidden camera in the projection room. Security just to make sure none of those films left the room. Duval's got them all over the gaff, because he's a surveillance nut – and a peeping Tom. But you know that yourself, don't you? You've heard about those parties he holds at his mansion. It's him and Dickie – oh yeah, the little fella's the same.' Tobin leaned forward, raised a beckoning forefinger, as if to hook him in. 'Between you and me, Treadwell, the little fella and Lionel are a couple of right heavyweight perverts. They like to watch the guests at it, all fucked up on booze, pills and dope. Men and women doing things, women and women dyking off, queer boys dressed up as birds. Duval's got cameras all over his house, and Dickie, too, I wouldn't be surprised. What do you think is going on downstairs now? Are you kidding? It's like a Roman orgy!'

Tobin was really hitting his stride now. His face was lavishly red, not at the prospect of joining in the fun and games downstairs, but at the power he now held over the young detective.

'You see, for all the little fella's big talk, Dickie doesn't like to fuck. He likes to watch others doing the dirty work, as he says. Lionel's the same: wouldn't cheat on his wife, but he likes to watch. You should see the people Lionel's got on film, doing stuff they shouldn't be doing with people they shouldn't be doing it with. How come you think he's buying up all of Soho, without the good people of Westminster Council batting an eyelid? Because he's got the dirt on the right people. And he's got it on you, too, Treadwell.'

Tobin stood up and walked around to the other side of the desk, to sit down again. He knitted his hands together and leaned forward, like a newsreader about to impart some very serious news. 'Don't you even want to know what happened to the fella you killed?'

Vince didn't answer, not wanting to give the whole story credence. He wasn't yet ready to allow that. He wanted it to remain a lie. But Tobin was dying to tell him, anyway, the words brimming around his thin-lipped mouth like drool.

'The projectionist was a nobody. No wife, no family. And no one really knew that he worked for Duval, or what he did. So he wouldn't be missed: just a piece of flotsam that got washed up in Soho. Occasionally had a few drinks in the Coach and Horses with the stagehands, but no one really knew him. He was a nothing.'

They were the only two in the room, but Tobin still panto-mimed looking around to check that no one was listening. 'I read the report on you from the psychologist, Treadwell. One of the best in the business. Wrote a book on it . . .'

'Dr Hans Boehm,' supplied Vince.

'That's right. The same report you weren't allowed to read. Oh, yeah, Scotland Yard's got a file on you. They're monitoring you very closely. Dr Boehm said you were prone to delusions. Fantasies. Said you was a nastysiss.'

'Narcissist, you moron.'

Tobin, unfazed by the insult, carried on. 'Yeah, like I said, a nastysiss. Bit like being a ponce, which I always thought you were, with your flash fucking suits and your oily dago good looks.'

The Mickey Finn must have been wearing off now, because Vince was becoming aware of his body again. And of the slurry of sickness in his stomach. It wasn't just the information spewing out of Tobin's mouth that made Vince nauseous, it was his actual mouth. It was him. While Tobin had been doing so much talking, foamy white spittle had formed in the corners of his thin lips. Even holding all the cards, as he professed to, the ex-copper still looked rabid with resentment, ugly with hate. Vince looked away from that gaping, foaming gob and glanced around the room.

'You're getting excited, Eddie. Wipe your mouth. I can smell your whore's breath from here.'

Tobin wiped the spittle off his mouth with the back of his sleeve. He rolled his shoulders, composed himself, then continued, 'OK, nice and easy. Dr Boehm reckons you always see yourself at the centre of things – things that don't exist. Prone to hubris and ego, he said. Most psychopaths and villains are nastysiss.'

Tobin was wrong, thought Vince, because Vince *was* smack bang at the centre of things, and they did exist, and it did revolve around him. He wanted to get it back on a cop footing. *Cop footing?* That didn't sound right either. As things stood, it was two ex-cops talking. One retired and one about to be permanently retired.

'Let's get this over and done with, Eddie, or else go brush your teeth.'

'Don't rush me, Treadwell. What's your hurry? You've got nowhere to go,' said Tobin, cracking his knuckles and stretching. 'The clear-up was easy. We gutted the place, turned the projection room back into a storage room, moved the cinema to another location. You probably guessed that already, right?'

'Right.'

'Here's the part that you're interested in. The part you'll never guess, and the part I like. Lionel called it *irony*. Me, I just think it's fucking funny! Lionel contacted Dickie Eton. Dickie contacted Henry Pierce. Pierce was good at getting rid of things, as he'd been doing it for Jack Regent for years.'

Vince felt his body gradually coming back to him, and it felt as if he had been on a weekend-long bender. Sweat prickled along his spine, his head throbbed and his chest tightened.

'Pierce picked up the stiff two days later, in an ice-cream van of all things. Good call, because the stiff was getting a bit gamy by then, stinking the whole place up, needed to be put on ice. Then he was driven down to Brighton.'

Vince was getting the joke; it was on him. And, whilst not enjoying it as much as Tobin, he was certainly appreciating the set-up and execution. It packed a hell of a punchline, a real killer.

'Pierce did his usual routine, chopped off the stiff's head and hands so he wouldn't be identified if anything happened. Only something did happen. Pierce messed up and the body got washed ashore. And the rest you know, Detective Treadwell. You're investigating a murder that you committed. A murder that's even been captured on film.'

Vince's mind raced – backwards – as he tried to remember what happened in the projection room that night. But nothing came to him. It was just the same as it had always been: the tall man entering the room, and then the big blackout. Then he recalled what Dr Hans Boehm had told him, about the mind being the ultimate trickster. It does whatever it takes to protect itself: it shuts down, edits out, compartmentalizes, and blocks the bad memories. But, try as he might, Vince couldn't block out Eddie Tobin.

'We got a bit concerned once we heard that Markham had sent you down here, what with you being such a bright boy, and such a smart copper. But, as Duval pointed out, there was the irony, the poetic justice. We laughed. We got the joke. What were you going to find, Treadwell . . . the killer?'

Vince began to laugh, and it might have turned hysterical, except the door opened and in walked Nick Soroya, with one hand behind his back. A gun? A knife? Vince stopped laughing and tried to stand up. He felt more life in his body now, and managed to haul himself out of the high-back chair. Tobin was already on his feet and moving fast from around the desk.

Nick Soroya revealed his weapon – a spike. He held a hotshot syringe in his hand. It was brimful with bad brown liquid, just like the killer gear that had been doing the rounds.

Eddie Tobin was at Vince's side now and he pushed the straining and grunting detective back into his seat. He clasped his arm and yanked up his sleeve. Nick Soroya made like a doctor and held the syringe up for a closer inspection. He then gave the glass cylinder three quick taps with his fingernail. Satisfied with the deadly concoction, the spike was driven deep into Vince's vein.

There was no time for Vince to say anything. Time had already slowed for him, as it inevitably does when it's about to stop altogether. And the detective's final thought, as the needle sank in, was just about the act itself. It was fast and professional. The malice and enmity had gone. It was like an execution.

Nick Soroya, the lad with the pleasant face, revealed the true nature beneath his pleasant smile, and Vince recognized the darker purpose behind his eyes as he pushed death home.

CHAPTER 25

SAWDUST CAESAR

Vaughn sat in a grotty pub in the parish of Portslade, which remained a stubbornly unfashionable part of town. That was the extent of his escape route. A backstreet pub he'd never visited before, therefore a pub where no one would know him. For hours he sat in the corner snug with pints and whisky chasers, draining both his glass and wallet. Not getting drunk, just more skint, and thus narrowing his options. But this pub in Portslade still wasn't far enough away. He listened to the men idly chatting at the bar. The news filtered through that 'the plague' was still in the air, and threading its way through the town in needles of despair. A young girl this time.

As Vaughn lifted the glass to take a final swig of his latest pint, the dregs at the bottom looking like organisms viewed through a microscope, his life came into sudden focus. As if surfacing through a glass drunkenly, a sudden sober clarity: he now had nothing. No girl, no money, no hope. The girl didn't bear thinking about. She'd already slipped into the past. A past he no longer possessed. A past he hadn't seen coming . . . *if that made any sense?*

So he sat there thinking about how he could extricate himself from the shit he was in. Nothing came to mind, apart from what he'd done all his life, to act as a foil for others. But that wasn't his plan. Because real patsies, suckers, mugs, gulls and foils, they never see it coming. His plan was to kill himself. Go the way of Wendy. Join her in the Big Nod. It seemed like the best plan of action, the best way ahead. It even seemed like the decent thing to do.

In the brief moments he had thought of the girl, it was only to think how little he had thought about her, and how much he had always been thinking about himself. He'd felt sporadic spasms of guilt, only to be usurped by long underlying feelings of self-centred fear. Now he thought about topping himself, he could give his impending demise a dignity: he was doing it to be with the girl. And for the girl.

He went to the toilet and locked himself in a cubicle, to hang himself with his belt. But then he realized he was wearing elasticised braces. It was his best suit, worn with red socks to complement his new loafers – just like his heroes, Frank, Dino, Sammy and Peter Lawford. But in a pub pisser in Portslade, even Vaughn, with his hyperactive fantasy life and lazy reality, could appreciate the sheer redundancy of that detail. He sank down on to the grimy seat of the bog, his head buried in his hands, and he cried. He cried for the girl and for the others that had died. But most of all he cried for himself. And then he pissed himself, terrified. He was sure death was going to hurt.

There were about forty of them. They tore up deckchairs and used their wooden struts as coshes, or just sent them flying through the air. '*We are the Mods! We are the Mods!*' they chanted. The handful of Rockers didn't stand a chance. They jumped over the promenade railings to escape a kicking or the flying deckchairs. The drop on the other side was about thirty foot but, fortunately for them, the wall came in at an angle, and they managed to scuttle down safely to the next level and make their escape. The BBC and British Movietone News cameras caught it all. It was chaos, mayhem, anarchy and excellent copy! Moral indignation kicked in as the 'Sawdust Caesars' were seen to be taking over the entire town. Some cynics claimed that the filmed riots were stage-managed.

Most social commentators said this drunken hooliganism wasn't anything that hadn't been seen before; just take a look at a Hogarth print.

'We are the Mods! We are the Mods!'

They'd gathered by the entrance to the Palace Pier. It seemed like the place to be: an epicentre, a potential flashpoint and, more importantly, yet another potential photo opportunity. Police on horses tried to disperse them but, as the cameras rolled, the publicity-astute Mods were eager for their close-ups and refused to budge. They protested. They staged a sit-down. Arguments about infringement of civil liberties were quickly gathered by the more politically minded and hurled at the mounted coppers. The not so erudite or politically minded, and generally more pissed, made do with stones. What a performance!

'We are the Mods! We are the Mods!'

Further along the seafront, by the kiddies' paddling pool, heads were being pummelled, wrists were being cuffed, paddy wagons were being loaded. The boys in blue had contained about two hundred of them on the beach. They threw stones, beer bottles, deckchairs and finally charged the police.

'We are the Mods! We are the Mods!'

Away from the seafront and the cameras, shop windows had been kicked in, pubs turned over and motorbikes set on fire. As most of the Rockers had gone home, the Mods now fought amongst themselves, divided by areas, football teams. All accompanied by a perennial chorus of 'What are you screwing at?'

'We are the Mods! We are the Mods!'

They'd given the movement a name, Mods, and anyone who was up for a bit of a debacle on the bank holiday weekend had gathered under its banner. It was a truncated and punchy little moniker that seemed a million miles away from the élan of the original Modernist movement that had cut a dash through the subterranean culture of Soho's coffee bars and jazz clubs, carrying a well-thumbed copy of Jean-Paul Sartre in the back pocket, watching Jean Paul Belmondo up on the big screen, favouring the Italianate-style clothing found in the glossy magazines, and turning away from American bubblegum culture towards a new European aesthetic.

'*We are the Mods! We are the Mods!*'

Vaughn wasn't a Mod. Even though he was wearing an Italian-style mixed-fibre Montague Burton suit with three buttons and a single vent, a skinny-brimmed trilby, a pair of suede tasselled loafers, and regularly ingested pills as if they were going out of fashion, he just didn't class himself as a Mod. That was the trouble with Mods, thought Vaughn; anyone with half a savvy about dress sense was considered a Mod. But he knew that he wasn't one, and he stood vehemently staunch on that little fact. Because, right now, he wanted to kill them. On his trudge away from the pub in Portslade, he'd planned on robbing a chemist (a Mod trick if ever there was one – even though he *wasn't* one). It was the perfect time for robbery, on a bank holiday. But the mobile alarms of the police force – on motorbikes, sitting in twos in panda cars, or mobbed up inside Black Marias – were thick in the air due to the Mods. And even though the overstretched cops, and the chaos in the town centre offered the perfect cover for such a caper, Vaughn just didn't quite trust his luck. Getting caught would kill him, and anyway he wanted to do the job properly. No, Vaughn *hated* Mods.

He had recently been avoiding Third Avenue, mainly because he'd been avoiding Henry Pierce. Now he didn't care, and he reckoned that by now Henry Pierce would be avoiding him, too, what with the bogies sniffing after Vaughn.

He pushed the button, pronounced his name and was buzzed up immediately. At the top of the stairs he was greeted by a tall West Indian he knew as Marcus Three. There were seven West Indians in Brighton called Marcus, and this one was number three. To Vaughn's knowledge none of them were related, yet they were all called Marcus. In fact, most of the West Indian men Vaughn knew were call Marcus, and he just couldn't figure out why. Marcus Three sucked his teeth, sniffed the air around him curiously, then sucked his teeth again and said, in his deep patois, 'You stink of piss, rassclatt!'

'You holding?'

'I don't deal what you're looking for, bwouy.'

'Barbs? You got barbs? I'll take barbs? Please . . . anything.' And he meant *anything* – and enough of it to kill himself with.

Marcus Three gave him a nod, and Vaughn stepped inside the flat. All the lights were out, so he couldn't see a thing. He walked into a fug as clouds of reefer lazed about the airless room. He didn't know what hit him, but something did.

When Vaughn came round, he found himself seated on a plastic chair. He was bound with a thin cord wrapped around his waist. His feet were also secured. It was a thorough job. Even he thought it was too thorough a job for someone as ineffectual as him. It was dark because the windows were painted over in matt black. The familiar mural on the wall depicting some loose-limbed Caribbeans dancing with not a care in the world.

He was still in Third Avenue, downstairs from the same flat, in the basement of the BBC or, to give it its full title, the Beach Bottle Club. There was the warm light of a flame flickering away behind him. As he recovered his bearings, he knew that behind him were tables with dead Jack Daniel's bottles masquerading as candlesticks, and layered with cascading stalactites of wax. He'd often sat mindlessly at one of those tables, stoned out of his box, thoughtlessly peeling strips of warm malleable wax off the bottles, feeling it crumble under his fingernails. Vaughn heard a noise behind him, chair legs scraping on the floor. He turned his head round towards the light and saw the bulk of a large object: Henry Pierce.

'Henry?'

Pierce slowly moved away from the light towards the other side of the room.

'Henry, what you doing?'

There was a theatrical pause, then Pierce's deliberate tones. 'Lurking in the shadows, what else?'

Pierce headed over to the makeshift bar, his white stick tapping away before him. His antennae located a bar stool and he sat on it, bolt upright, his feet still firmly on the floor. He laid his white stick on the bar, cracked his knuckles, then folded his arms. Ready now. He gave a knowing sigh of disappointment and said, 'So, it's come to this.'

Vaughn took in his situation, and asked the wrong question, 'How did I end up down here?'

Silence.

Vaughn nodded on realizing that the information was useless to him anyway. 'That gear you gave me, Henry, it's poison.'

'So it seems. And you're the one who's been knocking it out, putting it on the street.'

'You gave it to me! Said it was good!'

'It *was* good. Just *too* good.'

'I'm not taking the collar for this, Henry. You gave me the gear.'

'And why did I give you the gear?' Vaughn remained silent. 'That's right, what are you going to do, boy? Go to the bogies, tell them it's not your fault? They'll ask you where you got it. You'll tell them the truth, that you got it from me. They'll come to me, ask me why I gave it to you. I'll tell them the truth, how I gave you heroin as payment. Payment for services rendered, a job well done.'

'You *made* me!'

In a flash, Pierce was on his feet, the white stick was off the bar and raised in his hand. He bolted over to Vaughn and smashed it down across his lap.

Vaughn let out a primordial scream and closed his eyes until the initial agony subsided. Then opened them to find Henry Pierce was perched again on the stool and the white stick resting on the makeshift bar. Like nothing had happened.

Pierce continued: 'But the job wasn't well done, was it, boy?'

Vaughn, through the pain, whimpered, 'No.'

'Because the body was washed up on the beach. The *body of*

evidence was washed up on the fucking beach for some cunt to find it.'

Vaughn pleaded, through tears, 'I did what you said, Henry, I swear to God. You were there! I cut the head off.'

The misery was seared on to Vaughn's face, not from his burning lap, where the white stick had left a welt, but from the memory. The memory of that night. The lock-up turned charnel house, where Vaughn, under Pierce's guidance, had gone about his gruesome task. It was to be Vaughn's big break into the big time; and to be no longer just a lowly driver. But that night Vaughn had discovered something important about himself: he wasn't cut out for the big time. He didn't have the heart for it, or the balls for it, and he certainly didn't have the stomach for it. He had thrown up remorselessly throughout the whole ordeal.

Pierce, all matter-of-fact: 'I told you, boy, to stab his chest, puncture his lungs, let the fucking air out the tyres.'

Vaughn, hysterical now, and he would have stamped his feet if they weren't tied together, bawled out, 'You didn't, you didn't tell me that! You didn't tell me that you didn't tell me that you didn't tell me that you didn't tell . . . !'

Pierce, up again, the stick in his hand raised, and Vaughn, with Pavlovian obedience, stopped his whining and squeezed his eyes shut. But, unable to do anything about his ears, he heard the dead air around him slice open as the cane smashed down on to his lap. No cry of pain this time. Legs too numb, throat too sore. Just the burn of piss on his red-hot skinny legs. He'd thought he was all pissed out, but he was wrong. He now pissed like a racehorse. The excess – and there was excess – puddled up on the plastic chair. His eyes opened to the same routine: Pierce on the stool, cane on the bar. Like nothing had happened.

Vaughn realized that Pierce could keep up this routine all night. And realized that he himself couldn't. For a moment he thought that his plan had worked: Marcus Three had supplied him with the barbs, and he had killed himself, and he was dead. But, instead of being guided by seraph emissaries to the Elysian Fields to join his Wendy, he had gone to Hell. And this was to be his eternity. His personal divine comedy.

'Soiled yourself, boy?' Pierce said with a grimace and a tut-tut. But it was cartoon disgust, since he didn't expect anything else from Vaughn. He would have been disappointed with anything else. Vaughn's nervous disposition and his terrified bladder were the source of much amusement to those in the know when gathered in the pubs, clubs and around the card tables of Brighton. He very much took after his father in that respect.

Pierce continued, 'The truth, for you, isn't the best way forward in this case. And that's not even putting Jack into the equation.'

Vaughn's lips twitched, then shaped themselves into something that could loosely be described as a smile, as he was hit by a new thought. 'Like you said, Henry, you got me to do the work, get rid of the body. I was following your orders. You fucked up as much as me. And Jack will come after you as much as me. So, maybe you should untie me, Henry, and we'll call it quits, eh?'

As soon as the last word 'eh' was out of his mouth, he knew it was a mistake, and closed his eyes and waited for the cane. It didn't come. He opened his eyes and saw Henry Pierce still sitting on the stool, motionless and seemingly expressionless.

'No doubt I'll incur some wrath,' Pierce said, 'but I'm a man of good and long standing with Jack. Someone will have to take the fall, so who's it going to be? Me or you? Who's your money on?' Vaughn, tied firmly to the plastic chair, still managed to sink lower into it. Pierce, head tilted up as if he was addressing an audience in the gallery, continued in a vein that seemed well rehearsed, as if he'd gone over it a thousand times – his story, his alibi. 'I've got years of good service behind me. Diligently going about my work, never a complaint from the man. But you? You're not worth the piss in your pants.'

Pierce picked up the white stick from the bar, stood up and slowly circled his prey, twirling the cane in his heavy brutal hands. It resembled the laborious rotation of a propeller just started up, and Vaughn, leaning away as far as he could, viewed it as just as lethal.

'Still, today, you find me in a giving mood. I want to help you, boy.'

Vaughn looked through the propeller blades. 'You do?'

'Why wouldn't I?'

Vaughn really didn't know.

'Now you've killed the girl,' Pierce continued.

Through fresh panic. 'I swear to God, Henry, it wasn't me. She didn't get the gear off me. When I heard people were dying, I flushed away what I had left.'

'Then how did she get it?'

'Don't know.'

'Maybe she took it. Stole some before you flushed it?'

'She wouldn't.'

'She must have. While you were asleep, she must have stolen some for her own personal use.'

'No.'

'Never underestimate a slip. They'll rob the gold out of Granny's teeth to get what they want. And you know that, boy.'

Vaughn knew this wasn't true of Wendy, but he nodded in agreement anyway. He didn't want to feel the sting of that stick again. And it felt good agreeing with Pierce. It relieved what little guilt he had. *It was the girl's fault, not his.* Blame absolved him, and right now he'd take all the absolution he could lay his hands on.

'Let's not kid ourselves, boy, the girl's gone, God rest her soul. It's out of our hands. She's in a better place. She's done and dusted.'

There was a tremulous twitch of the bottom lip for the freshly grieving Vaughn as he said, 'I . . . I loved her.'

'Touched. But we must move on.'

'*Move on?* It's only just happened.'

'Time, in this case, is of the essence. When Marcus Three called me and said you was here, my first reaction was: call the bogies, let him hang! Then I thought again: "justice must be served".'

Pierce stopped circling and stood in front of him. The cane in his left hand, his right hand gripped the gnarled handle and slowly began to twist off the top of the cane.

Vaughn knew what was coming, because he'd seen that cane unscrewed, unsheathed and wielded before. *Justice must be served.* He closed his eyes and mumbled some prayers for the last-ditch get-out stakes: the ones that would get him back in good with God, and hopefully through the Pearly Gates.

Swoosh. The sixteen-inch razor-sharp blade sliced through the air and cut the cord that bound Vaughn to the plastic chair. Vaughn, and those who knew Pierce, always suspected his blind routine was exactly that, a routine. An act, shtick, like the Red Indian in the ring, and the black-clad villain on the streets. And if there was any doubt about Pierce's 20/20 vision in his one good eye, it was nixed at the point where Pierce spotted an opening of about half an inch between Vaughn's arm and the chair. Just enough to get the blade in, and cut the cord that bound him.

Vaughn opened his eyes to see Pierce cutting the other cord binding his legs. And, in a moment, he was free. He rubbed his wrists and looked up at Pierce, confused. But it was clear, even to Vaughn, that Henry Pierce had plans for him.

Pierce, pragmatic: 'Let's start then with Bobbie – Bobbie LaVita. What have you heard?'

'Nothing.'

'Not even from your brother?'

'We ain't that close. He's a copper.'

Pierce pulled a grin. 'Then you'll love this. He's been going, shall we say, beyond his brief. Not adhering to Scotland Yard's strict code of conduct.' Vaughn looked genuinely puzzled. Pierce gave an incredulous shake of the head and spelled it out. 'He's been giving her one, knocking her off, schtupping her. Showing the dog the bone. Sticking his—'

'I get the picture, Henry. Are you sure?'

'He's been seen, spotted. Observed. Clocked.'

For a man who was always a good few steps behind the game, and constantly caught in life's blinding headlights, there was no wide-eyed amazement from Vaughn at this information. He wasn't shocked. Bobbie and his brother did look good together. Even Vaughn could see that, in the drama that was unfolding, they were the two principals, the star turn. And he was happy to let them hog the stage as long as he could shuffle off it unscathed. 'So what's this got to do with me?'

'She's got to go.'

'Bobbie LaVita?'

Pierce gave a solemn nod.

'She's done wrong, Henry, they both have, but . . . but does she deserve to die?' Vaughn felt a genuine and overwhelming sadness that echoed his own loss. 'Maybe . . . maybe they love each other . . . ?'

'Like you and your girl . . . whass-her-name?'

'Her name is Wendy . . . *Wendy*,' he said, sinking down further and squelching about in the warm puddle on the bucket chair.

'Yours was a pure, decent love,' said Pierce, stepping around behind him and resting those violent hands on his bony, hunched shoulders. 'But theirs, their love is wrong. *All* wrong.'

Vaughn began to weep. Uncontrollable, chest-quaking, salt-wrenching sobs. 'I . . . I . . . I . . . I don't . . . I don't . . . I don't wer . . . wer . . . want to hurt anyone.'

'No one ever does,' said a soothing and avuncular Old Henry Pierce.

'Yer . . . yer . . . yer . . . *You* do.'

'That's true. Now, let's get you out of those wet clothes.'

CHAPTER 26

DIRTY WEEKEND

Crack!

Nothing.

Crack!

Nothing.

CRACK!

That one did it, and Vince's eyes opened. Bobbie was standing over him, the flat of her right hand primed and ready to smack him across the cheek again. His face stung, his vision going in and out of focus, but he could make out just enough to see he was back in his room at the Seaview Hotel.

Bobbie grabbed him by the lapels with both hands and sat him upright. His head lolled back again. She wrapped her arms around his waist and heaved him off the bed and on to his feet – only for his dead weight to fall back on to the bed. Not giving up, she repeated the manoeuvre. Again he fell back. And this is how it went on for about twenty minutes, but she persevered. She slapped him some more, she pulled his hair, threw cold water in his face, and thus she kept him awake. She brewed up cups of hot black coffee and forced it down his throat. Sometimes he puked it up, which was good; sometimes he kept it down, which was better. Eventually she got him to his feet. With his arms draped around her shoulders, she walked him around the room. She was exhausted and bruised, through him falling over and landing on top of her, or being pushed against the hard edges of the furniture under his collapsing weight. But she persevered and persevered until he had beaten whatever was running through him, and his body was again running, albeit shakily, under its own steam.

'Thank you,' were the first coherent words out of his mouth. He was sitting in a hot bath and Bobbie perched on the edge of it. With his vision no longer blurred, he saw she was wearing drainpipe blue jeans that were rolled up to just below the knee; ballet-pump style black shoes and a tight-fitting white and blue hooped Breton jumper. Although she was tired, devoid of her usual monochrome make-up with its pale powders and harsh black eyeliners, she looked younger than he'd ever seen her before, her skin taut and surprisingly olive-toned.

'What happened?' she asked.

Vince considered this, then after a few moments said, 'I went to a party.'

'Whose party?'

'Dickie Eton's.'

Bobbie's eyes widened. She looked alarmed. 'What are you talking about, Vincent?'

'You know about Dickie Eton's parties?'

'I've been to one,' said Bobbie. 'I left when everyone started taking their clothes off. What the hell were you doing there? And what the hell did you take?'

Vaughn shook his head and squeezed his eyes shut in concentration, until a memory spiked. 'They put something in my drink,' he said.

Bobbie, confused. 'You got drunk?'

'I don't drink.' He plucked the cigarette she was smoking out of her hand and took a long drag. He held down the fumes inside his chest, feeling the smoke scrape and scorch his lungs, then expelled it with a cough and a splutter.

'And you obviously don't smoke either,' she said, taking the cigarette out of his hand.

Vince looked at Bobbie and gave her a lazy smile. With his voice still smeary with the dope, he mumbled, 'You look beautiful . . . you know that? You really are a very beautiful girl. The most beautiful, beautiful girl I've seen . . . the most beauti—'

'Vincent!' she yelled, cutting him short. She wasn't smiling at the compliments, because the delivery was wrong – all wrong, slowed-down and vacant. This just didn't sound at all like the quick-witted and insightful young detective she'd found herself falling in love with.

He sensed her displeasure and ducked his head under the water.

'You look awful,' she said, as he resurfaced. 'Try and remember what happened.'

'They spiked my drink. Then . . . then I ended up back here . . .'

'Then how do you explain all this?' Her hand dipped into the bath and scooped away the soap bubbles covering his body. Vince saw bruising to his chest and arms, a gash across his ribs, his knees were torn to shreds, and he had welts to his body that looked like lash marks. The wound that caught his attention the most, and which his eye was oddly drawn to, was the smallest and the most imperceptible mark of all. In the fold of his right arm was a pinprick . . .

And then the memory of the previous night rewound and spooled into place.

The swimming pool, face down, naked, *dead* . . . The bodies crawling all over him . . . moving in on him . . . the boys and the girls . . . the doped-up sirens enticing him into the water . . . Vince rises to his bloodied knees . . . as bad a place to die as any, he'd thought . . . Dickie Eton, like Nero or Caligula, sitting on his poolside throne . . . shouts out to Tobin to stop . . . Eddie Tobin, can't help himself, follows through with more kicks to the gut . . . stamps his heel in his face . . . Vince chokes at the smell of dried dog shit . . . The cold white marble was surprisingly warm to the touch . . . the blow to the gut. Vince is chopped to the floor, doubled over . . . Like a movie set . . . Cecil B. DeMille . . . *Sodom and Gomorrah* . . . white marbled columns, fountains, a waterfall in the corner . . . The boys and the girls naked, fucking, an orgy . . . Pills ingested, powders snorted, dope smoked, dope shot and that crazy music whirling around his head . . . Vince thrown to the floor . . . The laughter getting louder, raucous, repellent, the music even more disorientating . . . Dragged through another long hallway, the paintings on the walls getting dirtier and dirtier, uglier and uglier. Sex and death, sex and death . . . Vince hauled to his feet, out of the chair, taken out of the wood-panelled study before the Big Nod kicks in . . . Tobin to one side, that pugnacious face, the spittle-webbed mouth laughing and snarling . . . On the other side, the lad with the soft smiling face and the darker purpose . . .

. . . His body contaminated, his blood polluted, forever corrupted. Shutting him down . . . That lethal dose of dirty brown in his bloodstream . . . The spike goes in, the bad heroin is injected into him, execution style. Just business . . . The door opens, Nick Soroya enters, hands behind his back. A gun? A knife? No . . . Vince in the chair, just his head floating, disembodied, limbs numb. Mickey Finn in the ice cool glass of Coke . . . Eddie Tobin sitting at the desk, his thin lips laughing. Oh the irony! . . . Tobin delivering the deadly joke with its killer punchline . . . 'You killed him, Treadwell. You *slaughtered* him . . .'

. . . Vince sat bolt upright, throwing off the sheet of bubbles that covered him; Bobbie jumped up as a wave of water splashed over the side of the bath.

'Vincent!' Bobbie's cry shook Vincent out of his recalled vision. 'What's wrong?'

Vince looked up at Bobbie and asked, 'How did I get here?'

'When you didn't come back to my place, I called the hotel. They told me that two men had delivered you to your room, said you'd been out drinking and you'd had too much. That's when I knew something was wrong, because you don't drink, do you?'

Vince gave a slow deliberate shake of his head, as he pieced it together.

'Tell me what happened, Vincent.'

He lay back again in the bath and rearranged the bubbles to cover himself. 'If I tell you what happened, you won't love me,' he said, not knowing if he was being serious or frivolous. He suspected it was the former, but his delivery suggested the latter. He took a big gulp of breath and ducked under the water again.

'If you don't, I *can't* love you,' said Bobbie as he resurfaced.

'I guess I have to take my chances, then.'

And he did. About everything. He laid out the whole thing from top to bottom (skipping over the bits she already knew). From Soho down to Brighton. From walking into the Peek-a-Boo Club with Tobin, to walking out of the Grand Hotel with Tobin. To being driven to Dickie Eton's party by Nick Soroya. To Dickie Eton and Lionel Duval's involvement with the porno films. To Eddie Tobin telling him about the death of the projectionist, and him being filmed committing the murder. Then finally, he, Detective Vincent Treadwell of Scotland Yard, being sent down to Brighton to solve the crime – the crime that he himself had committed.

It was at this point that Bobbie stopped the story. She had listened carefully, patiently. She was a good listener, and her own storytelling prowess, in reinventing her past, had made sure of that. She knew the devil was in the detail, but she didn't believe Vince had killed anyone. To her it was obvious that he had been framed. With or without the film, she reassured him that it was all a big set-up. And that, together, they would prove it. She was so strong and resolute in her beliefs that Vince believed her. The water was cold by the time Vince got out the bath, his skin the texture of coral. Bobbie wrapped a towel around him and dried him off.

'Are you hungry?' Bobbie asked him.

He gave a sluggish shrug.

'Good. Let's eat.'

The low-slung seagulls hovered over the town like marionettes in the hands of a lazy puppeteer, alerting all to a new day of fresh hunger, scavenging and survival, through their distressed, choric alarm call. Bobbie was exhausted, her body aching from the physical strain, and the desperation of seeing him slip in and out of consciousness and thinking she might lose him. But, as they walked from the Seaview Hotel and along the promenade, the sunrise's hallucinatory presence gave everything a fresh, invigorating glow.

Vince had his arm around Bobbie's waist, holding her close, feeling it was his turn to do the supporting. For all the new information he'd gleaned about himself and the murder case, he felt surprisingly at ease. Like he'd reached the end of something, and it was now out of his hands – the freedom of powerlessness. Whatever Nick Soroya had shot Vince through with, he was still feeling the hangover of. It was probably the same stuff he'd fixed his drink with. Either way, considering what he'd been told, Vince felt strangely at ease, almost serene. He certainly didn't *feel* like a killer, and he still had enough of the copper in him to feel innocent until proven guilty. And, even though he knew he had enough motive to commit the crime, and certainly enough righteous anger within him to carry it out, he needed to see the evidence, have it laid in front of him before he could condemn himself.

The town was scarred by the weekend's violence with the Mods and Rockers. Broken deckchairs littered the beach, smashed windows lined the high street, and there were bulging police cells. The papers were full of the weekend's mayhem, and moral indignation and shock. Questions to be asked in Parliament, and visiting politicians sent down to inspect the 'war zone' damage.

None of the cafés on the front were open yet, so Bobbie and Vince walked down to the beach and sat down, and there moulded themselves into the shingle. The beach was dotted with inhabited sleeping bags, which looked like recumbent walruses. Vince and Bobbie looked out to sea. Then the inevitable moved in on them.

'What are you going to do now?' asked Bobbie.

'I told you I've got some money stashed, and I'm owed some holiday pay, assuming I'm still a copper by the end of the week. Maybe go away, take that drive around Europe. You still want to come?'

'I didn't mean that. About the . . . the situation?'

Vince closed his eyes and lay back on the stones. 'Last night, Tobin said they were going to kill me, and they were going to get away with it. And if what Tobin told me is true, they *could* get away with it. Maybe leave me on a beach with a hotshot of bad heroin. Make it look like I dosed myself, like poor Wendy.'

'But you're a detective, Vincent, so they know you. Your colleagues know you, your friend Ray what's-his-name from Interpol knows you—'

Vince held up a halting hand and sat up again. 'That counts for nothing – they didn't believe what I saw the first time around. Even Ray thinks I'm obsessed with this case. There's also a medical report on me from an eminent Harley Street psychologist who treated me, claiming I'm a psycho. And apparently some film of me killing a man with my bare hands. They'll just think I've gone bad.'

She shook her head vehemently and said firmly, 'It's all lies. That's what *they* say, that's what they want you to believe. But it's not true, any of it. Where is this film of you killing the man? Where's the actual proof?'

Vince smiled, because her trust in him was heartbreaking. He lay back down on the stones. 'Like I said, Bobbie, if it's true, then last night was about showing me they've got me exactly where they want me. They could have killed me, could have shot me with that real bad heroin. But it seems I'm worth more to them alive than dead.' Vince rubbed his thumb over the soft skin where the needle had perforated. 'A corrupted copper is worth his weight in gold.' He emitted a slow heavy sigh, closed his eyes and let the morning sun warm his face and bruised body.

Bobbie studied Vince. He seemed almost *contented*, resigned to whatever was to play out. But she herself wasn't contented.

It was as if all Vince's rage had transferred itself over to her, so that she felt a burning resentment towards Lionel Duval, Dickie Eton, Eddie Tobin and all those who wanted Vincent beaten and laid out on the beach with his eyes closed. She stood up, wiped the damp clinging pebbles off her backside and purposefully insisted, 'Stand up, Vincent, I'm hungry.'

Vince and Bobbie were now sitting in a café. Eight tables covered in blue-check plastic tablecloths, with doors that opened out on to the esplanade, swivel racks selling cheap sunglasses, rubber rings, lilos, buckets and spades, flip-flops, postcards of the town and cheeky McGill cartoons, straw sunhats, and black-felt bowler hats with paper bands around them enticing passers-by to *Kiss Me Quick, Squeeze Me Slow*.

They had a full English breakfast arrayed in front of them. It was the biggest one they offered on the menu: 'The Big Brighton Gut-Buster'. Three sausages, three rashers of bacon, three runny fried eggs, three blood-dark discs of black pudding, three tinned tomatoes, a stack of chips and a pile of toast. Vince wasn't feeling hungry; it was Bobbie who had ordered up the breakfast. She knew Vince was running on empty, so his body needed fuelling and his mind needed firing. She watched as Vince dipped the corner of a piece of fried bread gingerly into the runny yolk of an egg, absentmindedly playing with his food.

Bobbie wanted to get him back on the case. 'Do you still think Jack has anything to do with all this?' she prodded. 'The dirty films . . . the girls?'

Vince didn't even acknowledge the question. He was caught up in the patterns he was making in the egg yolk, and probably more concerned with the age-old question of 'chicken or egg?' than Jack Regent's activities.

'Well?' she demanded.

His reply was mumbled, listless. 'Who knows.'

'*You're* the detective.'

He shrugged, and carried on staring down at his plate.

Bobbie dropped her knife and fork on her own plate with an attention-getting clatter.

They were the only ones in the café, so it was left to the two waitresses behind the counter to watch the good-looking young couple as the blonde slapped the dark-haired man around the face. The blow was struck with such power and velocity that they were surprised to see him ride it, then look almost grateful for it.

Vince raised his left hand to his face, and ran fingertips over his hot, numbed cheek; more to check that the cheek was still there than to soothe it. He looked at Bobbie. Her back was ramrod straight, her head cocked. There was a defiant, challenging look to her normally soft features. He'd already been slapped around the chops by Bobbie so many times during the night that he seemed resigned to it. Then, she'd only done it to stop him slipping into sleep and therefore the great void, the Big Nod. As for now, she'd done it to stop him slipping away from himself, slipping out of his identity as a detective. Maybe that was the thing she loved about him most, maybe not, but he wasn't going to take the chance.

He knew that Bobbie wanted Detective Vincent Treadwell back because he was strong, smart, resourceful and therefore could look after her now that Jack was gone. And because he could be all those things, and because he wanted her more than he'd ever wanted any woman before, he now did what he had to do.

He took two slices of toast, two sausages, two rashers of bacon, a disc of black pudding, a handful of chips, a dollop of ketchup, a dollop of brown sauce, and built himself a gut-busting sandwich. He opened his mouth as wide as he could, and took as big a bite as he could manage. Then worked his jaws for what seemed an eternity, and swallowed, before washing it down with several big glugs of black coffee. He put his plate to one side, took a tooth-pick and stuck it in his mouth, then folded his arms on the table. Finally, he faced her, ready for business.

'Jack must know about the dirty films?' Rhetorical, but Bobbie nodded anyway. 'First off, *dirty*. These films are beyond *dirty*. They're degenerate, OK?'

Bobbie nodded.

Vince manoeuvred the toothpick around his mouth with his tongue, and moved back into the mindset of a copper. 'Did Jack say anything about retiring?' he asked. 'About getting out of the game?'

'Jack's guarded. It wasn't chit-chat like with the boys.'

'Boys?'

Bobbie let out a sigh, as if she'd been caught out. 'Yeah, you know, Jack was an older man. He was more like a . . .' Her voice trailed off.

Vince stepped in and finished it, 'Like a father?'

She turned away from him, and thoughtlessly went about pressing her thumbnail into the plastic tablecloth, leaving a series of crescent-shaped imprints. She stopped vandalising the tablecloth after Vincent gave an admonishing cough.

'OK, Henry Pierce runs the operation along with Duval and Eton. He provides the *security*,' said Vince. 'It's a euphemism for dirty work – and, in a dirty business like the one they're running, that can get pretty dirty.'

'And your friend, Eddie Tobin.'

'Forget Tobin.' Vince gave a quick, dismissive shake of his head. 'Whatever he thinks he is, he's just a messenger. An ex-copper on the make who they'd never make a real partner. I think Henry Pierce is the answer. My guess is that Jack didn't know about the films.'

'That was my guess, too!'

He smiled. 'It's called team work. The team does the work, and the ones with the higher rank gets the credit. *Team work*.'

She smiled.

'Your guess, that he didn't know about the films, I agree with. Or, if he did know, he wasn't happy about it, and maybe that's

Jack's problem. He's made his money, wanted an easier life, then found love and wanted to settle down.'

They locked eyes. She won and stared him down.

'Or just wanted a quiet life,' ceded Vince. 'But you can't have a quiet life in this game. You're like a shark – stop moving and you're dead.'

'You think they killed Jack?'

Vince weighed it up. 'Doubtful . . . but they might have wanted him out of the way so they could carry on the operation without hindrance.' Vince took in a long breath, then let it out in a wistful sigh. He wasn't satisfied with his own analysis. 'Jack's smart, therefore why not let Pierce have a racket for himself and keep him happy? And Jack being Jack, why would he be opposed to that if it brought money in?'

Vince watched as Bobbie chewed this over. He handed her a toothpick. She, too, stuck it in her mouth and worked it around her lips with her tongue, resting her folded arms on the table. Sitting opposite, both deep in reflection, they were now mirror images of each other.

'And that's the reason,' said Vince, 'that Jack might not have wanted anything to do with the films. He didn't want it interfering with his new venture – his big-money venture. The one that would get him back in favour with his homeland and the Unione Corse. Heroin!'

Bobbie smiled, realizing he was back on track. 'So, Henry Pierce set Jack up with the . . . ?'

'With the body of the man I killed.'

She shook her head and spat out, 'Not true!' jabbing a finger in his chest. 'We don't know that.'

Vince smiled at Bobbie. She was no longer primarily defending Jack or his reputation – she was on Vince's side one hundred per cent. He was beginning to believe all that corny stuff he'd heard about the love of a good woman. '*We?* Are you my new partner, Detective LaVita?'

'Drinkwater. Detective Drinkwater. It sounds better . . . and I'd never thought I'd say that.'

'OK, Pierce took a knife that Jack had used on a past victim. It would be easy for him because that's what Pierce did: he cleared up Jack's messes. So, he had a stashed knife with Jack's prints all over it, took off the victim's head and the hands to stop it being identified.'

Bobbie looked down at her plate, where her fork lay, skewering bacon and black pudding, and covered in ketchup.

Vince saw Bobbie's uneasiness and, as she pushed her plate away, he rustled up a mischievous grin. 'Not so much fun now, is it: the nitty-gritty of murder?'

She returned his challenging look and said, 'I can handle it. Does Pierce know about you and . . . ?'

'Killing the projectionist?'

'We don't *know* that.'

Vince shrugged the smallest shrug available to him. 'I don't know.'

'Didn't you ask Tobin?'

Vince pulled a wry smile. 'You're forgetting my friend, Mickey Finn. I was groggy, not at my best, but I'm guessing Duval would have kept shtum. A copper in your pocket is a precious commodity that he can draw on any time he needs to. Duval and Tobin wouldn't have told a nut job like Pierce how the projectionist died. Pierce was merely in the disposal business.' Vince let out a sour little laugh. 'The poor bastard.'

'Who?'

'The projectionist. They certainly got their money's worth out of him. Duval uses him to set me up. Then Pierce uses him to set Jack up.'

All through this, Vince held on to the wry smile, till it was fixed to his face like wall cladding. But Bobbie saw through it to the anguish on the other side. She gathered up both his hands in hers, squeezed them and said, 'Let's stick with what we know, Vincent. And I know Henry Pierce isn't smart enough to outfox Jack.'

'Maybe not, but Max Vogel might be, and Pierce looked to me like he was taking his orders from him.'

Bobbie puckered her brow. 'I'm not buying it. Henry Pierce *loved* Jack – that's the only word for it. He would do anything for him. He didn't like me, not because I'd done anything to hurt him, but just because I got close to Jack. Or maybe closer than any other woman had ever got to him. It was jealousy, and I told Jack that once. He laughed, but he admitted it was true. I'm not saying Henry was queer for Jack, but he did love him.'

Vince gave a slow contemplative nod as he recalled Pierce's performance in the interview room, and his belief that Jack was either god or godless, the binary opposites that held equal power for Henry Pierce.

'Betraying Jack doesn't seem right to me, either,' said Vince. 'So you flip it. If that's the way it looks, maybe it looks that way because that's the way they want you to see it. Jack wants us to think he's finished. He wants us to think he's skipped town, retired to Corsica or wherever.'

Bobbie felt a cold chill. 'You think he's still here?'

Vince saw the fear backing up the question.

They went arm in arm as they walked out to sea. Or at least as far as the Palace Pier would take them. Past the fortune-teller's booth, the candyfloss concession, the fishing gear shop, the ghost train, the man setting out the deckchairs. Bobbie recognized the man who managed the arcade unlocking the doors for the day's trade. She smiled at him in acknowledgment, but he scowled and turned away when he saw her arm in arm with Vince.

'Who's that?' Vince asked.

'His name's Albert. He works for Jack.'

Vince glanced back at the man now walking into the arcade – lined with one-armed bandits, pinball, lucky dips and penny logs. Soon the place would be full of tourists putting their money into the machines, Jack's machines, Jack's pockets. You couldn't escape this town without paying tribute to Jack.

'Get used to it,' he said.

'What?'

'People turning away from you.'

'Doesn't bother me.'

Vince could see that it did bother her. And more so now after Vince had suggested that Jack hadn't left town.

'Anyway, it's a moot point,' she said.

'Why?'

Bobbie stopped walking, turned to face him and said, 'Because after you've cleared your name, you're going away from here, and I'm coming with you.'

'It sounds like you've made your mind up.'

'I have.'

'Do I have any say in it?'

'Not really. It's a done deal, signed, sealed and delivered.' She wrapped her arms around him and kissed him.

'Do you always get what you want?'

'Pretty much, these days. So you best be careful, because 1964 is a leap year. I could ask you to marry me.'

'Pick your moment and your scenery carefully. We could be anywhere we want to be by next week.'

They walked on until they reached the end of the pier. There they leaned over the rail and looked down at the black sea breaking around the barnacled iron girders, the spume leaping up to greet them.

'Legend has it there's a monster living down there, a thirty-foot Moray eel,' said Vince, staring into the black swell. He considered further this childhood exaggeration, then gathered up some spit in his mouth and let a slow gob fall into the sea below.

'Vincent!' She dug an elbow into his arm.

He gave her a mischievous grin. 'Everyone does it.'

'If you're *ten* years old.'

Bobbie leaned forward over the railing and spat, too. They stood spitting into the sea, watching those tiny flecks of themselves get swallowed up, until the clouds that had been gathering and darkening since they had stepped on to the pier burst open, and the gods spat back down on them.

They ran for cover.

CHAPTER 27

PIERS, QUEERS AND RACKETEERS

Vince stood before a large black oriental-style wardrobe that took up almost one entire side of the room. It was inlaid with silver wire and mother-of-pearl depicting exotic birds and insects. It was definitely top quality, not the knock-off stuff that Vogel was importing and peddling. Inside was a selection of Jack Regent's suits, shirts and ties. Like the wardrobe that contained them, the clothes were all top quality.

'Take your pick. You're about his size,' said Bobbie, who was standing behind him.

Vince's suit was a mess, crumpled, creased and carrying the sweat and strain of a long night.

'I'll go and get ready,' she said, leaving Vince to make a choice.

Vince eyed the suits lined up. He ran the back of his hand along their sleeves, making them ripple like keys on a piano. Shelves of laundered shirts, displayed like candy in a sweetshop, every colour available, stripes, check, different collar-and-cuff combinations; all hand-made Egyptian cotton from Jermyn Street. The suits were bespoke, run up by a tailor in Hong Kong: cashmere, fine wool, summer suits in linen and silk blend. Midnight-blue, Prince of Wales check, pin-stripe and chalk-stripe, shimmering sharkskin. Whatever else Vince thought about Jack, his taste was impeccable. And it all fitted him.

An hour later and Bobbie was ready. She'd soaked herself in a hot bath, got dressed again and painted her face and nails.

Vince had selected a midnight-blue suit, a powder-blue shirt, and a slim black knitted tie with subtle thin silver stripes woven through it. The shirt was monogrammed, and so was the hand-kerchief for his top pocket. Vince thought about the thief, Murray the Head, not wanting his name displayed on everything. Jack was different, however; he put his mark on the things he owned. Vince thought it strange at first that there were no shoes anywhere in the room, then he remembered Jack's disfigurement – the club foot. But even if the shoe did fit, so to speak, whilst he had no great compunction about wearing Jack's clothes, there was something about walking around in another man's shoes that just didn't feel right.

'You look great.'

Vince turned around to see Bobbie, who was wearing that turquoise silk dress, her mother's dress, with the brooch of the mythical bird. Vince was surprised to find her wearing it – knowing that there was a room in the apartment solely devoted to storing her clothes. It was probably crammed with expensive outfits.

'So do you.'

Three hours later they sat in a Wimpy Bar and ate Knickerbocker Glories. It had been a meal promised, and a date long overdue. Dressed to the nines, as they were, Vince had wanted to take her somewhere classy like Wheeler's, Prompt Corner or the Metropole, but Bobbie had visited these places with Jack, always getting the best table even if someone was already sitting there, and had the stodgy, genuflecting waiters fawn over them with a startling servility that made Bobbie uneasy. She wanted the brightly lit Wimpy Bar with its vinyl-buttoned booths and Formica tables, and its wholesome American hamburgers, multi-storey desserts with fan-shaped wafers and topped with chocolate and strawberry sauces, refreshing milkshakes served in tall glasses with a dirty joke waiting for you when you reached the end – for the bottom of the glass was stamped 'Duralex', and that sounded like a French letter.

As for the film, Vince had wanted to see *From Russia With Love,* but it was sold out. Bobbie wanted to see *Yesterday, Today and Tomorrow* with Sophia Loren and subtitles, but Vince argued that if he wanted to read, he'd go to the library. *A Shot in the Dark,* a comedy with Peter Sellers about a bumbling detective, was also playing, but Vince didn't fancy that, and *Zulu* with Stanley Baker and some new young actor. Bobbie had met Stanley Baker last year in the Astor Club in London, where he'd bought her and Jack a bottle of champagne, and told her this young blond actor was going to be big; meanwhile she'd forgotten his name. It was all enough to put Vince off that film, too. Bobbie thought Laurence Harvey was a dish, and wanted to see *Of Human Bondage;* but he was acting his socks off playing a man with a club foot, so that was a no-no. They settled on *The Fall of the Roman Empire.* It seemed to play out in real time, too, for by the time Rome eventually fell, Vince had himself fallen asleep.

So they left it early and went to a pub that Bobbie liked, by the Theatre Royal, knowing none of Jack's crowd would be there. In the upstairs, not so public, bar, the crowd was made up of queers and dykes and artist types. A black drag queen with the best legs Vince had ever seen was singing Eartha Kitt. 'She' invited Bobbie up to sing, and Bobbie joined him in a duet. They got chatting to a couple of theatrical types named Hugh and Dennis. They said Vince and Bobbie looked like a couple of film stars. When pushed, Vince had to admit he was a copper. Hugh and Dennis took that in their stride, and told him Brighton was full of 'Piers, queers and racketeers'. Vince bought them a drink.

As soon as Bobbie had twirled the key in the lock and they entered the flat, the phone started to ring. They looked at each other, and just let it ring. Neither wanted to answer it. It had broken the spell of their first date, during which time they had avoided all talk of the intrigue, deception and uncertainty that was uncontrollably spinning around them. They had talked about everything else a young couple might talk about on a first date. For, even though they had already been through so much, and been forced to reveal themselves so completely, they needed to catch up on the normal stuff. The frivolous stuff. Favourite books, films, music, first kisses, funny stories. There was an element of play-acting about it, mixing in with all the other dates waiting in line at the cinema; walking arm in arm along the street; being complimented by Hugh and Dennis; sitting in a booth at the Wimpy Bar. As with most young couples in love, there was a conceit about them. They knew they looked good together. Their bodies seemed to fit effortlessly, like missing pieces in a jig-saw puzzle finally put together and showing all the world what a dazzling picture it made. From an outsider's point of view, they looked as if they hadn't a care in the world.

And from the point of view of the man inside the black car who had followed them from destination to destination, and finally back to Adelaide Crescent, it looked just the same: not a care in the world . . .

The phone kept on ringing relentlessly, and seemingly getting louder and louder like an alarm. It demanded to be picked up, wouldn't take no for an answer. They both knew that once the call was answered, their 'date' was over.

Bobbie picked up the receiver, just to stop the noise, but left it hovering over its cradle. She looked up at Vince for guidance. He gave her the nod, and she put the phone to her ear and said, 'Hello . . .'

The caller refused to give his name, but Bobbie knew who it was. And so did Vince, by the look of contempt that crossed her face. He darted over to the phone and grabbed the receiver out of her hand.

'Vaughn!'

CHAPTER 28

BLIND MAN'S BUFF

Vince drove to the address that Vaughn had given him, a good half hour's drive east of Brighton, along the coast. He followed his brother's directions, but he lost precious time, driving in the dark, while trying to find the unmarked, narrow country lane that led to a dirt road that accessed the house. The road wasn't private, there being no gate, but the house was all there was at the end of it. Bumpy, with jagged flinty stones, the path was not lit up – puncture alley. The flinty road fizzled out and opened into grassland. And there was the house itself, standing almost at the edge of the cliff.

It was a small bungalow, no more than a chalet really, and at first sight it looked like a small farmhouse with a weatherboard facade. Seeing as there was nothing to farm here on the edge of a cliff, Vince took it as a holiday home or a little weekend bolthole. It sat all alone, no cars parked outside, and no lights inside to indicate that anyone was home.

Vince killed the engine and stepped out of the car. He heard the surf breaking, crashing on the rocks below the cliff, then drawing back out again, to repeat itself like some mighty perpetual drum roll. Before knocking on the door, he checked around the back and saw some large sliding glass doors. He decided that in daylight it might be worth while having a place with such a

dramatic sea view. But its isolation made him nervous, thus working in reverse of its intention: it seemed all too obvious a place
to hide out in. It almost warranted a huge neon sign proclaim-
ing: Hide-Out! The glass doors were locked, and he couldn't see
anyone inside, so he went back around the front and softly
knocked on the door.

'Vince?' came Vaughn's hushed voice from behind the door.

'Yeah. Open up.'

The door opened and there stood Vaughn. He led Vince through
to the living room. It looked as if it hadn't seen a lot of living in.
Vaughn lit a couple of candles, not for ambience but because the
light bulbs were blown. Otherwise the room was more homely
than the outside suggested. An armchair and a small covered settee;
a wooden rocker sitting in the corner of the room; a small television set in the other corner; a side table with an old black 1940s
telephone resting on it; and a small wooden coffee table. On the
last were some magazines: a couple of *Reader's Digest*s, a *Titbits* and
a *National Geographic*. The kind of reading material you'd find in a
dentist's waiting room. And that's exactly what it felt like – a place
for waiting for something potentially unpleasant.

'Sit down,' said Vaughn, gesturing to the settee.

Vince sat down. Vaughn took the rocking chair in the corner,
giving him a view of the room, the front door and the front
windows. He sat perfectly still in it, hands stuffed in his jacket
pockets.

'Took a while to find,' remarked Vince.

'Directions no good?'

'They were fine. It's just the type of place that takes a while to
find.'

Vaughn nodded, as if pleased with himself.

'How did you find it, Vaughn?'

'It's a mate's.'

'A mate's?' Vince echoed, looking around the place, uncon-
vinced. There wasn't much to it, but what there was didn't strike
him as it might belong to the kind of company Vaughn normally

kept. The magazines, the wooden mantel clock, the crocheted throw draped over the settee, the wooden rocking chair, the Home Sweet Home rug on the well-swept wooden floor, the armchair with an embroidered cushion. 'Can you be more specific?' Vince asked.

'You don't know him.'

Vince gave a nod towards the cushion on the armchair and said, 'No, but I'm admiring his needlework.'

'It's his mum's place.'

'OK, you want to tell me about it?'

'What's to tell? The bogies are looking for me.'

'That heroin, where did you get it from?'

'I didn't! It's not me!' snapped Vaughn, setting in motion the rocking chair.

'I saw it, Vaughn – and your girl, Wendy.'

Vaughn cast his eyes downwards on hearing her name. Vince could see the pain of her loss was genuine. 'I'm sorry about her, Vaughn. But that's what happens when you mess with that stuff.'

Vaughn's eyes shot up urgently. 'I had nothing to do with that, I swear to God, I got rid of . . .' His unthinking voice trailed off.

'You got rid of the heroin?'

Vaughn, knowing he'd already said enough, gave a guarded nod.

'Then what was a stash of it doing in your flat?'

'What stash?'

Vince saw that his brother was genuinely surprised by this. 'Machin found some of the junk stashed behind a cupboard in your flat. It's bad junk that's been doing the rounds and killing people.'

'That's not true!'

'Why would I lie?' asked Vince, impatient and angry. 'I'm here to help, you idiot!'

At that point, Vaughn pulled out the gun. It wasn't like Bobbie's old cannon but a sleek and lethal German 9mm Parabellum, perfect for up-close work.

'Easy, Vaughn, take it easy.'

'*You* take it easy, copper!'

Vince gave three meditative nods at this new development.

'Who's the idiot now?' Vaughn sneered.

'I guess that'll be me.' Vince dead-panned it. 'Did you know it was bad junk, when you were selling it?'

'What d'you take me for?' Vince didn't answer. 'I didn't find out till I read about it in the paper. I knew it was strong stuff, needed cutting, but not *that* bad.'

'If you really got rid of it, Vaughn, how come Wendy got hold of it?'

'Because she was a lying bitch!' exclaimed Vaughn, nodding his head now as if he was hammering in nails with it. 'She must have stolen some off me before I could unload it. She deserved what she got.'

'You believe that?'

''Course, I do!' he snapped, trying to sound as resolute as his shaky voice would allow. 'It ain't my fault. She lied to me! You can't trust junkies!'

'And who turned her into one?'

'She knew what she was doing . . . She lied, she stole the junk off me, she got what she deserved.'

'That's the company line, is it?'

'What company?'

Vince sighed, forgetting just what a dispiriting dumbshow talking to his brother could be. 'The company you're keeping, Vaughn. Machin found about half a pound of heroin. I was there and he showed it to me. I don't know how much you unloaded, but you'd have known if you were that short, wouldn't you say?' Vaughn clearly would have known, but he didn't say. Vince sat up and leaned in closer to the candlelight, to get a good look at his brother and make things as clear as possible.

'You've been set up, Vaughn. Little Wendy didn't steal anything off you. She didn't inject herself with the heroin either. She was dosed, given a hot shot. The heroin was stashed behind a cupboard, which is one of the first places coppers would look. Also they were working off a tip. The person who stashed it there was the one who dosed her. Any ideas who that might be?' Not giving Vaughn time to think or answer, he continued, 'Then, let me tell you, it was whoever put you up to this — sticking a gun on me and getting me out the way.'

Vaughn shook his head. 'Not true!'

Vince's brow creased in disdain. 'You know it's true, because it hurts, because it shows you for what you are. Deep down, you know poor little Wendy didn't steal that heroin. She didn't have it in her. That wasn't what she was about. Because she was OK — better than that, she was decent. A girl that got a tough break in life, born with that stain on her face. But little Wendy was an all-right kid. She deserved better. She deserved better than you.' Vaughn held the gun but it was Vince who was firing the bullets. 'But you're taking the easy way out, Vaughn. You're rewriting her sad little history to suit your own purposes. You want to believe she stole it because you're too weak to punish the man that did it to her.'

Vaughn shook his head vigorously in denial, but it just looked as if he was trying to shake the truth out of his ears.

'What was the easy way out, Vaughn? What deal did you make? Kill me and you get off the hook?'

'What if it was? I owe you nothing!'

'Maybe not, but you owe the girl. You owe Wendy — and so do I. Because she got killed in order for them to get at me. Because she was with you. You're being used, Vaughn, and it stinks. It stinks of Henry Pierce. What did he offer you?'

Vaughn's pallid, pockmarked skin had begun blotching and reddening up, tears brimming in his eyes. He cried out, 'More than you could, copper!'

Vaughn pulled back the hammer.

Death at his own brother's hand? It had a twist to it.

'Not you, Vaughn. Not you.'

Vince had a hunch he would have to make his move before a car, Henry Pierce's black Cadillac, drove down that flinty dirt lane and parked outside. Because by that time it would be too late . . .

CHAPTER 29

THE BLUE ORCHID

Vince had dropped Bobbie off at the Blue Orchid. She didn't want to go there, didn't want to leave the flat. There was still a large part of her that was in denial, holding on to the idea that no harm would come to her because of Jack. Vince understood all too well how that kind of patronage from a powerful man like Jack could become addictive, and hard to break free of. But he also knew that nothing stays the same in this game, and the world was littered with corpses of those who had held on to a delusional and deadly belief that it could. But Vince had insisted. He'd originally wanted her to go somewhere public, like to the pictures where they were showing a double bill. But she had refused, and settled on going to the club, as there she would at least know some people. He dropped her off at the bottom of Oriental Place and promised her that, as soon as he was finished with Vaughn, he would call by and pick her up. He would only be a couple of hours, at the most.

The first sign that all wasn't right was the actual sign itself. The neon sign that read 'The Blue Orchid' above the entrance wasn't switched on. And the door was locked. She rang the bell; there was no answer. Gino, the manager, should have been there by now to open up. She had given him firm instructions: it was business as usual until further notice. She fished around in her handbag and hooked out the keys, turned them in the brass lock and the door opened. It was dark and silent inside. She threw on the lights and saw the place was empty. She went into the back office and discovered the safe open – nothing had been taken, as no money was kept there, just some legal documents – and drawers had been searched. She felt spooked and went straight back home.

Once inside the flat, she went to call Gino and find out what was going on. The address book was a novelty one: red Bakelite with a silver dial. She put her finger in the 'G' slot for Gino – and was thrown into darkness as the lights suddenly went out. They had gone out in the whole building. She started going downstairs to check, but heard someone climbing the stairs and ran back inside, bolted and double-locked the door. She tried to call the police but, as soon as she put the receiver to her ear, she realized the line was dead. With a waxing moon and the street lights outside, Bobbie soon adjusted to loss of light inside the flat, and clearly saw, and heard, the front door handle turning quickly.

A pause. Someone, moving back from the door. Not to walk away from it, but to enable a run-up. Then a forceful weight against the door, the dull but powerful thud of someone trying to shoulder his way in. A second, harder, attempt indicated the intruder really getting into his stride. Under its impact, the whole wall groaned, joists screamed and paint cracked. As strong as the door was, as new and secure as the locks were, Bobbie was losing faith in them holding out. She could now see movement: the door buckling under the force. Such was its power that she imagined a charging rhinoceros outside.

She went over to the heavy black-lacquered bureau, the one Vince had slid across the door before there was a lock. It *was* heavy, however; just as heavy as it looked. She put all her weight behind it, which wasn't a lot, and tried to push it over to the door, to act as a barricade. The next onslaught on the door saw wood splitting along the frame. Inching the heavy bureau across the parquet flooring of the front-door entrance, she was filled with a sense of dread and impending doom that sapped her strength. On the next muscular ram from the rhino, the doorknob flew off. With a good four feet still to go, Bobbie gave up on her makeshift barricade, ran to the kitchen, opened a drawer and pulled out a carving knife. Then she remembered the gun that Vince had stashed away in the heavy black bureau. She also remembered Vince's advice about never firing it, and knew this was no time for props that might blow up in her face. If she had to have a weapon, she wanted one that at least worked. There was a heavy torch in the cupboard under the sink, so she picked it up, too.

Gripping the torch and the carving knife in either hand, she went back out to the living room; and took an intake of breath that hit the back of her throat like a blast of freezing air. The door was wide open. *The rhino was in the room.* She turned on the torch, her hands shaking, and shone the beam of light erratically. Slashes of light tore through the dark until the beam settled on something unfamiliar. In one corner of the room, a closed eye. With its complex of scar tissue, it looked like a small plate of spaghetti. The eye then opened. Milky, marbled and dead. Henry Pierce was standing in the corner of the room. Not expecting the torch to pick him out amongst the heavy black shapes of the furniture in the room, his plan to locate his prey and then pounce was now foiled. But no matter.

'Hello, my dear.'

He'd always referred to Bobbie in such terms as *My dear*, and it always made her skin crawl. He reminded her of some benevolent old uncle who would always turn nasty once the parents were away and the lights were out. And now they were. And now he was about to start.

'What's that in your hand?' Pierce asked.

'What do you want?' A stupid question. And one he didn't bother answering.

'I've got one of those, too. Sharp and pointy.'

'One of what?'

'One of' – *swooosh* '– these!'

298

Pierce held up the sword stick that he had drawn from its white wooden sheath. The ruse walking stick that hid a much darker and deadlier purpose.

Bobbie moved backwards, hoping to circumnavigate this nightmare and make it to safety downstairs.

'Stay right there – right where I can *see* you.'

She froze, never having expected to hear those words come out of Pierce's mouth. Then she realized that his black glasses were off. She slowly sidled to the left, then to the right, but his one good eye, like an annoying portrait, continued following her around the room. His bad eye was frightening her even more.

'You're not really . . . *blind*?'

'None so blind as those who cannot see.'

He moved out from the corner and loped over to the heavy black wooden bureau, and with just one hand he pushed it up against the doorway, as if it was a mock-up, movie-set prop fashioned out of balsa wood.

Bobbie now knew she was in for a long and painful night.

Vaughn sat back in the rocking chair, the gun still trained on his brother.

'Now what?' asked Vince.

'We wait.'

'Whilst we're waiting, d'you mind if I run a few things by you? Just for my own curiosity.'

'Like what?'

'Like who gave you the heroin?'

Vaughn gave a sour smile. 'Guess.'

'The stuff comes from Jack Regent, brought in by Max Vogel, is my guess. But you wouldn't be dealing with either of those two – no offence, Vaughn, but you're too far down the pecking order.'

Vaughn's sour smile curdled and then died on his face.

'So, that leaves Henry Pierce. Why would he give it to *you*?'

'I did some work for him.'

'Driving?'

'And other stuff.' Eager to impress now. 'Wanna know?'

'I'm all ears.'

'The body on the beach, that was me.'

Vince didn't move a muscle, involuntarily or otherwise. It seemed that the age of great surprises was over for him. This was the time for twisted ironies.

Vaughn, back with the smirk, proud of his job. 'I chopped its head and hands off and dumped it.'

'That makes sense. The job was botched.'

'I followed Henry's instructions, to the letter.'

'The blind leading the blind.'

'Henry ain't blind. It's just an act to keep the coppers off his back. Who's gonna mess with a blind man?'

All Vince's hunches were coming to pass. The intruder in Bobbie's flat could only have been Pierce. That wasn't the work of a blind man stumbling around in the dark. 'The body was meant to be found then, because the job was meant to be botched. That makes sense. If you want a botch job, you're the man to do it, Vaughn. In fact, I'm surprised you didn't even botch the botch job by doing it right and never having the body turning up.'

Vaughn took a few moments to work out that it was an insult, then he spat out, 'Shut your mouth!'

'Do you know who killed the man you buried?'

Vaughn nodded, savouring his gangster moment. 'Top London boys. We picked up the stiff in Soho.'

Vince feigned impressed. 'Friends of yours?'

Vaughn took a cigarette out of his coat pocket, lit it from one of the candles on the table, then took a long, satisfied and noisy drag. He left that question hanging in the air for Vince to answer.

Vince answered it silently, but didn't share it. Because it wasn't the answer Vaughn would want to hear. Because Vince knew that his brother was strictly a 'wait in the car' man. So Vaughn would never have met Duval and Tobin. They wouldn't have wanted to meet him. Vaughn was the kind of low-level hood that a smart cookie like Duval would have insulated himself from. It would have all gone through Pierce.

So Duval and Tobin would never have made the connection that Vaughn was Vince's brother.

Instead, Vince said, 'The stiff you got rid of, you picked him up in Wardour Street, at a club called the Peek-A-Boo? You did the driving for Pierce, using an ice-cream van.'

Vaughn felt a chill at the memory: Mister Whippy. Henry Pierce had made him wear the white uniform with the cardboard hat, just in case they got pulled over. The blood on his coat looked conveniently like raspberry sauce.

Vaughn, incredulous, demanded, 'How do you know that?'

'I'm guessing you weren't introduced to the men involved, but one was a grey-haired smooth-looking fella, goes by name of Lionel Duval. He owns that club, the Peek-A-Boo. Owns a lot of Soho, for that matter. The other man, stockier, older, red-faced, looks like an ex-pug. His name's Eddie Tobin, my ex-beat partner in Vice.'

Vaughn gave an imperceptible and involuntary nod of acknowledgement to these facts.

'*You* know who killed the stiff?' Vaughn sat there, his mouth gaping in ignorance.

Vince couldn't help the wicked grin that waxed around his mouth, as he told him, 'It was me. I did it.'

Vaughn sat bolt upright, stirring the rocking chair into motion. He quickly steadied it with his feet, scared that Vince would take this opportunity of jumping him and snatching the gun. Vaughn was under no illusion that, if he got jumped, he would end up with nothing in his hands and it would be Vince pointing the gun. He rubbed his left eye quickly with his balled fist, as if he couldn't believe what was laid in front of him. 'You . . . ?'

Vince nodded, calm as you like. 'That's what I've been told, but of course, I don't remember a thing about it. And deep down I don't think I did do it, but they say they have a film of me that proves otherwise. So, you see, I'm just as fucked as you. Even more so, I'd say. Let's be honest, Vaughn, nothing much was ever expected from you, and you didn't disappoint. But me turning bad? Well, I've got further to fall. One thing we do have in common, Vaughn, is that we're both being stitched up. So, wise up, put the gun away and let's work out a way to get out of this. We never did do much together as brothers and this could be our big chance.'

Vaughn picked up on the sarcasm. 'Fuck you. I've got a way out.'

'Henry Pierce?'

A quick, unsure nod from Vaughn.

Vince laughed. 'For dumping the stiff, Henry Pierce paid you in bad junk, hoping that you'd take it and kill yourself.' Vince now saw that Vaughn really hadn't worked that one out.

A candle fizzed and spat like a cheap firework, and seemed to burn brighter, throwing an unforgiving light on to Vaughn's face. He had nowhere to hide. Not even when behind a gun.

Vince, notching it up, knowing he had to make his move soon, continued. 'And you trust him, you mug?'

'I'm no mug! I've got stuff on Pierce!' barked Vaughn, setting the rocking chair off again.

'You're disposable, Vaughn, always have been. Now put the gun—'

'Bastard!' Vaughn screamed, jumping to his feet. The gun was held in two trembling, intertwined hands, two twig-like fingers on the trigger. His expression was glowering, the skin of his face almost rippling with rage.

Vince had intended to rile him, to get him off balance, but he didn't want to receive a bullet. He slowly raised his hands in the surrender position.

'Put the gun down. You're not going to shoot me.'

'Don't bank on it, copper.'

Vince shot out of the chair, one hand on the gun, the other hand around his brother's throat. He smashed Vaughn into the wall, then threw him to the floor with such force that he seemed to slide along the polished wood.

Vaughn lifted his head, dazed, eyes popping, but still clutching the gun. He lifted both arms to take aim. Vince dropped to the floor, snuffing out the candle with his hand on the way down. Vaughn squeezed off a shot. *Bang!*

Vince distinctly felt the cold slipstream of where the bullet had passed. He clamped his hand to the right side of his head, felt blood. But it was a glancing impact that had just grazed his ear. Close enough, though, for Vince to mouth a silent *Fuck!* and to know what he had to do next.

Vaughn called out, 'Vince! You OK?'

Vince didn't answer, remained down behind the coffee table, playing possum. Bullet-in-the-brain dead. He could see Vaughn get up on one knee, but couldn't still see the gun. Then he heard the click of the hammer being pulled back. That sound annulled any brotherly love that may have been felt in Vaughn's last utterance. His brother was just checking his status as a corpse, and was now about to finish the job by putting a fresh bullet in him.

Vince eased himself up carefully into a crouch, making sure he stayed lower than the coffee table. As soon as he saw Vaughn rising, the coiled Vince sprung. With his head kept down he felt his cranium connect with Vaughn's chin. There was a grinding and snapping of ill-set teeth, followed by a low yelp of surprise and pain. Vince had launched himself with such force that he'd almost thrust Vaughn through the wall. A palpable tremor ran through the prefabricated bungalow. With one hand around Vaughn's throat, Vince sent his brother's head smashing against the skirting board as he fell. There was blood on the wall from his brother's injured head, and around his mouth where the splintered teeth had pierced his tongue.

Vince reached down with his other hand to search for the gun that might still be in Vaughn's hand. Meanwhile he squeezed his brother's throat to stop him calling out. In the tormented silence that followed, he heard the gargle of blood from within Vaughn's throat. Still Vince squeezed tight, unprepared to listen to any pleas.

Down on the floor it was even darker yet he could distinguish the expanding whites of Vaughn's eyes as they bulged, almost cartoonishly, turning his wretched features into some type of cheap Halloween mask. Vince turned away from the sight, felt his brother squirming underneath him. Those bony legs trying to kick out, doing the death dance, the last dance – the one you do on the end of a rope. Vince wanted to be sure of having the gun in his hand, before the last breath left Vaughn's body.

Then he found the weapon, as he felt the hard metal of it pressing into his chest. The butt or the barrel, he couldn't tell.

Then it gave its report.

CHAPTER 30

MAE WEST'S LIPS

Bobbie was sitting on the red-lipped sofa. Henry Pierce sat in the chair opposite, a high-backed armchair with gilt-painted woodwork and red-velvet upholstery. Ornate, altogether over the top, and Jack's. His chair, his throne. Pierce had seen him seated in it many times. He recalled looking up at Jack, whilst he himself sat below his level, on the feminised sofa, awaiting his boss's instructions. Over time he'd grown to resent the arrangement – not Jack being boss, for that was never in question – but merely the seating arrangements. Jack on his burnished throne, all-powerful and talking down to him, while Pierce perched on a pair of girly fucking lips. Naaaa, no way to conduct business, Pierce thought, not dignified. Jack Regent? Jack Regina more like! *She* really knew how to lord it, sometimes! But now the chairs had been turned and he was on the throne. He had control.

Pierce had poured himself a glass of brandy, a Vieille Reserve, Jack's favourite tipple. He held the swordstick in his hand, its point rotating and boring a hole into the thick blue carpet. Pierce savoured the spirit, and the moment. As far as he was concerned, everything had now gone to plan. Even though he hadn't actually planned any of it. But he satisfied himself that, if he had planned it, he couldn't have executed it any better.

305

He looked down at Bobbie. She stared at the hole he was making in the carpet. He considered the carving knife that she was holding so unconvincingly. They both had weapons, but, even with the best will in the world, you'd be hard pressed to call it a Mexican stand-off. She might as well have been wielding one of Murray the Head's nail files. Bobbie looked down at the knife in her hand – and had a nasty feeling it would soon be out of it.

'What do you think Treadwell will do when he comes back here to find that knife you're holding buried in your skull?' asked Pierce.

Bobbie dry-swallowed but said nothing.

'Young Vincent has got one of two options,' he said. 'One, he'll call the bogies and report a murder, then Machin will do a thorough investigation. A certain film will fall into his hands, showing Treadwell killing a man with his bare hands. Machin will put two and two together, because that's what coppers are wont to do, and come up with a suitable conclusion: crime of passion. Copper falls for and then kills a gangster's inamorata. The same gangster that he was sent down here to nick. Or, option two, the more likely but less bleedin' newsworthy scenario: he'll cut off your head, your hands, drive the knife into your chest to puncture your lungs to get all the air out of you, and then bury you somewhere at sea. Then he'll go back to London like nothing ever happened, and carry on with his good work for the Metropolitan police service.' Pierce smiled contentedly on reaching this conclusion.

Bobbie bit her bottom lip, hoping the pain would distract her from thinking about the latter fate just laid out for her. Then she shook her head. 'It's all a lie, because Vincent wouldn't do that. He's not a killer.'

'That's what I thought,' said Pierce, reaching into the inside pocket of his black Crombie overcoat and pulling out a long cardboard tube, 'until I was shown these today. They're enough to make you wish you was blind.' Pierce tut-tutted and threw the tube over towards Bobbie.

It bounced off the plump bottom lip of the sofa, and fell on to the floor next to Bobbie's feet. She glanced down at it, then fixed her eyes straight back on Pierce. He carefully rested the sword-stick on the arm of the throne, then mockingly raised his hands, palms upwards, in a fey gesture of surrender, knowing that he could take the carving knife off her in a none-too-bothersome second.

Vigilantly, Bobbie leaned down to pick up the cardboard tube, making sure that the pointy end of her knife was constantly aimed at Pierce, as though it was a wand that could ward off evil spirits. With one hand, she popped off the white plastic cap as if it was a big tube of Smarties and stuck a finger inside. Instead of sweets, she found two A4-sized, rolled-up glossy black-and-white photos. Sliding them out of the tube, she laid them on the coffee table. About five seconds was all it took for the knife to fall from her trembling grip. The tremble took over, reverberated around her body, shook tears from her eyes. She buried her head in her hands.

As Pierce stood up, the carving knife was already in his hand . . .

Vince placed the receiver down on its cradle. He had just called an ambulance for Vaughn, who was laid out on the floor with a pillow under his head, and his jacket tied around him by its sleeves to stem the blood. The bullet had caught him on his right-hand side, just below the ribs. No major organs there, but enough of a hole to empty him out. Apart from the bloodied mouth, smashed teeth and cracked cranium, his eyes were as wide as saucers. A permanent eddy of tears streaked his pockmarked cheeks, as Vaughn had not accepted the consequences of his actions stoically. Vince thought he might have to knock him out to stop his screaming and squirming so he could then tie something more effective around the wound to stem the blood. It had been fifty-fifty who would get shot, but Vince knew that if anyone were to take a bet on it from past form, their money would be on Vaughn buying the bullet. Vince picked up the gun from the floor, emptied it of the remaining bullets, then threw it on to the sofa.

'I didn't want to be the one to bring you in, Vaughn, but that's what I would be obliged to do, so maybe this is the best result.'

'Tell me about it, copper.'

'Nothing to do with being a copper. Whatever you think of me, I'm still your brother, and I don't want to see you dead. And Pierce and the others, they'll kill you, and they'll do it properly so that you'll never be found. You've got nowhere to run, Vaughn.'

'I'd have killed *you*, so what do you care what happens to *me*?'

'You would have, yes, but you didn't. As for caring what happens to you, Vaughn? I don't know that I do any more. But we shared the same mother, so . . .'

Whatever was left of Vaughn's tough-guy schtick had pretty much evaporated now. 'What's . . . what's going to happen to me, Vince? Will they hang me?'

Vince walked towards the door.

'Vince . . . please, Vince, will they?'

'The ambulance will be here soon. Don't try and move. You won't get very far.'

Vince opened the door and exited without looking back at his brother. He stared up at the moon, which was clouding over. Dark swathes covered its face. It looked angry.

'Vince! . . . Vince! Please, don't let them. Please . . . !'

Vince walked over to the car, his brother's pleas falling on deaf ears. He got in the vehicle and drove off.

CHAPTER 31

THE HALF OF IT

'They're what they call "stills" in the picture business,' said Henry Pierce, eyeing the glossies. 'When they want to advertise a coming attraction, they take photos of the best bits, and hang them in the foyer. "Publicity stills",' he elaborated in an enlightened, learn-something-new-every-day kind of way.

Bobbie still had her head buried in her hands, still too torn apart inside herself to look at the photos. So Pierce forced the issue. He bent down, grabbed her by the hair, pulled her head up, picked up one of the photos and shoved it in front of her face. 'See how photogenic young Vincent is?'

Bobbie yanked herself free, grabbed the photo out of his hand and tore it in pieces.

Pierce tut-tutted. 'Shouldn't have done that. I was hoping to get the young star himself to sign it. But, don't worry, plenty more where they came from. Enough copies to last a lifetime. His lifetime at least. You see, they don't want to kill Vincent, because, since he's a copper, much as I'd like to, you just can't. Not the done thing. And you certainly don't kill the goose that lays the golden eggs. I've heard good things about the boy, headed for the top of his chosen profession. Of course, the boy obviously needs looking after, to be handled with care. He has violent tendencies, but none of us is perfect, I say. I did a stint in Broadmoor meself, would you believe? They wanted to call me "Mad" Henry when I got out – you know how villains love snappy monikers – but I soon nipped that one in the bud. Everyone's a "mad" something or other in my line of work.'

Pierce dragged Bobbie to her feet by her hair. She was nearly on tiptoes when he remarked, 'You've got a lovely head of hair, my dear. That lustrous, it would make a nice addition. I collect scalps, you see. Maybe Jack told you? Maybe young Vincent told you?'

She spat in his face.

He threw her weightless body on to the big red mouth of the sofa that she wished would swallow her up. You never give up on the cavalry, thought Bobbie desperately. Vincent would come through the door and save her . . . At this point, she would have taken Jack coming through the door – even if she didn't see a happy ending to that scenario either.

Pierce started to move in.

Delay!

She now gave up on the cavalry. It was up to her now. She knew she had to talk to him, engage him, prolong whatever life she still had left.

Delay!

'You've always hated me, Henry, from the first time you set eyes on me. But what did I ever do to you? Please, just answer me that.'

'One of you has to go. And, as they say, better a bent copper in the hand than a dirty bird in the bush.'

Delay!

'The brooch? When I first met you, Henry, you wanted to take a closer look at my brooch. Why was that? Tell me why?'

Pierce readjusted his grip on the carving knife into the killing position.

'Was it the dress?' Though she was riddled with fear and desperation, her voice held firm. 'What was it you saw, Henry . . . *please* tell me!'

310

Pierce stared down at her. She didn't cower any more but met his gaze head-on. Usually no one looked at Henry Pierce's good eye. They were too mesmerized, too horrified, by his bad eye. But Bobbie now peered into it, and found something. A glimmer, a hint of hidden treasure. *His Tell*. Henry Pierce was hiding a secret, and now Bobbie knew she had him. Because she herself knew the nature of secrets, and how the best ones are seldom kept. A good secret is an even better story that's just waiting in the wings – waiting to burst on to the stage. Stories *need* to be told, and she saw that Pierce was dying to spill.

And who better to spill it to than someone who was about to die?

'There's something you want to tell me, isn't there? I know there is.' She smiled at him, her eyes wide like a child. She said softly, conspiratorially, 'You can tell me, Henry. *Anything*.'

Pierce stood there unmoving, as if rigor-mortic in thought. As that bad old brain of his ticked over, he realized a golden opportunity had just presented itself. And on that realization his mouth twitched and creased into a grin. He hooked the thumb of his left hand under the fob chain hanging from the buttonhole of his lapel, yanked out a half-hunter gold pocket watch from his top pocket and gave it a glance. He had time; it wouldn't take long. And he knew it would only add to the occasion, which made this time well spent. He sat back down on the burnished throne.

'Anything?' he echoed.

'*Anything*.'

'There is something, yes. Something I need to unburden myself of, and who better . . . ?'

Pierce looked genuinely grateful to her for giving him this opportunity. He just hadn't thought of it, and it was so obvious. *To kill Bobbie without telling her? No, that would never do*. He would never have forgiven himself.

Pierce cleared his gummy throat and began, 'It was 1939 and I remember it like it was yesterday. Christmas Eve, snow on the ground, fairy lights, decorations, chestnuts roasting on an open fire. Picture the scene. Lovely time of year, if you like that kind of thing. Means nothing much to me, but there you go. Jack, just out of nick, eighteen-month stretch for malicious wounding. He got out early, 'cause he saved a screw's life in a riot. It was all a put-up job. They only had the riot so Jack could save the bloke's life. Anyway, he's out early, so I picks him up. I suggested a slap-up meal, drinks, a club, some whores – if you like that kind of thing. Means nothing much to me, but there you go. Not Jack, oh no, he's all business. Business first. Take care of business. Someone he had to see, someone who had been taking liberties, besmirching his reputation. Had to be straightened out, taken care of . . .'

. . . 1939. A black Rover 8 with blood-red leather interior pulls up outside St Michael's Place. The front door of number 27 had a red and green festive wreath attached to its heavy brass knocker. The door was off the latch and the two men made their way inside to the dark hallway. Without turning on the light, Jack made his way up the stairs. It was on the stairs that Jack's heavy-booted foot pronounced itself, the light foot levering its way upwards, while taking the weight of the other, which then landed with a distinctive thud.

Four floors up and they were on the desired landing. Jack stood at the door he was about to enter and listened for signs of life. All he heard was his own breath, measured and calm. The climb had taken nothing out of him, nor did the thought of what he was about to do unnerve him. He stepped back a couple of paces, raised his clubbed foot, then hammered it home, sending the door flying off its lock.

Inside, the startled voices of a man and woman rudely awoken were heard. A light went on in a bedroom. A sliver of it escaped under the door and feebly illuminated the living room where Jack and Pierce now stood.

Jack scanned the room, which was tatty and depressing. Threadbare carpet, damp and mottled peeling wallpaper, cheap painted furniture. As an attempt at seasonal cheer, a small tinsel-covered Christmas tree stood in the corner of the room, shedding pine needles on to a handful of wrapped presents. Some cards stood on the mantelpiece.

'What the bloody hell is—!' A woman's voice, fearful, as she started getting out of bed and pulling on a dressing gown. Jack entered the room and the door slammed shut.

'No . . . please, God, no!' Her panic-pitched voice scorching the ceiling, but going nowhere.

Jack grabbed her hair and reeled her in towards him. Her long, shiny auburn tresses were wrapped around his hand like silk rope as he forced her to her knees. Her head was pulled back, the long white neck exposed, her green eyes wide open and so alive. Jack's other hand gripped the ebonized hilt of a long slim knife. Her cries quickly muted to gargles and bubbled out in blood as the knife sliced back and forth; fast, savage, severing the spine. Her lifeless body, almost in two parts now, fell to the floor.

Jack then turned his attention to the corner of the room . . . And there he crouched, cowering on the floor. Bollock-naked and well and truly backed into a corner. He still had the sweat of his exertions with the woman on him. No doubt he was cocksure, felt he could handle himself in the right circumstances. These weren't the right circumstances. He looked up at Jack. The inevitability of it all took away some of the fear. He knew what was coming, because he knew Jack Regent.

Jack held the man's gaze as he approached, then slowly drew the knife down to the level of his face. With a steady hand he placed the tip of the blade on to the black pupil of the man's hazel eye. The pupil dilated and contracted – flashing on and off like an emergency signal. The tip of the blade now slowly punctured the membrane that covered the jellied lens – yet still the man didn't squeeze his eyes shut, or even blink. He couldn't take his gaze off Jack and time slowed for the kneeling man. His life didn't flash before him, because what he was watching was so much more compelling than anything that had gone on before – a front-row seat for his own execution.

Jack gave the man a soft smile, almost an adieu. *And in one swift, powerful movement drove the knife into his eye, through the soft grey matter until it reached the bone at the back of his skull. His body juddered and twitched as Jack rotated and twisted the blade buried in his head;*

skewering his brain, shutting down the fear, the thoughts, the memories, until his life faded like a diminishing signal . . . over and out.

Jack came out of the bedroom. switching off the light. Henry Pierce eyed him admiringly. Hardly a drop of blood on the long, perfectly tailored camel-hair overcoat. Pierce knew what came next. Whilst it wasn't exactly routine, this was how they'd done it before. Jack would depart and leave Pierce to his work: the clean-up, the getting rid of the bodies. The tools were in the car. Take them apart and bury them at sea. Pierce cracked his knuckles inside his black leather gloves, showing his readiness for the task ahead.

But Jack didn't go immediately and leave Pierce to his work. He held out the knife and fixed him with a challenging look. Henry Pierce took the weapon simply because it was offered to him. This unexpected move threw him slightly, and his heavy brow furrowed in confusion. He didn't know what came next, so he looked to Jack for further instruction.

Jack didn't say a word. He pulled out his silver cigarette case, took out one of his French cigarettes, put it to his lip, and fired it up with the engraved gold lighter. The flame illuminated the dark hallway. Jack inhaled the rich smoke, then plumed it like an instruction towards a door.

Pierce was no longer confused; he had got the message. Sweat prickled his top lip. He quickly wiped it away with the back of one leather-clad hand. He knew Jack might take that for weakness – maybe even insubordination, a questioning of his judgement. Pierce gave him three slow, considered nods and conceded it was the right thing to do. The only thing to do. By the time he reached the third nod, he wondered why he hadn't thought of it himself. But that was Jack, always one step ahead. It would join them, bond them in blood: a shared deed they would carry together to the grave. Pierce savoured this morbid thought. He gripped the knife in a hand which still trembled. He reckoned even Jack could forgive him this minor weakness, considering what he was tasked with . . .

Jack went out of the flat. Pierce listened as those uneven footsteps faded away, heading down the stairs. He then headed towards the bedroom door and pressed his ear against it. The only sound he could hear was his own jagged breath. He reopened the door. The room was pitch black, seemingly windowless. No light from the street lamps below or the three-quarter moon above made its way into the room. But darkness, and whatever it held, never bothered Henry Pierce. Dressed in black, as always, he even felt an affinity with it.

The long knife in his hand was steady now, as he stepped over the threshold, and closed the door behind him . . .

Bobbie exhaled a dispirited and disgusted sigh, then asked timorously, 'Please, I need to know . . . who were they?'

Pierce slowly raised a knotty forefinger to his lips, and then said in a tone of someone chiding an impatient child, 'First things first, my dear. There's more to come, much more.' He lowered his hand and carried on . . .

. . . A black wall. He stands stock-still, waits until his eyes adjust to the darkness and the wall crumbles before him. The room is cluttered with clothes, women's clothes. Dresses and other garments draped over every piece of furniture, lynched on wire hangers, scattered around the room; long gowns and fur coats hang from curtains rails, blocking the street lights below and three-quarter moon above.

Then a noise, crying and mewling. The waking cries of a baby. Pierce stands over a large cot, but he can't look. He holds the long knife ready, raises the knife over the cot. The baby's cries grow louder, swelling for attention. He doesn't look into the cot, but knows it's there. A clean kill, for God's sake, a clean kill. He grabs an evening gown hanging on the door of a bulging wardrobe, and throws the turquoise silk evening dress over the mewling object inside the cot. He looks down for the first time, takes aim at the small moving mound under the fabric. He adjusts the knife in his hand into a stabbing position. His hand shakes, so he tightens his grip around the ebonized hilt. He closes his eyes . . . mutters . . . 'God forgive me' . . . then brings the knife down.

'Stop!' screamed Bobbie.

Pierce snapped out of his storytelling reverie.

'You didn't *kill* the baby?'

'Yes, and I've regretted it ever since,' said Pierce, his head drooping in shame, full of repentance for the past. Racked with guilt, he had never been able to forgive himself for what he did that night. And now he was confronted with the consequences.

Bobbie tried to block out the unfathomable horror of the Herodian atrocity. Her mind desperately scrambling around for hope, found some solace in those words he'd uttered: *regretted it ever since.* A chink in his insanity perhaps? Some degree of humanity creeping in . . . and some hope for herself?

Pierce raised his bowed head, and lowered his heavy brow so his features sank into a satanic V. Then he said, 'Yes, I didn't kill the baby.'

Bobbie was at first confused. Then she remembered the old wartime song, *Yes! We have no bananas, yes we have no bananas today.* Bobbie felt both blasts of that double negative, as hope disappeared and insanity returned.

'And I've regretted not killing the baby ever since,' snarled Pierce, shaking his head as if in disgust, while he continued the story . . .

. . . Pierce, his eyes squeezed shut, lifts the knife from out of the cot. He opens his eyes and sees there is no blood on the blade. He looks down into the cot, and sees the turquoise-silk dress shift shape. Still alive . . .

'I missed.'

'Missed?'

'*Missed.*'

A numbness spread around her body like a ghost. She didn't want to know any more, but she had to keep going – had to keep Pierce talking and keep herself alive. 'What happened?' she asked in almost a whisper.

Pierce gave a burdensome shrug. 'Madness? Weakness? Superstition mainly. In fact, you could say that superstition was my weakness, and my madness. I've been prey to it all my life. It stems from my wrestling days. You'll find that most professional performers and sportsmen are superstitious. And having Red Indian blood in me probably didn't help, them being a superstitious lot and no mistake. Not walking under ladders, or hats on the bed, or black cats crossing your path, that sort of thing. So, you see, I couldn't stab the little mite again any more than I could walk under a ladder or put a hat on a bed. So I said to myself, I said, Henry, if it's still alive, then maybe it was meant to live.'

Bobbie wrapped her arms tightly around herself, as if an Arctic chill suddenly pervaded the room. She began rocking slightly on the lip of the sofa, as she pieced it together, sensed where this story was heading. She looked down at her dress, the turquoise silk dress. Her mother's dress. Pierce leaned in and brushed his hand over her breast, and over the brooch. She didn't flinch.

'Take off the brooch, my dear.'

'No,' she said, her mind now a montage of memories, piecing together the times she had spent with Jack. Him asking about her past, her mother and father . . . the mother and father she never knew . . . the mother and father *he* had killed.

'Take it off!'

Bobbie, trance-like, turned the brooch over and slid the long, thick fastening pin from its catch, then withdrew the pin through the material till the brooch was off. Revealing the repaired gash where the knife had entered. Scarcely an inch long, but undeniably there.

Pierce smiled in recognition of the slashed dress as the memories rolled back for him, too. 'The minute I saw that dress, I knew it was you. I remember your mother. Never forget a face, and a real beauty she was. And you, my dear, are your mother's girl. Same face – the image of her. Got a touch of your father about you, but you're a spit of your mother. A beauty.' A snide, knowing smile spread across his face. 'Easy to see why Jack would fall for you.'

Tears forced their way through her closed eyes and fell freely on to the silk dress and soaked into it like big spots. Her parents, the young couple, now became vibrant to Bobbie, almost alive to her as her imagination joined up the dots. She wondered what might have happened to incur Jack's wrath. Her father might have owed Jack some money and couldn't pay it back. But would Jack *really* kill him over that? She didn't know, because Jack was a black mystery to her now. Maybe her father had said something out of turn, something to cause Jack offence. Bobbie at once recoiled from the thought, a wave of repulsion moving over her. Was she making excuses for Jack, her lover? If Pierce was to be believed, he had slaughtered a whole family: father, mother and, for all he knew, their baby daughter. As inconceivably evil as it seemed, and as undeniably mad as Pierce was, she unquestioningly believed it. Deep down, she knew it was true. She *did* believe that Jack Regent, the man she'd lain with, had butchered her own parents . . .

'You want to know what happened next?' Pierce asked, disrupting her thoughts.

She didn't want to know, but she did want to live. So she nodded.

'I wrapped you up in that dress and drove you out of Brighton that night. It was dawn when I found the church where I left you on the steps.' Pierce gave a throaty chuckle. 'Christmas Day, I should have left you in a barn, to keep up the nativity theme. So, you could say, my dear, I saved your life.'

Her eyes still closed, the heavy sobs has subsided into sharp little intakes of breath, and her hands still clasped the brooch. 'You should have killed me.'

Pierce gave a slow, harmonious nod of accord, then gripped the arms of the throne and hauled himself to his feet. He stretched himself to his full height and bulk, and issued a plangent sigh that marked the end of the conversation and his confession, and signalled that the bloodletting would commence. He moved slowly towards her, carving knife in hand.

His words echoed in Bobbie's mind: *If it was still alive, then maybe it was meant to live.* She wanted to live.

'You bastard!' she yelled. 'Jack Regent killed my mother and father, and you . . . you want me to be grateful?'

At these words, Henry Pierce stopped in his tracks and stood stock-still. His mouth twitched, a smile teetering across his dry old lips, then it transformed itself into a fully fledged grin. And then he laughed. He laughed loud and he laughed hard, till he was doubled up in his mirth. Eventually, after he'd exhausted it, he stilled himself. He calmed his breath that was still wheezy from laughter. He felt this moment needed silence, because he felt a weight of responsibility for what he was about to do. It felt good to him, he felt like God, not only having her life in his hands, her future, but also her past. He was about to tear it all away from her and leave her with nothing. Henry Pierce had killed before . . . but not like this. Not from the inside out. This solemn moment needed time, more time than they had, but still . . .

He drew closer to her.

Bobbie, her head bowed, gripped the brooch in her hand, squeezing it tight. The end of the thick pin had sunk into the base of her thumb, boring into the flesh, the tendon, the muscle, towards the bone. The warm blood coursing down her fingers felt good to the touch. She wanted to feel more of it.

Pierce bent down to meet her gaze, his neck seemingly extending out of the grimy collar of his shirt; an unnatural and dangerous position for him to be in, like a giraffe grazing in the long grass. But this was the real moment he had been waiting for: to study the wretched creature he'd caught and trapped under glass, as he delivered the denouement, the final part of her destruction.

And then he could finally kill her. Everything inside out.

'My dear, you don't know the half of it. *The half—*'

'*The half of it!*'

The all-powerful, all-knowing, all-seeing Henry Pierce was now stopped, unsure and blind. The brooch pin sank into his eye. The good eye. The seeing eye.

Bobbie had heard enough of what emerged from Pierce's mouth, enough to last her a lifetime. She was ready. Coiled ready on the mouth-shaped sofa, she sprang. Her only warning was those hissed words, '*The half of it!*'

At that, Pierce took his first backwards step. He'd seen something in her eyes, something fresh, something new. An expression that sent a jolt of uncertainty through his powerful body. And, in that backward step, and in a flash, she leapt up and was straddled around him. Her left arm was around the back of his head, grabbing a hank of his inky-black hair. In her bloodied right hand, the brooch was buried within her fist, its long pin sticking out from between her fore and middle fingers, a deadly protrusion like the sting on the scorpion's tail. And, with her legs wrapped around his waist, she jabbed the pin straight into his eye, moving her balled fist around and around, digging deeper, as it shredded the jellied lens.

Pierce gave a scream, surprisingly high and shrill for the brutish bulk of his body. But it soon faded as he worked on ridding himself of the lacerating limpet that had attached itself to him with such speed and surprise, and was now destroying his only good eye. The unfavoured eye that paled in comparison with the scary-looking eye. The eye that he'd never shown too much interest in went up in his esteem now that he realized he was losing it.

But it was too late. The work was done.

His arms flailed and flapped about, like some dreadful old albatross trying to take flight, as she gripped him tightly. They were thrashing around the room, engaged in a ghastly dance, clattering into furniture, smashing ornaments, knocking into gilt-framed mirrors and taking paintings off the walls. But Pierce had played the blind man for so long now that he was well rehearsed in the role, enough to get his bearings. Somehow he felt as if he still had his good eye and, working on the memory of sight, that's what led him towards the doorway. He regained his balance, and charged for the door.

Bobbie, her eyes still closed, still hanging on, trying to push the entire brooch into his bloody eye socket, felt a first crushing blow as her back slammed into the heavy black bureau that stood blocking the doorway. She let out a scream of pain.

Pierce, alerted to the doorway by her knife-like scream directly into his ear, shuddered helplessly in pain and rage. He didn't want her attacking any more of his senses, and he knew he would be desperately needing his ears. Realizing that he'd run into the bureau, from hearing her pain, he stepped backwards, then charged at it again. Another scream, and the sound of cracking just in front of him, either bone or wood.

Then release, her grip was gone. She was off him.

Bobbie was now on the floor, crawling away from him. Pierce, blood coursing down his face, still wanted to finish the job he'd started. He gripped the black bureau, braced himself and, with a loin-stretching groan, heaved it up over his head. Henry 'Redskin' Pierce, like his grandfather before him, the supposed Sioux warrior, used his tracking senses. He listened. He sniffed the air around him, hoping to pick up her scent: Chanel No. 5. He was now doing all the things he pretended to do when he was pretending to be blind. The irony wasn't lost on him – but it still wasn't *fucking* funny.

His head tilted downwards. The bad eye and the new *really* bad eye were superfluously directed towards Bobbie, sprawled in a crawling position on the floor. She looked up at Pierce and, seeing she was about to be crushed by what seemed like a monolith, carefully, silently, took off her shoe and tossed it about five feet across the room. Hearing the noise, Pierce turned his attention in that direction; shifted his stance and, with a belting grunt, hurled the black block of wood in the direction of the fallen shoe. The bureau, brittle and old, exploded on to the parquet floor. Then Pierce stood in silence, listening for the last sounds of the crushed and dying girl.

And heard . . . *nothing.*

Pierce stared out into this new-found blackness. *Was this it?* he asked himself. His shoulders collapsed; it had all gone wrong. This would never have happened to Jack. For him, the girl would be dead by now. Maybe he now wanted to cry? But this was not the time for experiments. Pierce stood there wondering if anything else came after the blackness. Wondering if this was all a bad joke and the lights would come back on again. He didn't know what to do next.

Then he realized it was over. The lights weren't coming on again – and this was it. That black garb he'd dressed himself in all these years, even during the most inappropriately sunny of days, was never coming off now. There was no respite from the dark-ness that had once defined him. The dress rehearsal for the old performer playing the blind man was over – this was opening night for the rest of his life. He was at one with the part now. And in a soft, sad, almost involuntary voice, he said 'Goodbye' to the girl.

Gripping the ornate banister, operating on falls, rolls, bumps, twisted ankles and gravity, he bruisingly made his way down the unforgiving marble stairs. With arms outstretched in front of him, like Frankenstein's sad old monster, he stumbled out into the street, groping his way into the night and into the middle of the road. He lifted his head to the sky and let the rain beat down on his face to wash the blood away and cleanse his brand-new eye. The fantastic new jewel he wore glistened in the rain and moonlight. The light from the moon and the street lamps playing on the silver and the cut-glass stones. The brooch was now firmly implanted in his eye socket. The dead diamanté eye was as much a part of him now as the dead marble eye. Neither of them pretty, but both fitting.

'SPIDER!'

. . . Spider had been instructed to park on the opposite side of the crescent, and that's exactly where he was, in Pierce's car, a black 59 Cadillac sedan Deville with red interior. Spider liked tooling around in Pierce's Caddy – typical of Pierce to have a yank tank. Fuck-off fins, fuck-off V8 engine and fuck-off white wall tyres. Nice and conspicuous, a real eye-catcher, it was the only Cadillac in Brighton now. A local car dealer had owned one, too, different colour, white interior. Pierce had the car stolen, then compacted. The other Cadillac, now about the size of a television set, was then dumped on to the car dealer's front lawn; along with a warning not to be such a flash cunt. The town wasn't big enough for two of them: Cadillacs that is, not flash cunts. The town was full of flash cunts. And Spider was one of them.

Spider had known that Pierce was planning to kill Bobbie, because Pierce had filled him in on the details. Not *all* the details, not what happened twenty-five years ago, because that was private between him and Bobbie. Pierce had told him that the order came from up high, and it made Spider feel good that Pierce was part of a bigger picture, and not just acting under his own psychotic volition. It made Spider feel good that he himself was part of a bigger picture. And a murder. That felt really good, really villainous. That Pierce was taking his own sweet time to do the job didn't worry Spider unduly. He knew that Pierce, a sadist at heart, would savour his work, indulging his depravity. So, once Pierce disappeared into the house, Spider had lit up a joint and turned on the radio. Maybe that's why he didn't initially hear his boss, Henry Pierce, as he called out into the night.

'SPIDER!'

The black 59 Cadillac Deville with red trim pulled up. The back door was duly opened. Pierce, his hand covering his newly ornamented eye, was guided into the back seat. But there seemed to be someone next to him. Confused, he called out to his driver. 'Spider!'

Spider didn't answer. Spider was next to him in the back seat. Dead.

With a heavy foot on the accelerator, the car sped off into the night.

CHAPTER 32

SNAP!

The street-entrance door was ajar. It was dark inside. Vince tried the lights – dead. He walked towards the stairs and felt a stickiness underfoot. He looked down to see a tar-like substance on the marble floor. As black as it was, he soon recognized it as congealing blood. Without hesitation, he raced up the stairs.

The door to the apartment was closed, but almost hanging off its hinges. Vince needed to lift the door to open it and enter the flat. He tried the lights; again they were dead. To his left he saw a twisted heap on the floor: it turned out to be the smashed black bureau. He called out Bobbie's name. No answer.

Vince went down one of the passages and noticed a soft warm light flickering from inside one of the rooms. He put his ear to the door, and heard a young girl's voice. She was softly singing a lullaby that was carried along on the hushed, jagged breath of sobs. He opened the door into a large white-tiled bathroom, and saw that Bobbie was lying in the bath. A single candle lit the room. Her precious photo album lay on the floor.

She didn't seem to notice him as she stared straight ahead, her toes playing with the taps. The bathwater was pink with blood. He looked at her body, but saw no wounds.

'What happened, Bobbie?'

She carried on staring at her toes and humming her lullaby.

Vince braced himself for the worst, but stayed calm. 'I went to the Blue Orchid, but no one was there . . .' Still she kept on with the lullaby. 'Bobbie?'

'The bad man,' she said, pulling an exaggerated, frightened-child grimace. 'The bad man dressed in black came.'

Vince bent down and grabbed her under the arms and lifted her out of the tepid water and on to her feet. She was as light as a rag doll, lifeless as if all that spirit that keeps us from floating off into the ether had evaporated. Bobbie didn't say a word to all this manhandling. She seemed stoned but he sensed she hadn't taken anything. Then he saw the bruising, the colour spectrum of pain: black and blue and brown and yellow. It stretched from her shoulder blades down to the base of her spine, like a mottled cape. He held her close, her limp body swaying in his arms. He squeezed his eyes shut and whispered, 'Sorry sorry sorry sorry . . .'

Grabbing a white towel off the rail, he wrapped it around her. Then he picked her up in his arms and carried her down the passage, into the living room, and laid her gently on the red lips of the sofa.

'My pictures . . . ?' she said softly.

He went back into the bathroom and retrieved her photo album. She held it close, hugging it in her arms.

'The lights, Bobbie? Do you know where the fuse box is?'

'Vincent, sit down with me, just for a moment,' she uttered in a childish voice, opening her photo album.

Vince tried to suppress his impatience. 'Come on, Bobbie, please, where is it? Is it downstairs? Do you know?'

Not looking up from the album, 'Downstairs under the table, I think,' she replied perfectly calmly, as if nothing had happened.

Vince went downstairs and located the fuse box. The fuses themselves were all in place, just switched off. He pressed the switch and the hallway lit up.

Back upstairs, he found Bobbie sitting bolt upright, peering at the photo album. She was smiling at the pictures and muttering, not just to herself but to the people in the photos. She was asking them questions, giving instructions, chiding and laughing. The images had come to life and she was now absorbed in the world of her photo album, as the memories swarmed back to her. Borrowed, stolen, fake, but memories nonetheless; formed in her imagination, forged out of the darkness and nightmares of her childhood. They were hers, and right now they were better than the ones Pierce had left her with.

Vince surveyed the damage. The bureau lying there like a stack of firewood for a bonfire about to be lit, the broken ornaments, shattered mirrors, upturned furniture, the glass-fronted clock lying smashed on the floor. And the blood, thick and dark like tar or spat tobacco. He went over and stood beside her.

'Bobbie?'

She didn't answer, her focus still on the photo album. Vince put his forefinger under her lightly dimpled chin, and gently lifted it until her eyes finally met his – or tried to. Those brown eyes that always seemed so alive and switched on, now wore an emulsive sheen and looked vacant and lost. He wondered if this was an act to put him off asking her the questions he needed to ask. The little actress trying to escape reality?

'Bobbie, the blood? What happened?'

'None so blind as those who cannot see,' she recited and winked at him. 'Well, *he* would say that now, wouldn't he?' It was a joke, and she was smiling, but it was underpinned by a steely dead-eyed coldness. She turned her attention back to the photo album.

Vince looked about the room for clues to Pierce's demise and spotted the carving knife on the floor. He bent down and picked it up, finding there was no blood on it. Then he noticed Pierce's swordstick lying under the tall throne-like chair. No blood on that either. Pierce didn't play by the Queensberry Rules, and most women don't know them, anyway. *None so blind as those . . .*

'Sit down with me, Vincent. We can look at my photos,' trilled Bobbie in a childish cadence, unnecessarily shifting over to make space for him on the sofa.

Too late. Vince had found his own photos. He bent down and picked up the torn glossy prints scattered on the floor. Realizing what they were, he put them on the coffee table and pieced them together. The evidence laid out in front of him, undeniable. He sank to his knees, not only to get a closer look but because he physically had to. His life had drained away from him and was now spilled all over the coffee table. He inhaled deep and sombre breaths and stared at the evidence before him, caught in black and white. He thought of the possibilities of the photos being mock-ups. With the right equipment, it's easily done. While working Vice Squad he'd seen porno mags, photos of movie stars performing gross acts with smiles on their faces as if they were in a Lassie movie. But he knew *these* weren't forged. He looked at himself, hoping he wouldn't see himself there. But it *was* him, just as Eddie Tobin had said. Vince was kneeling directly over the man on the floor, his right hand raised, balled into a fist that was about to smash down into the waiting face of the projectionist. Vince wore a twisted scowl of righteous anger, during a moment frozen in time. A single frame of film. But what had happened next? That was what Vince couldn't see.

His mind raced ahead, writing a scenario for himself, putting himself in the dock and making his defence. He wasn't a killer, he assured himself. He didn't feel like a killer! But what did a killer feel like? Vince had sat in on interviews with real sociopaths, and the experience had always left him cold. Their moral compass was so out of sync with the rest of the world. They talked about their murders as if they were everyday and commonplace actions; couching the atrocities in emotionless language possessing the monotony of a read-out shopping list or an errand run. And then you had your schizophrenics, who remember nothing when they kill. They wash the blood off their hands and wake up forgetting it ever happened: a tabula rasa.

Vince looked around the wreckage of the room, at the girl sitting on the red lips looking at the photo album. It all presented a surreal aspect of insanity. He thought of the good Dr Boehm, whose diagnosis not only had Vince pegged as schizophrenic sociopath but also a narcissist. He guessed that narcissists would like nothing better than to sit around looking at pictures of themselves, yet here Vince was looking at pictures of himself that he wished didn't exist. And Bobbie was looking at pictures of herself that never did exist. Surreal insanity.

Vince stood up, stamped the blood back into his feet and shook off the feeling of unreality. He paced around the coffee table displaying the photos and wanted to kick it over, but didn't want to add to the carnage of the room, or the madness. He was determined not to get dragged under. Vince knew, somewhere deep down, that none of it was true. It was all a set-up. He knew that it was only telling him half the story. What about the girl on the screen? Where were the pictures of her in this collection? If she was alive, he could find her and thus discover the truth. She could tell them, how he was trying to save her. As for the projectionist, maybe he had been justified in killing him? Maybe he was merely defending himself? And if he did kill that sicko who was putting such vile obscenity up on the screen, then what of it? Maybe he was *justified* . . .

The phone rang and broke his train of thought.

'Don't pick it up,' said Bobbie firmly, her eyes suddenly alert. She put down the photo album and stood ready to block his way.

He gave her a soothing smile. 'Nothing to worry about,' he said, padding over to the phone.

'Please . . .' she said, following him, wrapping her arms around him, burying her face in his chest. 'Let's go. Let's get out now, leave now . . .'

Vince unpeeled her arms from around his neck, then carefully picked the receiver up as if it was a stick of dynamite about to go off. He didn't say a word, just listened hard. He heard panting – more like a dog than a human. The breathing was erratic, and the caller was trying to control it and put words in its place.

'Hell . . . hello . . . hello?' came the voice at the other end. There was interference on the line, a crackling static that broke the voice up.

'Is . . . is . . . is anyone there?'

The well-brought-up voice was unmistakable, no matter how hard the interference tried to distort it.

'Terence?' Vince asked.

'Yes . . . s.'

Vince took the phone from his ear, beat the earpiece against the hard edge of his lower palm, hoping to dislodge the static, then put it back to his ear. 'Terence? Can you hear me?'

'I can hear you.'

'Where are you?

'The harbour.'

Terence sounded so faint and remote that Vince felt as if he himself should be saying, in a plummy BBC voice, 'Go ahead, Hong Kong. We're receiving you.' Instead, he shouted down the blower: ''Fucksake, Terence, speak up! I can't hear you!'

'I'm in Shoreham harb—'

Vince, loud and annoyed: 'I got that part. What are you *doing* there, Terence?'

'He's here!'

'Who's here?'

'Jack.'

Vince gripped the stick of dynamite which had now just blown up in his ear. Then he tried to compose himself, not wanting to alert Bobbie to what he'd just heard. But he needed to double-check what he'd just heard.

'Say that again.'

'Jack Regent. I've seen him . . . Called the hotel, but you've not been there, so I called this number you gave me. You don't mind, do you, Vince?'

'No, Terence, I don't mind. Tell me exactly what you saw.'

'I was standing about thirty yards away, between the loading pallets. I was staking out the warehouse.'

In normal circumstances, Vince would have raised a smile at Terence's use of the term 'staking out', obviously culled from one of *The Black Mask* detective magazines he avidly read. But these weren't normal circumstances, and this wasn't the time for fictional heroics.

'A car pulled up at the warehouse. It was American. No one got out. They waited for about a minute, then the warehouse doors opened, and they drove in.'

'OK, you're forty yards away—'

'Thirty.'

'Thirty, then. It's dark. How do you know it was . . . ?' Vince, conscious of Bobbie listening, didn't even want to use the pronoun *him*, because she'd instantly know who *him* was. Because there was only one *him* in this story.

'I made my way along the quayside and spotted the man in the driving seat. He was wearing a hat, but he lit a cigarette. I then saw his face. It was Jack Regent.'

Vince was concerned. 'Did he see you?'

There was a pause.

'No no no, I was very careful.'

'Terence, are you wearing those shoes with the Blakeys?!'

'No, I thought of that, Vince. I'm on surveillance, so I wore my plimsolls.'

'Jesus Christ, Terence . . . get out of there.'

'But it was him, Vince. It was—'

'Get out of there. That's an order!'

Beep-beep-beep. The pips went.

'Vince, I'll call—'

Vince, urgent. 'Give me your number.'

The line went dead.

Vince paced around the room, waiting for Terence to call him back. Bobbie was pacing after him.

'I'm not giving up.'

'Giving up what, Vincent?!'

'Giving up who I am.'

As soon as Vince put the phone down, Bobbie had said, 'Jack's here, isn't he?' She'd been watching him speaking on the phone with his back towards her, talking quietly, not giving anything away. She'd seen his back straighten, the muscles of his shoulders tighten. Even before Vince had shouted, 'Get out of there!' it was obvious.

She demanded the truth, and eventually he told her. He saw fear invade her face, and heard anger disfigure her voice. Mixed emotions blending into pure hatred. He tried soothing her by insisting that he was going to get Jack and put him away for life so she'd never have to see him again. But that didn't allay her fear, or assuage her raw hatred. Vince didn't understand where this fresh burst of hatred came from, but he accepted it. He was getting used to not asking questions.

'I came down here to do a job, Bobbie. I'm still a detective until I'm told otherwise.'

'Even if it means ending up in the pay of the men you're supposed to be going after? They've got you trapped now, Vincent. Your life's not your own.'

Vince stared at her, noticing her eyes – alert, lucid all of a sudden. 'I'm not going through the rest of my life living in fear of something I don't even know I've actually done.'

She pointed to the pile of evidence on the table – the torn-up photos and said, 'Those are just the stills. Pierce said they have the whole thing on film—'

Vince cut in, 'I know what they say, Bobbie!'

'You've done your job, Vincent. It's over. You came down to find a killer, and you found him. It's you.'

Vince's head dropped and he couldn't meet her gaze.

She went over to him and clasped his face in her hands. 'I'm sorry I'm sorry I'm sorry. It's not true, it's not true, Vincent. You're a good man . . .' she crooned, peppering his face with kisses. She felt guilty, knowing that Vince had given up all his secrets, while she still held on to her own. She had no right to throw it all back in his face. If Vince knew what she knew about Jack, then he'd have righteous justification in destroying him. She'd even expect Vince to do so. And that's one reason she didn't tell him. The other reason was clear to her: she felt ashamed at once having loved the man who had slain her parents and destroyed her childhood.

Vince broke away from her and went over to the coffee table, collected the torn-up photos and headed into the kitchen. He put them all in the sink, took some matches and set them alight, watching his torn-up past turn brown, blacken, then curl up and die.

CHAPTER 33

THE WORLD'S PROP STORE

A large case sat in the back of the Triumph Herald. Vince had helped Bobbie pack, knowing that, even in these circumstances, to ask anyone to pack a bag for a lifetime, especially a woman with a wardrobe so full and fancy as Bobbie's, would be futile and time-consuming. He misjudged her, however, because she was fast and ruthless with her possessions. She packed only her own clothes. All the really expensive outfits were courtesy of Jack, and now she didn't want them. She was ridding herself of the past, shedding the skin that signified Jack. The turquoise silk dress, her mother's dress, was taken into the kitchen and placed on the funeral pyre that Vince had started with the photos, then unceremoniously lit. Vince noted that the phoenix brooch wasn't pinned on the dress. He also noted how the burning of the garment, that last vestige of her mother, was not a problem for her. It rather surprised him, but he didn't question it. And the photo album? Bobbie left it behind on the sofa. Before they turned out the lights and left the flat, Vince asked her if she was sure she had everything? Bobbie glanced at the photo album for a moment, then gave him a firm 'Yes' and they left.

The rain beat down on the windscreen in a steady thrum as they made their way to the Seaview Hotel. It was the middle of the night and the coast road was empty of traffic. The street lights, distorted by the rain, lit up the long straight empty road in a bright orange hue, like an aeroplane runway.

Vince glanced around at Bobbie, who was smiling. But it was a vacant smile; it had little joy about it and wasn't pleasing to see. It was the same faraway and lost look she had carried on her face when he'd found her in the bath. She had been slipping intermittently in and out of it, ever since.

'Bobbie? Bobbie?' he called softly. Her head leaned against the window, but her eyes were closed and she was mumbling the lullaby again. It unnerved him seeing her like this. The bruising on her back, the destruction of the flat, he didn't know exactly what had passed between her and Pierce, but a nightmare made flesh he imagined.

They passed the West Pier, where some tramps were gathered under the available shelter, sharing a bottle. Standing by the railings, Vince thought he saw a man clasping what looked like grey sludge in his outstretched hands. He was yelling out to the almighty sea that was battering and tearing at the beach before him. Vince realized it was Billy 'the Schnozz' Riley, the tormented town crier, the ghost from his past. The rain had washed the curse from his forehead, and pulped the newspaper held in his hand, but he was still calling out the names of the town's dead.

Vince felt exhausted too. He felt as if he was out in the middle of that pitching sea, flailing around and trying to get ashore. Above him hovered the seabirds, big web-footed scavengers, waiting to pick his bones. And in front of him was Billy the Schnozz, calling out his name from his book of the dead.

This brought his thoughts back around to Terence. Vince shook his head and rapped his knuckles against the steering wheel in frustration.

Bobbie sat up from her reverie, suddenly alert. 'What's wrong?'

'Terence,' he said solemnly. 'He didn't call me back.'

'Maybe he didn't have change.'

'He had change, believe me. Terence is an ex-boy scout,' said Vince with a wry smile – though he didn't know that for sure.

'Terence is the kind of kid that always has spare change, stamps, maps, a compass, and his gloves sewn into the sleeves of his jacket.'

They reached the Seaview Hotel and parked.

'You told him to go home. I heard you.'

'I know what I told him, Bobbie,' said Vince, shaking his head at the dangerous impetuousness he and the young scribe shared. 'But Terence is a stubborn little bastard, and sometimes he doesn't really know what's good for him.'

There was no one at the reception desk of the Seaview Hotel. There was no one in the bar either. The entire place seemed deserted, eerily quiet. No sounds of people creaking about upstairs. Vince wondered if it was just him, seeing things that weren't there, and not hearing things that were there. It was the middle of the night, after all. He rang the bell on the desk. No response.

They went upstairs. He fished out his room key and opened the door. Vince hit the switch and saw that the room had been neatly made up. But sitting on top of the plump pillow on the bed were two small boxes, jewellery boxes. One was a hexagon-shaped ring box in green tooled leather, the other oblong-shaped in red leather. Vince and Bobbie, in almost comic unison, looked at each other with quizzical frowns. Then they opened the boxes. Vince found a gold pendant hanging from a gold chain, Bobbie found a gold signet ring. Realizing that the pendant was for the girl, the signet ring was for the boy, they wordlessly swapped over. Both items of jewellery carried the same engraved image: a Moor's head. Vince picked up the two boxes and examined them, to find both were stamped, on the silk lining, with the name and address of Max Vogel's antiques shop.

Bobbie put the pendant around her neck, and examined more closely the engraving. 'It's the same as the picture you drew.'

'It's a gift from Jack,' said Vince.

She held the pendant in her hand, her eyes widening as the news sank in. The Moor's head seemed to metamorphose into

Jack's head. She tore it roughly from her neck, the gold links scattered as she threw it to the floor.

'Let's get out of here,' she said in a resolute voice.

Vince bent down, picked up the pendant and put it back in the box. He had not been a hundred per cent sure about Terence seeing Jack at the harbour – considering it was dark, there was a sea mist and it was raining. Whilst the young scribe wasn't the type to make up stories, his writer's imagination might lead him astray. But now Vince was sure that the Corsican was here.

'I have to find Terence first. To make sure he's OK.'

'No, please, Vincent, let's go. Let's go now!'

'I have to find him, Bobbie. I have to.'

'Please—'

Vince held her tightly in his arms and whispered in her ear, 'Do you trust me?'

'Yes.'

'Do you *trust* me?' he repeated.

'Yes.'

He sat her down on the bed, then calmly, as if he was laying out the most routine of itineraries, he continued, 'Then, here's what we're going to do. Now, listen . . .'

Bobbie listened. It took some convincing her, but here's what they did. Vince sat her down with her case in the bar of the hotel. She didn't want to be left alone in the room, but the man who was tending both the bar and the desk had returned. Nothing sinister, he had just been taking a snooze. When Vince questioned him on who had been up to his room, he hadn't seen anyone, nor had anyone asked for him. Vince believed him because he looked genuinely surprised when Vince showed him the gifts they had received. When the man offered to put the jewellery in the hotel safe for safe keeping, Vince handed over the two boxes, knowing that he would never return to collect them.

Vince assured Bobbie that he would call her in thirty minutes. He was just going out to check on Terence, nothing more. He genuinely wasn't going after Jack. And if he found out that Jack was in town, he would call his friend Ray Dryden, at Interpol, and let him deal with it. Having reassured her with everything she wanted to hear, he kissed her gently on the forehead, then departed.

In search of Jack.

As Vince passed a lone milk float pootling along, it reassured him that his life wasn't playing itself out in some alternate universe. Up ahead lay the harbour. At the entrance stood the red phone box. Vince slowed the car, seeing no sign of Terence. He made the turn and entered the harbour. No one about: no nightwatchmen, no barking dogs, no lights. Apart from a fence, there was no security to protect the precious cargo that Vince was convinced lay inside the warehouse. He opened the glove compartment and fished out his torch. He weighed it in his hand for potential use as a weapon. Even with the two heavy batteries tombed up inside the long aluminium casing, it still didn't possess sufficient heft to be used for such a purpose. He thought about Bobbie's gun – was it worth going back and fetching it? No, it was uncleaned, uncared-for and would probably explode in his face. He'd improvise, and felt sure he could pick something up along the way: something with a bit of heft, an edge or a point.

He continued along the quayside and found Terence's hiding place, the stack of pallets ready for the fork-lifts. No Terence in sight. Vince switched on his torch and checked for any signs of the young scribe. He didn't even know what he expected to find, almost treating him as if he was a nesting bird or a messy pet. Maybe pencil shavings, a crisp packet or a big cartoon footprint. But nothing.

Torch switched off, he turned around and headed back towards the warehouse. The gate through the perimeter fence was chained and padlocked. The mesh fence itself was about eight feet high, easy to scale apart from a vicious-looking roll of barbed wire festooning the top of it. Through the fence, he could see Henry

Pierce's Cadillac Deville parked in the middle of the forecourt. It looked like a big black shark, a fish out of water, incongruous and a set-up made to be noticed. Vince had the feeling it had been deliberately parked there as an obstacle or as a challenge – the first test he must pass before getting into the warehouse and facing his quarry.

Vince accepted the challenge. He took off his jacket, gripped it between his teeth, jumped up and scaled the fence and spread the jacket across the barbed wire. He then eased himself carefully over the top, feeling the spikes beneath the cloth as his weight shifted. Levering himself safely over the fence, he dropped and landed on his feet. Reaching up, he retrieved the jacket and put it on.

Certain he was being watched, he headed towards the car, torch held in hand like a cosh. He was about twenty feet away from the car before he turned on the torch and raked the windows with its beam. He detected no sign of movement inside.

He reached the car, peered inside, saw the keys still in the ignition. He shone the torch beam on to the red leather back seat and saw blood.

The boot wasn't locked, but Vince already knew that it wasn't an oversight by the driver. He pressed the button and slowly lifted the lid, its jaws creaking as the gap got wider and wider, letting out a yawn of death. The smell was instantly recognizable: rancid urine, faeces and the earlier stages of decomposition.

As pungent as the air was around him, Vince still took a deep breath and held it. He held it in preparation for what he might find: Terence, the young scribe, so in awe with the intrigue and the mythology created around the *real* underworld.

Inside, curled up, with his throat cut, was Spider. But no Terence. Vince breathed a sigh of relief and slammed the boot shut.

Vince turned to the warehouse, shot a glance up at the small circular window set in the facade. There was a light burning somewhere inside; not strongly but enough to interrupt the uniformed darkness. He thought he noticed a flicker of movement behind the window itself. Vince strode to the entrance under the sign: Tartarus Storage Ltd. There was a normal-size door set within a larger door used for vehicular access. He turned the handle, found it unlocked and entered the warehouse.

Amid the darkness within, he located four light switches just beside him on the front wall. Four metal-caged bulbs as big as footballs were suspended from wires hanging from the ceiling. They threw out an industrial-strength light, and Vince took a step backwards to get a better perspective. The three separate buildings with three separate entrances were merely a facade, for in fact it was one very big warehouse. The immediate area was a large open space with a concrete floor, stained with machine oil from the trucks and forklifts parked just inside. There were three large, gated goods lifts and three sets of wrought-iron stairs spiralling upwards. He could instantly spot some of Vogel's antique furniture, but the other racks nearby were laden with all manner of goods. Naked and bald female shop mannequins with their heads sticking out of wooden crates, rolls of carpet, old radio sets, slot machines, new fridges, racks of clothes . . . Vince soon stopped looking, for the inventory was dizzying. Long aisles divided each floor into sections, with walkways and metal ladders giving access to the various floors, stretching all the way to the back of the warehouse. It looked like a maze, somewhere to get lost in or, more fittingly, somewhere to hide in.

Vince's compass had already been set for him: the top floor, towards the light he had noticed in the window. He approached the lift in the central section, but saw that the gate was padlocked – as were the other two lifts. So he took the stairs, trying to be as quiet as possible, but his footfalls on the metal seemed to ring out like a sharply struck xylophone.

Reaching the first floor, he glanced along the aisles that seemed to stretch forever until they disappeared into darkness. Nothing to be seen. He carried on up to the fourth level. Once he reached the top, as if on cue, the main overhead lights went out. He could just make out a dim light at the end of the aisle in front of him. This was clearly no accident: he was being guided. Vince no longer felt like the hunter and that made him nervous. He persevered nevertheless and followed the source of light along the walkway. Its sides were lined with metal shelves, all of them crammed with disparate objects like a junk shop or a prop store. The only theme here was that it was theme-less. Books, bicycle wheels, cricket balls, wooden sledges, cartons of light bulbs, bowler hats, yet more mannequins, a horse's saddle and all the musical instruments suitable to kit out an entire orchestra.

Reaching the end of the walkway, he found himself standing in a lit-up space, looking back at himself. It was a room full of mirrors, gilt-framed like the ones adorning the walls of the flat in Adelaide Crescent. They hung on the walls or were stacked up in piles. Everywhere he looked he could see himself. Then the lights here went out.

Swallowed in blackness suddenly, he shuddered and dropped his torch. He heard it roll away, then begin a clanging descent down metal stairs to the ground floor. The noise echoed around the warehouse. But it wasn't the noise that bothered Vince; it was the enveloping dark. He had never quite overcome his fear of the dark, and his terror of something deadly hiding in its layers. He stood rooted to the spot, as if waiting for further instruction.

As his eyes adjusted, Vince found himself looking into a face that was twisted, ugly and surreally grotesque. It looked as if it was melting. Then he remembered the old adage: never look into a mirror in the dark.

A light went on, illuminating another walkway leading off to the right side of the mirrored space. The shelves on either side of the aisle were stacked high with antiques: silverware, old clocks and small items of furniture. The type of wares sold in Vogel's shop, therefore he was getting warmer.

It was another twenty yards until he reached the end of the walkway and found himself standing on a balcony. About thirty foot in diameter, with waist-high railings running all the way round, it was a viewing gallery that looked down into a black abyss. A pit!

It was official, thought Vince: Jack Regent was the Devil, and he himself was now standing at the gates of Hell!

On closer inspection, he realized that the pit, about fifteen foot deep, was merely a room on the level lower down. Not quite the entrance to Hades, but certainly unusual enough, the black room below was covered floor to wall in black plastic sheets. In the centre of the plastic-clad floor stood about fifty pieces of black-toned furniture. Heavy bureaus, bookcases and tables, it was the same ebonized furniture he'd seen in Jack's flat and in Vogel's container. To one side of the gallery there was a ladder that led down into the same room. Above his head extended a huge black plastic canopy secured by ropes attached to a winch. It was now clear the canopy could be lowered to form a kind of tent. Whatever its purpose, it was undeniably a room that could be sealed off. Vince sniffed the air, detected a sharpness about it; the tang of chemicals of some description, though Vince couldn't place them.

The final instruction. A flicker of flame guided Vince's eyes up and away from the black pit and over to the gallery opposite, where a man now stood. Vince couldn't see his face, because it was obscured by the wide brim of a hat. A grey fedora with a black band encircling it. It matched the long grey gabardine trench coat that was knotted at the waist and worn with the collar turned up, over an open-neck black shirt. Vince realized he couldn't see his feet. The light was weak, and the man's movements were playing to it perfectly; he wanted to be obscured, half lit and half in the shadows. The wide-brimmed fedora dipped down to meet the flame of the slim gold lighter that was igniting a cigarette. Even before Vince smelled the smoke from the pungent French cigarette, he knew this was Jack Regent.

Vince felt his chest tighten and his guts seize up, as if being clenched in a giant fist. A jolt of adrenalin shot through him and his hands gripped the gallery rail. He took a deep intake of breath, and slowly exhaled, steadying himself. The dark room below Vince really did feel like an abyss now. They were only a short distance apart, but it felt like a chasm was opening up. The closing of distance in the hunt meant nothing, for Vince had no control. He hadn't tracked Jack. Jack had led him here.

Vince wanted to see his face clearly, but the lighter's flame was extinguished, the wide brim of the fedora pulled down further. Then Jack retreated from the gallery, moving further into the darkness.

'Jack Regent?'

No response. Just the glowing tip of the cigarette.

Vince swallowed, then announced, 'My name is Detective Vincent Treadwell.'

'I know who you are, my boy.'

'Of Scotland Yard.'

'Please, Vincent, I ask that you not speak to me in the procedural patter of a policeman. The time for that has passed, has it not?' Without giving Vince time to answer, he continued, 'It's not the job I object to, you understand, it's the method of the delivery. Yet you, I hear, are an educated, intelligent young man, so don't bore me with your "Treadwell of the Yard" affectations. Ask me whatever you like, Vincent.'

The tone of the voice was low but strong. It could have been the acoustics that gave it strength, but Vince doubted that. It belonged to a man who didn't have to raise his voice to be heard. The constant flow of cigarettes had also worked their magic. His accent, whilst not strong, worked to endow his voice with a cut-crystal pronunciation that gave it a natural authority which Vince never doubted.

Vince glanced down into the pit. 'Is this how you're smuggling in the heroin – in Vogel's furniture?'

'That's right. Morphine paste flown in from Indochina, with help of the French colony there. Then processed, to some degree, in Marseilles. Then shipped over here.'

Vince made a point of not appearing too impressed. 'How long do you think you'll get away with it?'

'Until I'm caught, I suppose, is the answer you want. If I could give another, more truthful, guess, it would be, for as long as I choose. But you know, Vincent, we two are just specks of dust in the great scheme of things. I have no more control over my fate than you do of yours. We're all just playthings for the gods. That's something I've suspected all my life, but really, really only just found out for sure tonight.'

'Your turn to do me a favour, Regent – spare me your philosophical insights. You're a low-life killer, nothing more, nothing less.'

The fedora-wearing head remained dipped, as he took a long draw on the cigarette, before pluming a vapour trail of smoke across towards Vince, as if it held a bullet.

'Very well, cards on the table. How are you going to catch me?'

'Interpol already possesses a lot of information on heroin smuggling by the Unione Corse.' Vince looked for some reaction to the mention of that crime organization, but none was forthcoming. 'I got your present, *Rinieri*.' Again, no reaction from Jack to the mention of his birth name. 'The Moor's head. I've heard all your clan wear it.'

'Max Vogel told me you had a fascination with such tokens. I hoped you'd appreciate it. A gift from me to you.'

'What do you wear yourself, Jack, the ring or the pendant?'

'You want me to tell you if I'm a member of a secret society? If I did, I wouldn't be much good as a member, would I? Yet again, Vincent, your imagination is at play. There's no intrigue involved, just business. Corsicans have been smugglers all their lives. It's in our blood.'

'Smuggling the heroin in furniture isn't exactly foolproof.'

'But it is if the fool isn't listening. I didn't say *in* the furniture.' Jack left that hanging in the air to be processed, then continued. 'I've found a secret formula, able to turn dust into gold. Better than alchemy, my dear boy, simple chemistry. The morphine paste is carried in the lacquer painted on the furniture. Therefore invisible to the naked eye. First the furniture is painted black, as befits the oriental style. The morphine paste is then painted on to the furniture, the flat surfaces, table tops and drawer panels. Then it is sealed with lacquer. As I say, invisible to the naked eye. So, you see, even if the furniture is confiscated, they can chop it to pieces but they'll never find anything. In fact, they'll have to pay us to replace it. Only to bring in the next shipment.'

Vince thought he heard a small laugh from Jack – as if playing to the gallery. Vince looked back down into the pit. The sealed plastic room made sense now. The lacquer was sanded off the wood, coming off in a white powder that was collected. Being as precious as *gold dust*, the powder must then be protected from the elements or contamination within the sealed pit. And, coming off in a white powder, the black plastic would show it up clearly. Perfect, apart from one thing:

'You must lose more of the morphine than you retrieve.'

'When we first started, we lost about sixty per cent. Still enough to make a profit, but not enough considering all the effort. Through trial and error, we're now down to a mere ten per cent loss. And there's still room for improvement. We're working towards and will settle for a loss of five per cent. The process of separating the morphine from the lacquer involves a new discovery. The lacquer itself is a natural gum harvested from seed, like rape seed. I won't bore you with the science but, needless to say, like all genius solutions, it's deceptively simple.

'By the time it's stripped off the furniture and the powder is processed, it comes out at seventy-five to eighty per cent pure. Again, there's room for improvement, and we think we can do better, refining the process towards a purity of ninety per cent. By the time it's been packaged for consumption, it will give us a yield of a million and a half, two million, pounds for each shipment. Enough to trade off for a year, all over this country, all over Europe. But we won't get greedy: we'll make sure our product is easily available and reasonably priced at first. That way you build up your market, build up an appetite, create a hunger.'

Vince considered Jack's plans, reckoned they were no more than he expected of him – brilliant. But the fact that he was laying them out for him made the next stage of Jack's intentions clear. Vince was never going to leave this warehouse alive.

'The trouble, is Regent, your junk kills people the minute it hits their bloodstream. That's diminishing returns. Bad economics to kill your customers.'

'I take it you're referring to the plague, as the papers are calling it.'

'I'm no poetic hack. I call it heroin. I call it *your* heroin.'

'That was most unfortunate. But you're wrong, it has nothing to do with me.'

'Everything has something to do with you in this town, Regent, and all of it bad. Why should the bad junk be any different?'

Again, Vince thought he heard a low laugh, or maybe a sigh of derision.

'You're a very literal young man. What I meant was, that batch was the product of experimentation as we were refining the process. And, yes, some of it went bad, fatally bad. Very unfortunate, and indeed *very* bad for business. I could do without such publicity. It was never meant to be put out on the streets, and I myself certainly didn't put it out there. I would have been a fool to do so. It was stolen from me, you see. From what I hear, your brother had a part to play in that.'

'It was given to him by Henry Pierce.'

Vince watched as Jack, his expression still obscured by the brim of the hat, took a moment to reflect.

Then he stubbed out the cigarette. 'Ah, Henry.' Jack's voice denoted the wistful disappointment you'd feel for an errant child. 'Henry told me he gave it to your brother as a reward for getting rid of a body in Soho. But, of course, you know all about that, Vincent.'

He was still unnerved by Jack calling him 'Vincent', as if Jack had known him all his life. When in fact it was the reverse: it was Vince who had known Jack all his life. From a hallowed distance, of course, like you would know about a legend, or even a movie star. Was that it, thought Vince, was he star-struck? Awed by the very presence of Jack Regent? Vince knew what a dangerous state of mind that could be, and shook the thought from his head.

'By the way,' said Jack, 'I had nothing to do with the Soho business. I know Duval, just like I know a lot of people. But those films he and Eton and Henry were involved in, it wasn't to my tastes.'

Vince gave a sour laugh. 'Bit late to get morals, Regent.'

'Morality has nothing to do with it. Not enough profit involved. But those films are not what you think they are. They're flights of fantasy. Degenerate flights, but fantasy all the same. No one dies in them. That just comes from *your* imagination. After all, you're the one being accused of murder.'

Vince grabbed the rail so hard that he dislodged it from its spindles.

'Take it easy, my young friend. You don't want to fall in.'

'I know what I saw. And I know that I didn't kill anyone.'

Jack issued an audible sigh and shook his head, seeming almost to pity the young detective. 'I didn't say you did kill anyone – just that you were accused of it. Just like you're accusing me. You think too highly of me, my young friend. I didn't even know Henry was involved with the film business – not until some of my heroin went missing. That bad heroin he paid your brother with. Most regrettable.'

'Is that why Pierce wanted to get rid of you?'

'No, that's not why.'

'Then why did Pierce set you up?' asked Vince, as he slowly began to move around the gallery towards Jack.

'You still want to play the policeman?'

Vince carried on taking steady strides, knowing he had to make his move and not wait for Jack to move first. Knowing he couldn't be awed by Jack.

'Look behind you, Vincent . . .'

'Oldest trick in the book. You can do better, Regent.'

'No tricks.'

Vince halted, but kept his eyes on the Corsican.

Jack pointed to a side passage leading away from the gallery. 'Through there you'll find a room, and in that room you'll find the answers to all your questions. You'll find out if you're the killer. You might not like what you hear, but that's the lot of a detective, I guess.'

Vince quickly looked around and saw that the passage led to a door. When he turned back again, Jack was gone. *The oldest trick in the book.*

But it was no trick, since Jack could have disappeared into the shadows of the warehouse any time he wanted to. He was now offering him two doors: an entrance and a exit. A past and a future.

CHAPTER 34

THE OTHER HALF

He was still the detective, and he still wanted answers. So Vince moved on down the passage and towards the door to another storage area. Another compartment in a building with so many, with so many things stored away, with so many secrets. Vince slowly opened the door. In the darkness beyond, he reached around to the nearside wall, groping for a switch. A light bulb fizzed into life, illuminating the room with a fierce magnesium light. The juice must have been running off a separate generator, because there was an uneven humming noise in the room, and the light seemed to wax and wane along with the irregular rhythm of a machine. The room was the size of an average family garage, windowless, with its walls painted gloss-white. Though it didn't look freshly painted, there was a cloying, acrid odour. The harsh light made the surfaces reflective, like the inside of an ice box.

The room was empty apart from a naked figure crouching on the floor. The figure was that of Henry Pierce, sitting on his haunches, with his hands cupped before him as if in prayer. His eyes were closed – or at least one of them was. His lips rippled in mumbled prayer. His body looked old and decayed, pouches of flesh hanging off his arms, with a flabby, corrugated belly and wrinkled dugs. The skin hung over his once powerful frame like a crumpled dust sheet thrown over one of Jack's opium-infused heavy black bureaus. It was colourless, almost transparent, so that his face, which had always struck Vince as pallid and bloodless, looked healthy and tanned in comparison with the rest of his body. In the white room, this had the effect of making his face and hands, the parts that normally emerged from the black sheath of clothing he was constantly encased in, look disembodied – or at least separate, as if he was wearing a balaclava and gloves.

And he stank. Vince now realized that the sickening odour wasn't paint drying; it was Pierce dying.

And then there was the eye: the phoenix rising from the flames. The brooch that Bobbie had worn to cover an unsightly tear on her mother's dress, which had once so caught his eye, was now caught in Pierce's eye. And now covered his own unsightly tear. Vince could see the muscles above and below the ruined eye twitch, attempting to blink. But the lids were long gone, like torn and frayed curtains that gave no coverage to a bauble that needed no moisture. The muscle contractions were working on memory, the memory of eyes that needed lubricating; a lens that needed cleaning in order to maintain a clear picture.

Pierce, obviously under instruction, and working on blind faith that Jack would have done what he had said he'd do and have the young detective standing before him, stopped muttering his prayers. He sniffed the air.

'Hello, Henry.'

'Narcissist?'

'So they tell me.'

Pierce smiled. 'Good-looking boy, granted. Handsome, but not a narcissist.' He stopped smiling. Pierce's voice, usually varied and theatrical, was now one note only and raspy. It was, like himself, dying. 'No, no, not you. You didn't kill him.'

'The projectionist?'

Pierce gave one slow nod.

'What happened?'

Pierce's shoulders rose and fell in an expressionless shrug. 'They set you up when you was out cold. Duval killed him. They put one behind his ear. That's what Eddie Tobin told me. That's all I know.'

Vince considered this news. A burden lifted from his shoulders. Then, just as quickly, rested back on them. A false dawn? Vince was still a dead man. His killer waited outside. Vince turned towards the door.

'There's more.'

Vince looked around at Pierce, noting there was a fresh desperation on his face. Not just the desperation of dying, but the desperation of unburdening.

'It's about the girl.'

Again, Vince looked around at the door, saw there was no lock on it. For some reason he didn't feel this was a trap; or any more of a trap than he was already caught in. He looked back around at Pierce and nodded for him to continue. Then he looked at the marbled and diamanté eyes, and remembered that Pierce really was blind now. 'I'm listening,' he prompted.

Henry Pierce then told the story of what happened that Christmas in 1939. He told his story exactly as he had told it to Bobbie. But slower and not so playfully. His delivery was altogether more deliberate. He wasn't doing it for his own sadistic amusement this time. He was under orders from Jack, and it was killing him. Vince had to draw closer to him to hear the fading voice. Pierce only really sparked into life when it came to his own part in the drama. When Jack handed Pierce the knife and tasked him with the killing of the infant.

Vince listened intently, but he wasn't playing for time, like Bobbie; instead his mind was rushing ahead. Still with the conceit of a detective, he didn't want Pierce to finish the story or furnish all the answers. Vince wanted to solve the riddle and crack the puzzle himself. He wanted his brushwork to feature on the picture being painted, his signature added in the corner. So when Pierce got to his part of the crime: entering the infant's room, throwing the turquoise dress over his intended target, and then raising his knife to kill the infant in the cot, Vince firmly ordered: 'Stop!'

Pierce, compliant like an obedient robot, stopped.

'That baby. The baby is Bobbie?'

Pierce nodded.

The puzzle almost completed, Vince put the last pieces together. Now he understood Bobbie's new-found hatred of Jack. Now he knew why Bobbie was slipping away from him, slipping into another world. The world of innocence, the world of the photo album, make-believe and borrowed memories.

'Jack killed her parents.'

'Yes . . . and no.'

Vince had been here before with Pierce, and he didn't have the time. He looked behind, checking for the Corsican, but the door was still closed.

'I've no time for your riddles, Henry.'

'It's no riddle. Jack killed her mother, but he didn't kill her father.'

Vince felt his legs give way. He crouched down, then sank to his knees, joining the noisome Pierce in a position of prayer. Vince's head was now bowed, his hands rested on the floor, supporting his body. Pierce must have known that Vince was kneeling, because he adjusted his head, lower, towards him.

It all made sense to Vince now. The man cowering in the corner of the bedroom, with a knife in his eye, was not the main target of Jack's anger. He could have been any one of her lovers. It was the woman . . .

'The woman, she was Jack's . . . ?'

Pierce nodded.

'And Jack is Bobbie's . . . ?'

Pierce didn't nod this time, and Vince kept hoping there was another twist that would divert it all from its inevitable conclusion. There wasn't, of course. As if a nod wouldn't suffice, Pierce said, 'Her father. And then her lover.'

Vince studied Pierce's face for the truth. But Pierce had worn the same fixed death-mask expression since he'd started this story and, of course, Vince could tell nothing from his eyes. But Vince could sense that Pierce was working on something else now. His present admission was fuelled by a fear freshly instilled into him by a power greater than himself: Jack Regent. Pierce was doing as instructed, being rigorously honest and telling the truth. This was the get-out stake for the old gangster, that old monster from his past. Pierce knew he was dying, and confessing and making his peace now was lightening his load for wherever he was headed. Vince reckoned it was somewhere hot.

'Jack's wife was a real beauty. A passionate woman. Too passionate. She started cheating with other men when Jack went away. She made a fool of Jack. But she was his weakness. Once he found out what she'd been up to, he knew she had to go. That's why he didn't want anyone to know he was out of prison. He wanted to catch her at it, and I think he derived some pleasure from it. Pity the poor bastard who was with her. He got his . . . in the eye.'

'What about Bobbie?'

'She was born just after Jack went away. He'd never set eyes on her, so getting rid of her wasn't such a chore. Jack did what he had to do: he cut out the weakness, the ties that bind. No dependants. That way, no one or anything can get at you again. He'd turned to stone, invincible, until *she* came along.'

'Does Bobbie know all this?'

Pierce's lips rolled inwards as he bit down on them, seemingly suppressing either laughter or pain. For his sake, Vince was hoping it was the latter.

'Does she know this?' he insisted.

Pierce wasn't laughing. He was crying. But these weren't tears drawn from the well of some deep emotion. They were from his body reacting against the bejewelled phoenix parasite that was so closely attached to him. The brooch was only cheap costume jewellery, silver-coloured base metal, and it was clear that Pierce was suffering a reaction to it. His brow was beading up with sweat. His pallor, never healthy, was greying. Pierce was being poisoned. His brain, slowly, toxically, turning off. Vince almost felt sorry for him. *Almost.*

'Bobbie . . . beautiful baby . . . she's the image of her mother . . . almost the same face . . . same eyes . . .' said Pierce, his voice slowing.

Vince looked at the brooch, which seemed to be losing its sparkle. If Pierce was reacting against the brooch, the brooch was also reacting against him.

'You're dying, Henry. You know that?'

'Know it? I can *feel* it.'

'You want to make your peace with your maker, don't you?'

'Why do you think I'm telling you this? I've made my peace . . . and Jack knows it all. He knows why I did it. He forgives me. He forgives me . . . Jack is . . .'

Vince almost laughed. But he saw the look of beatification on Pierce's face, as he uttered his false prophet's name, and he couldn't deny the dying man his faith. And Vince realized now that Pierce didn't set Jack up to take over his rackets. He wouldn't dare. He set Jack up simply to atone for the crime he'd committed all those years ago; the crime of *not* committing the crime of murdering Bobbie.

Vince realized that it was no coincidence that brought Bobbie to Brighton. She believed her mother was from the town, her only clue being a turquoise dress that she had been wrapped in, bearing the label 'Penelope of Brighton'. And Vince also knew that it was no coincidence that she had met Jack. It was down to Fate. Like Jack said, they were all playthings for the gods.

When Pierce first met Bobbie in the Blue Orchid club, he knew instantly who she was. She was the image of her mother, and was wearing the turquoise silk gown. With the brooch carefully positioned to hide the tear where the knife had entered . . . and *missed*. It was soon after that Henry Pierce had gone into his 'blind man' routine.

A suitably poetic and dramatic gesture from the seasoned old performer, but it served a practical purpose: it retired him from Jack's services. It gave him distance from the man. Because Pierce couldn't bear to witness the crime that Jack and Bobbie were unknowingly committing. A crime that Pierce was responsible for. Henry Pierce didn't act straight away, thinking it was just a crush between the older man and the ingénue and it would soon pass. But Jack fell further and further, deeper and deeper in love with Bobbie, and her fate was sealed. She had to die. And to do that, Pierce had to get Jack away from her.

And that's where the projectionist came in. Pierce was asked by Duval to do for him what he'd been doing for Jack all those years: the dirty work. Dispose of the body. Did Pierce hold on to a knife that Jack had used in a previous killing, a knife that still had his fingerprints on it? Of course he did, either as a memento or an insurance policy. Vince suspected the former, but didn't dismiss the latter. Pierce took the knife with Jack's prints on it and planted it on the body of the projectionist, knowing it would soon be found. Pierce may even have kept the knife that Jack used on the woman who had betrayed him all those years ago. The very same knife that he gave to Henry Pierce to kill the baby daughter he'd never met. The knife that would bond them in blood. The bond that never happened, not that night anyway. But, no matter, there were to be plenty of other nights.

Vince stared back at Pierce, losing what little pity he had for the dying man. He was too incomprehensible, too twisted to deserve any real compassion. And if Pierce did have any remorse in his voice, it was for *not* killing. Vince repeated his question, 'Come on, Henry, tell me. Does Bobbie know all this?'

A rictus grin spread across Pierce's face. There was a halting rattle as he drew breath into his throat, and his toxic lungs filled for the last time. Fuelled by a fading breath, the words clawed their way out of him. 'I was going to . . . but . . .' Pierce raised his hand and rubbed his forefinger across the phoenix jewel. 'I was going

354

to tell her . . . but she got the better of me. I . . . I . . . lost my concentration . . . She knows only . . . *the half of it . . .*'

Then silence.

Vince looked up and saw that a thick tar-like substance was oozing out of Henry Pierce's nose and mouth, a mouth that was now fixed in a rigor-mortic grimace. Vince couldn't tell if the expression was one of joy or pain. It didn't matter; *ask no man if he's happy until he's dead.*

CHAPTER 35

BOBBIE AND VINCE, POUR TOUJOURS

The whirl of the generator slowed to a stop, and the light went out. Vince turned his head. Standing above him, framed in the doorway, was Jack, the light from the rooms behind throwing a halo around him. He held a long blade, which seemed like a natural extension of his arm. Hilt and hand welded together; imperceptibly extending and retracting, accommodating his every breath and movement. Maybe it was just an optical illusion, because the point was hovering and hesitating over Vince's eye.

Vince blinked, adjusted his eyes, and looked beyond the blade, right up to Jack's face. It was still obscured by the gloom and the brim of the hat, but he could make out the lower half of it. His lips hadn't thinned with age, were still full, but dry. His jaw was solid, defined, cradling a chin that held a dimple, a deep line indent, as if someone had sliced a knife down it.

Jack noticed that Vince was paying too much attention to his face, and he leaned back into the darkness.

'So you see, Vincent, we share a lot more than just being set up for murder with the same victim. We share the same woman . . . and just as deadly.'

'Bobbie doesn't know . . . ?'

'She must *never* know,' said Jack. 'I can live with her despising me, but not despising herself. She doesn't deserve that.'

'What have you got planned for her, Regent?'

'Vincent, you think you love her?'

'I'll do anything to get her away from you.'

'She *is* me.'

Vince could feel something pass through the blade like a current. The point moved, quivered. A tremble? Hesitation? *Nerves?* Vince stared up at the Corsican's face. There was no smile, no cruelty, no emotion that could be attributed to it. Jack's eyes were wide open, hungrily taking in the young detective.

Vince held his gaze. Jack blinked.

And in that blink, Vince's hand shot up and diverted the blade away from his face. He was instantly on his feet, but with his head down, as he charged at Jack, driving him back out of the room.

Jack was trying to get a foothold, his hands grabbing at the shelves to his side, pulling them down. Vince felt the sharp and bruising clunk of heavy objects falling and hitting his back.

They were now on the gallery. Vince, still with his head down, worked at Jack's gut with vicious jabs. Shovelling punches into his kidneys, his liver, his heart. As fast and furious as they were, they were almost scientific in their execution. Body blows to slow him, tire him and keep him busy and in pain. Vince didn't know if Jack still held the knife, as he drove him harder against the rail, hoping it would give way and send him down into his pit.

Jack must have regained his footing. His body tensed as he soaked up the jabs to his stomach. There was no soft underbelly on the older man, and it was like punching a wall. Then Vince felt a blow to the back. The knife? No, too dull, just Jack's balled fist in his spine, but powerful enough to send Vince back to his knees. Jack grabbed a hank of Vince's hair, pulled his head back.

Vince now saw that the knife was gripped between Jack's teeth, like a pirate; then the fist came thundering towards him. Vince closed his eyes to receive the blow, and it smashed into the bridge of his nose. *Crack*. He felt – and always worse – heard the bone splinter. On his back now, the sweet sickly taste of blood in his mouth became overwhelming. His mouth was filling up with it,

357

leaving him gurgling, choking, drowning. He opened his eyes, only to see Jack remove the knife from his mouth, grip it ready to plunge. Vince spat a gobbet of blood straight into the older man's face. Jack recoiled, withdrawing his head in order to wipe the blood from his eyes.

'You fight well, Vincent. Shame that your mind is not so astute. Always the tiresome policeman with his pathetic quest for the truth. We haven't any of us told the truth since the apple was taken from the tree. And what good would it do her now, anyway?'

Vince kept quiet, preserved his breath. He knew he'd need it. He felt their potency was equal – he could still win. He thrust himself forward and screwed his thumb into Jack's eye. Jack's head jolted back. Vince lunged his arms around to Jack's side, enough to throw him off balance, then heaved himself up and pushed Jack away. He twisted over on to his front, lifted himself further and, like a sprinter out of the blocks, surged to his feet and gripped hold of the rail. He spun around and saw Jack lying on his back, his left hand covering one eye, his right hand still holding the knife ready to stab downwards.

Vince hurtled towards the Corsican, raised his right foot ready to stamp his nose into his skull. Just as the raised heel was ready to do the damage, in a flash Jack spun out of the way. Vince's foot slammed down and, almost as soon as his boot hit the floor, he felt a burning sensation. The Corsican was up on his haunches, and with almighty force had driven the knife into Vince's foot. Through the leather, the flesh, the tendons, the muscle and bone, pinning his foot solidly to the floor. Jack scuttled back like a satanic spider, then was back up on his feet.

Blinded with pain, Vince threw his head back and gave it voice. Then he crouched again and, feeling the blade inside his foot severing new tendons with each movement, he grabbed the ebony hilt with both hands, squeezed his eyes shut, pulled a face that was a dress rehearsal for the pain that was due to follow, and in one movement hauled the knife out of his foot. Burning hot blood began oozing through the black leather, like lava from a volcano.

Now with the knife firmly in his grip, Vince stood up, ready to plunge into his enemy.

But Jack was gone.

Even with the knife in his hand, Vince knew he didn't stand a chance against the Corsican in the darkness of the warehouse. This was his milieu, his web, and there were enough lethal objects sitting on the shelves for Jack to make use of.

On the floor, Vince's eye caught a glint of metal and realized it was the gold lighter. He bent down and picked it up, flipped the lid and ignited it. As the flame burned, he rubbed his thumb over the cartouche containing the etched message, '*Jack, Pour Toujours*'. Vince silently translated it: 'Jack, Forever'.

The smell of chemical vapours from below was strong, as he threw the lighter into the black pit. The flame met the fumes and it ignited immediately, sending a column of fire shooting up towards the roof. The wooden frame caught fire, the black plastic canopy instantly melting. It was an impulsive action, for the place was a powder keg, literally. Dynamite and petrol could be stored in the warehouse, for all he knew. But Vince didn't give a damn, knowing he had to do it – to spite the Corsican, put a dent in his operation. And hopefully send him to Hell with Henry Pierce.

As fast as he could travel, Vince made his way along the walkways to the stairs. A left, then a right, another left, then straight on. The pain in the foot was gathering momentum. It advanced up his legs, kicked into his stomach, beat on his chest, then burned its way up his oesophagus. It was a quickening and sickening pain, each footfall more painful than the last. Vince wondered when the body's natural defences would kick in, take charge and eject the invading trauma. He closed his eyes and imagined the cool flow of his natural anaesthetic washing over him, numbing the burning pain in his foot, freezing the nauseous acids in his gut, and soothing his buckled brow. The stratagem worked: he opened his eyes and the stairs were in front of him. He felt the heat behind him, and looked around to see a corridor of fire rolling towards him, greedily burning up everything in its path.

There were constant explosions as stored fireworks sparkled, banged and rocketed around. He choked on the spiky black smoke filling his lungs, finally dropped the knife and covered his nose and mouth with his hands, squeezed his eyes shut and carried on blindly along the corridor; as fast as he could manage until he finally reached the stairwell. The heat on his back seemed to propel him, guiding him onwards to freedom. It seemed the fire, like himself, wanted to escape into fresh oxygen so that it could breathe. Sensing his position, Vince groped around until he found the stair rail. One hand on the rail, pressure off the injured foot, he made his way down to the ground floor, hobbled over to the light switches and threw them. The huge light bulbs sparked up, throwing a light on the scene for the last time. Vince scoped the warehouse one last time.

No sign of Jack. Just fire.

He opened the door, and was standing in the forecourt. Rain beat down on his face, cooling and cleansing, getting rid of the musty smell of all the old things stored in the warehouse, of the chemicals in the black pit, and the deathly decaying stench of Henry Pierce.

The Cadillac was still parked outside. It was closer than his own car, and Vince could do with the ease of driving one-footed in an automatic. The keys were still in the ignition and Vince climbed inside. He sat for a moment, got his breath back and his bearings. He looked back at the warehouse, where the small round window at the top was aglow – like the spinning disk of the sun. He smiled. *Jack, pour toujours?* Not any more.

Vince had never driven an automatic before, but it looked easy, like the dodgems, he decided. He adjusted the rear-view mirror to assess the damage to his face. The nose wasn't broken, showed no blood or marks at all. The thick black hair had lost its lustre and was now peppered with grey. His brow was strong though, casting a shadow over his eyes. It gave him a somewhat cadaverous look, but this was because the cheekbones were so pronounced. His skin was strangely olive, and had lost the suppleness of youth. He recognized the shape of the mouth, like his own, but the lips were not as full. A hand went to the bottom lip, forefinger and thumb pulled it down, exposing twin rows of strong, straight ivory-coloured teeth. And there, on the inside of the bottom lip, in black ink, was a tattoo of the Moor's head.

Vince felt an arm reach around and grip him. An ivory-handled open cutthroat razor was at his throat.

'You know where to go, so drive,' instructed the Corsican.

Vince knew exactly where Jack wanted to go – wherever Bobbie was – and he knew he could never let that happen. He dragged his eyes away from the Corsican, and got down to the job at hand. He turned the key and gunned the engine, put the gearstick into drive. Right foot down hard: the car jolted forward. The razor pressed into his throat. Vince looked in the mirror, blood on his Adam's apple. Jack narrowed his eyes, the crow's feet spreading into the gullies that ran along his cheekbones.

'I've never driven one of these before.' As true as it was, to Vince's ear this excuse sounded so prosaic as to be almost laughable. Jack passed no judgement. As Vince edged back in his seat, the edge of the blade followed suit. He drove forward, building speed, while heading towards the quay. Then foot down hard, then a burst of speed. Vince slammed down the brake and the car screeched to a stop. The razor jolted forward, then jumped back to slice open Vince's chin. The blade dropped to the floor. Jack fell backwards. Vince slammed down on the accelerator. Jack sprang back up, went to grab Vince around the throat. Vince bit hard into his hand – the soft flesh between thumb and forefinger – and tasted Jack's blood in his mouth. Vince kept his foot pressed on the accelerator. The quayside was disappearing fast on both sides, just the black sea ahead of them. Vince opened the door at the last moment, and rolled out of the car. He hit the ground with a dull ache, a hammer blow to the head, burning white light, then stars. The car pitched into the sea.

Despite the pain, Vince rolled towards the edge of the quay, opened his eyes and watched the fins of the Cadillac disappear like those of a black shark diving into the murky swell. In two heavy gulps, the shark was swallowed up.

Vince got to his feet, and took on a heavy gasp of night air for ballast to steady himself. He put a hand to the back of his head, which felt warm and worryingly soft. Blood oozed down the back of his neck, warm and sticky and sickening. He turned to haul himself towards his own car, felt his foot wasn't hurting so much now, perhaps because it was in stiff competition with the searing pain of his broken nose and sliced chin, while his cracked cranium didn't even bear thinking about.

As his foot moved with increased ease across the tarmac of the parking lot, he heard exploding glass behind him. The fire inside the warehouse had finally punched its way through the top windows like a glowing orange fist. Vince would've loved to have watched the whole place go up, but he didn't have time. He reached his car, took out his keys and climbed in. Taking a deep breath – and holding it – he peered in the rear-view mirror. No Jack. Just himself. Vince started the engine and drove slowly along the stretch of road leading out of the harbour and on to the coast road. Reaching the telephone box at the entrance, he stopped.

Ray Dryden was at home in bed, but he was still happy to take the call. Vince laid out the bare bones of the case, telling him how Duval and Tobin were responsible for the body on the beach. And how Duval had the killing on film. He told Ray that he suspected Dr Hans Boehm, Vince's psychological assessor, had been in on it too; that he was the weak link in this case, who would give everybody up under the right pressure. Finally, Vince told Ray that Jack Regent was dead.

Ray wanted further details, but Vince was in a hurry, said he'd call in after he got home.

Vince put the phone down, then took a deep breath and called Bobbie as he had promised. He wanted at least to tell her that he was all right. He wanted to tell her . . .

'The Seaview Hotel.'

'This is Detective . . .' No, not any more, that was over, in another life. 'Vince . . . Vincent Treadwell. The lady's waiting for me in the bar. Can you tell her—'

'Oh yes, but she's not here, sir.'

Vince, in alarm, exclaimed, 'What do you mean?'

'She said she had to go home.'

'When?'

'A taxi picked her up about ten minutes ago, sir.'

'Where . . . where did she go?'

'She said she had forgotten something . . . a photo album, I think she mentioned.'

She couldn't forget. Bobbie had sat in the hotel bar nursing a brandy, her suitcase sitting next to her. She had tried to empty her mind of what had gone before and think only of her future with Vincent. But her past wouldn't let her go; it kept pulling her back in.

So there she now sat, on the floor of the apartment, surrounded by the world of Jack Regent: the fine art on the walls, the antiques, the books and the past. That past she had invented for herself in the world of the photo album. As she turned its tired, faded pages, it still called out to her. The images of the family came to life like a film featuring the happy narrative of a fictional world. The sprawling farm house in the New Forest, horses nuzzling in the stable, black Labradors foraging around in the grounds. Her mother, the headmistress in the local school, with her joyous smile. She seldom wore any make-up, occasionally some lipstick to bring out the pleasing shape of her mouth when she and her father went up to town to see a show. And then here was her loving father, the doctor with the kind face; shirtsleeves rolled up at the weekend, being the keen gardener. He was her *real* father . . .

★ ★ ★

The street-entrance door was off the latch, as he made his way into the dark hallway. Past the old-fashioned gated lift that wasn't working. And if ever he had needed the damn thing, it was now. It was on the stairs that his swollen foot announced itself. The light foot kept levering its way upwards, taking the weight of the other, which then landed with a distinctive thud . . .

They say it's darkest just before the dawn; it was certainly the quietest. A vast silence seemed to be compressed and distilled into one moment. And in that moment, she heard it – like she'd heard it so many times. The uneven footfalls of the nightmare climbing the stairs. And now she knew who it was, who it really was, who it had *always* been. And she knew what would happen when the door opened and he entered. She put the photo album down. Nothing could hurt her now, because she was already dead. She died the night that man came up the stairs and took her . . . She died, didn't she? Henry Pierce – on *his* orders – had killed her, hadn't he?

The blood still wasn't stemmed. With each new step it oozed up through the punctured leather like molten lava. He gripped the banister, focusing deliberately on its ornate metalwork decoration: cherubs and satyrs picked out in gilt. He pulled himself up its cold, polished rail as if it were a rope securing him to the mountain he was ascending. The adrenalin, the fear, the hatred, the sheer bloody excitement of the battle and the joy of victory against the monsters of his past, all of them had worked as an anaesthetic. But now it was fading as the pain returned and kicked in. Surging up from his foot, running through his body and twisting his brow. It was becoming unbearable again. It even took away his voice. He would have called out to her, but he didn't want her to hear him weakened like this, beaten and breathless. He had to stay strong for her. That was his job now. He had to get her away and look after her. Vince knew that things had changed. He knew that the two of them had changed. But she didn't know just how much – *only the half of it* . . .

Her eyes squeezed shut, she shook her head violently, trying to shake those ascending footfalls from her ears. But still they approached, relentless. When her eyes opened again, her gaze fell upon the glint of a metal object amid the broken black heap in the middle of the room . . .

Four floors up and he was finally on the right landing. He took it in slow steps, part of him never wanting to reach the door, never wanting to have to confront Bobbie. Thinking that even if he didn't tell her the truth, she would see it in his eyes. Something that men like Jack could never understand is that the truth is something you can never fully conceal. It lives, it breathes and it needs to be told.

And then there was the crime back in 1939, Bobbie's mother and . . . and her lover. Didn't *they* deserve the truth? Didn't they deserve to have their story written up as a matter of record? Their murders solved? As Vince had told Bobbie when he first met her, *People don't just disappear. They go somewhere and eventually we find them.* He was still a policeman, still a detective.

He finally stood at the door he was about to enter, and listened for signs of life within. All he heard was his own breath, low and unsure and fading fast. He looked down at his shirt, soaked red with blood from the razor cut to his chin and from the broken nose. He ran his hands through his hair, and as he reached the crown he felt the blood there, too. His vision blurred. He felt sweat prickle down the back of his legs, his breath becoming laboured . . .

★ ★ ★

She was standing up now, the gun clasped in her hand. Firm, resolute and wide awake. She aimed it at the door. *Did it work?* Vincent had warned her that it should never be fired . . . but she had no choice now. Her breathing was measured. She was calm. She knew what she had to do, and pulled back the hammer . . .

The handle turned.

She saw the door gradually inch open. She didn't even want to see his face. She squeezed the trigger.

Bang! Bang! Bang!

Three shots. Three bullet holes clustering in the centre of the door. Her ears ringing. The *bang, bang, bang,* was so loud it filled the room, echoing and ricocheting around the apartment as if trying to find release. The smell of cordite and sulphur, her eyes stinging and watering. She had absorbed the gun's recoil and held her position, ready to fire more shots if necessary.

'No! Please God, no!' she cried out as she saw him.

Vincent stumbled into the room. He dropped to the floor. Bobbie dropped the gun, ran over and joined him. She held his bloody and beaten face in her hands and peppered it with soft kisses; kissing away the blood, cleansing him with her lips and trying to void his pain. Her voice juddered and broke up, hot tears salting her eyes, blinding her. 'I thought . . . thought it was him, Vincent.'

Vince hushed her, putting his forefinger to her lips. 'He's gone, Bobbie. He's gone forever.' His eyes flickered, his pupils dilating and contracting, sliding in and out of consciousness.

'Kiss me. Please, kiss me,' she said, her tears splashing on to his upturned face, the blood dissolving wherever they fell.

He lifted his hand towards her, his fingertips traced her profile: those black pencil-line eyebrows, the tip of her nose, the dips and curves of her lips. He smiled her a smile that was comforting, reassuring and strangely serene. 'It's all right, Bobbie, he's gone . . . Listen to me, Bobbie, it's all over. It's all over, baby. No one can hurt you any more. You don't need your photos any more.'

Vincent noticed the dark roots of her bleached-blonde bob were just showing through. He studied the eyes, the dimple in her chin – not deep like her father's, but still there – and the full rich lips and olive skin. That face, that was the face he'd recognized the first time he saw it. A face he'd known all his life. Did she know who she was? Did she maybe know the truth? Could she see the truth . . . could she see the truth in his eyes?

Vince's eyes closed, he lost consciousness and was gone.

Bobbie held him in her arms, gently kissing his forehead. Vincent was only sleeping, she told herself. And now she would join him. The nightmare was over. Her head thrummed with the lullaby that was lodged inside. Her broken body ached, her tear-saturated eyes were sore; a finality of sorts was setting in now, and a tiredness was spreading through her. And she knew, as she always knew, how her pain would ebb under languid folds of anaesthetizing sleep.

Bobbie picked up the gun, held it in both hands . . . and was about to put it in her mouth . . .

When she heard it again. Those uneven footfalls on the stairs. But they were swifter this time, more assured.

The left foot was distorted. A club foot. He had a certain gait when he walked, but the club foot and built-up shoe he wore over it worked like a slipper, never affecting his swiftness. Never disabling him from what he had to do. It was on the stairs that the swollen foot pronounced itself. The light foot levering its way upwards, taking the weight off the other, which then landed with a distinctive thud . . .

But now she was awake, alert, ready. She stood in front of Vincent, protecting him as she would always do. The door, hanging off its hinges, was half open. She gripped the gun, still hot from its last discharge . . .

The door handle turned.

With the poise of a well paid-for and practised assassin, she assumed the killing position. She took aim, forefinger nudging on the trigger.

The broken door swayed slowly open, scraping across the polished floor like death calling out with a grating, parched caw . . .

Her thumb eased back the hammer until the firing lever silently slotted into place.

The swollen foot crossed the threshold.

A smile curled across her lips, like a kiss, as she squeezed the trigger.

. . . *click* . . . *click* . . . *click* . . .

THE DETECTIVE

Three weeks later. A private sanatorium in the Kent countryside.

'And then I blacked out.'

   'And that's all you remember?'

   'That's all I remember, Ray.'

   'Nothing else?'

Vince gave an internal groan of boredom; he'd been over this a hundred times since he had shown signs of recovery in the private sanatorium in the Kent countryside, where he had been lodged for the last three weeks. But he knew that Ray Dryden, like all good detectives, craved information and filling in the gaps, so Vince played along and said, 'Nothing else.'

Ray pulled a full-beam smile. 'Then Vince, you're going to love this. Just gimme a second.'

Ray went about setting up the film in the portable projector he had brought with him from London. On the wall he had already pinned up a white sheet that the nurse had kindly lent him for a screen.

Vince was sitting on the bed in his private room, with its pleasant views of the lake and the ducks and swans messing about on the water. It was the same room in the same sanatorium that he'd spent a month convalescing in once before. Life plays out twice, it seemed: first as tragedy, then as comedy. Vince didn't know about the comedy, but there was certainly irony this time around. The relatively small lump he'd taken the first time, in Soho, had left him in a coma for three weeks. His latest head trauma, which had well and truly cracked open his cranium, had involved a four-hour operation bolting in a steel plate to replace a section of his smashed skull. When the anaesthetic wore off, he felt groggy, but he was up and about in a few days. His broken nose had been reset to look as good as new. His chin had needed stitches, and it would always carry a small vertical scar. The nurses told him it looked sexy, but every time he looked in the mirror, it reminded him too much of Jack. Nevertheless, all in all, Vince felt good: no constant headaches, no feelings of nausea. And also not being fed pills and lies by that crooked quack Dr Hans Boehm had helped. And, through this uncorrupted clarity of thought, he was able to truthfully piece together most of how he'd come to be in this sanatorium in the first place:

As the three shots hit the centre of the door, Vince watched as the bullets flew past and studded the wall. He himself was leaning against the door jamb, doubled over while trying not to pass out. The next thing he remembered was being in Bobbie's arms. He was pretty sure he remembered telling her that every-thing was OK, and that Jack was gone, and that she no longer had anything to fear. And then . . . then the next thing he remem-bered was waking up in the hospital three days later. The first face he saw was Ray's. The first sentence out of his mouth was, 'Where's Bobbie?'

Ray shifted uncomfortably in his seat, smiled nervously, and then told him that Terence Greene-John, who had heeded Vince's advice and scarpered after setting eyes on Jack, was now back at Cambridge and attending his studies. As happy as Vince was to hear that the young scribe was safe and staying out of trouble, he knew that Ray was stalling, and repeated his question: 'Where's Bobbie?'

Ray broke the news that Bobbie was gone. What happened to her was a matter of conjecture and speculation. Vince was sure that

Jack had perished in the black Cadillac, but then he admitted to Ray, he hadn't actually witnessed with his own eyes the last breath leaving the Corsican's body. Ray confirmed to Vince that Jack *was* indeed related to a powerful Unione Corse clan that was part of an emerging world-wide heroin smuggling and distribution ring.

But it was Bobbie that Vince was worried about. Ray explained that when they found Vince unconscious inside the flat, his shirt covered in blood from the wounds he'd received, and with three bullet holes in the door, they assumed at first that he had been shot and killed. And Ray reckoned that Bobbie must have assumed the same thing, and that she had killed him, and so she had fled.

On considering this, Vince had bought the first half of the story. Bobbie might well have thought she killed him. She'd heard him limping up the stairs, his wounded foot resembling the crippled footfalls of Jack Regent, the same ones she'd heard a thousand times before. Her nightmare again climbing the stairs. But he didn't buy the second half of the account. Or didn't want to. That Bobbie would ever leave him . . .

'OK, Vince, here goes, showtime.' Ray closed the room's curtains and switched off the light. He had the film already cued up to the last moments Vince could remember of that momentous night in Soho. After the projectionist had entered the room and closed the door. And before the big blackout . . .

On the screen, Vince watched as the tall figure of the projectionist entered the room. It is too dark for Vince to distinctly make out his face. He and Vince exchange words. The projectionist swings for Vince and his fist connects on the jaw. A sucker punch. Vince is sent reeling back into shelves of film. Canisters fall to the floor. The projectionist is on to Vince fast, getting him with some good shots to the body. Vince rides them, then gets back at him with a powerful left hook. The projectionist goes down like a big-branched tree, arms outstretched; he does what Vince was about to do, and takes his wretched projection machine with him to the floor. It smashes to pieces. The projectionist tries to get up, but Vince is on top of him. Vince pulls back his fist ready to—

Ray froze the film.

'Recognize this bit?'

Vince nodded. The film was frozen at exactly the same spot as the still he had seen at Bobbie's.

Ray starts the film moving again.

Vince brings down his fist, but the projectionist moves his head, and Vince misses. Vince goes to hit him again, and misses—

Ray freezes the film and laughs. 'Tough guy Vince Treadwell doesn't even manage to get a punch in!' Ray starts up the film again.

Eddie Tobin and Lionel Duval are now standing at the door. Duval has the cosh in his hand and smashes it down on to Vince's head. Vince struggles to stand up, Tobin cracks him again, and Vince goes down. He's out cold. The projectionist gets up off the floor and starts kicking Vince in the ribs. Tobin pulls him off. Then Tobin, Duval and the projectionist begin what looks to be an animated conversation, that soon boils over into a full-on, finger-jabbing argument. The projectionist storms out of the room. Tobin and Duval exchange looks, and then go after him.

Ray stopped the film. 'You didn't lay a finger on him, Vince, never mind kill him.'

'So what happened next?'

'What happened next is that the projectionist gets shot. Off screen, unfortunately. We did like you said, and the first person we picked up was Dr Hans Boehm. He tried to tell us that he only watched these films for research purposes. But you were right, Vince, he gave the whole case up. He was terrified. We raided Duval's house, found his stash of films. Reels and reels of the stuff. There's enough film footage from his parties, and from the private booths in his club, to keep the entire village of Westminster shit-scared for a long, long time.'

'So who killed the projectionist?'

'We know what happened – but not who. Tobin and Duval both blamed each other. First of all we thought Tobin did it, him being the muscle, after all. But then we found that Duval had a nice gun collection at his home. Either way, the projectionist had to go. Once he found out you were a copper, he panicked, and didn't want anything to do with it any more. Tobin and Duval knew they couldn't have him just walk away, knowing what he knew – so they shut him up. Shot him. Like you said, it was easy to make him disappear – no friends or family.'

'So that just left me,' said Vince.

'Duval wanted to throw you down the stairs – make it look like an accident. Apparently, Tobin was a little nervous about that.'

'Because he likes me so much? Or because he knows very well that, once murder squad start digging around with forensics, the whole thing could unravel?'

'The latter, I fear. Tobin's been around long enough to know you can't rush these things; you need to work out all the angles. So they wrapped a chloroform rag around your face to keep you good and unconscious, whilst they discussed your fate down in Duval's office over a glass of Scotch. Duval looked at the film and liked what he saw. That's when he had his big idea. If the projectionist can disappear, never exist, what then if everything disappears, never existed. The cinema, the films, everything. No evidence at all.'

Vince smiled. 'My word against theirs – a senior copper, about to retire with an unblemished record, and a rich businessman with friends in high places.'

'And they have the film for back-up. If you did start convincing other people, they'd show you the film. Not all of it, of course, just the start of the fight, but still enough to convince you that you killed the projectionist. And the bonus is that they also get another copper in their pocket.'

'And that's where Dr Hans Boehm comes in?'

'Yeah,' said Ray, smiling. 'They got extra lucky when you went into a coma. Boehm says that he tried everything on you, like drugs, hypnotherapy, but you still wouldn't give up your story.'

'It wasn't my story to give up, Ray,' said Vince. 'It was the truth.' He thought about the hypnotherapy Boehm had tried on him, the sleep-suggestion tapes he'd made him listen to at night. Boehm claimed all these things would open up his mind and then the truth would come out. Vince now realized Boehm was trying to bury the truth, and mire what Vince had witnessed in darkness, disbelief and, ultimately, madness.

'I'm sorry I doubted you, Vince.'

'Forget it. Not strictly true what Boehm's said, though. That's why I doubted myself. Because the truth is, I *did* want to kill the projectionist for putting that girl up on the screen. If my eyes had adjusted to the dark, maybe I would have succeeded.'

'But you didn't do that, Vince. Instead, you brought the case in. We've now traced some of the girls and it's clear they were drugged and then raped. You know, when I watched some of those films, I felt like killing the projectionist, too – and Duval and the rest of them. I've got some more news for you.' Vince glanced up at Ray in expectation. 'Eddie Tobin hanged himself in his cell yesterday.'

Vince looked away in disappointment, not because of Tobin's plight but because it wasn't the news he'd been waiting to hear. He therefore paid it just the right amount of respect it deserved – which was not a lot. Anyway, it wasn't much of a surprise: police time was the hardest time to do – and Eddie had just retired again for good.

'Any news on Bobbie?'

Ray shrugged.

Vince saw more in the shrug than Ray wanted him to, so he repeated the question: 'Come on, Ray, any news?'

'There's been a sighting of a girl that fitted her description – but nothing solid.'

'Was she with anyone?'

'A man, they say, but that's not unheard of, Vince.'

'An older man?'

'We don't know. And if you're going to ask if he had a club foot, that wasn't mentioned.'

'Where was this?'

'In Rome.' Ray went over to the makeshift screen and started dismantling it.

Vince smiled at the thought of Rome. The scene of her last reinvention: *La Dolce Vita*. But what if Bobbie really was with Jack? He knew that the Jack Regent file was now with Interpol. International crimes. Out of his jurisdiction, so officially he had no right to go after her. That's what he told himself, at least.

There in Bobbie's flat, as she held him in her arms and kissed the blood from his face, her fate had seemed something from another age. Out of his hands, and his sphere of being. Almost biblical in proportion, and seemingly only punishable or forgivable by God. If such a being existed, and it didn't feel like it to Vince. He saw no sign of greater order or good in the world that ferociously encircled her. And in that moment, before his eyes closed, he knew that Jack was right: to tell her the truth would be to destroy her. For the pain would never go, and she would have to live with it forever. It coursed constantly through her veins, it was embedded in her bones, it coloured her flesh and made up every fibre of her being. To survive, he knew, she would have to reinvent herself, like she had before, again, and again, and again . . .

On the bedside table sat Bobbie's old photo album. Vince had asked for it, somehow knowing that she would not have taken it with her. As he glanced at it, his mind raced back to the shop in the Lanes, where he and Max Vogel had discussed the work of the artist Jacob Radlington, and the brutal crime depicted in his painting.

'Detective, may I turn the tables on you and ask you a question?'

'Be my guest.'

'Do you know who you are?' asked Vogel.

I   up. 'How do you mean?'

*   who you are in the painting? Where you stand in the   Treadwell?'*

'*Detective Treadwell.*'

'*Sorry, Detective.*'

'*Yes, I'm standing at the door. And I'm about to tear it down and then put an end to it all.*'

Vince considered the resolute answer he had made, and knew that when he gave it he was still uncertain – uncertain about so many things. He now allowed himself a small smile because, at last, the young detective knew exactly where he stood in the picture.